GIANTS BEWARE!

For my beautiful boys, Diego and Pablo, and my beautiful wife, Carla
—J.A.

For the three girls in my life: Amelia, Avery, and my beloved, Darlene
—R.R.

We would like to thank our editor, Mark Siegel, for his invaluable support and enthusiasm for Claudette. We also want to thank the talented crew at First Second: Calista Brill, Colleen AF Venable, and Gina Gagliano. And finally, here are some folks who gave us vital feedback along the way: Carla Gutierrez, Vijaya Iyer, Elizabeth Neal, John Novak, Juan Carlos Perez, Raul Rosado, and Darlene Rosado. Thank you! —Jorge & Rafael

Fi**rst Second**

Text copyright © 2012 by Jorge Aguirre
Illustrations copyright © 2012 by Rafael Rosado
Published by First Second
First Second is an imprint of Roaring Brook Press, a division of Holtzbrinck Publishing Holdings Limited Partnership
175 Fifth Avenue, New York, NY 10010

Distributed in the United Kingdom by Macmillan Children's Books,
a division of Pan Macmillan.

Cataloging-in-Publication Data is on file at the Library of Congress
ISBN:978-1-59643-582-7

First Second books are available for special promotions and premiums.
For details, contact: Director of Special Markets, Holtzbrinck Publishers.

First edition 2012
Book design by Colleen AF Venable and Rob Steen
Printed in China by 1010 Printing International Limited, North Point, Hong Kong

20 19 18 17 16 15

GIANTS BEWARE!

WRITTEN BY
JORGE AGUIRRE

ART BY
RAFAEL ROSADO

STORY BY
RAFAEL ROSADO &
JORGE AGUIRRE

COLOR BY
JOHN NOVAK

ADDITIONAL COLOR BY
MATTHEW SCHENK

:01

First Second
New York & London

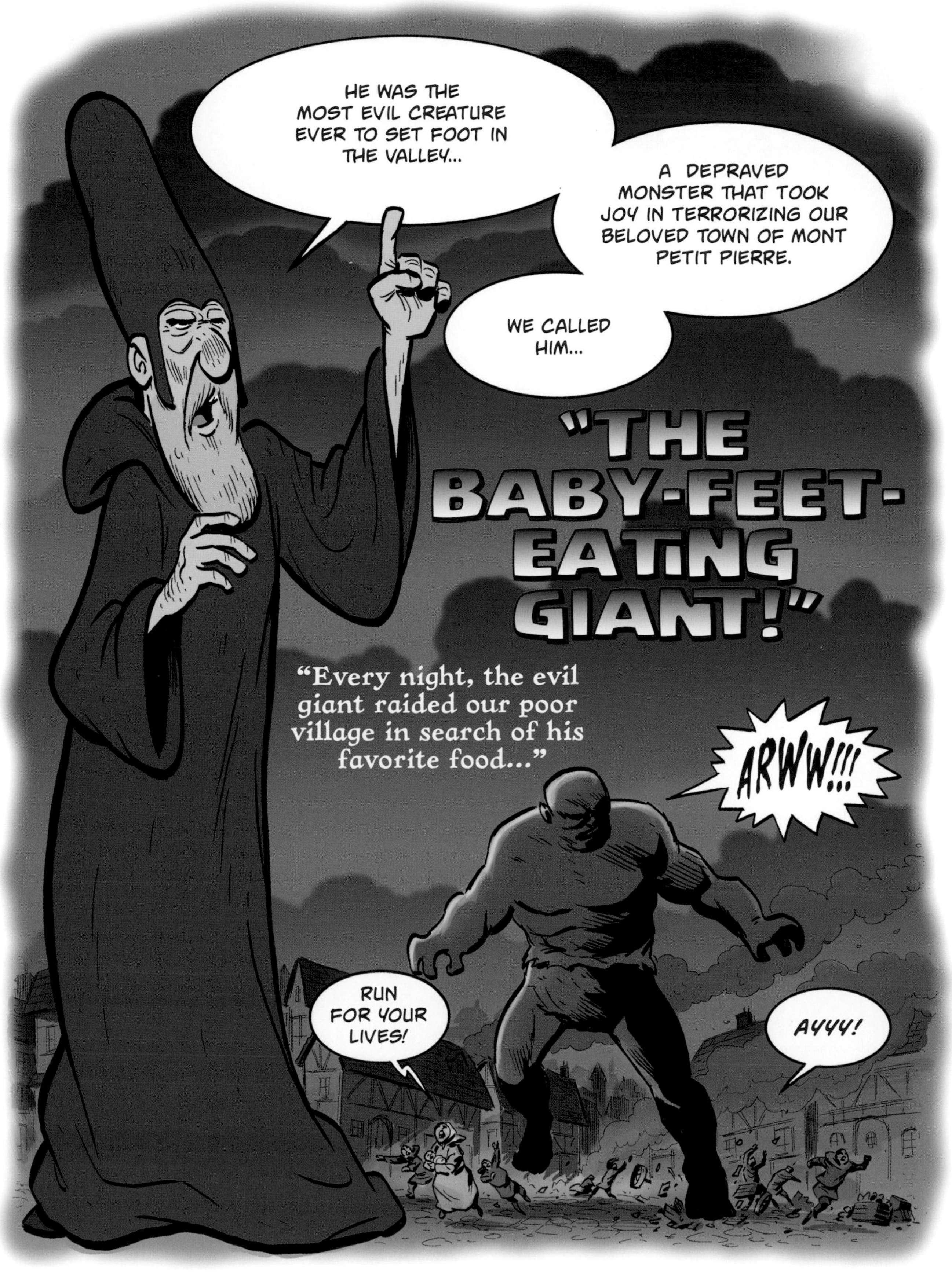
HE WAS THE MOST EVIL CREATURE EVER TO SET FOOT IN THE VALLEY...
A DEPRAVED MONSTER THAT TOOK JOY IN TERRORIZING OUR BELOVED TOWN OF MONT PETIT PIERRE.
WE CALLED HIM...
"THE BABY-FEET-EATING GIANT!"
"Every night, the evil giant raided our poor village in search of his favorite food..."
ARWW!!!
RUN FOR YOUR LIVES!
AYYY!

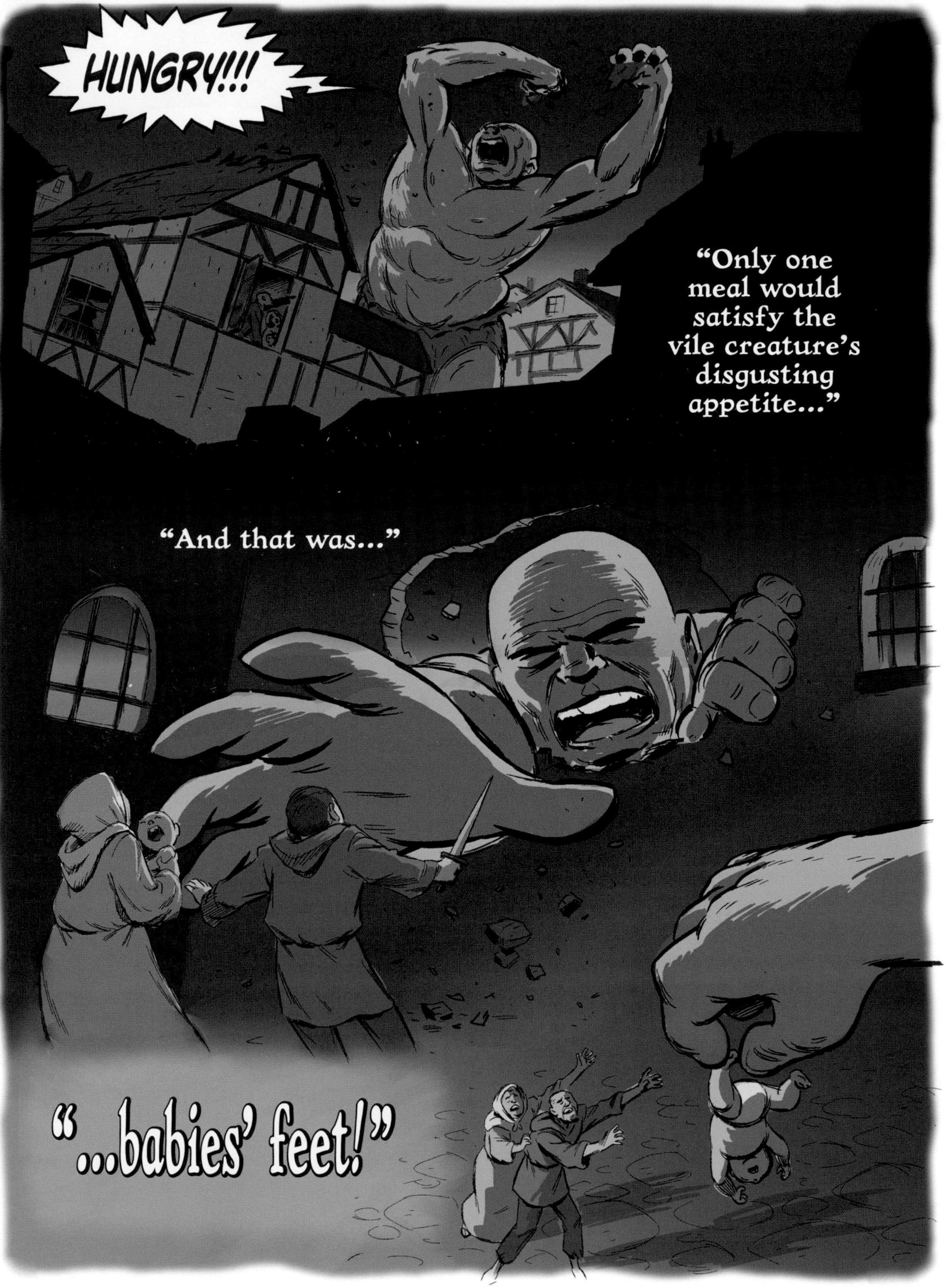
HUNGRY!!!
"Only one meal would satisfy the vile creature's disgusting appetite..."
"And that was..."
"...babies' feet!"

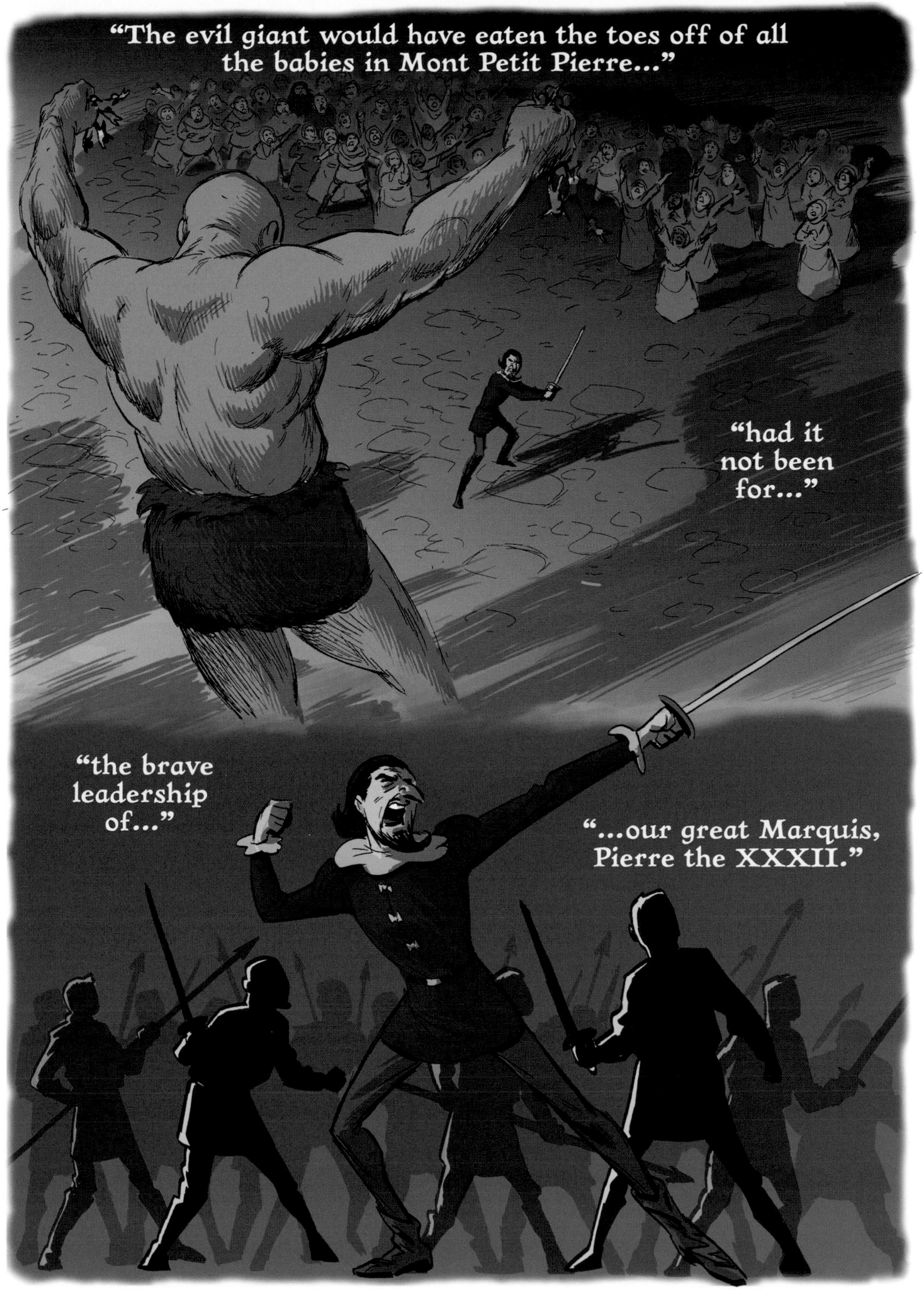
"The evil giant would have eaten the toes off of all the babies in Mont Petit Pierre..."
"had it not been for..."
"the brave leadership of..."
"...our great Marquis, Pierre the XXXII."

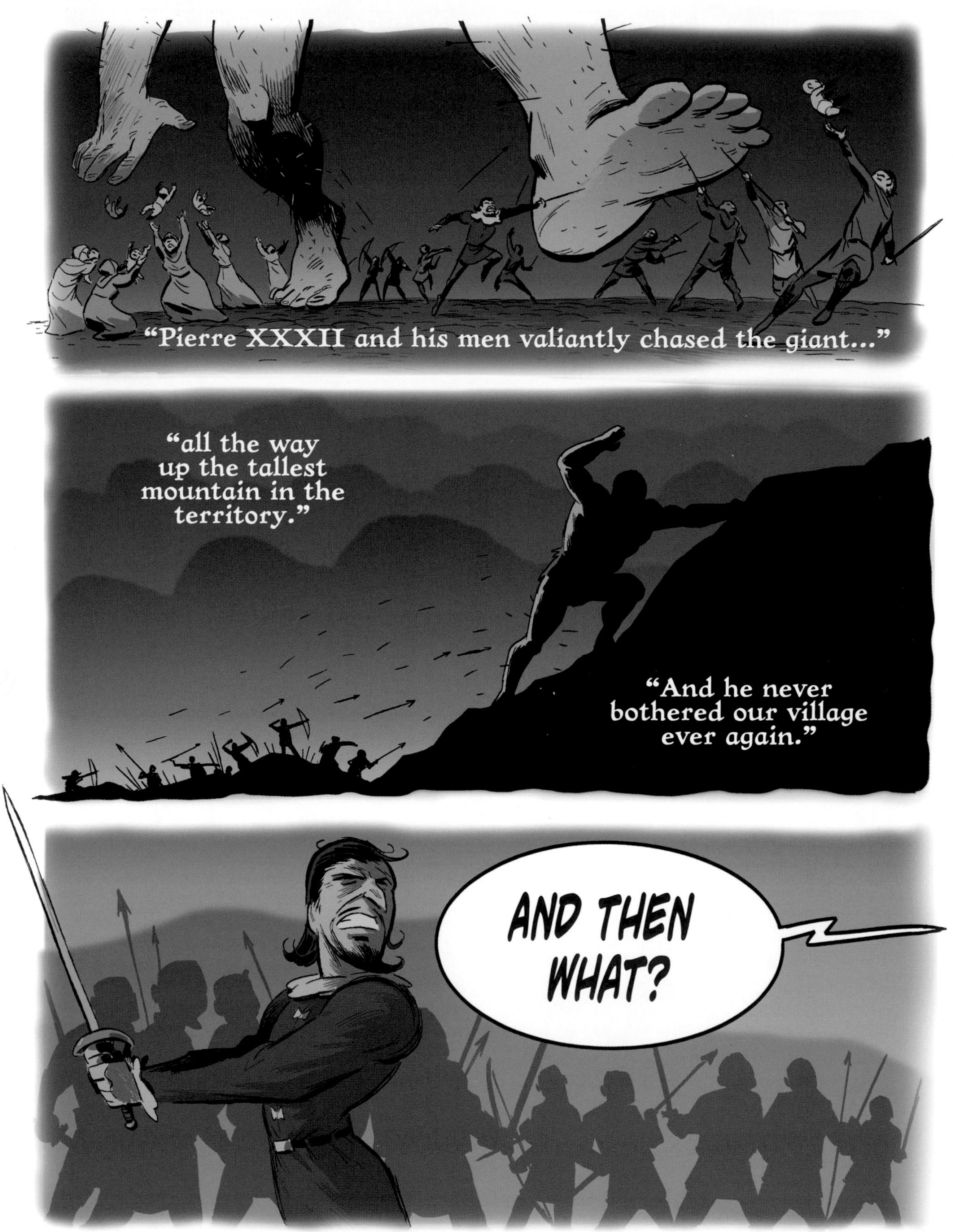
"Pierre XXXII and his men valiantly chased the giant..."
"all the way up the tallest mountain in the territory."
"And he never bothered our village ever again."
AND THEN WHAT?

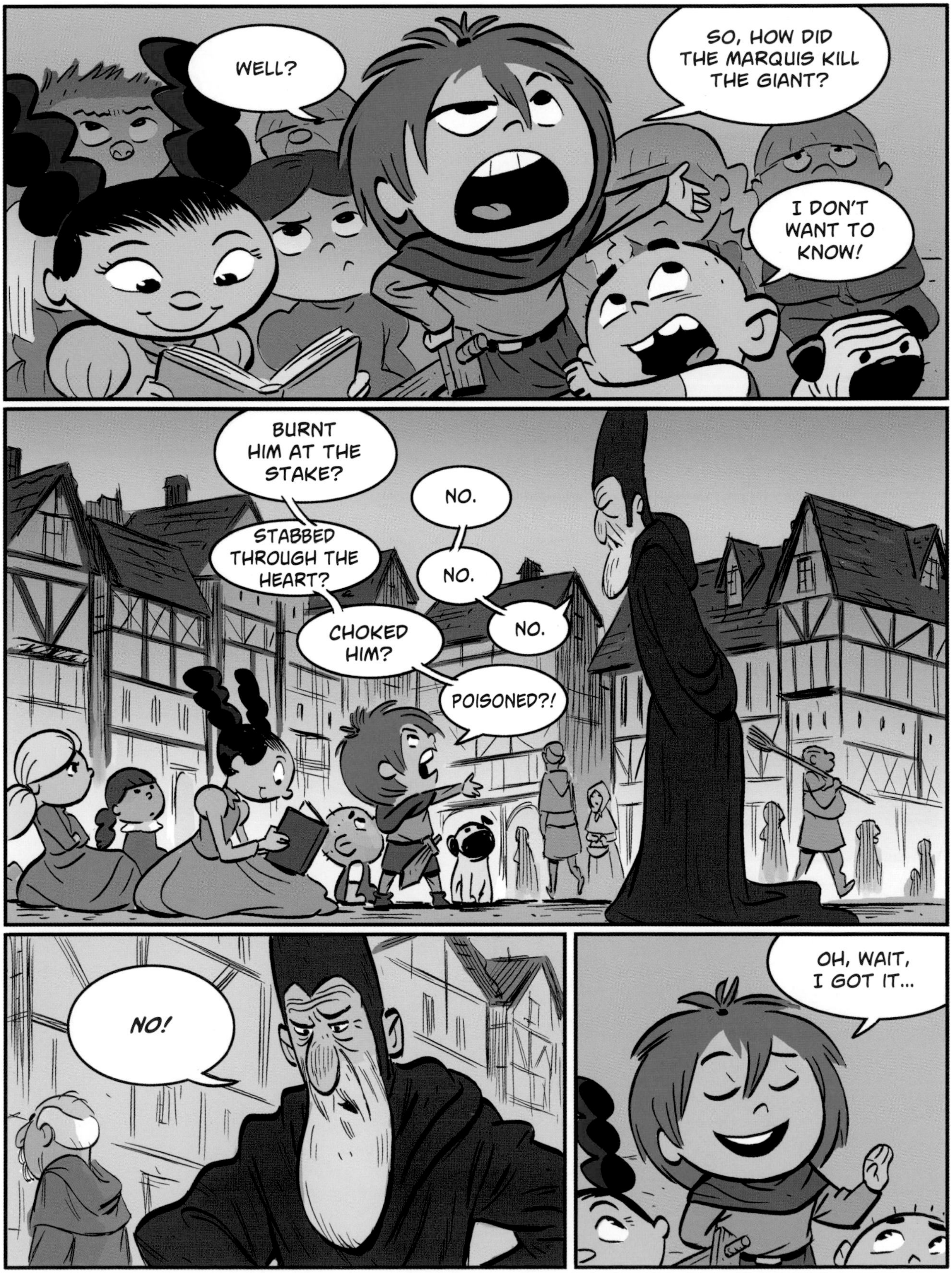
WELL?
SO, HOW DID THE MARQUIS KILL THE GIANT?
I DON'T WANT TO KNOW!
BURNT HIM AT THE STAKE?
NO.
STABBED THROUGH THE HEART?
NO.
CHOKED HIM?
NO.
POISONED?!
NO!
OH, WAIT, I GOT IT...

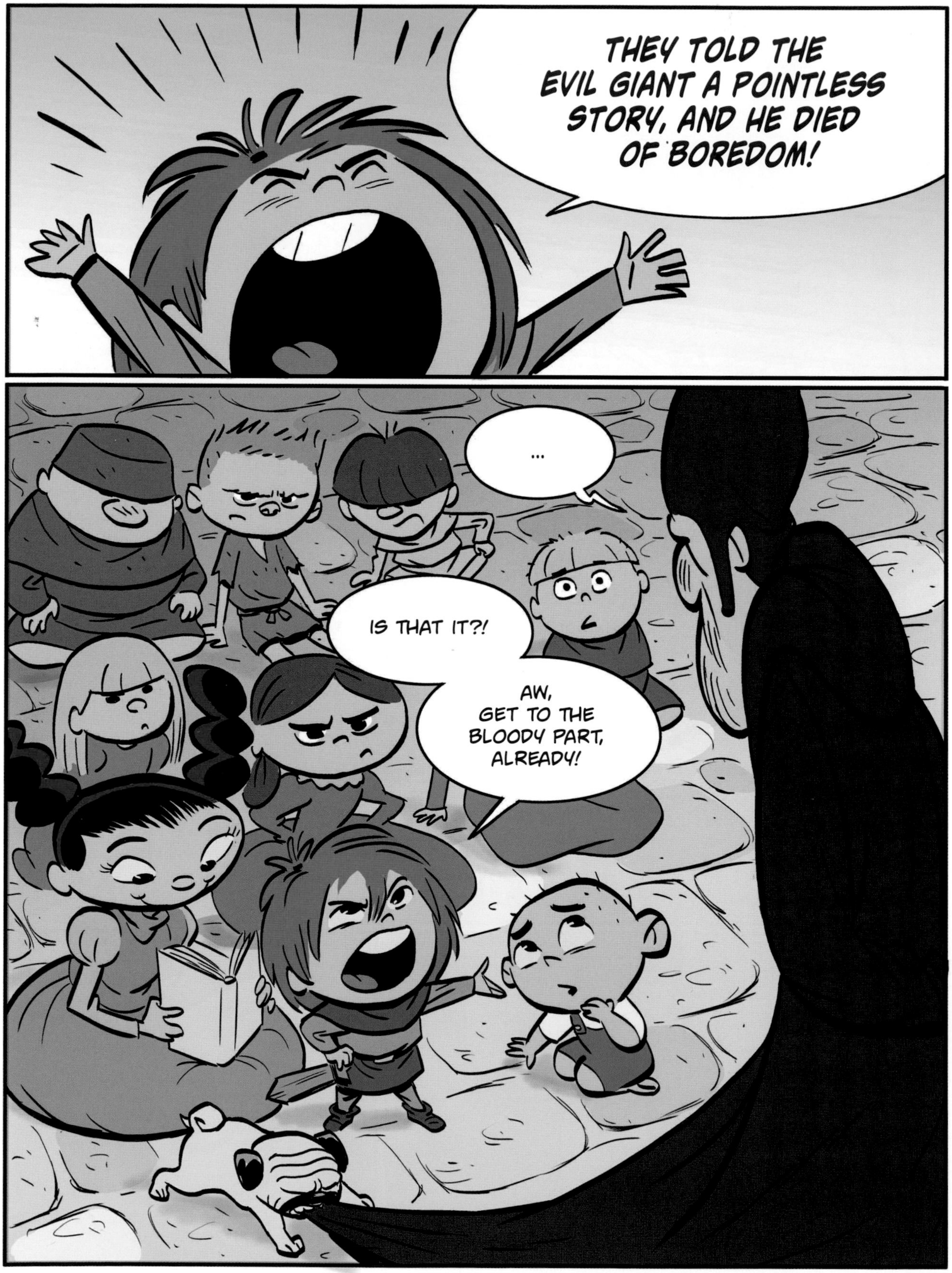
THEY TOLD THE EVIL GIANT A POINTLESS STORY, AND HE DIED OF BOREDOM!
...
IS THAT IT?!
AW, GET TO THE BLOODY PART, ALREADY!

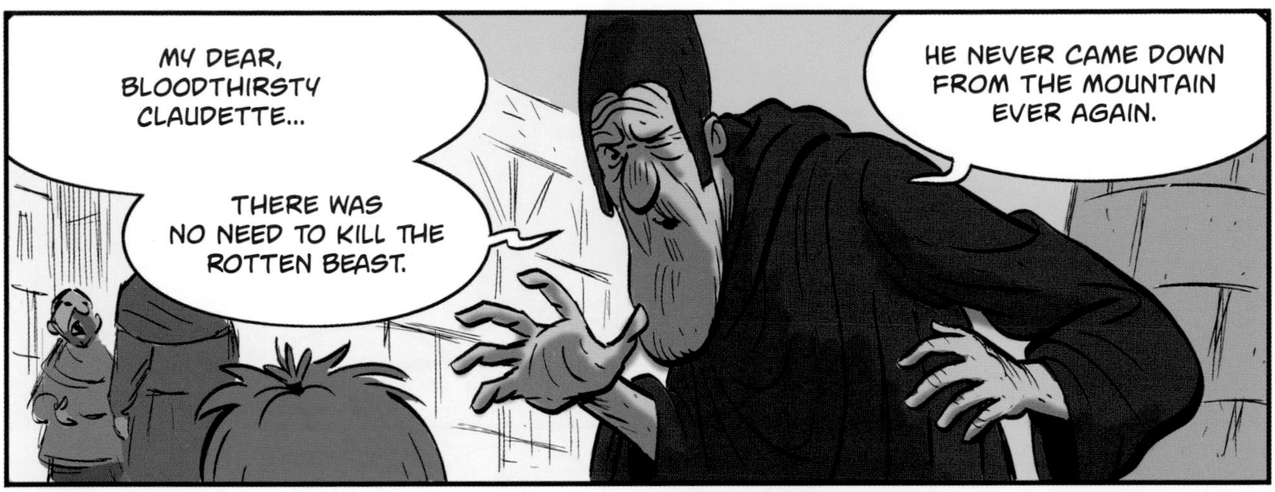
MY DEAR, BLOODTHIRSTY CLAUDETTE...
THERE WAS NO NEED TO KILL THE ROTTEN BEAST.
HE NEVER CAME DOWN FROM THE MOUNTAIN EVER AGAIN.

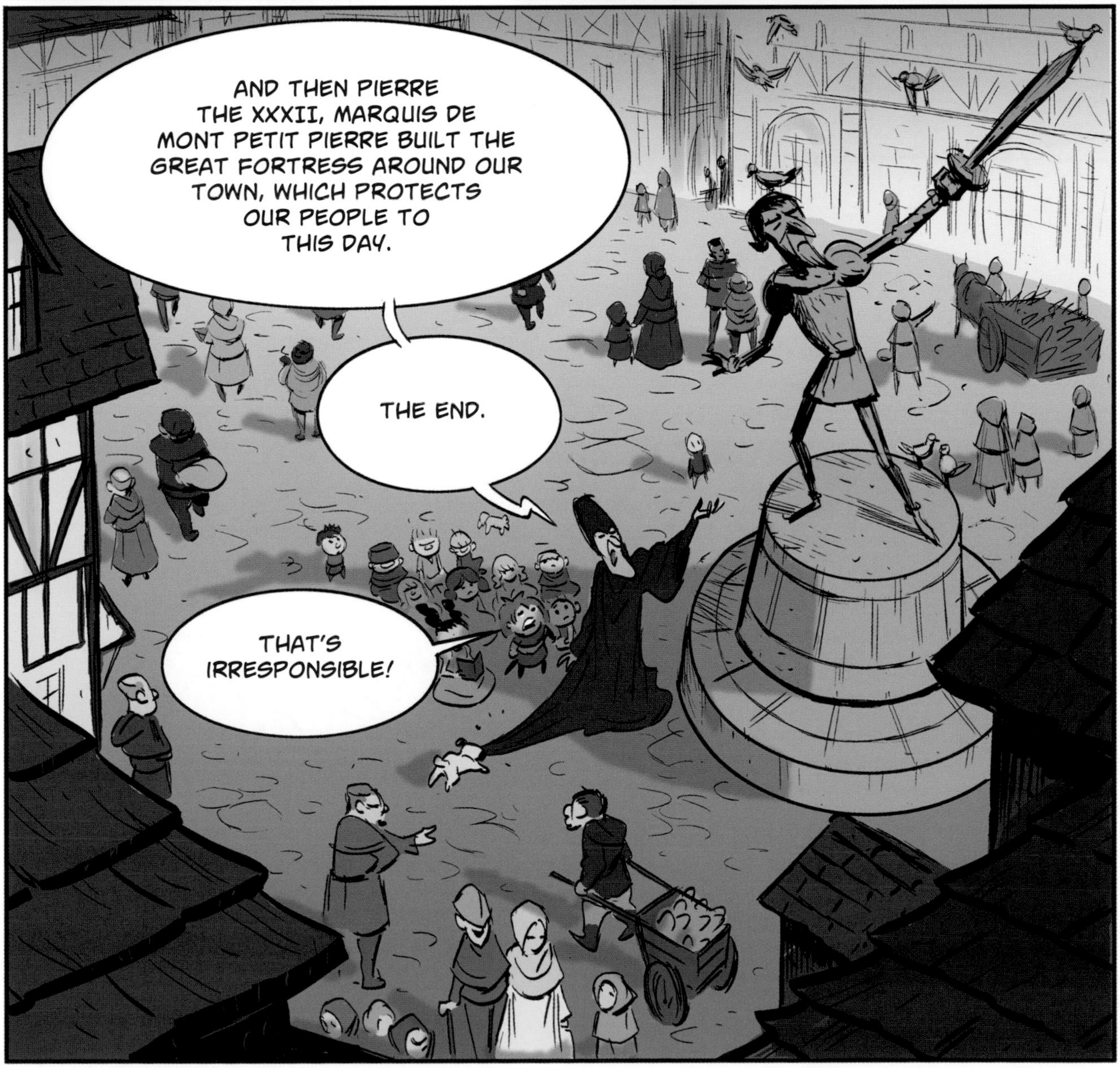
AND THEN PIERRE THE XXXII, MARQUIS DE MONT PETIT PIERRE BUILT THE GREAT FORTRESS AROUND OUR TOWN, WHICH PROTECTS OUR PEOPLE TO THIS DAY.
THE END.
THAT'S IRRESPONSIBLE!

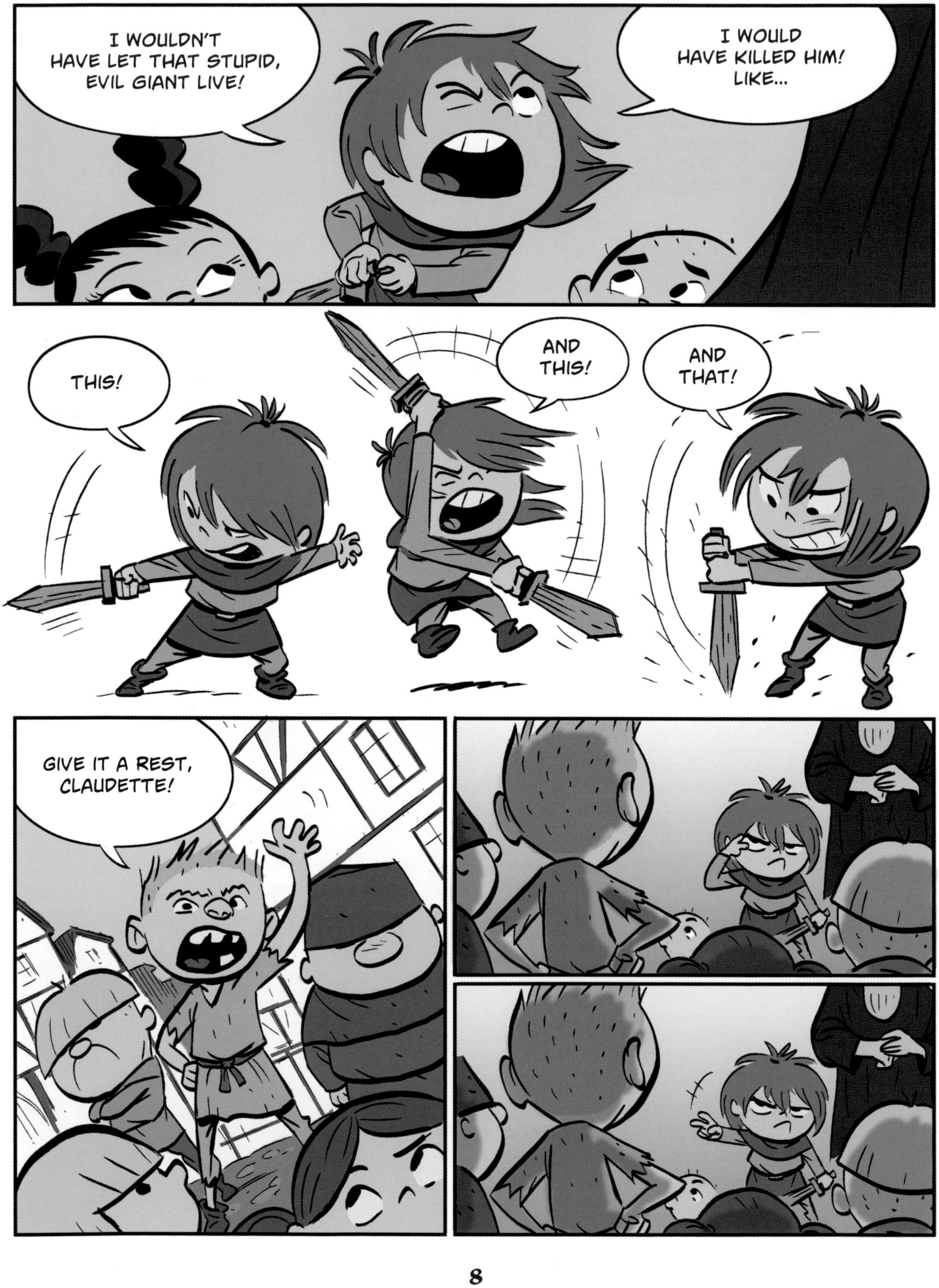
I WOULDN'T HAVE LET THAT STUPID, EVIL GIANT LIVE!
I WOULD HAVE KILLED HIM! LIKE...
THIS!
AND THIS!
AND THAT!
GIVE IT A REST, CLAUDETTE!

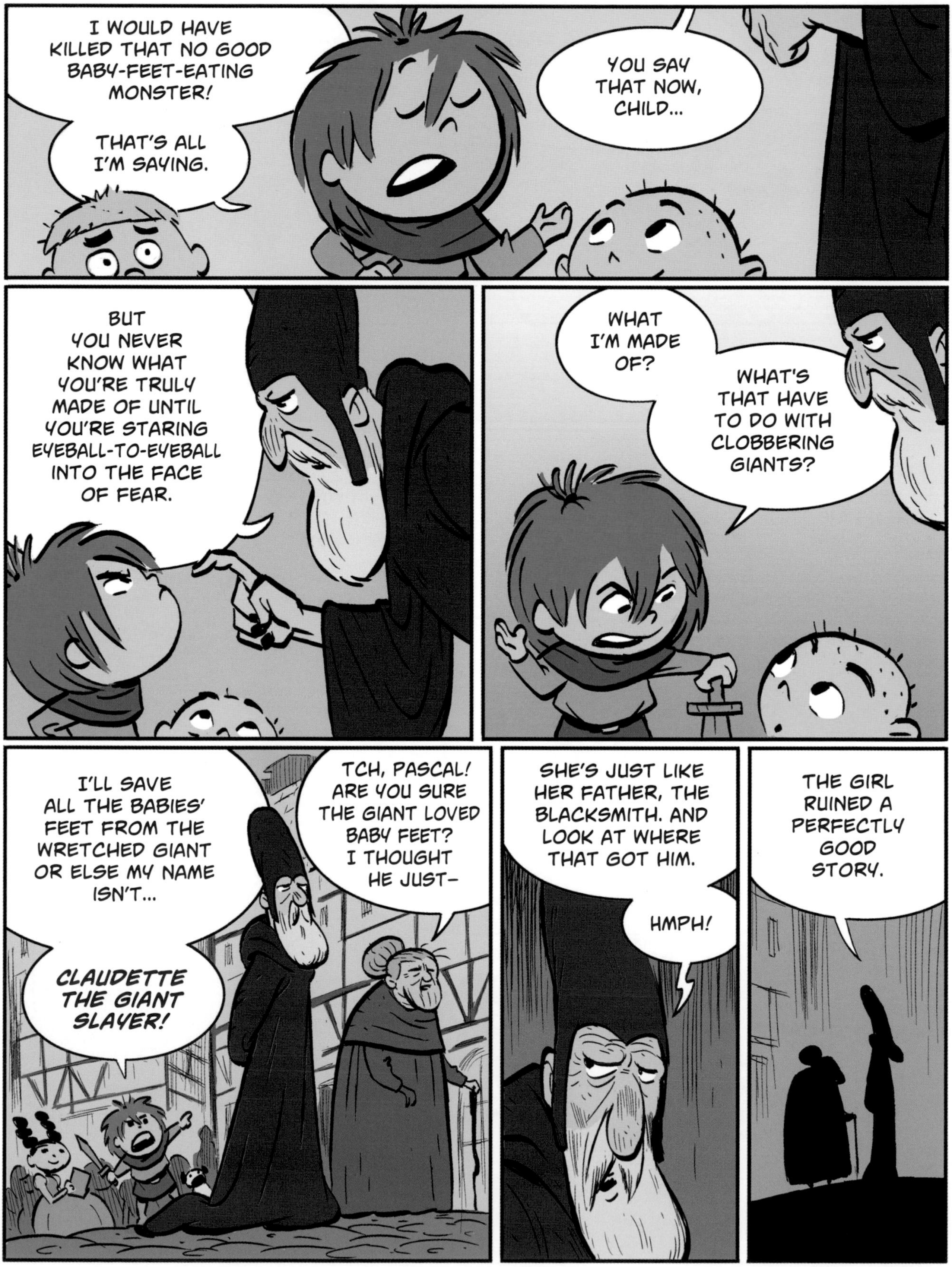
I WOULD HAVE KILLED THAT NO GOOD BABY-FEET-EATING MONSTER!
THAT'S ALL I'M SAYING.
YOU SAY THAT NOW, CHILD...
BUT YOU NEVER KNOW WHAT YOU'RE TRULY MADE OF UNTIL YOU'RE STARING EYEBALL-TO-EYEBALL INTO THE FACE OF FEAR.
WHAT I'M MADE OF?
WHAT'S THAT HAVE TO DO WITH CLOBBERING GIANTS?
I'LL SAVE ALL THE BABIES' FEET FROM THE WRETCHED GIANT OR ELSE MY NAME ISN'T...
CLAUDETTE THE GIANT SLAYER!
TCH, PASCAL! ARE YOU SURE THE GIANT LOVED BABY FEET? I THOUGHT HE JUST-
SHE'S JUST LIKE HER FATHER, THE BLACKSMITH. AND LOOK AT WHERE THAT GOT HIM.
HMPH!
THE GIRL RUINED A PERFECTLY GOOD STORY.

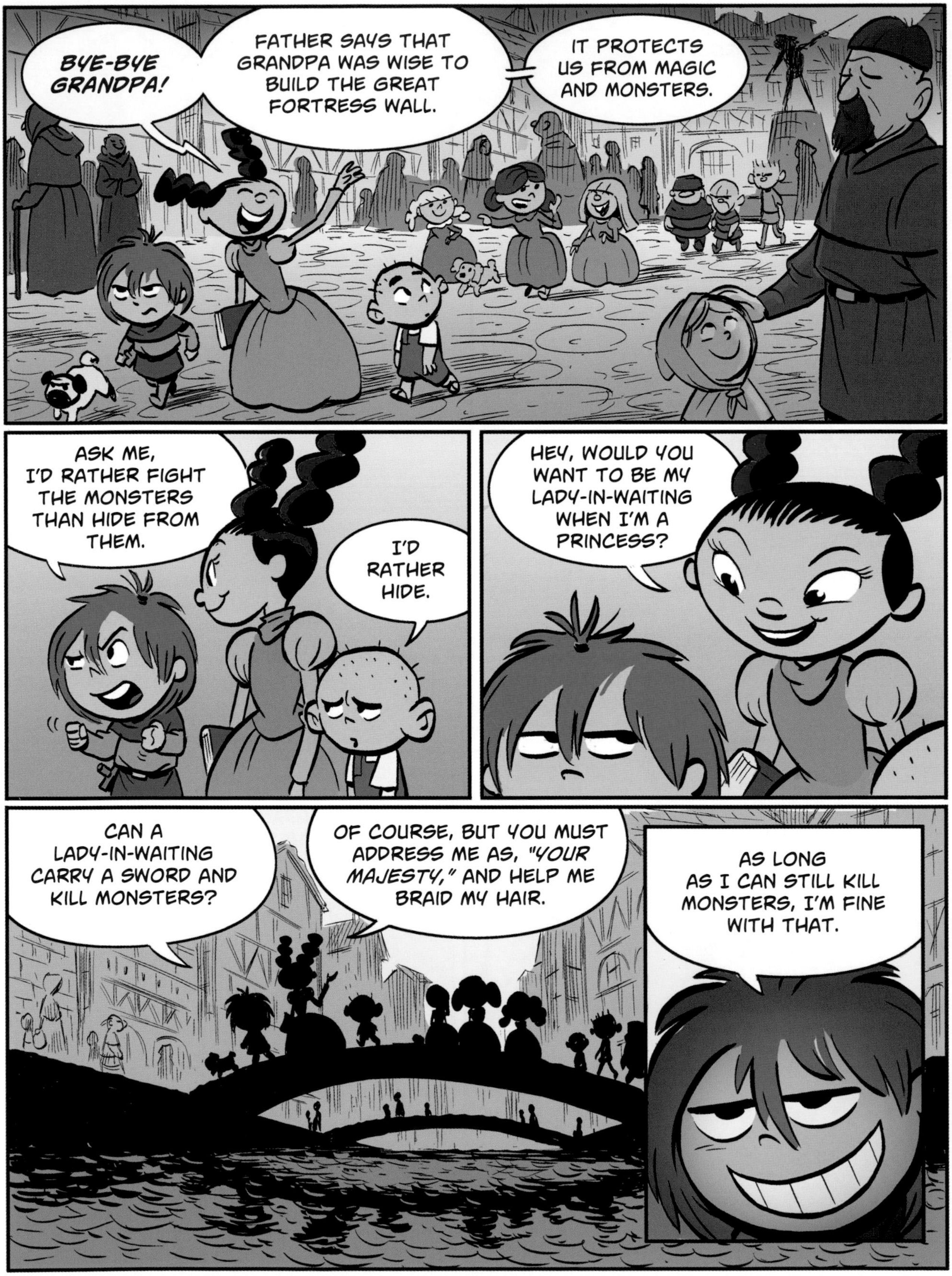
BYE-BYE GRANDPA!
FATHER SAYS THAT GRANDPA WAS WISE TO BUILD THE GREAT FORTRESS WALL.
IT PROTECTS US FROM MAGIC AND MONSTERS.
ASK ME, I'D RATHER FIGHT THE MONSTERS THAN HIDE FROM THEM.
I'D RATHER HIDE.
HEY, WOULD YOU WANT TO BE MY LADY-IN-WAITING WHEN I'M A PRINCESS?
CAN A LADY-IN-WAITING CARRY A SWORD AND KILL MONSTERS?
OF COURSE, BUT YOU MUST ADDRESS ME AS, "YOUR MAJESTY," AND HELP ME BRAID MY HAIR.
AS LONG AS I CAN STILL KILL MONSTERS, I'M FINE WITH THAT.

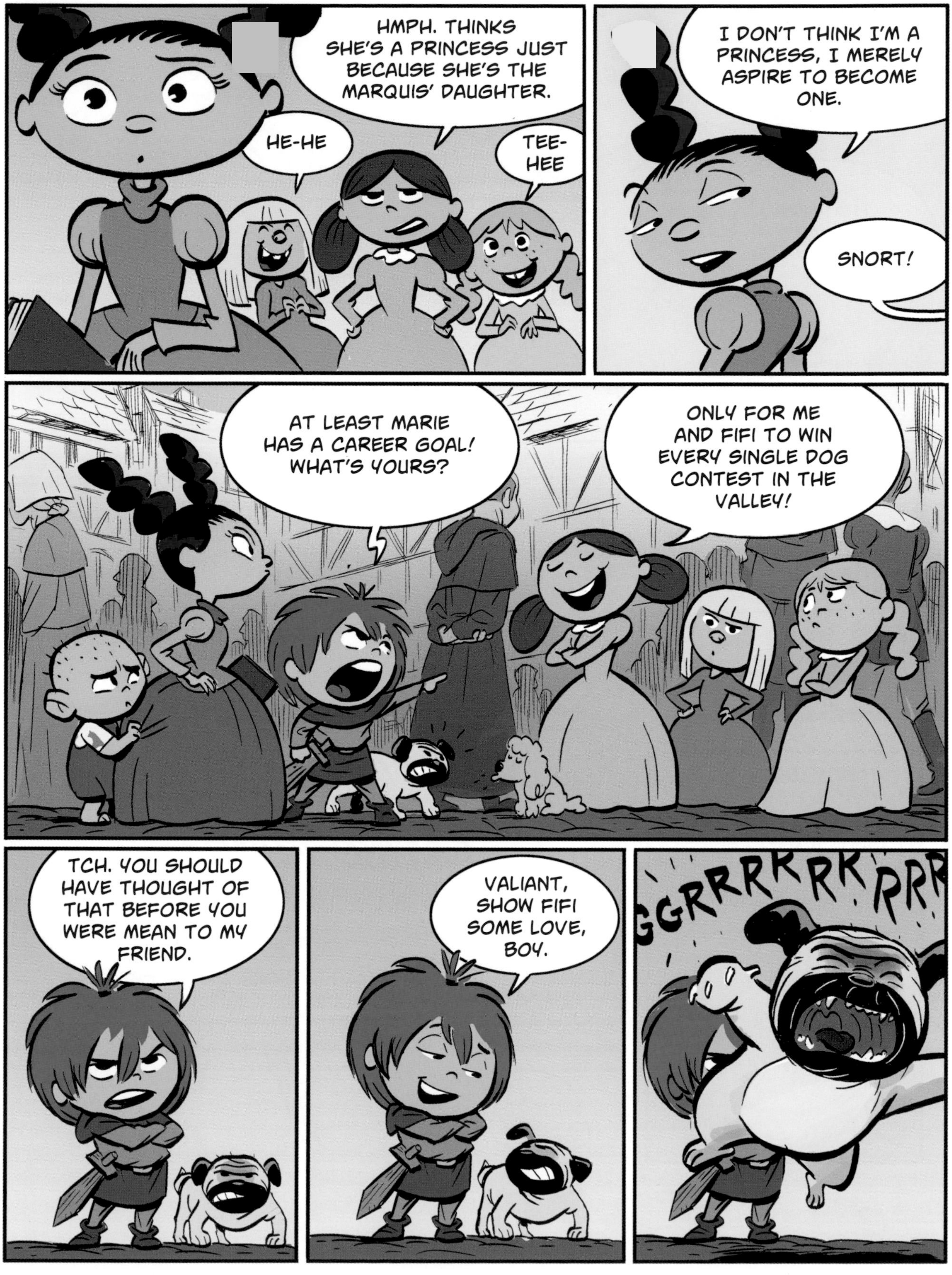
HMPH. THINKS SHE'S A PRINCESS JUST BECAUSE SHE'S THE MARQUIS' DAUGHTER.
HE-HE
TEE-HEE
I DON'T THINK I'M A PRINCESS, I MERELY ASPIRE TO BECOME ONE.
SNORT!
AT LEAST MARIE HAS A CAREER GOAL! WHAT'S YOURS?
ONLY FOR ME AND FIFI TO WIN EVERY SINGLE DOG CONTEST IN THE VALLEY!
TCH. YOU SHOULD HAVE THOUGHT OF THAT BEFORE YOU WERE MEAN TO MY FRIEND.
VALIANT, SHOW FIFI SOME LOVE, BOY.
GGRRRRKRKRRR

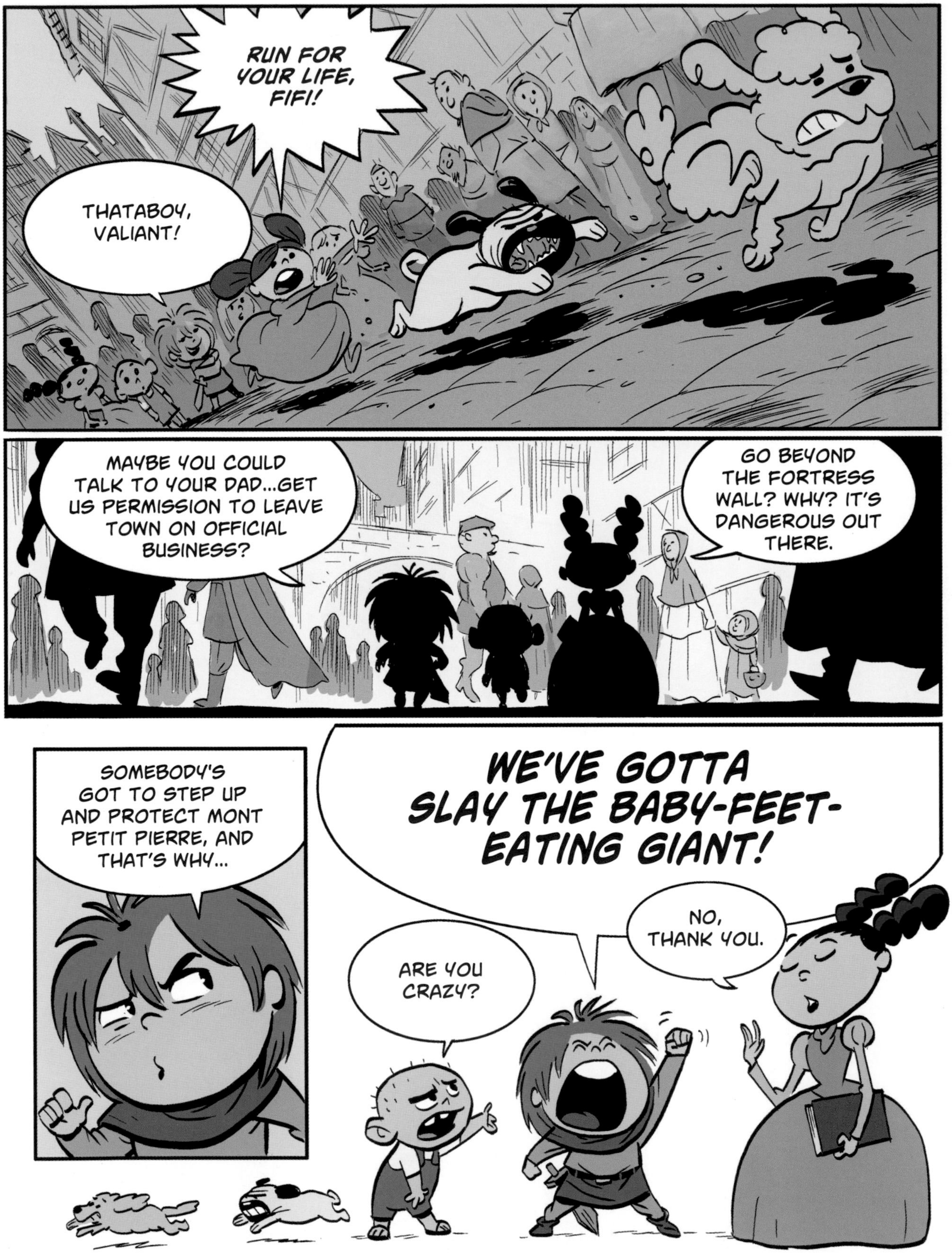
RUN FOR YOUR LIFE, FIFI!
THATABOY, VALIANT!
MAYBE YOU COULD TALK TO YOUR DAD...GET US PERMISSION TO LEAVE TOWN ON OFFICIAL BUSINESS?
GO BEYOND THE FORTRESS WALL? WHY? IT'S DANGEROUS OUT THERE.
SOMEBODY'S GOT TO STEP UP AND PROTECT MONT PETIT PIERRE, AND THAT'S WHY...
WE'VE GOTTA SLAY THE BABY-FEET-EATING GIANT!
ARE YOU CRAZY?
NO, THANK YOU.

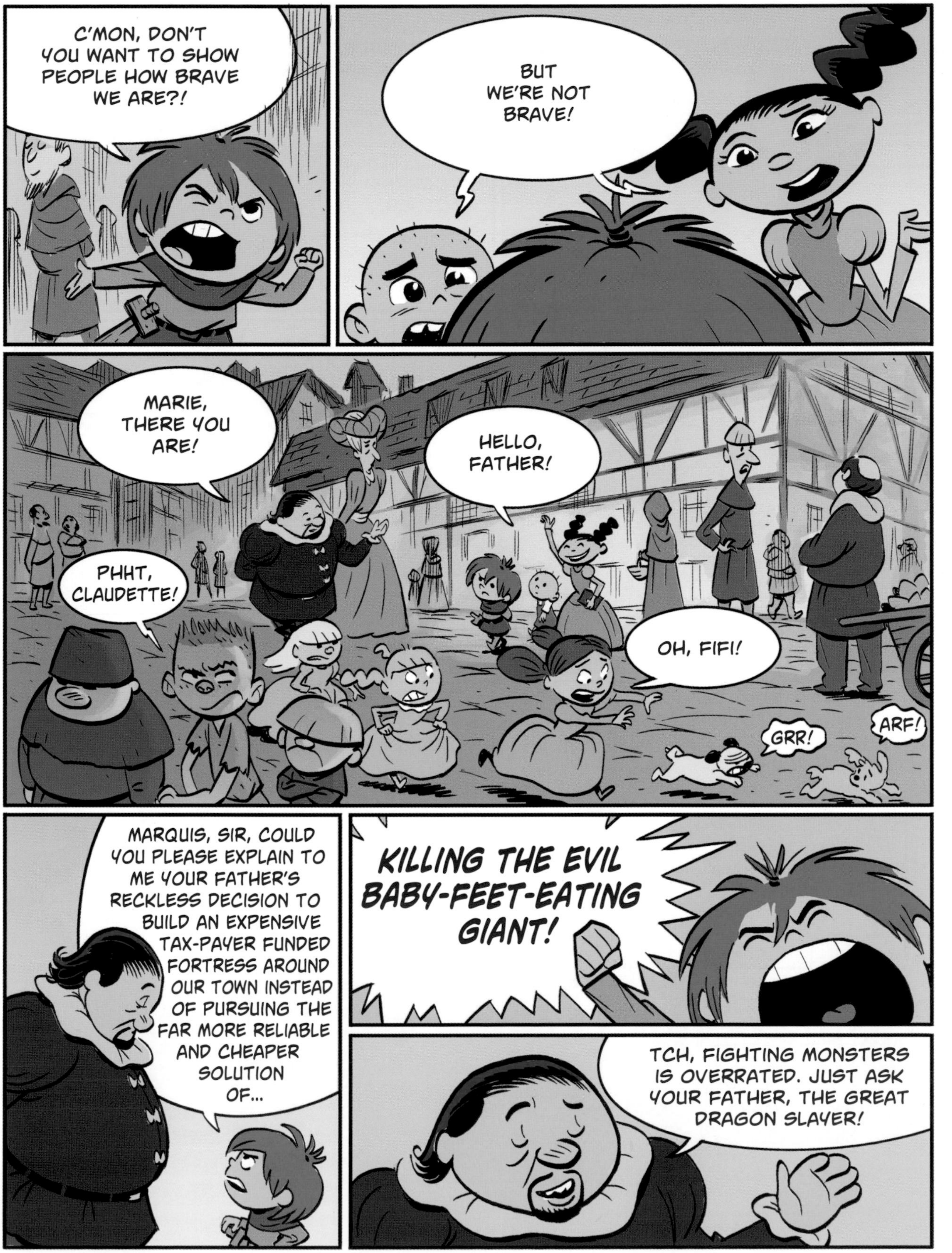
C'MON, DON'T YOU WANT TO SHOW PEOPLE HOW BRAVE WE ARE?!
BUT WE'RE NOT BRAVE!
MARIE, THERE YOU ARE!
HELLO, FATHER!
PHHT, CLAUDETTE!
OH, FIFI!
GRR!
ARF!
MARQUIS, SIR, COULD YOU PLEASE EXPLAIN TO ME YOUR FATHER'S RECKLESS DECISION TO BUILD AN EXPENSIVE TAX-PAYER FUNDED FORTRESS AROUND OUR TOWN INSTEAD OF PURSUING THE FAR MORE RELIABLE AND CHEAPER SOLUTION OF...
KILLING THE EVIL BABY-FEET-EATING GIANT!
TCH, FIGHTING MONSTERS IS OVERRATED. JUST ASK YOUR FATHER, THE GREAT DRAGON SLAYER!

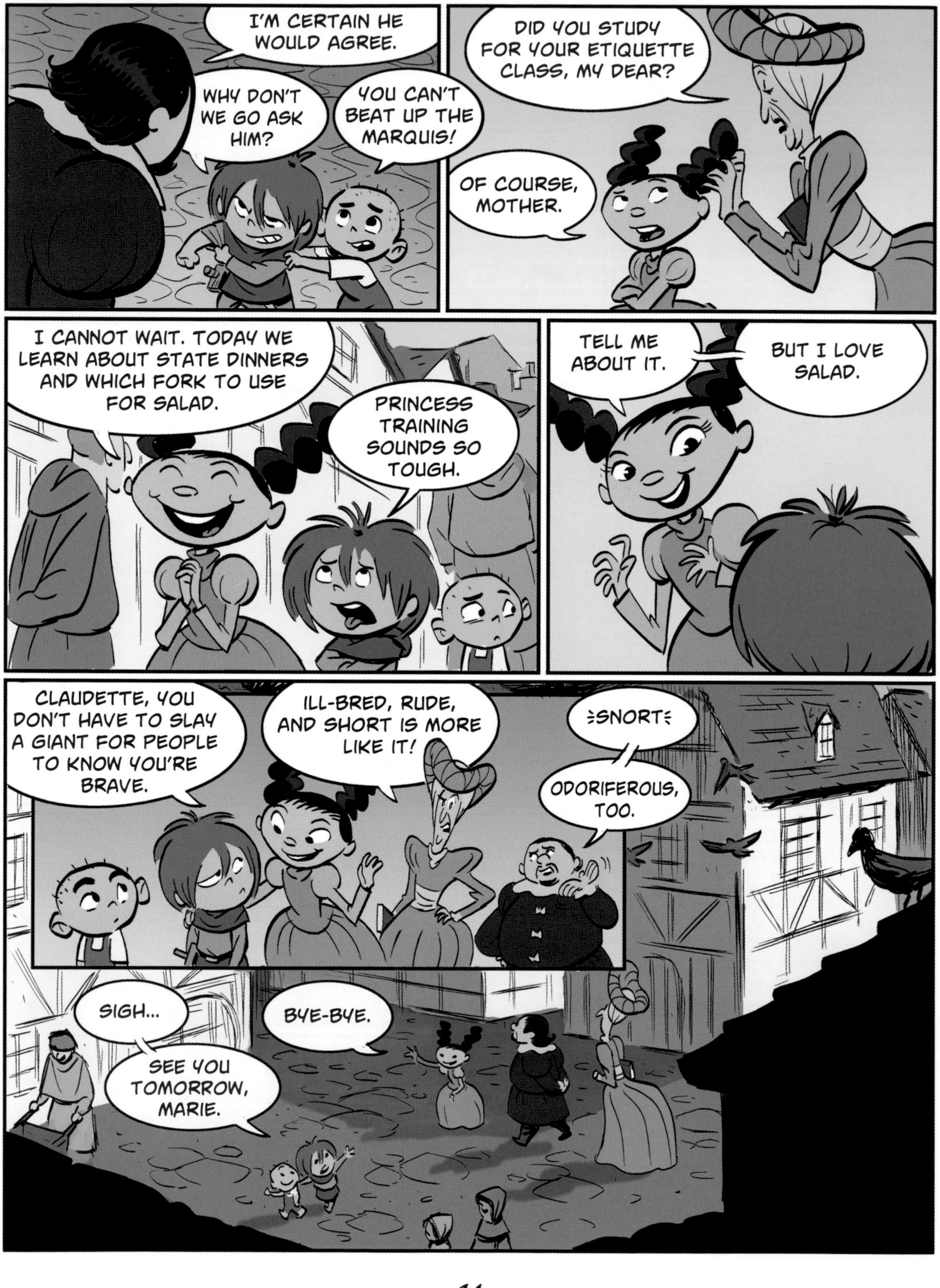
I'M CERTAIN HE WOULD AGREE.
WHY DON'T WE GO ASK HIM?
YOU CAN'T BEAT UP THE MARQUIS!
DID YOU STUDY FOR YOUR ETIQUETTE CLASS, MY DEAR?
OF COURSE, MOTHER.
I CANNOT WAIT. TODAY WE LEARN ABOUT STATE DINNERS AND WHICH FORK TO USE FOR SALAD.
PRINCESS TRAINING SOUNDS SO TOUGH.
TELL ME ABOUT IT.
BUT I LOVE SALAD.
CLAUDETTE, YOU DON'T HAVE TO SLAY A GIANT FOR PEOPLE TO KNOW YOU'RE BRAVE.
ILL-BRED, RUDE, AND SHORT IS MORE LIKE IT!
SNORT
ODORIFEROUS, TOO.
SIGH...
SEE YOU TOMORROW, MARIE.
BYE-BYE.

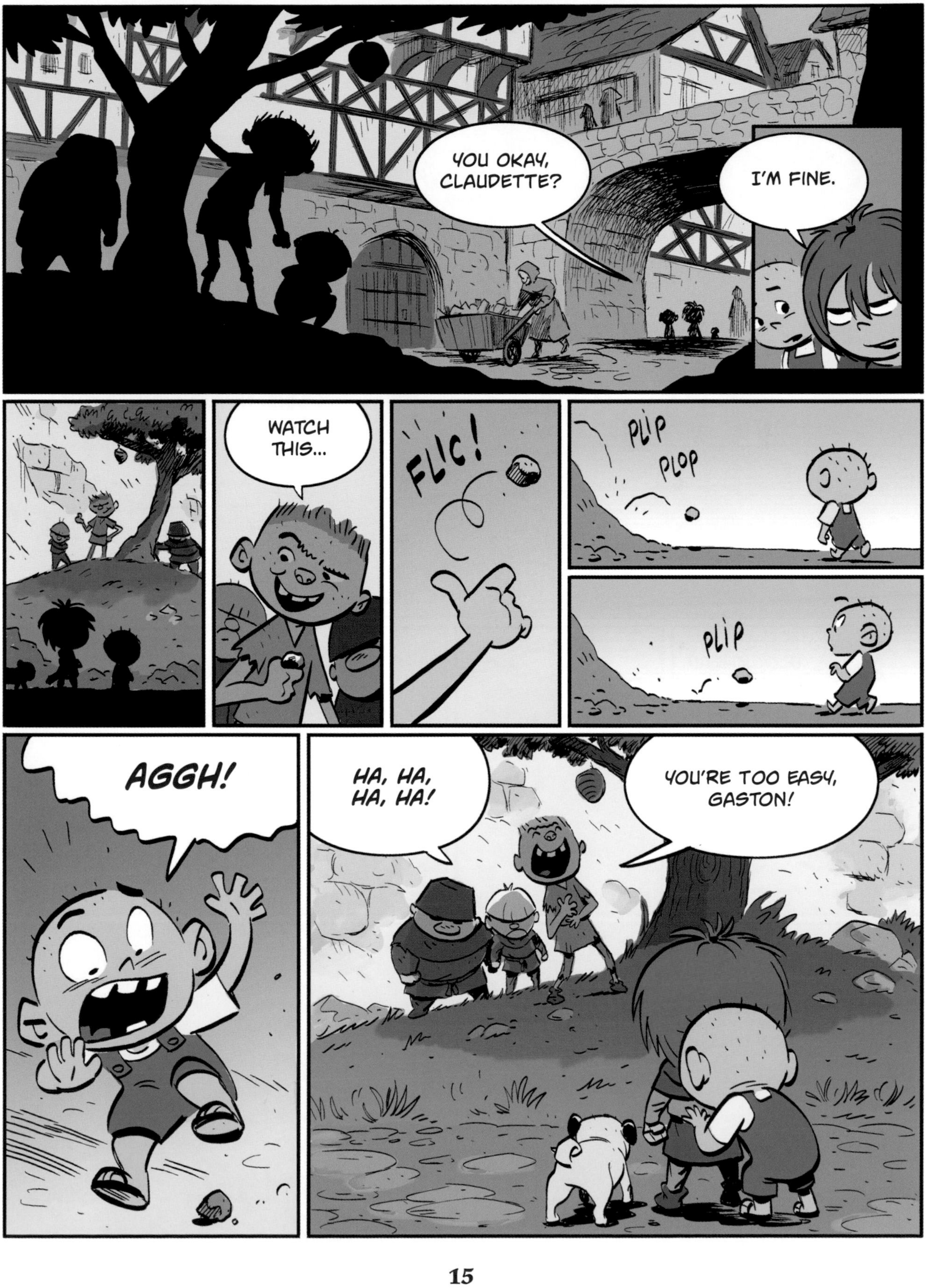
YOU OKAY, CLAUDETTE?
I'M FINE.
WATCH THIS...
FLIC!
PLIP
PLOP
PLIP
AGGH!
HA, HA, HA, HA!
YOU'RE TOO EASY, GASTON!

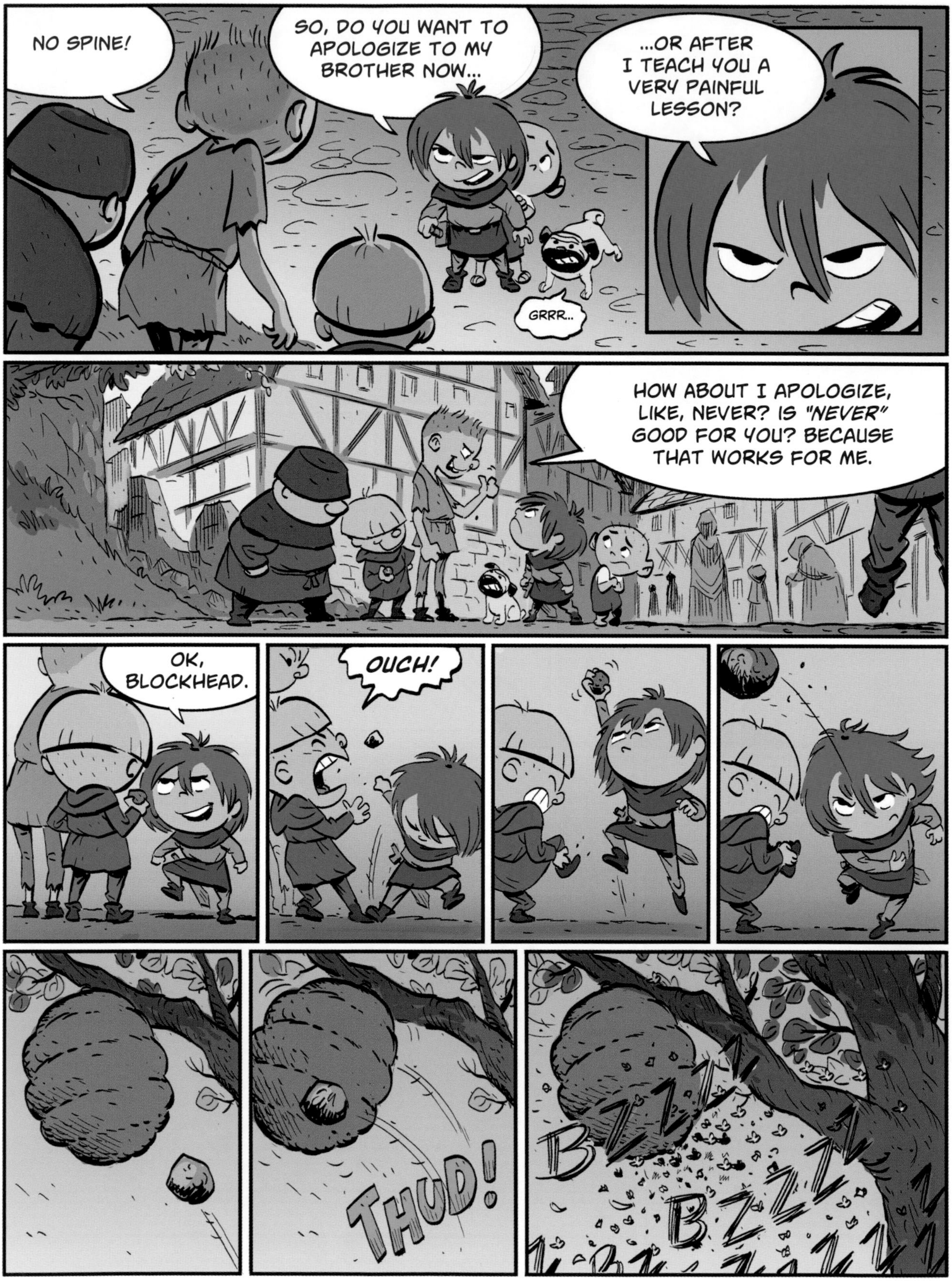
NO SPINE!
SO, DO YOU WANT TO APOLOGIZE TO MY BROTHER NOW...
...OR AFTER I TEACH YOU A VERY PAINFUL LESSON?
GRRR...
HOW ABOUT I APOLOGIZE, LIKE, NEVER? IS "NEVER" GOOD FOR YOU? BECAUSE THAT WORKS FOR ME.
OK, BLOCKHEAD.
OUCH!
THUD!
BZZZZ
BZZZZ

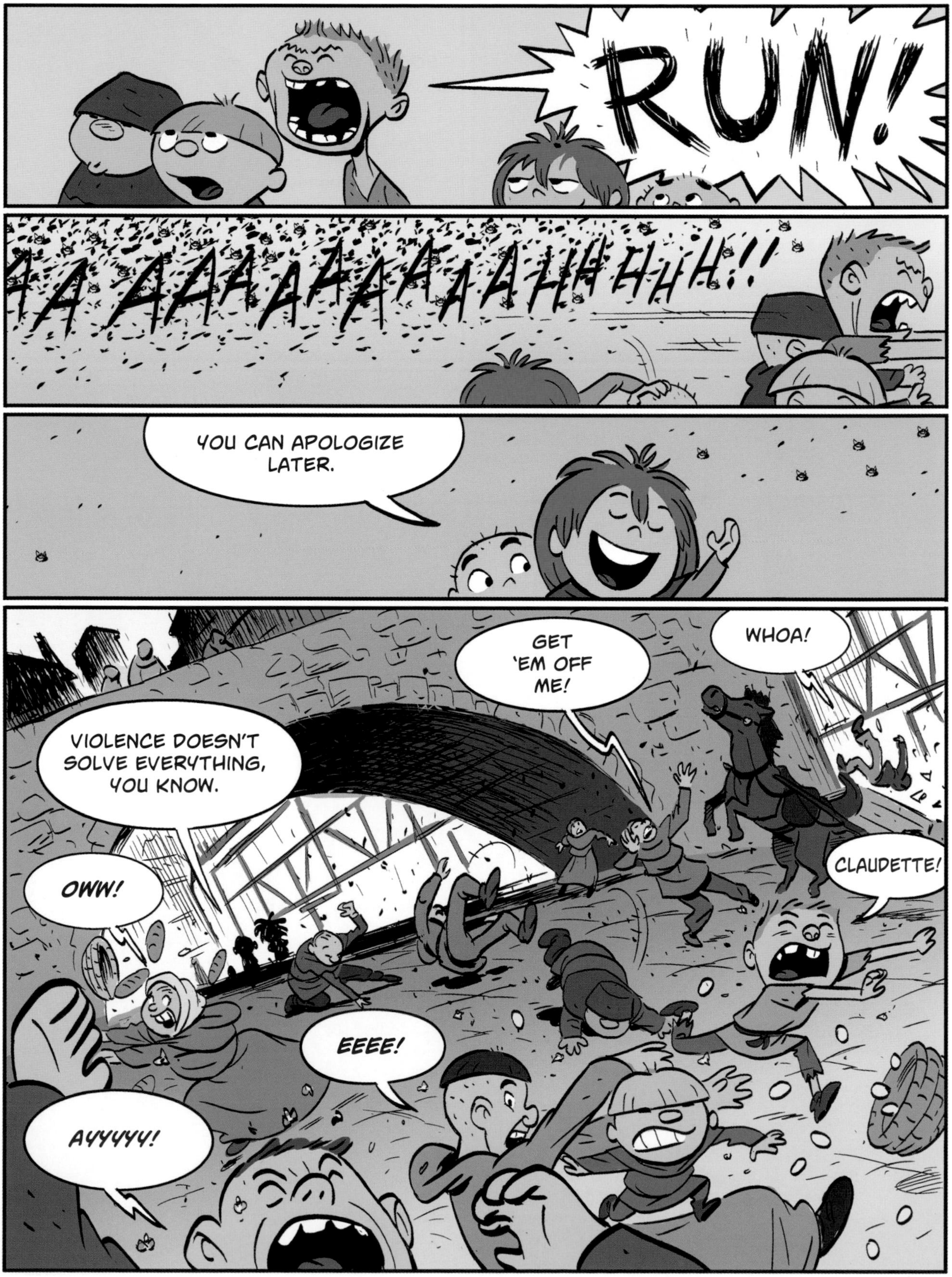
RUN!
AAAAAAAAAAAHHHHHH!!
YOU CAN APOLOGIZE LATER.
VIOLENCE DOESN'T SOLVE EVERYTHING, YOU KNOW.
GET 'EM OFF ME!
WHOA!
CLAUDETTE!
OWW!
EEEE!
AYYYYY!

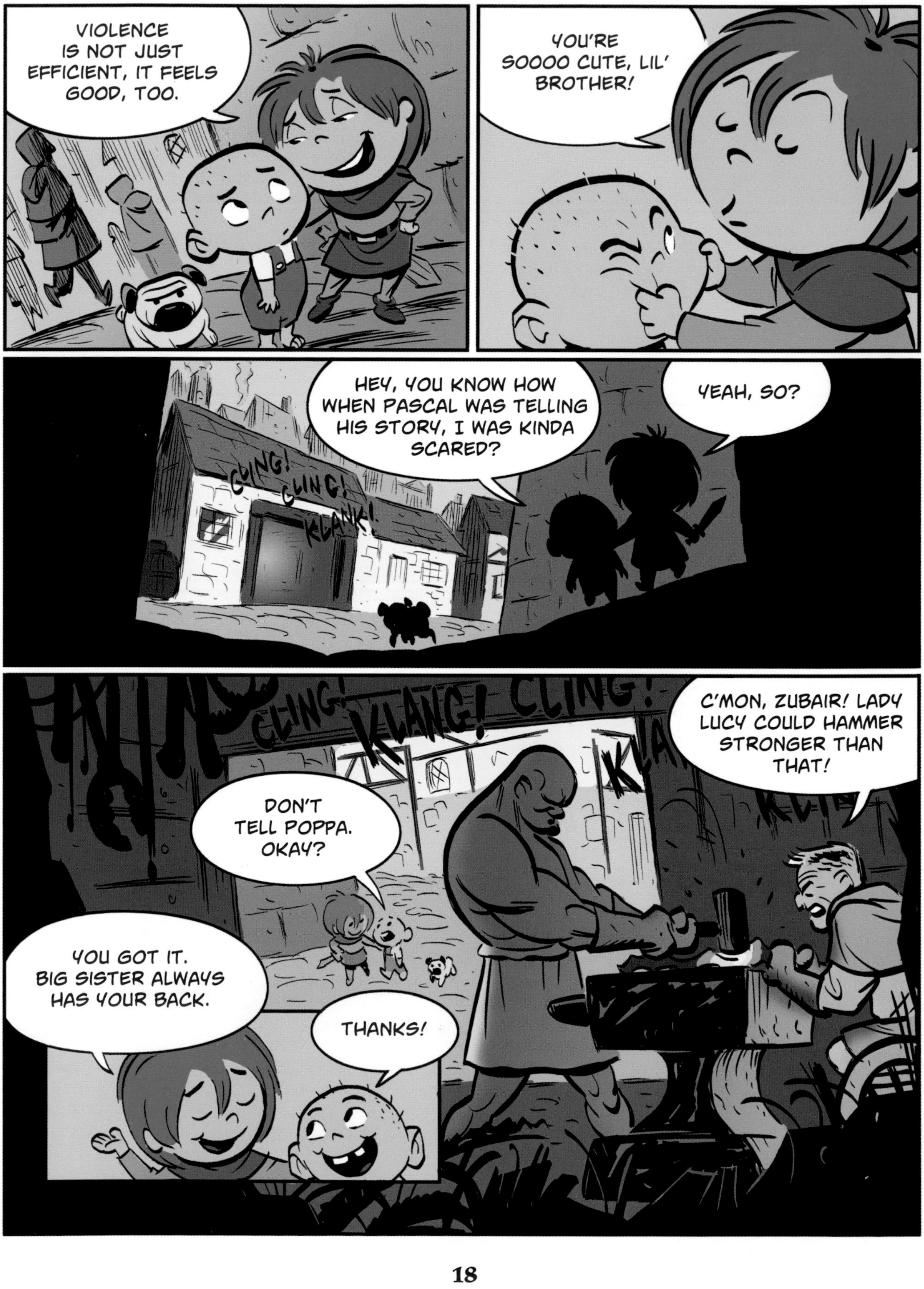
VIOLENCE IS NOT JUST EFFICIENT, IT FEELS GOOD, TOO.
YOU'RE SOOOO CUTE, LIL' BROTHER!
CLING! CLING! KLANK!
HEY, YOU KNOW HOW WHEN PASCAL WAS TELLING HIS STORY, I WAS KINDA SCARED?
YEAH, SO?
CLING! KLANG! CLING!
C'MON, ZUBAIR! LADY LUCY COULD HAMMER STRONGER THAN THAT!
DON'T TELL POPPA. OKAY?
YOU GOT IT. BIG SISTER ALWAYS HAS YOUR BACK.
THANKS!

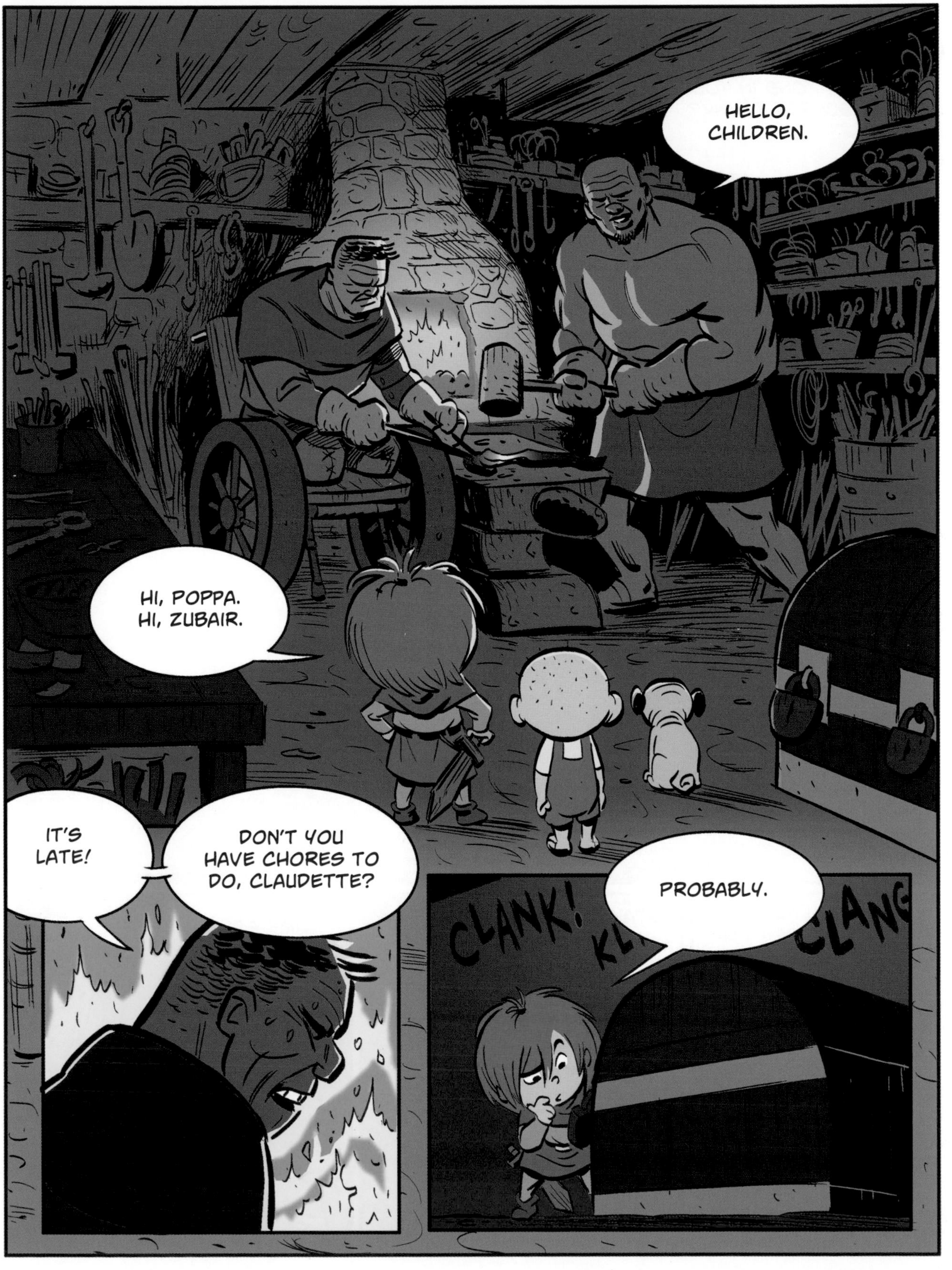
HELLO, CHILDREN.
HI, POPPA. HI, ZUBAIR.
IT'S LATE!
DON'T YOU HAVE CHORES TO DO, CLAUDETTE?
PROBABLY.
CLANK!
CLANG

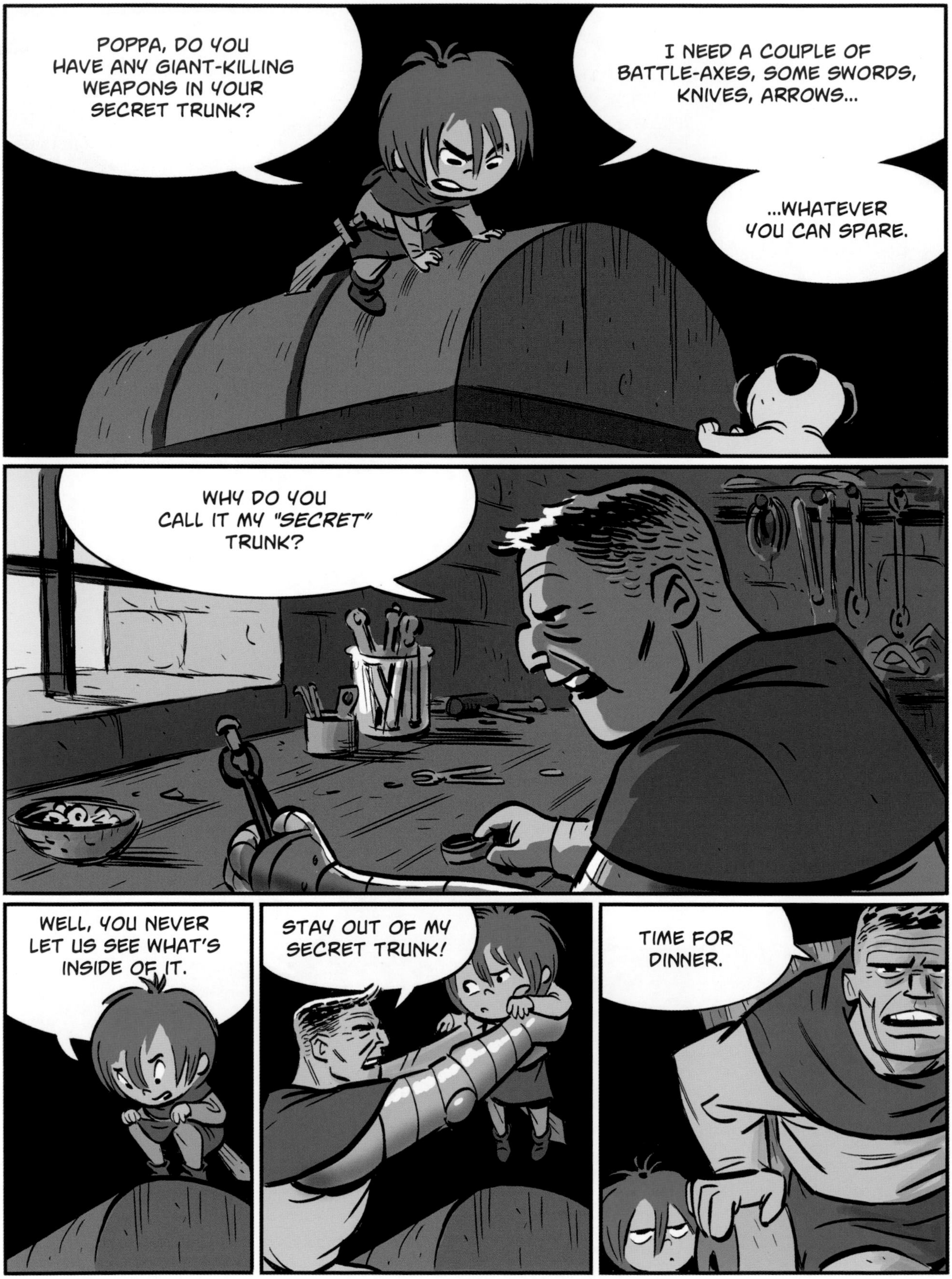
POPPA, DO YOU HAVE ANY GIANT-KILLING WEAPONS IN YOUR SECRET TRUNK?
I NEED A COUPLE OF BATTLE-AXES, SOME SWORDS, KNIVES, ARROWS...
...WHATEVER YOU CAN SPARE.
WHY DO YOU CALL IT MY "SECRET" TRUNK?
WELL, YOU NEVER LET US SEE WHAT'S INSIDE OF IT.
STAY OUT OF MY SECRET TRUNK!
TIME FOR DINNER.

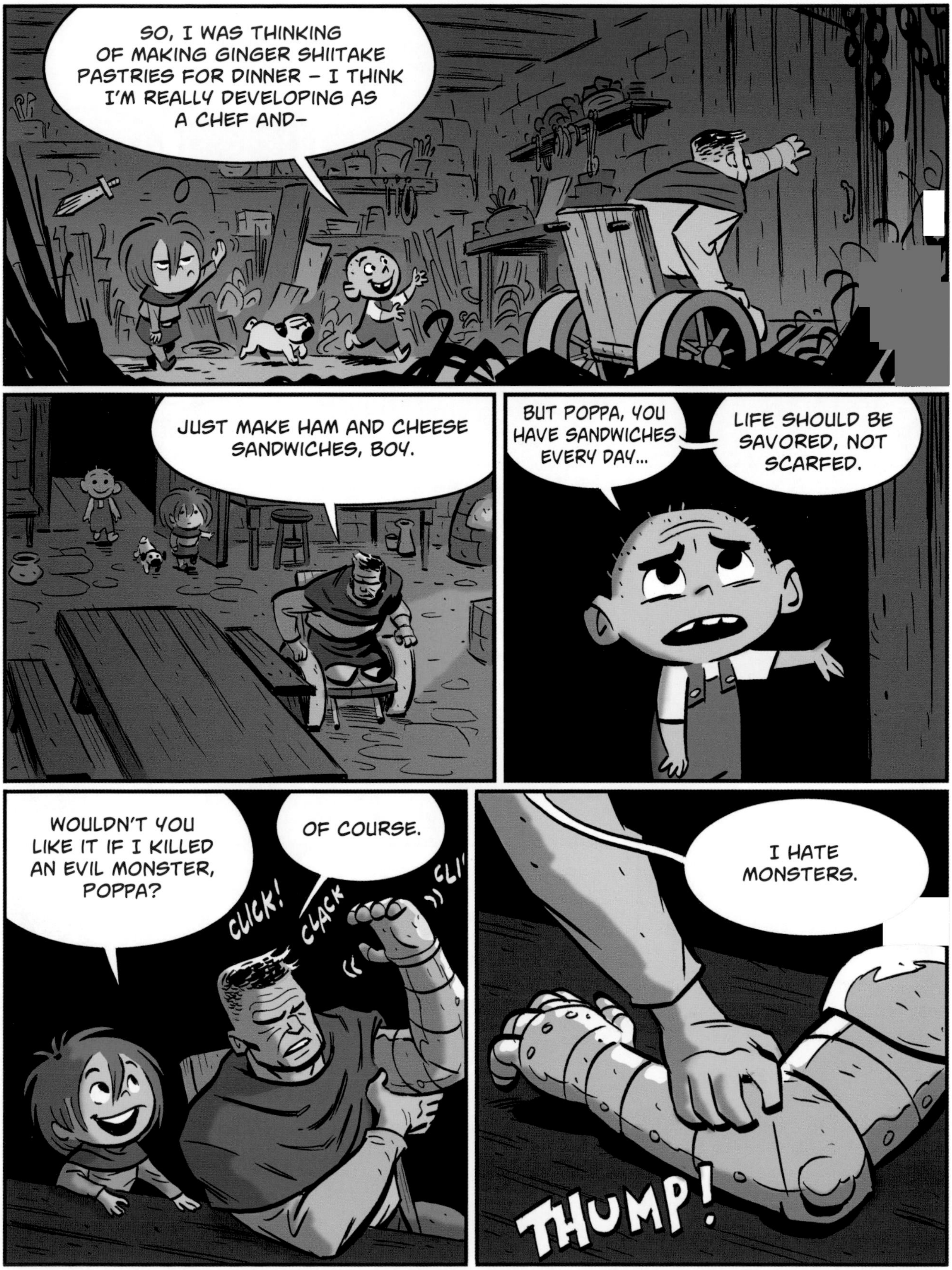
SO, I WAS THINKING OF MAKING GINGER SHIITAKE PASTRIES FOR DINNER – I THINK I'M REALLY DEVELOPING AS A CHEF AND–
JUST MAKE HAM AND CHEESE SANDWICHES, BOY.
BUT POPPA, YOU HAVE SANDWICHES EVERY DAY...
LIFE SHOULD BE SAVORED, NOT SCARFED.
WOULDN'T YOU LIKE IT IF I KILLED AN EVIL MONSTER, POPPA?
OF COURSE.
CLICK!
CLACK
I HATE MONSTERS.
THUMP!

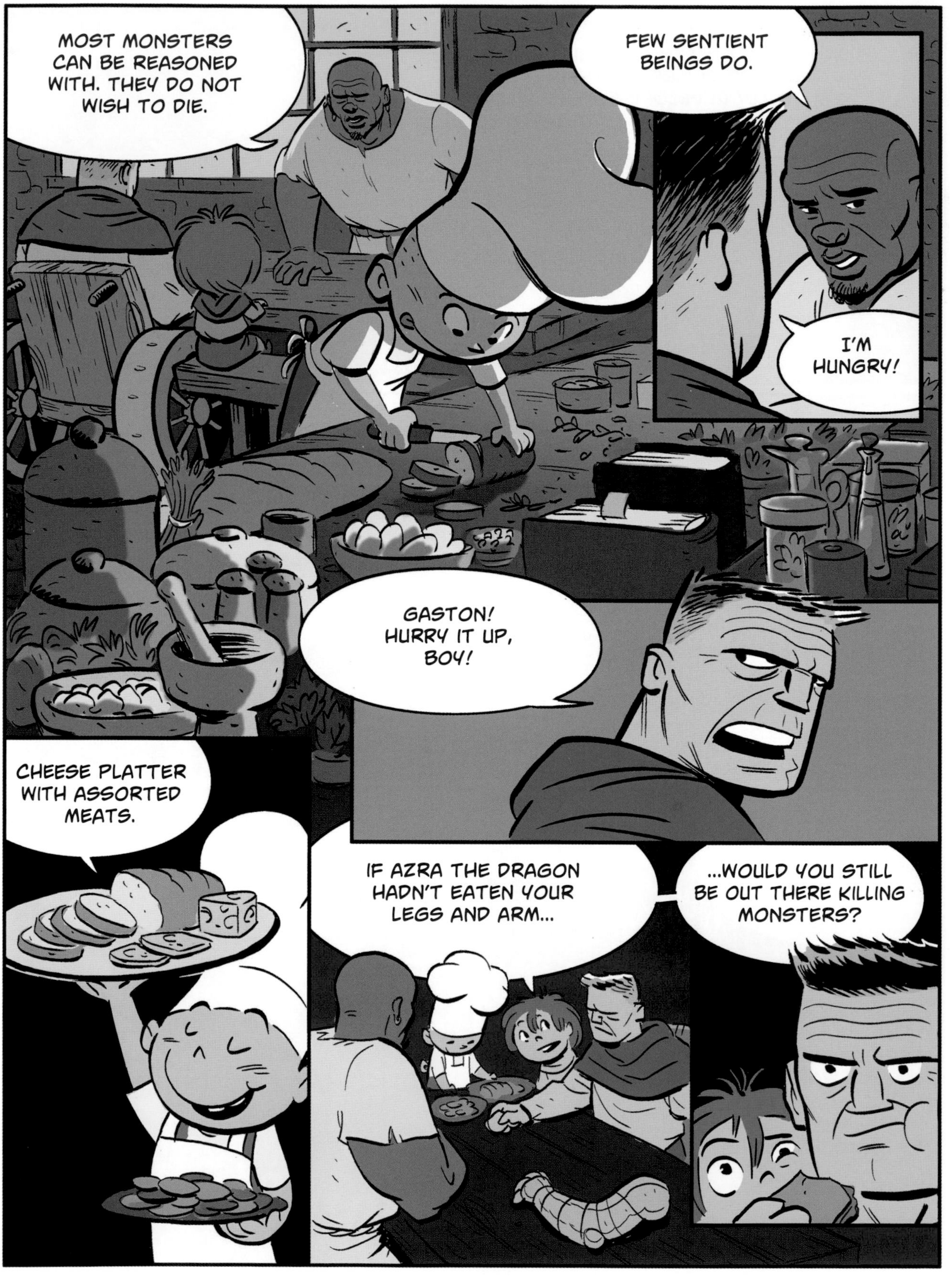
MOST MONSTERS CAN BE REASONED WITH. THEY DO NOT WISH TO DIE.
FEW SENTIENT BEINGS DO.
I'M HUNGRY!
GASTON! HURRY IT UP, BOY!
CHEESE PLATTER WITH ASSORTED MEATS.
IF AZRA THE DRAGON HADN'T EATEN YOUR LEGS AND ARM...
...WOULD YOU STILL BE OUT THERE KILLING MONSTERS?

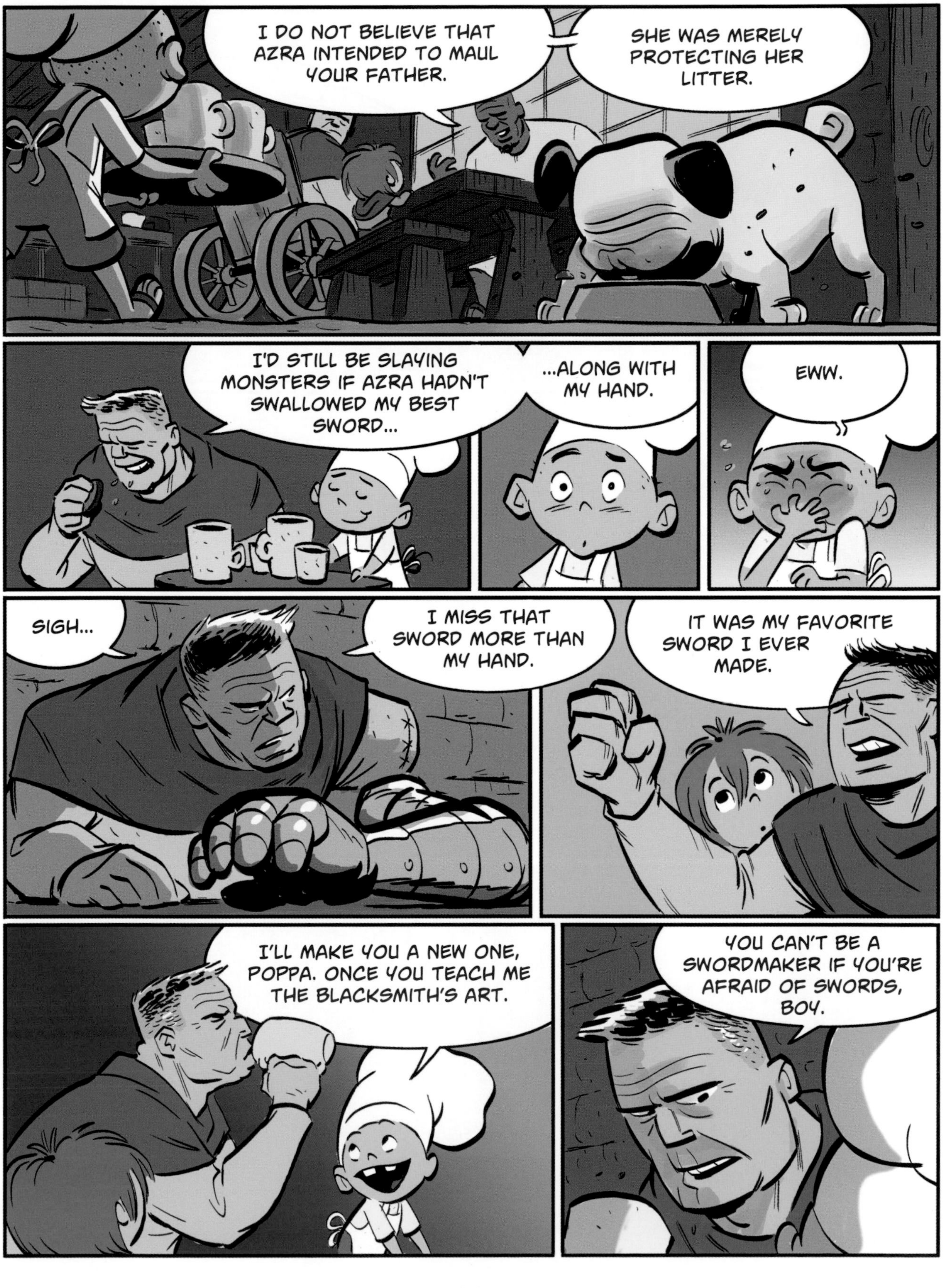
I DO NOT BELIEVE THAT AZRA INTENDED TO MAUL YOUR FATHER.
SHE WAS MERELY PROTECTING HER LITTER.
I'D STILL BE SLAYING MONSTERS IF AZRA HADN'T SWALLOWED MY BEST SWORD...
...ALONG WITH MY HAND.
EWW.
SIGH...
I MISS THAT SWORD MORE THAN MY HAND.
IT WAS MY FAVORITE SWORD I EVER MADE.
I'LL MAKE YOU A NEW ONE, POPPA. ONCE YOU TEACH ME THE BLACKSMITH'S ART.
YOU CAN'T BE A SWORDMAKER IF YOU'RE AFRAID OF SWORDS, BOY.

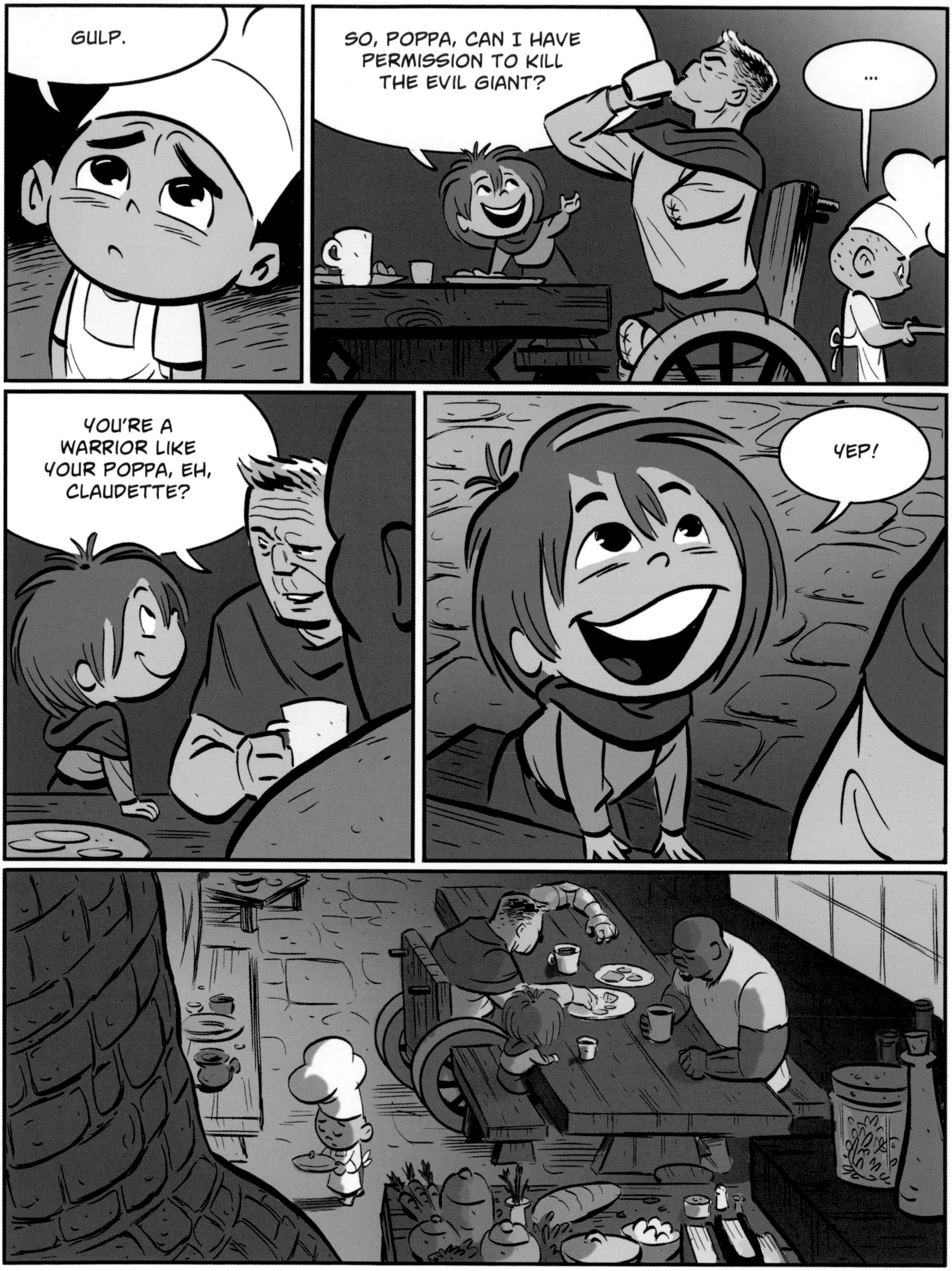
GULP.
SO, POPPA, CAN I HAVE PERMISSION TO KILL THE EVIL GIANT?
...
YOU'RE A WARRIOR LIKE YOUR POPPA, EH, CLAUDETTE?
YEP!

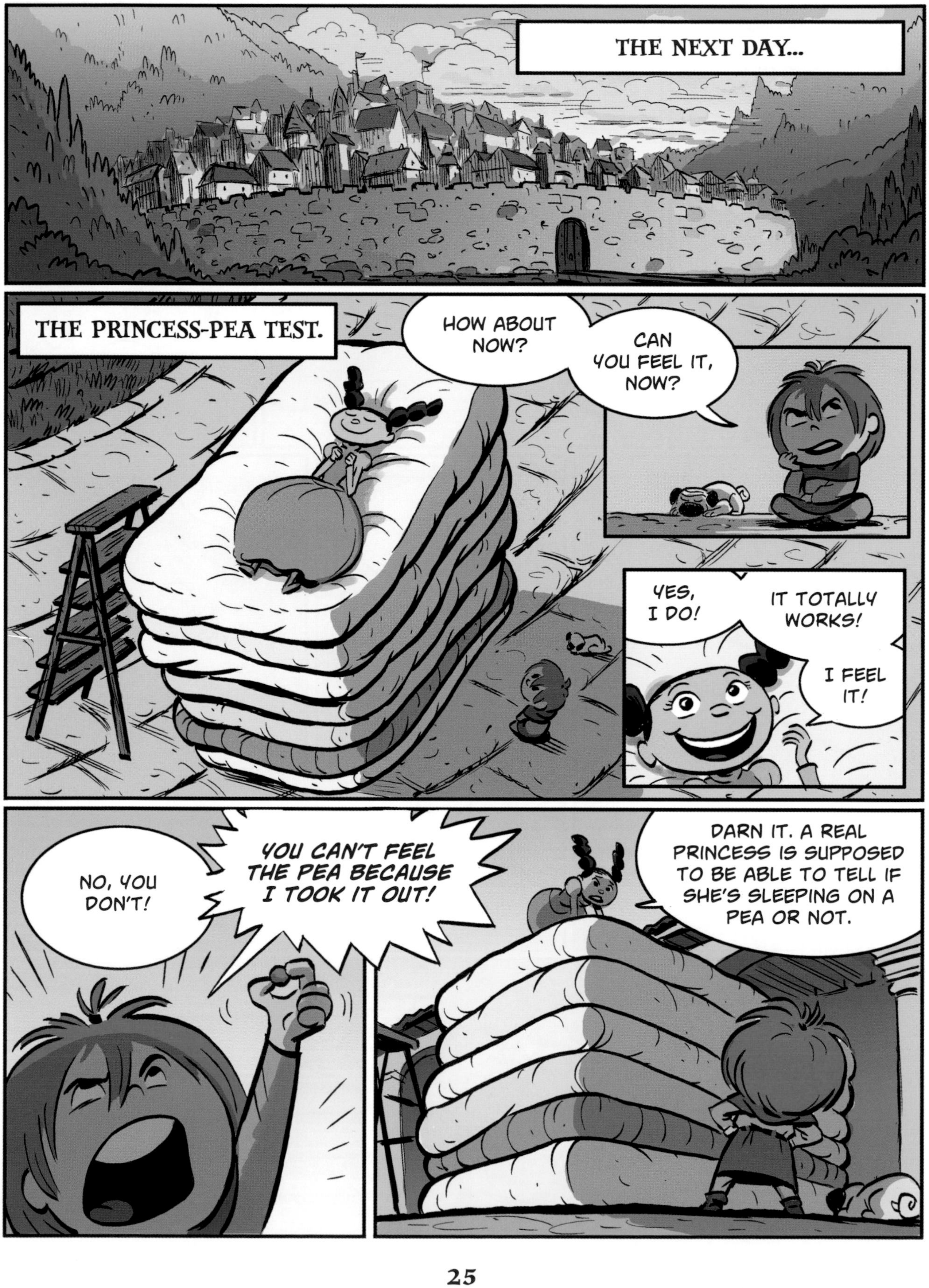
THE NEXT DAY...
THE PRINCESS-PEA TEST.
HOW ABOUT NOW?
CAN YOU FEEL IT, NOW?
YES, I DO!
IT TOTALLY WORKS!
I FEEL IT!
NO, YOU DON'T!
YOU CAN'T FEEL THE PEA BECAUSE I TOOK IT OUT!
DARN IT. A REAL PRINCESS IS SUPPOSED TO BE ABLE TO TELL IF SHE'S SLEEPING ON A PEA OR NOT.

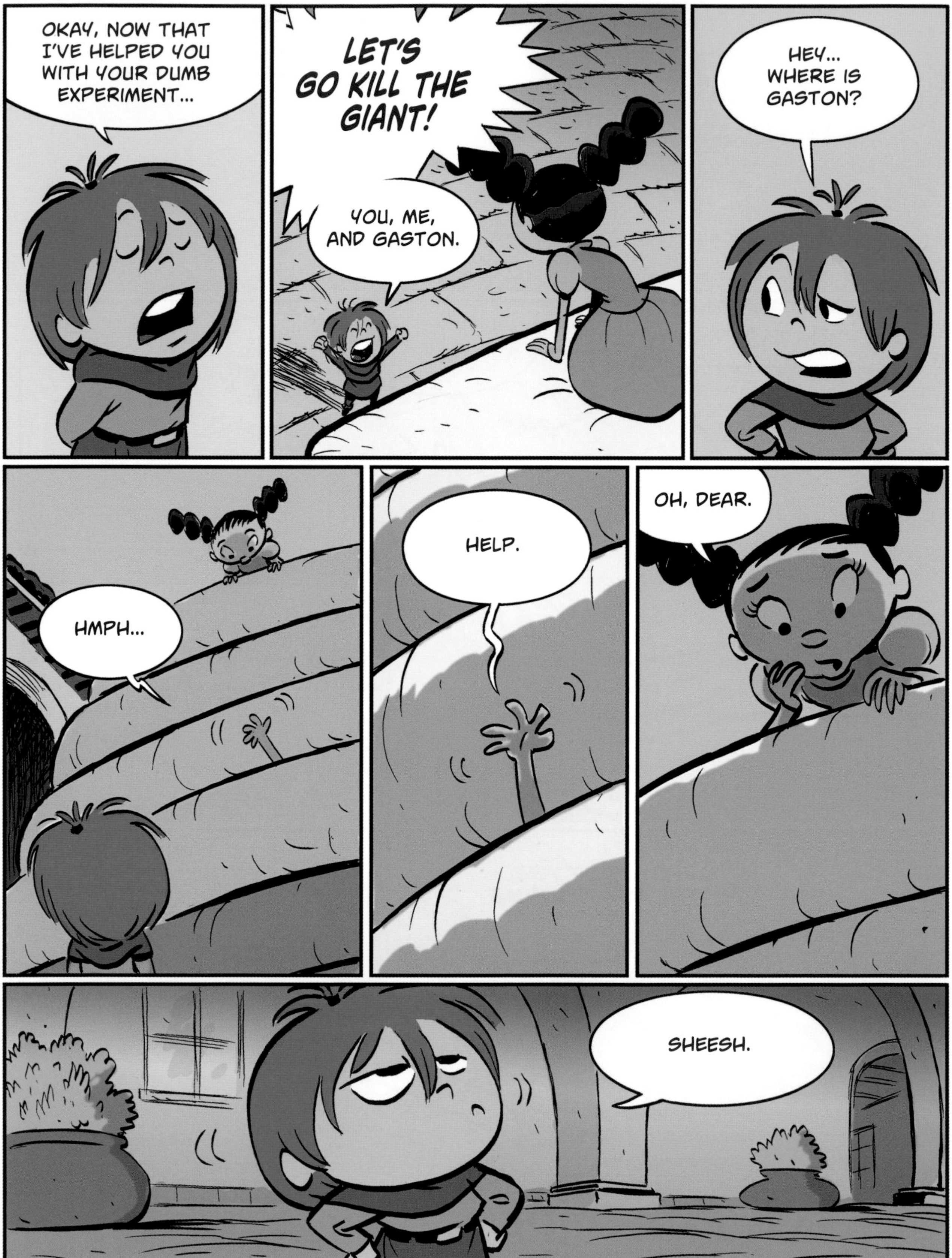
OKAY, NOW THAT I'VE HELPED YOU WITH YOUR DUMB EXPERIMENT...
LET'S GO KILL THE GIANT!
YOU, ME, AND GASTON.
HEY... WHERE IS GASTON?
HMPH...
HELP.
OH, DEAR.
SHEESH.

HMM?
GOOD HEAVENS!
UMPH!!!
POP
MARIE NEEDS NEW FRIENDS.
SLAM!
OW.

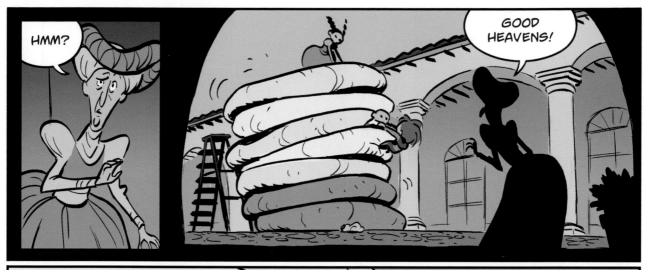

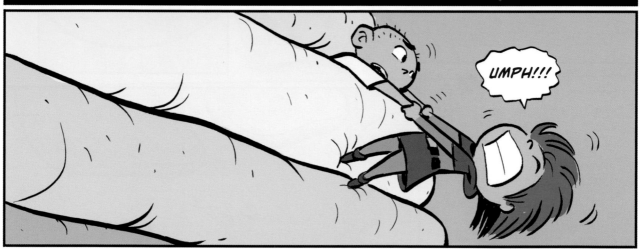

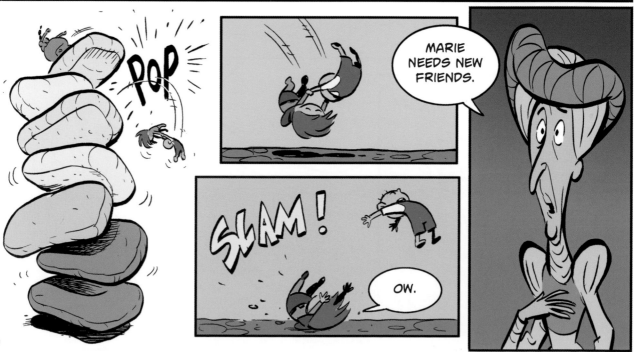

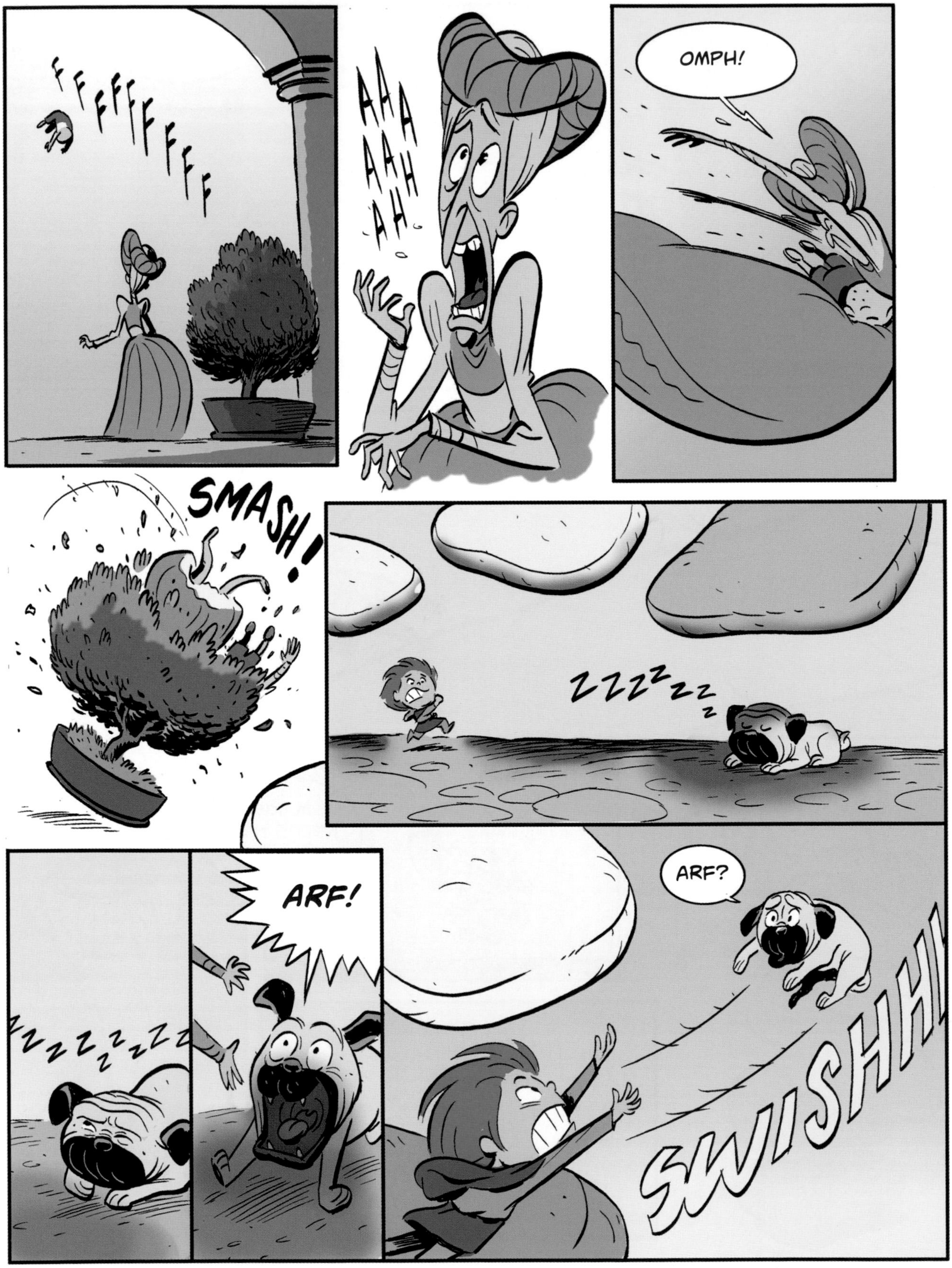
FFFFFFFFFF
AAAAAAAAH
OMPH!
SMASH!
ZZZZZZZ
ZZZZZZZZZ
ARF!
ARF?
SWISHH

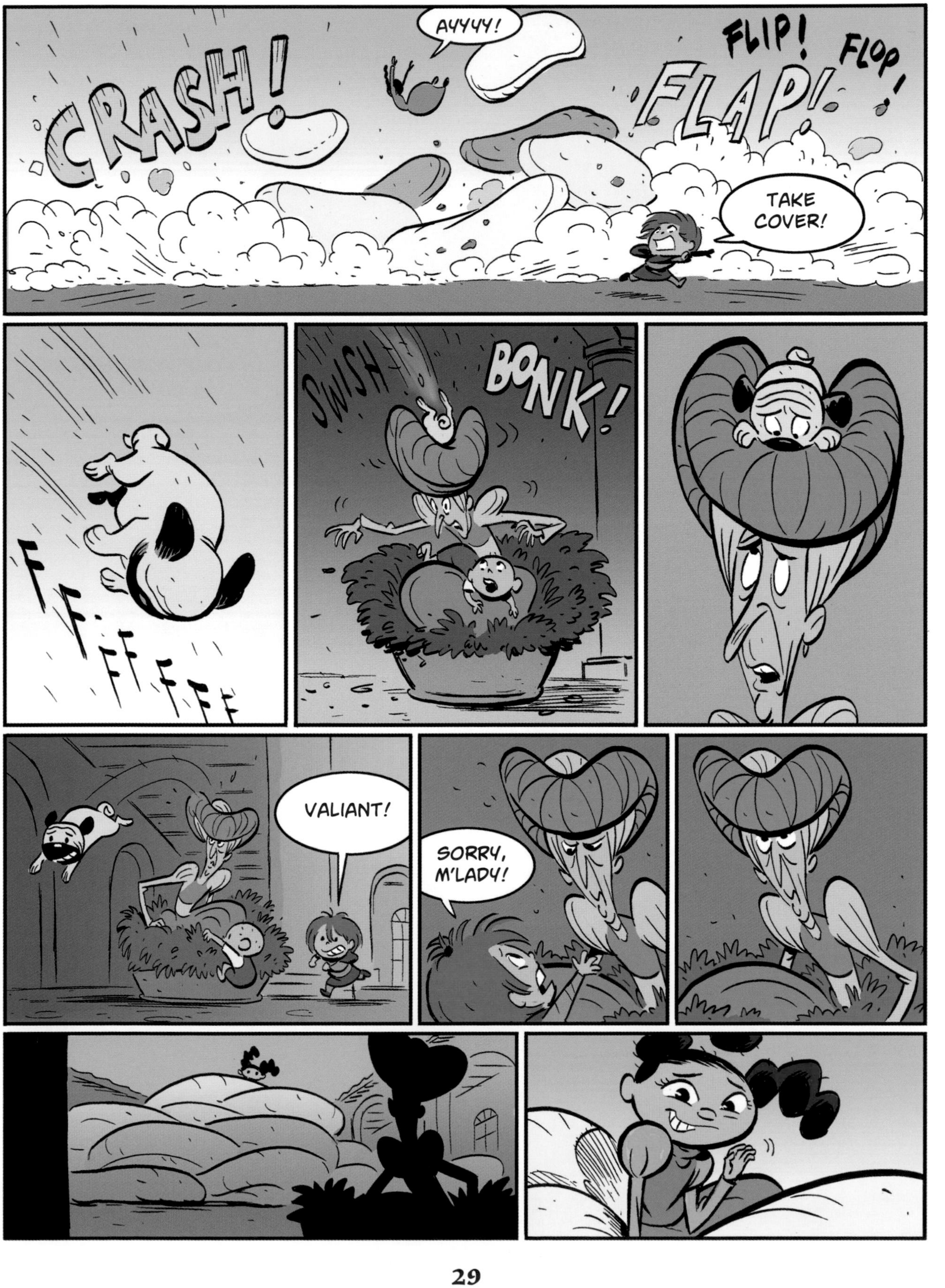
CRASH!
AYYYY!
FLIP!
FLAP!
FLOP!
TAKE COVER!
FFFFFFFF
SWISH
BONK!
VALIANT!
SORRY, M'LADY!

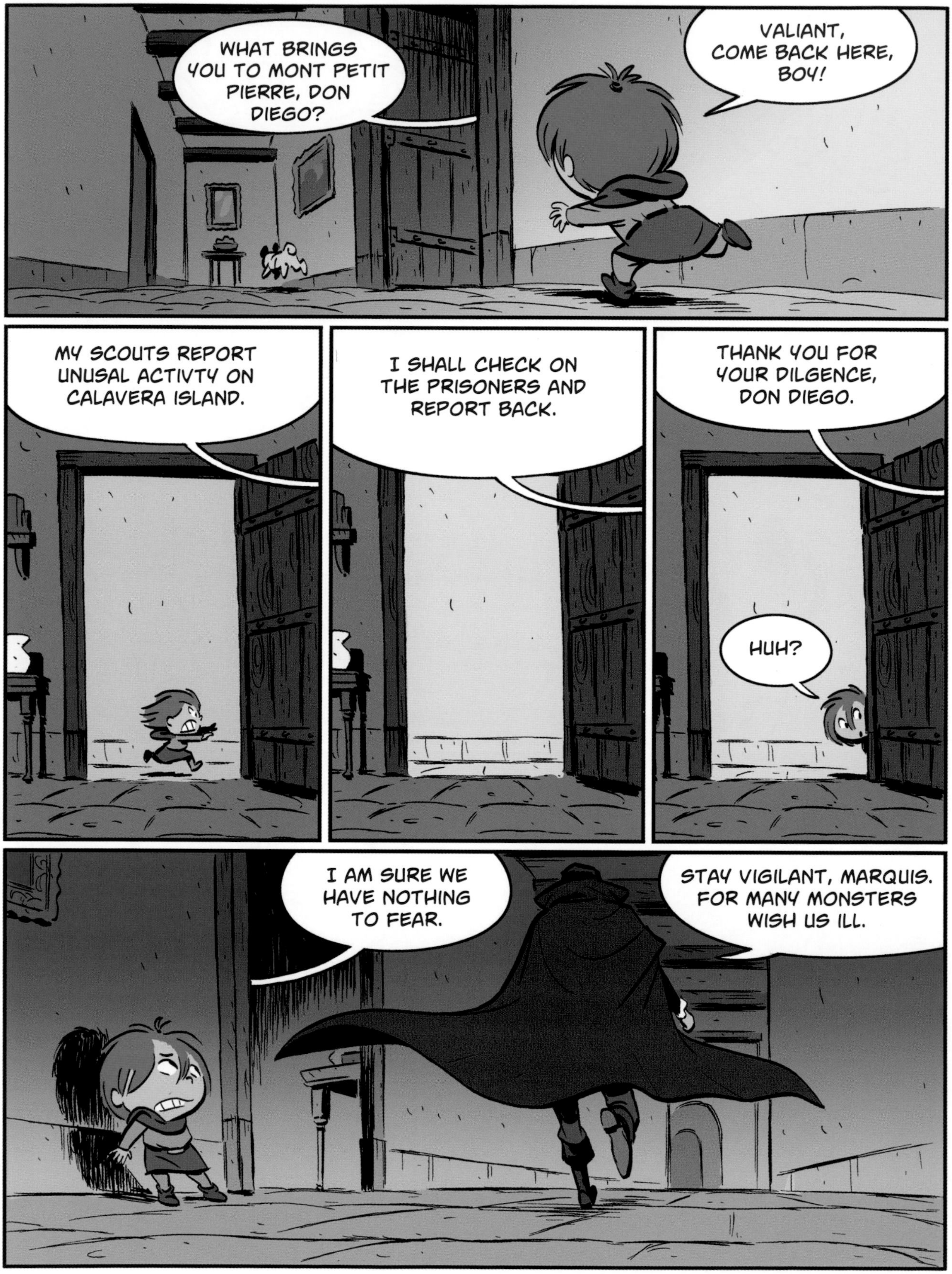
WHAT BRINGS YOU TO MONT PETIT PIERRE, DON DIEGO?
VALIANT, COME BACK HERE, BOY!
MY SCOUTS REPORT UNUSAL ACTIVTY ON CALAVERA ISLAND.
I SHALL CHECK ON THE PRISONERS AND REPORT BACK.
THANK YOU FOR YOUR DILGENCE, DON DIEGO.
HUH?
I AM SURE WE HAVE NOTHING TO FEAR.
STAY VIGILANT, MARQUIS. FOR MANY MONSTERS WISH US ILL.

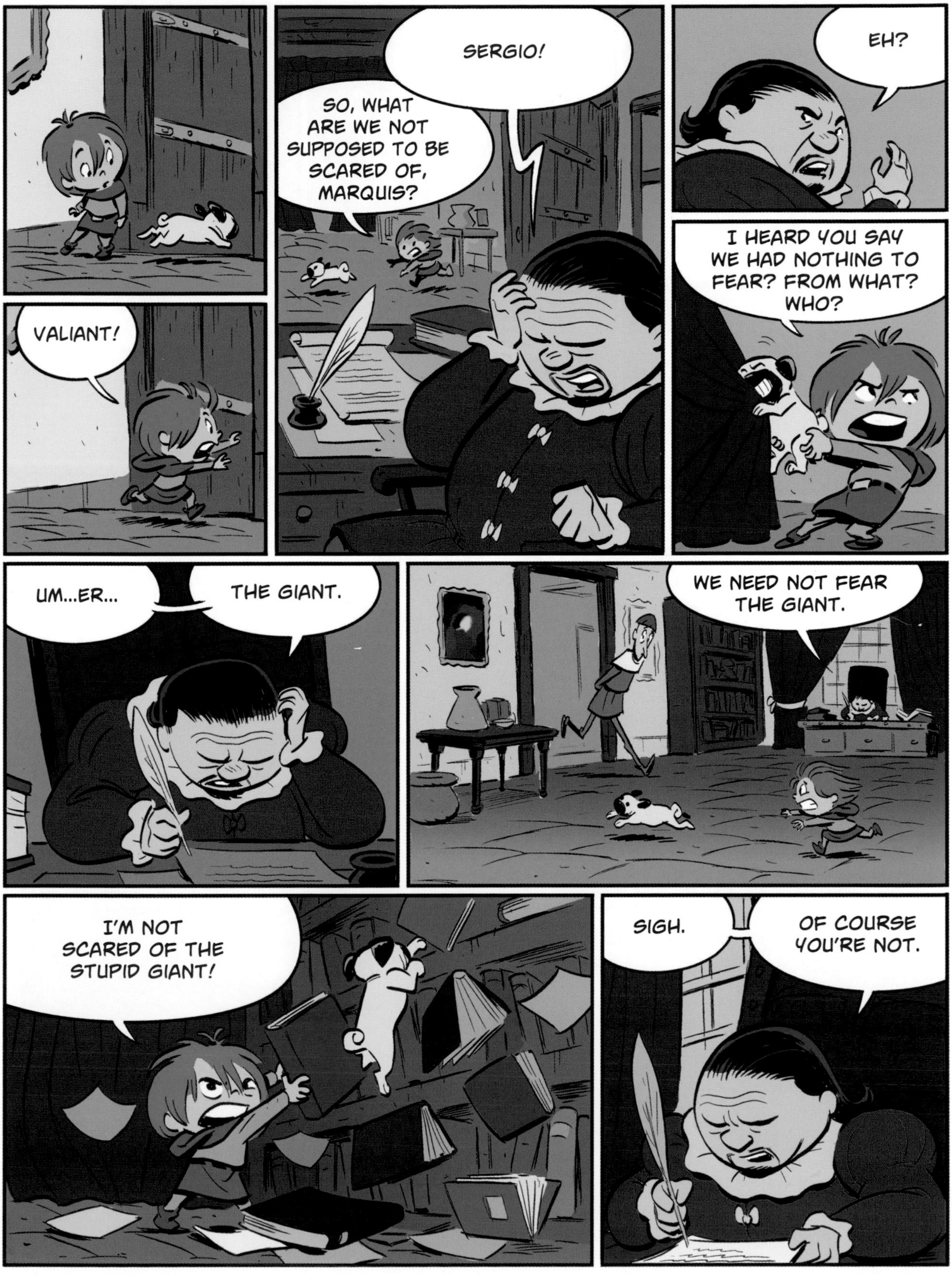
SERGIO!
SO, WHAT ARE WE NOT SUPPOSED TO BE SCARED OF, MARQUIS?
VALIANT!
EH?
I HEARD YOU SAY WE HAD NOTHING TO FEAR? FROM WHAT? WHO?
UM...ER...
THE GIANT.
WE NEED NOT FEAR THE GIANT.
I'M NOT SCARED OF THE STUPID GIANT!
SIGH.
OF COURSE YOU'RE NOT.

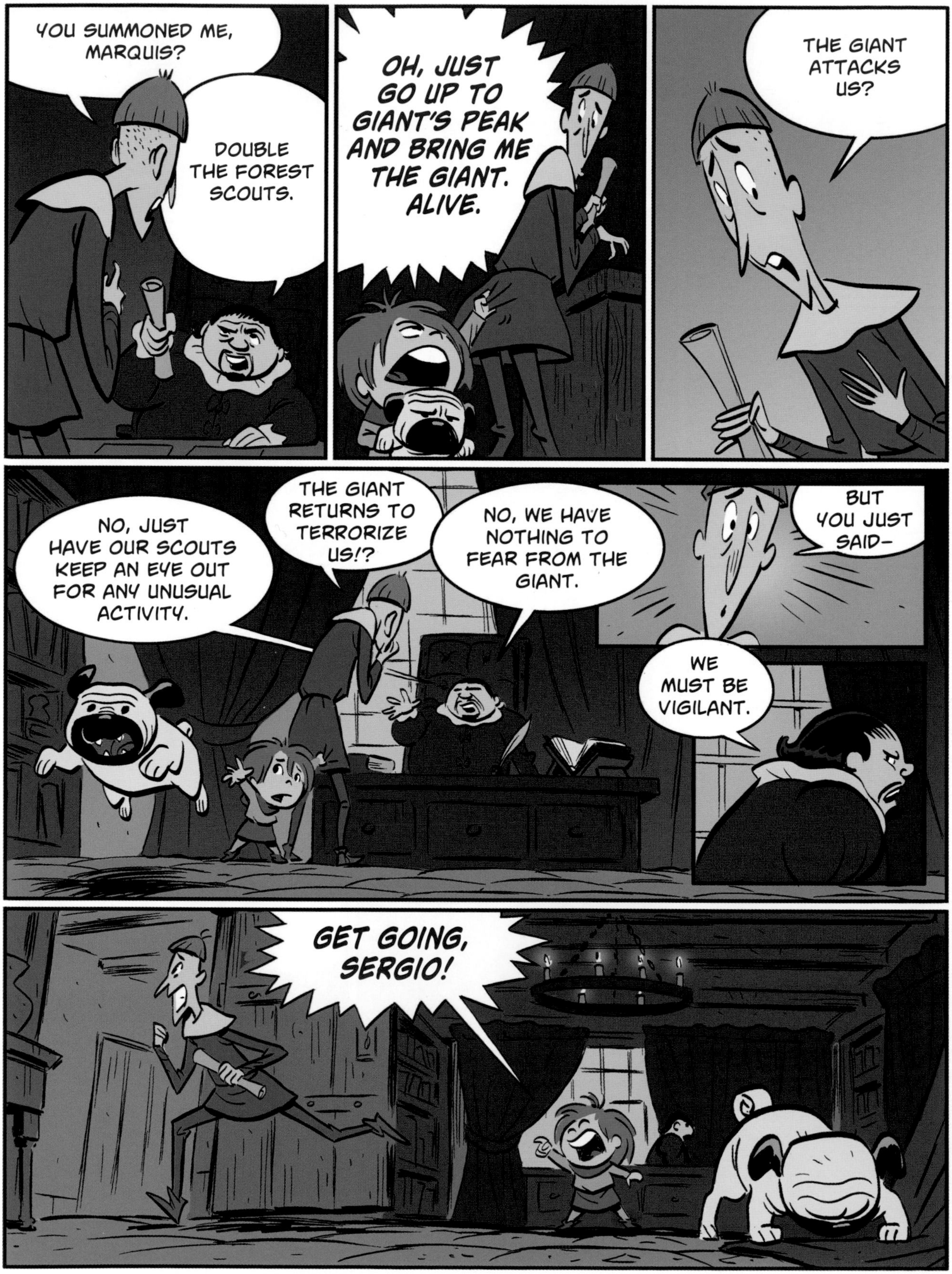
YOU SUMMONED ME, MARQUIS?
DOUBLE THE FOREST SCOUTS.
OH, JUST GO UP TO GIANT'S PEAK AND BRING ME THE GIANT. ALIVE.
THE GIANT ATTACKS US?
NO, JUST HAVE OUR SCOUTS KEEP AN EYE OUT FOR ANY UNUSUAL ACTIVITY.
THE GIANT RETURNS TO TERRORIZE US!?
NO, WE HAVE NOTHING TO FEAR FROM THE GIANT.
BUT YOU JUST SAID–
WE MUST BE VIGILANT.
GET GOING, SERGIO!

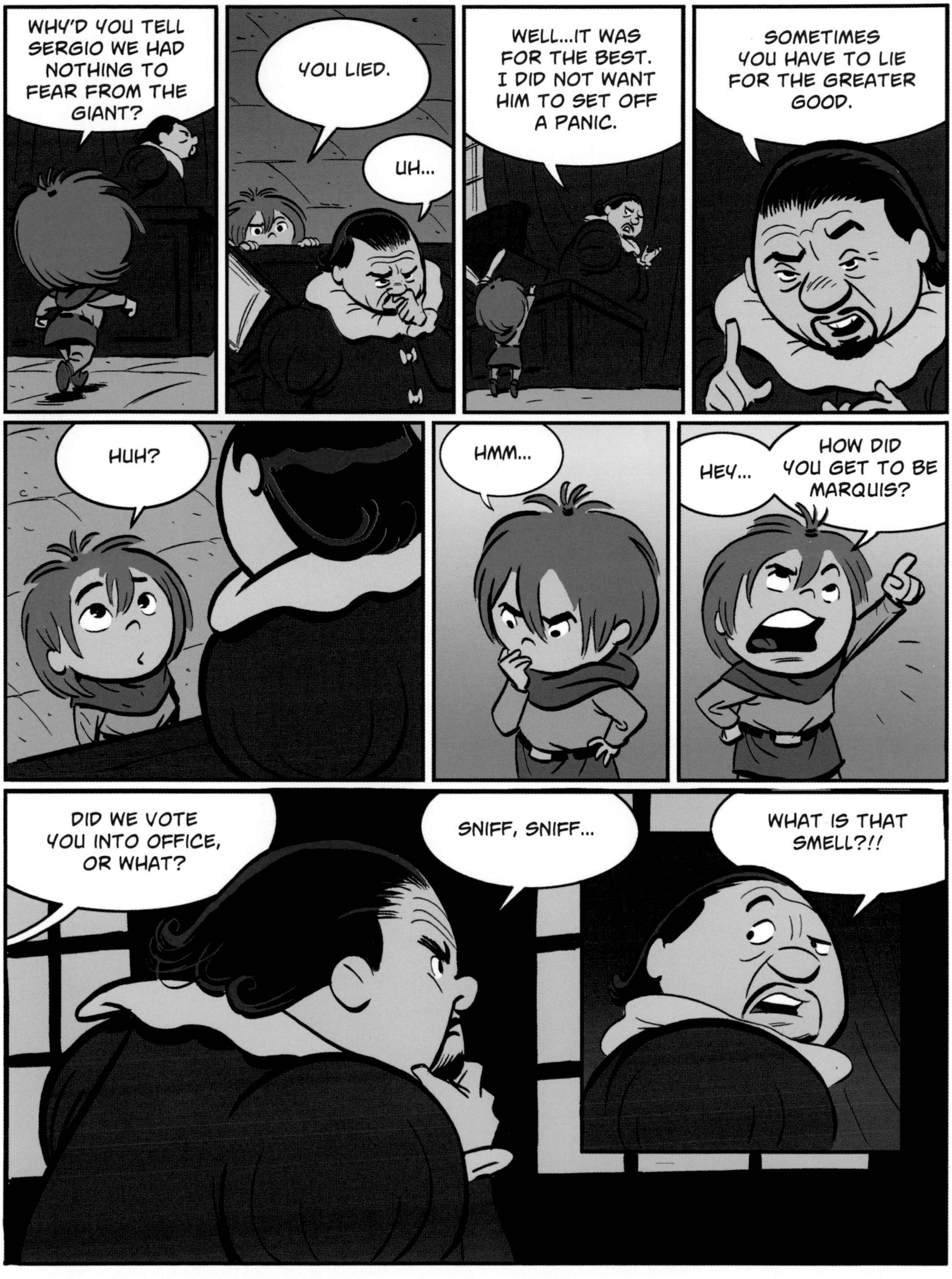
WHY'D YOU TELL SERGIO WE HAD NOTHING TO FEAR FROM THE GIANT?
YOU LIED.
UH...
WELL...IT WAS FOR THE BEST. I DID NOT WANT HIM TO SET OFF A PANIC.
SOMETIMES YOU HAVE TO LIE FOR THE GREATER GOOD.
HUH?
HMM...
HEY...
HOW DID YOU GET TO BE MARQUIS?
DID WE VOTE YOU INTO OFFICE, OR WHAT?
SNIFF, SNIFF...
WHAT IS THAT SMELL?!!

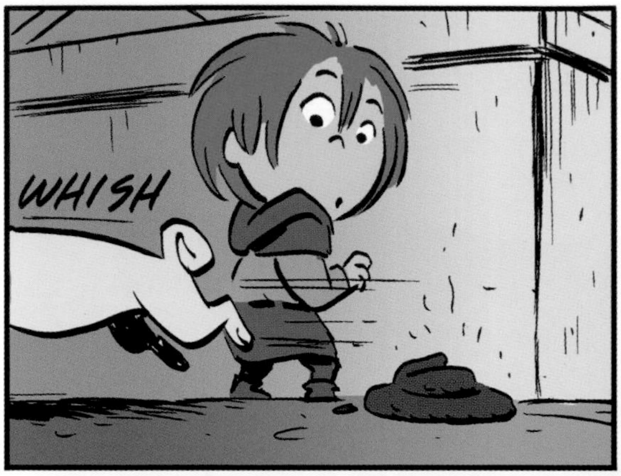
WHISH

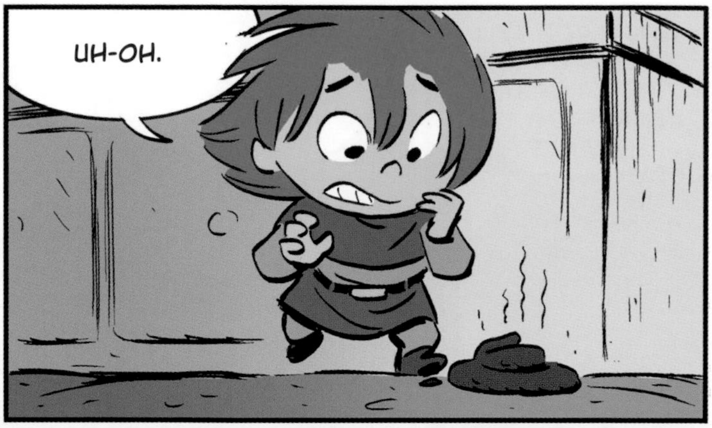
UH-OH.

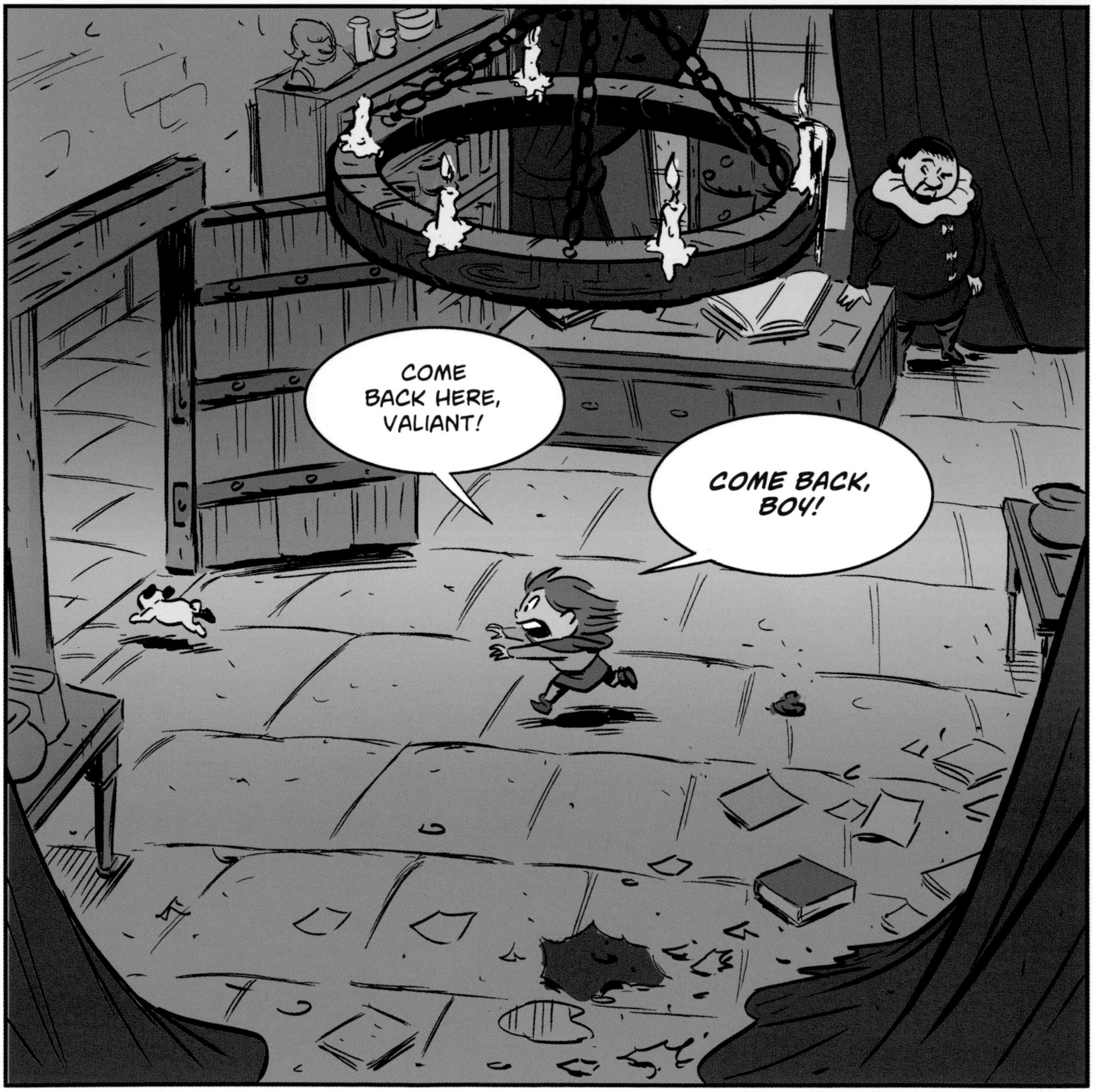
COME BACK HERE, VALIANT!
COME BACK, BOY!

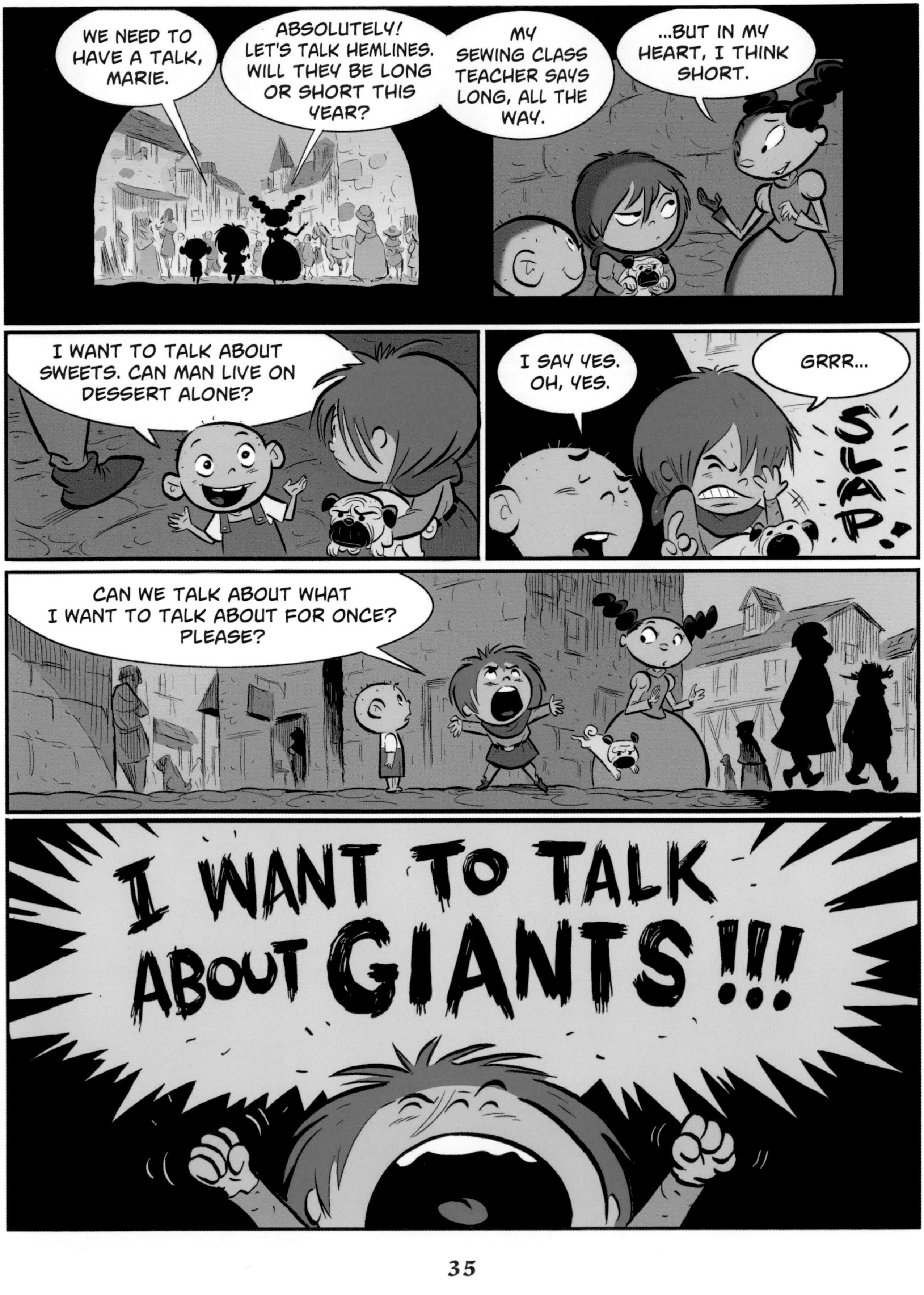
WE NEED TO HAVE A TALK, MARIE.
ABSOLUTELY! LET'S TALK HEMLINES. WILL THEY BE LONG OR SHORT THIS YEAR?
MY SEWING CLASS TEACHER SAYS LONG, ALL THE WAY.
...BUT IN MY HEART, I THINK SHORT.
I WANT TO TALK ABOUT SWEETS. CAN MAN LIVE ON DESSERT ALONE?
I SAY YES. OH, YES.
GRRR...
SLAP!
CAN WE TALK ABOUT WHAT I WANT TO TALK ABOUT FOR ONCE? PLEASE?
I WANT TO TALK ABOUT GIANTS!!!

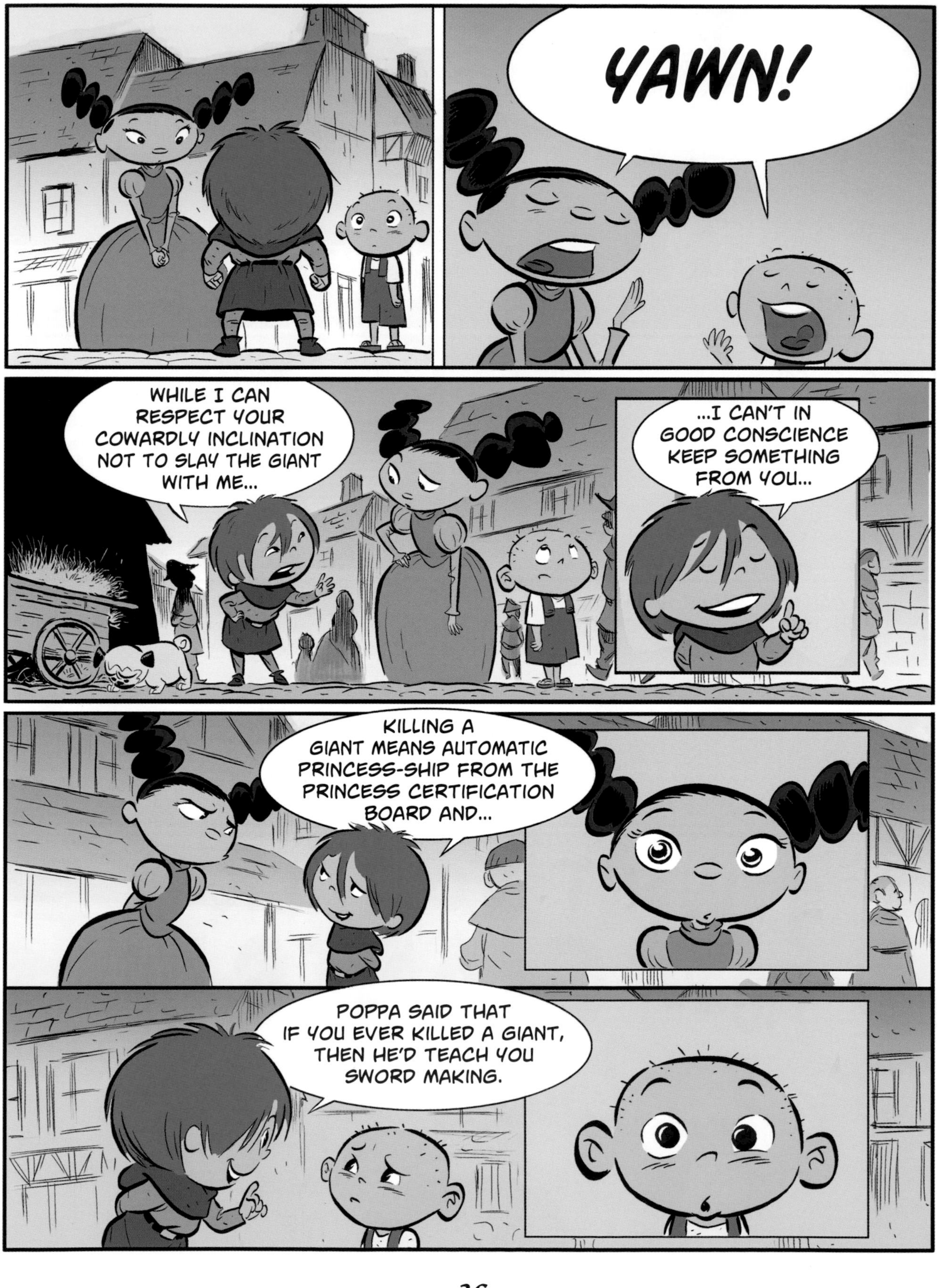
YAWN!
WHILE I CAN RESPECT YOUR COWARDLY INCLINATION NOT TO SLAY THE GIANT WITH ME...
...I CAN'T IN GOOD CONSCIENCE KEEP SOMETHING FROM YOU...
KILLING A GIANT MEANS AUTOMATIC PRINCESS-SHIP FROM THE PRINCESS CERTIFICATION BOARD AND...
POPPA SAID THAT IF YOU EVER KILLED A GIANT, THEN HE'D TEACH YOU SWORD MAKING.

FOR REAL?
COME ON...
WOULD I LIE TO YOU?
HMMM, EXACTLY, HOW HARD IS IT TO KILL A GIANT, ANYWAY?
PHHT! IT'S A WALK IN THE PARK.
THE GIANT LIVES IN A PARK?
NO. HE LIVES IN THE MOUNTAIN.
SO, WHO ARE WE GOING TO KILL IN THE PARK?
FORGET THE PARK! OKAY?
SO, ARE YOU WITH ME OR NOT?
WE'LL BE LIKE THE THREE MUSKETEERS!

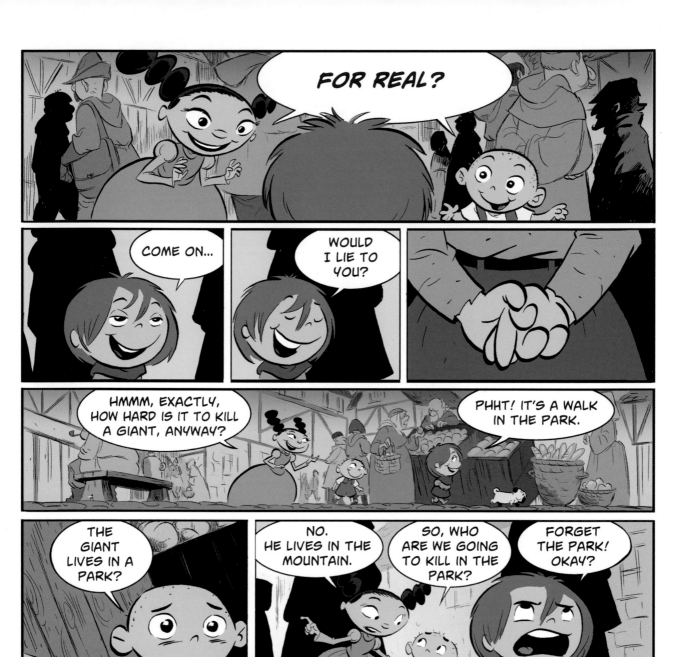

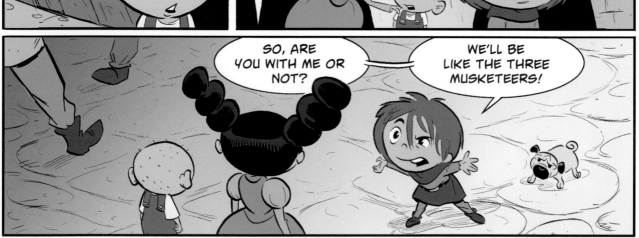

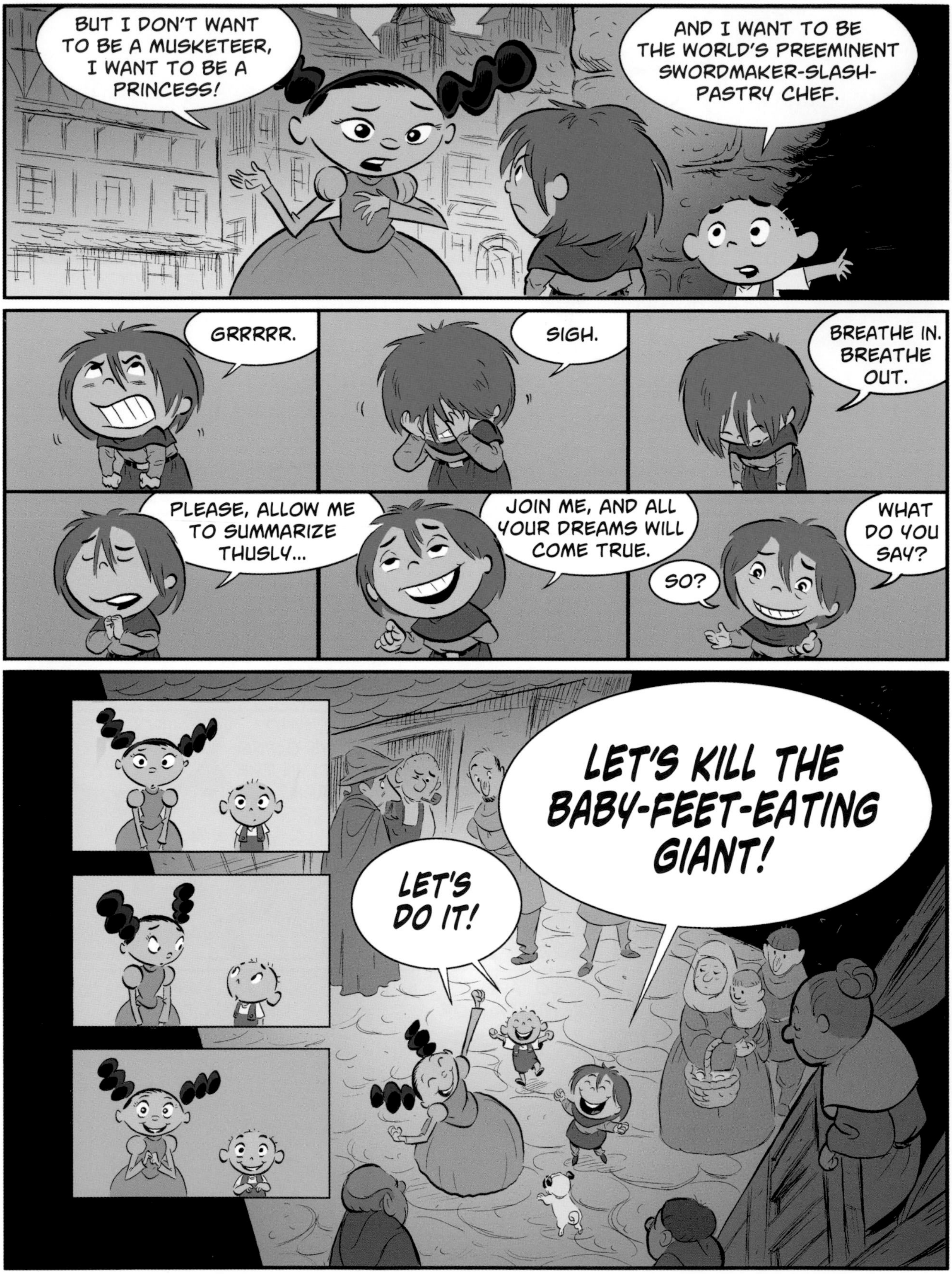
BUT I DON'T WANT TO BE A MUSKETEER, I WANT TO BE A PRINCESS!
AND I WANT TO BE THE WORLD'S PREEMINENT SWORDMAKER-SLASH-PASTRY CHEF.
GRRRRR.
SIGH.
BREATHE IN. BREATHE OUT.
PLEASE, ALLOW ME TO SUMMARIZE THUSLY...
JOIN ME, AND ALL YOUR DREAMS WILL COME TRUE.
SO?
WHAT DO YOU SAY?
LET'S KILL THE BABY-FEET-EATING GIANT!
LET'S DO IT!

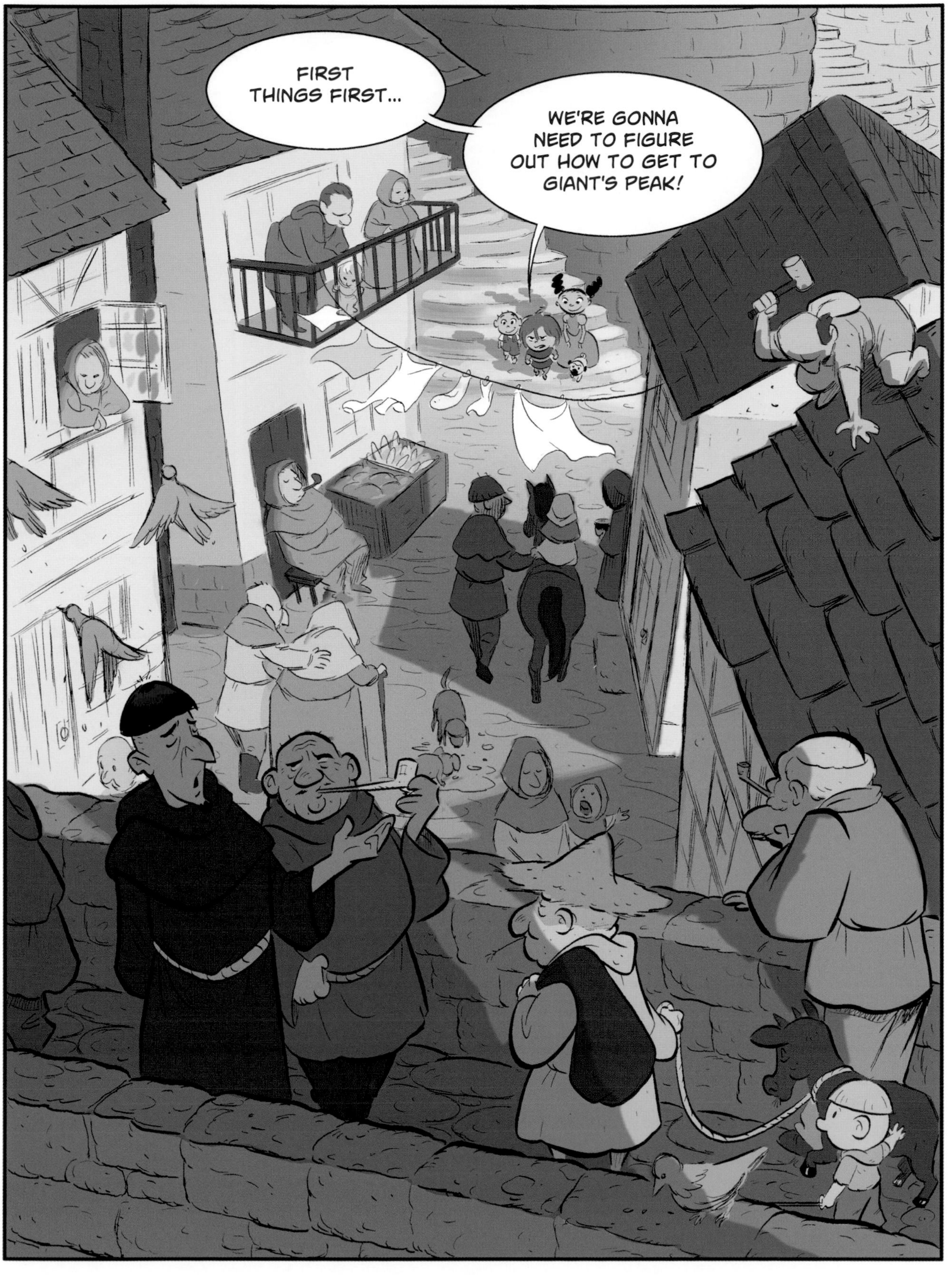
FIRST THINGS FIRST...
WE'RE GONNA NEED TO FIGURE OUT HOW TO GET TO GIANT'S PEAK!

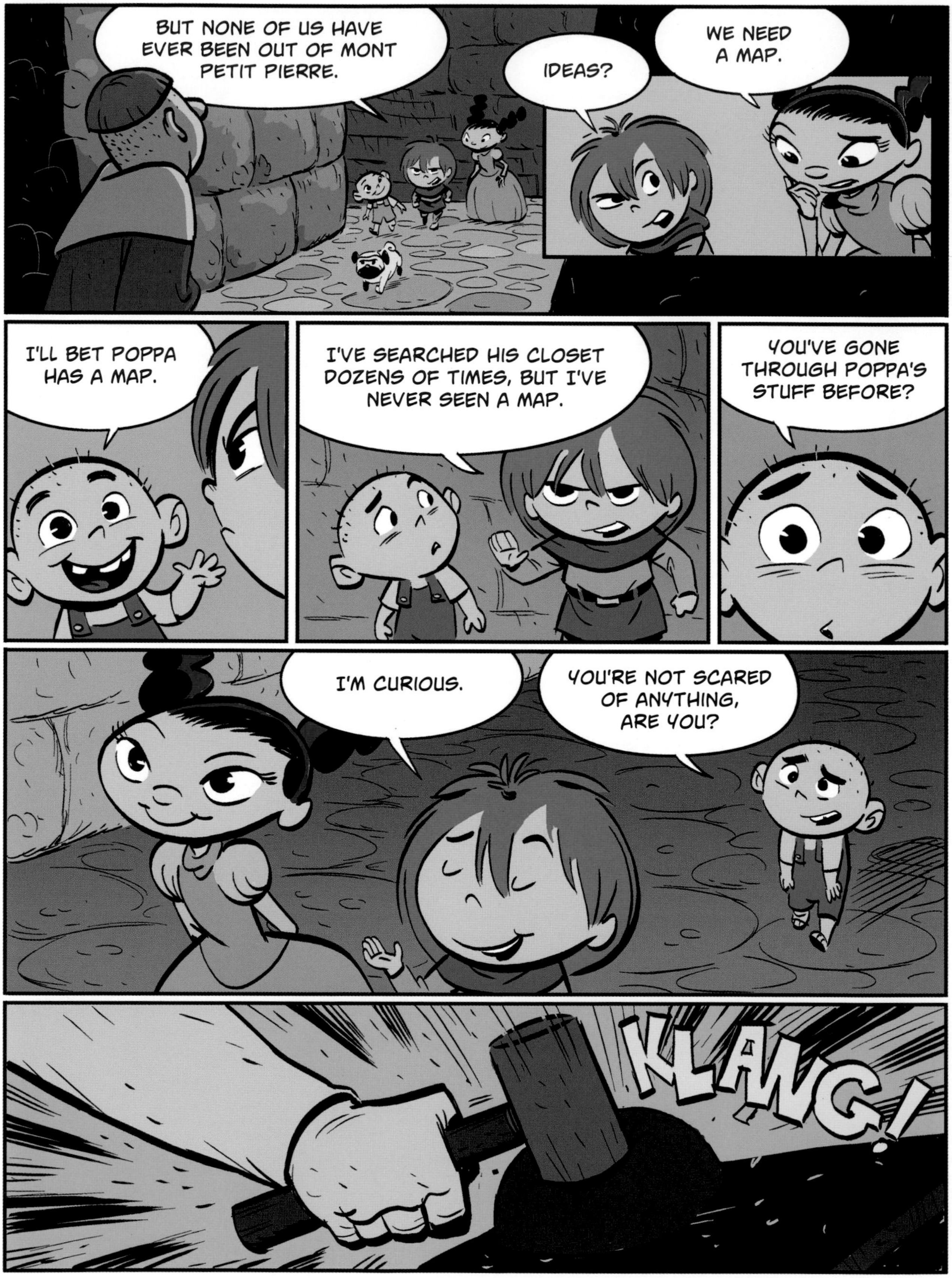
BUT NONE OF US HAVE EVER BEEN OUT OF MONT PETIT PIERRE.
IDEAS?
WE NEED A MAP.
I'LL BET POPPA HAS A MAP.
I'VE SEARCHED HIS CLOSET DOZENS OF TIMES, BUT I'VE NEVER SEEN A MAP.
YOU'VE GONE THROUGH POPPA'S STUFF BEFORE?
I'M CURIOUS.
YOU'RE NOT SCARED OF ANYTHING, ARE YOU?
KLANG!

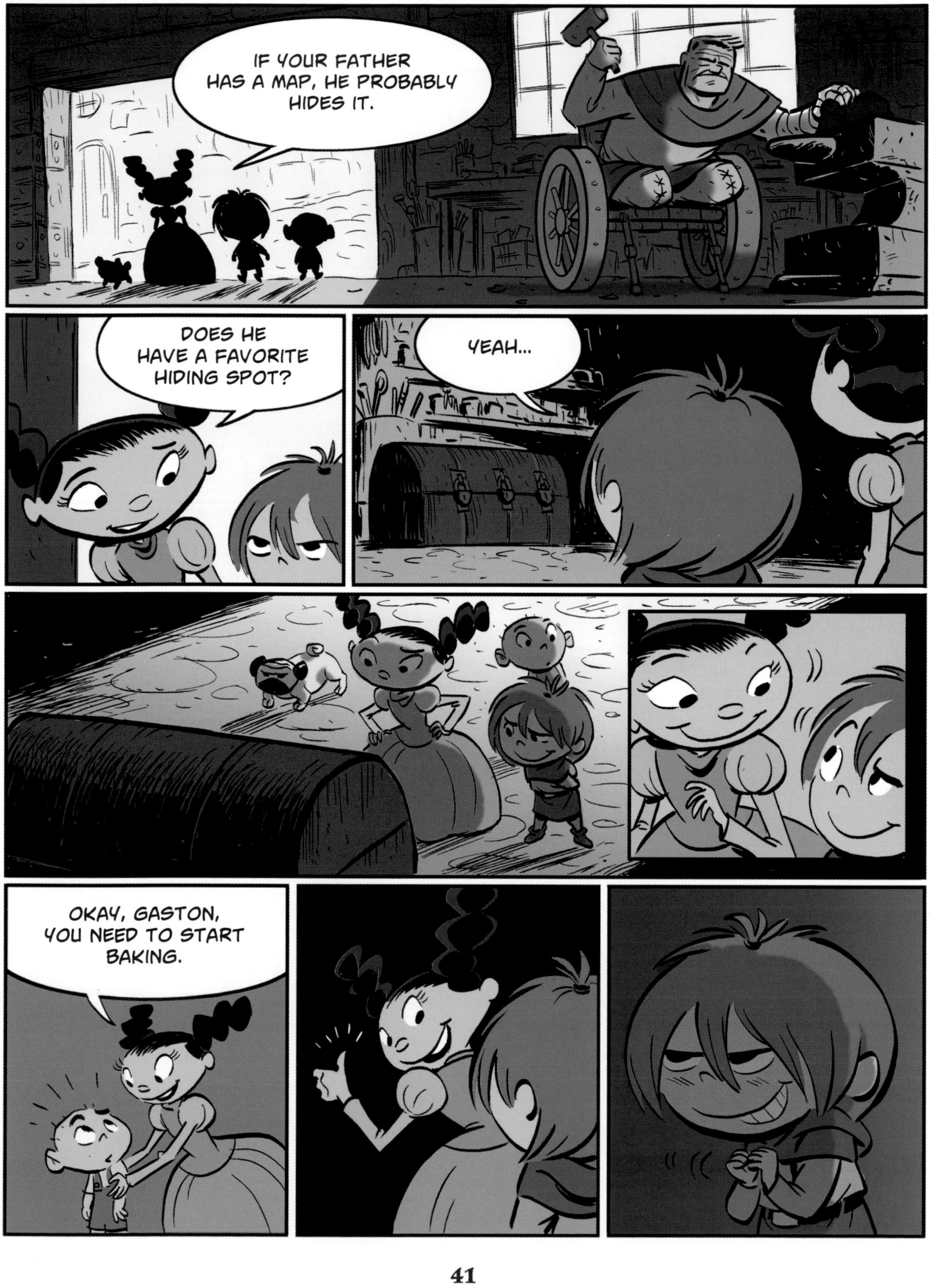
IF YOUR FATHER HAS A MAP, HE PROBABLY HIDES IT.
DOES HE HAVE A FAVORITE HIDING SPOT?
YEAH...
OKAY, GASTON, YOU NEED TO START BAKING.

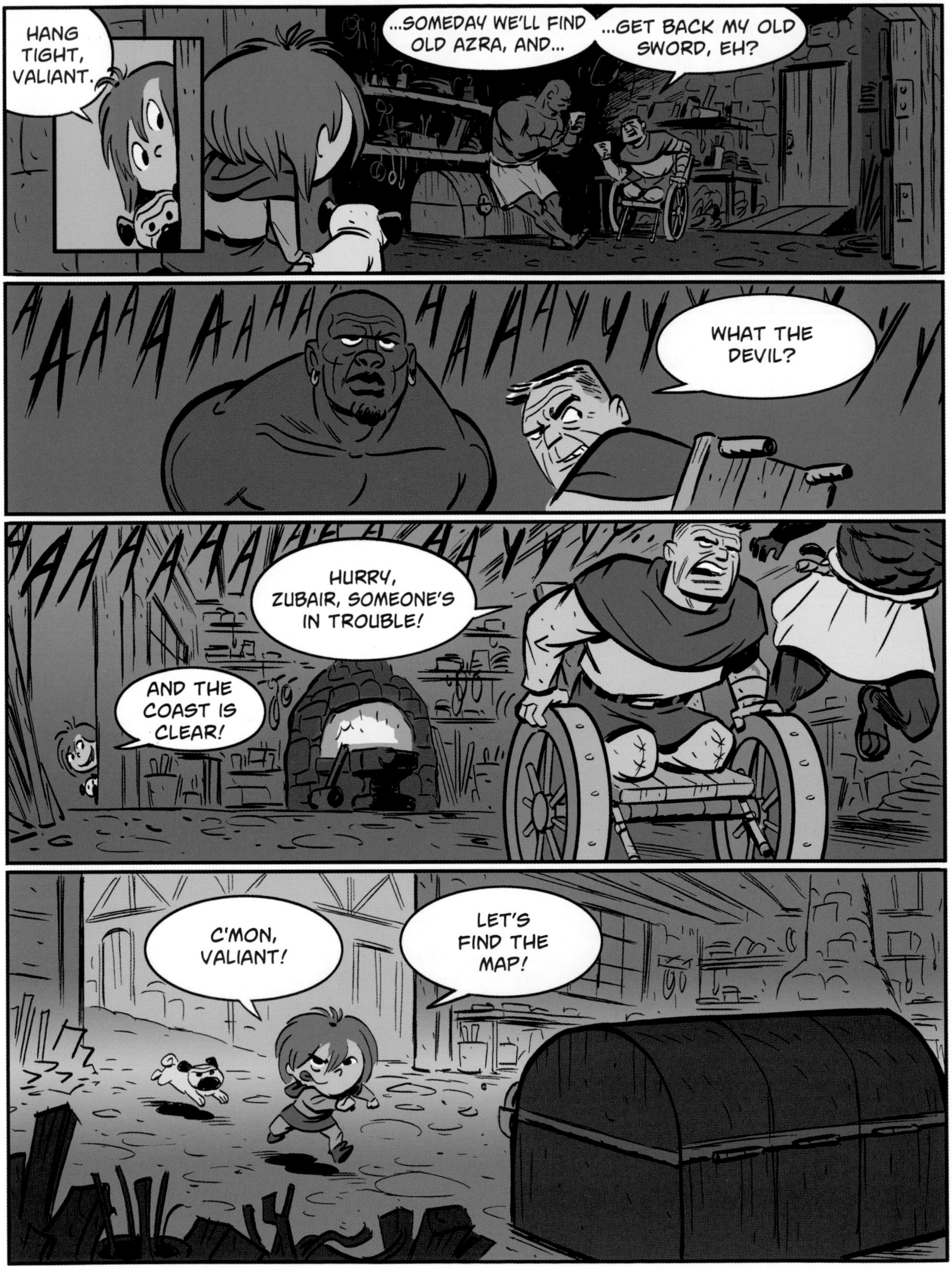
HANG TIGHT, VALIANT.
...SOMEDAY WE'LL FIND OLD AZRA, AND...
...GET BACK MY OLD SWORD, EH?
WHAT THE DEVIL?
HURRY, ZUBAIR, SOMEONE'S IN TROUBLE!
AND THE COAST IS CLEAR!
C'MON, VALIANT!
LET'S FIND THE MAP!

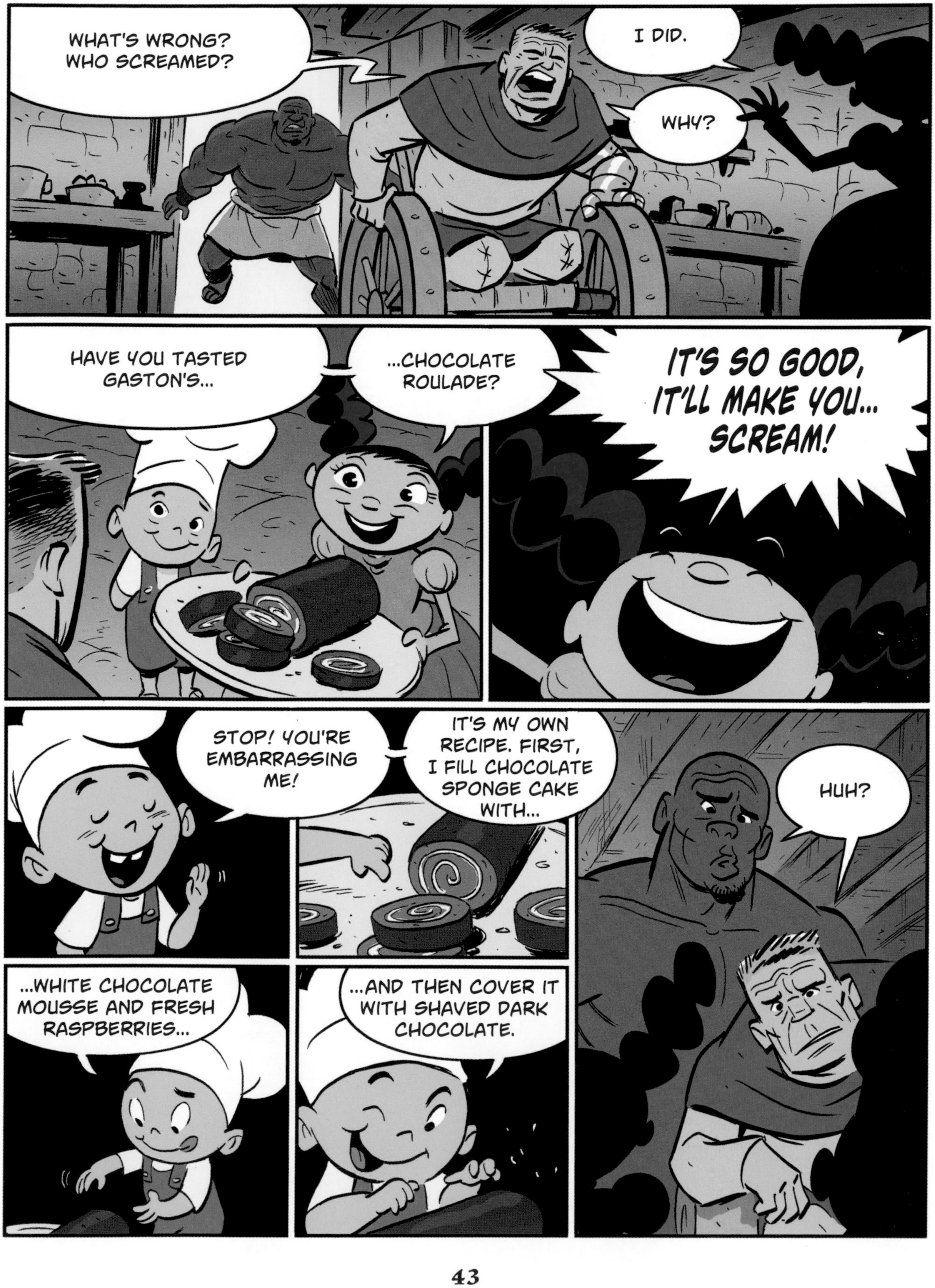
WHAT'S WRONG? WHO SCREAMED?
I DID.
WHY?
HAVE YOU TASTED GASTON'S...
...CHOCOLATE ROULADE?
IT'S SO GOOD, IT'LL MAKE YOU... SCREAM!
STOP! YOU'RE EMBARRASSING ME!
IT'S MY OWN RECIPE. FIRST, I FILL CHOCOLATE SPONGE CAKE WITH...
HUH?
...WHITE CHOCOLATE MOUSSE AND FRESH RASPBERRIES...
...AND THEN COVER IT WITH SHAVED DARK CHOCOLATE.

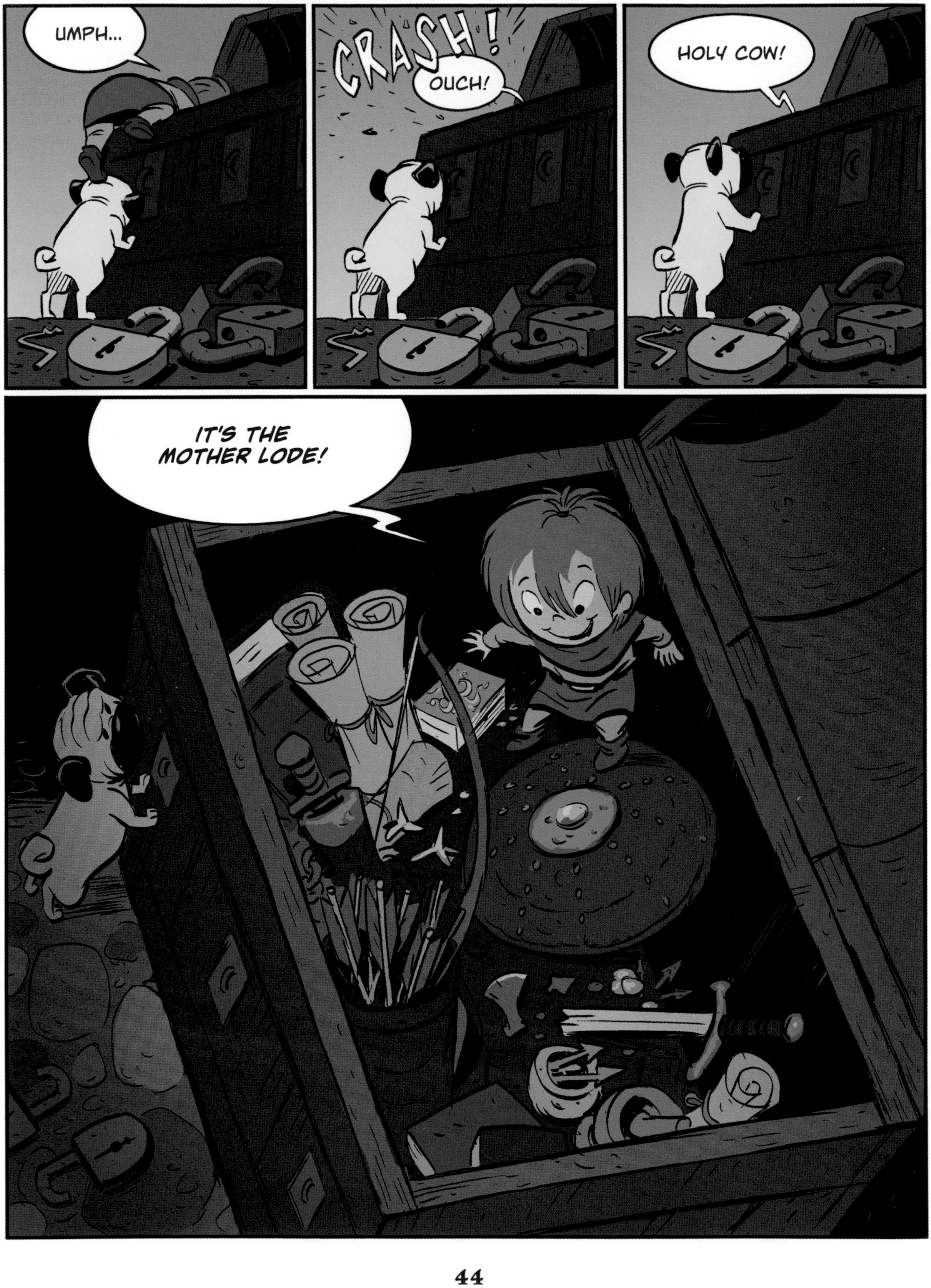
UMPH...
CRASH!
OUCH!
HOLY COW!
IT'S THE MOTHER LODE!

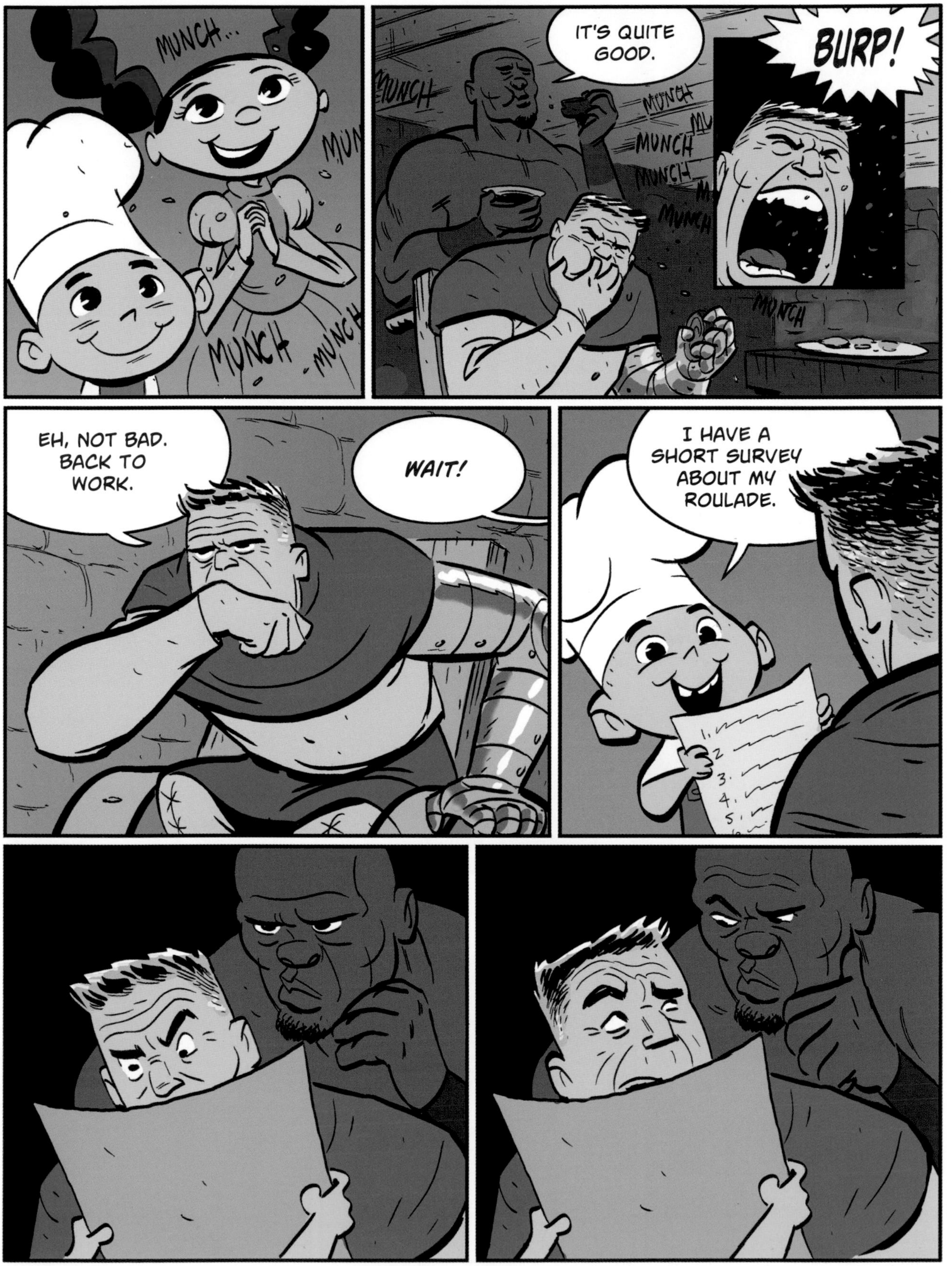
MUNCH...
MUNCH
MUNCH
MUNCH
IT'S QUITE GOOD.
BURP!
MUNCH
MUNCH
MUNCH
MUNCH
MUNCH
EH, NOT BAD. BACK TO WORK.
WAIT!
I HAVE A SHORT SURVEY ABOUT MY ROULADE.

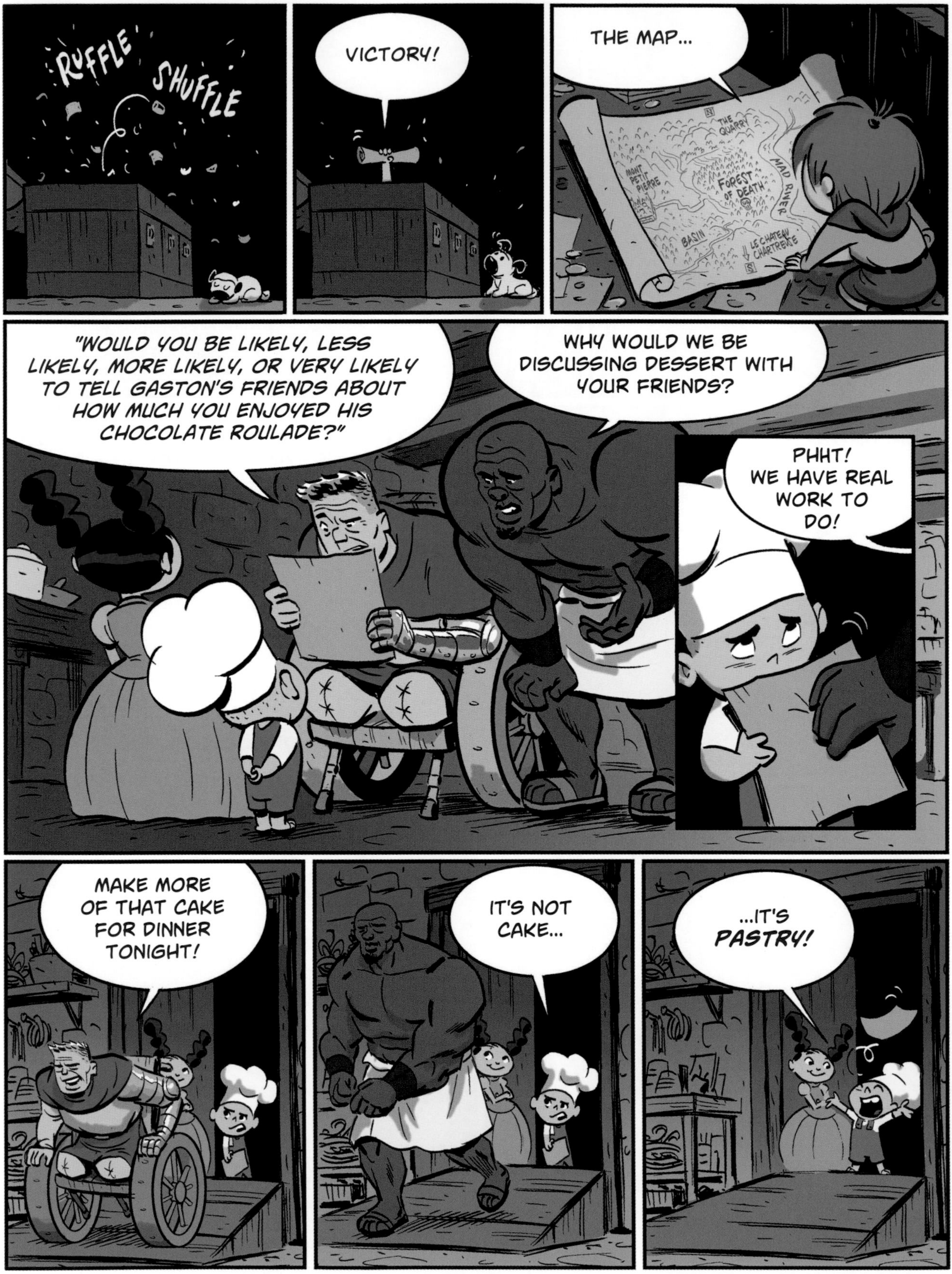
RUFFLE
SHUFFLE
VICTORY!
THE MAP...
N
THE QUARRY
MONT PETIT PIERRE
FOREST OF DEATH
MAD RIVER
BASIN
LE CHATEAU
S
"WOULD YOU BE LIKELY, LESS LIKELY, MORE LIKELY, OR VERY LIKELY TO TELL GASTON'S FRIENDS ABOUT HOW MUCH YOU ENJOYED HIS CHOCOLATE ROULADE?"
WHY WOULD WE BE DISCUSSING DESSERT WITH YOUR FRIENDS?
PHHT! WE HAVE REAL WORK TO DO!
MAKE MORE OF THAT CAKE FOR DINNER TONIGHT!
IT'S NOT CAKE...
...IT'S *PASTRY!*

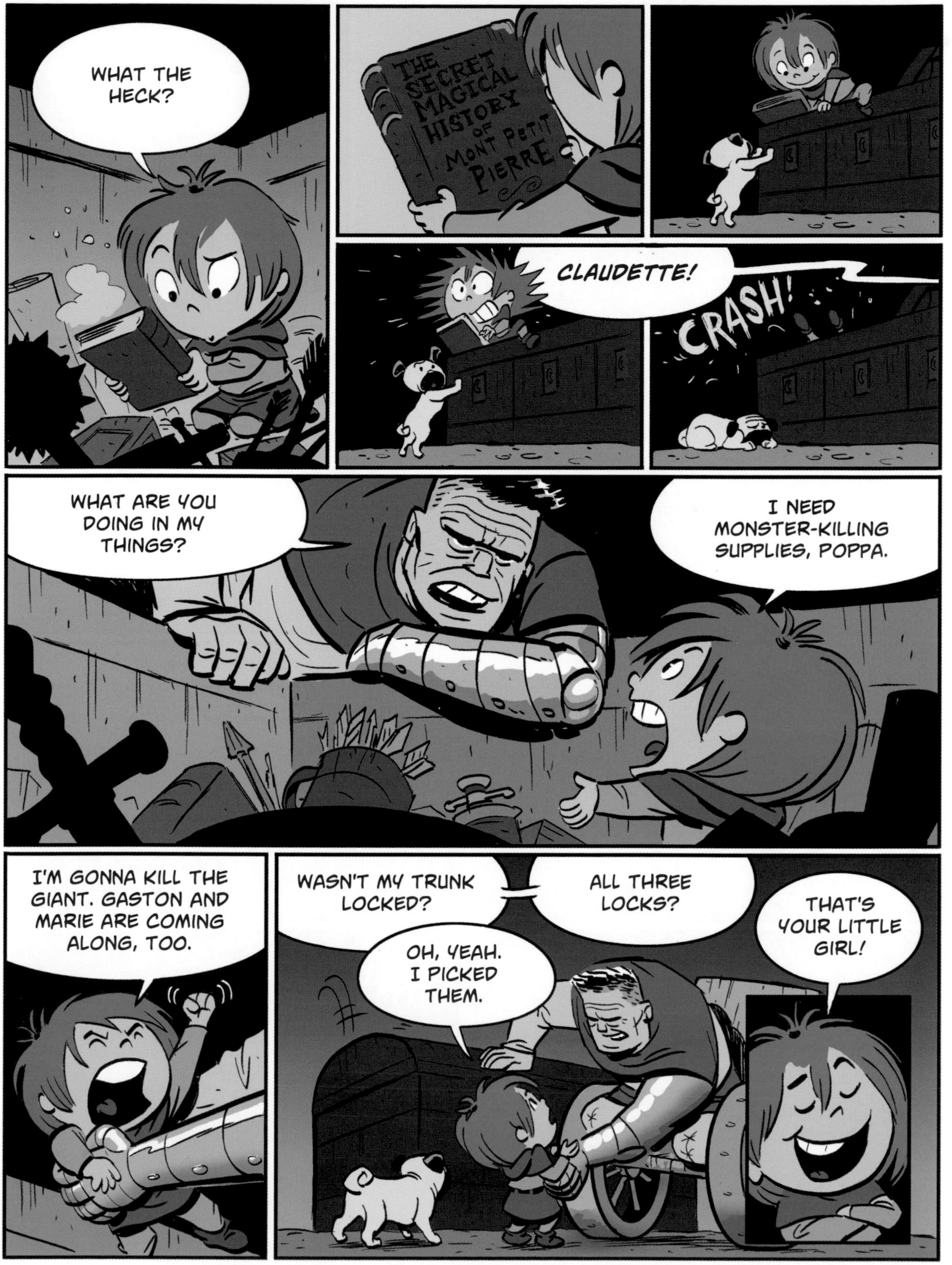
WHAT THE HECK?
THE SECRET MAGICAL HISTORY OF MONT PETIT PIERRE
CLAUDETTE!
CRASH!
WHAT ARE YOU DOING IN MY THINGS?
I NEED MONSTER-KILLING SUPPLIES, POPPA.
I'M GONNA KILL THE GIANT. GASTON AND MARIE ARE COMING ALONG, TOO.
WASN'T MY TRUNK LOCKED?
ALL THREE LOCKS?
OH, YEAH. I PICKED THEM.
THAT'S YOUR LITTLE GIRL!

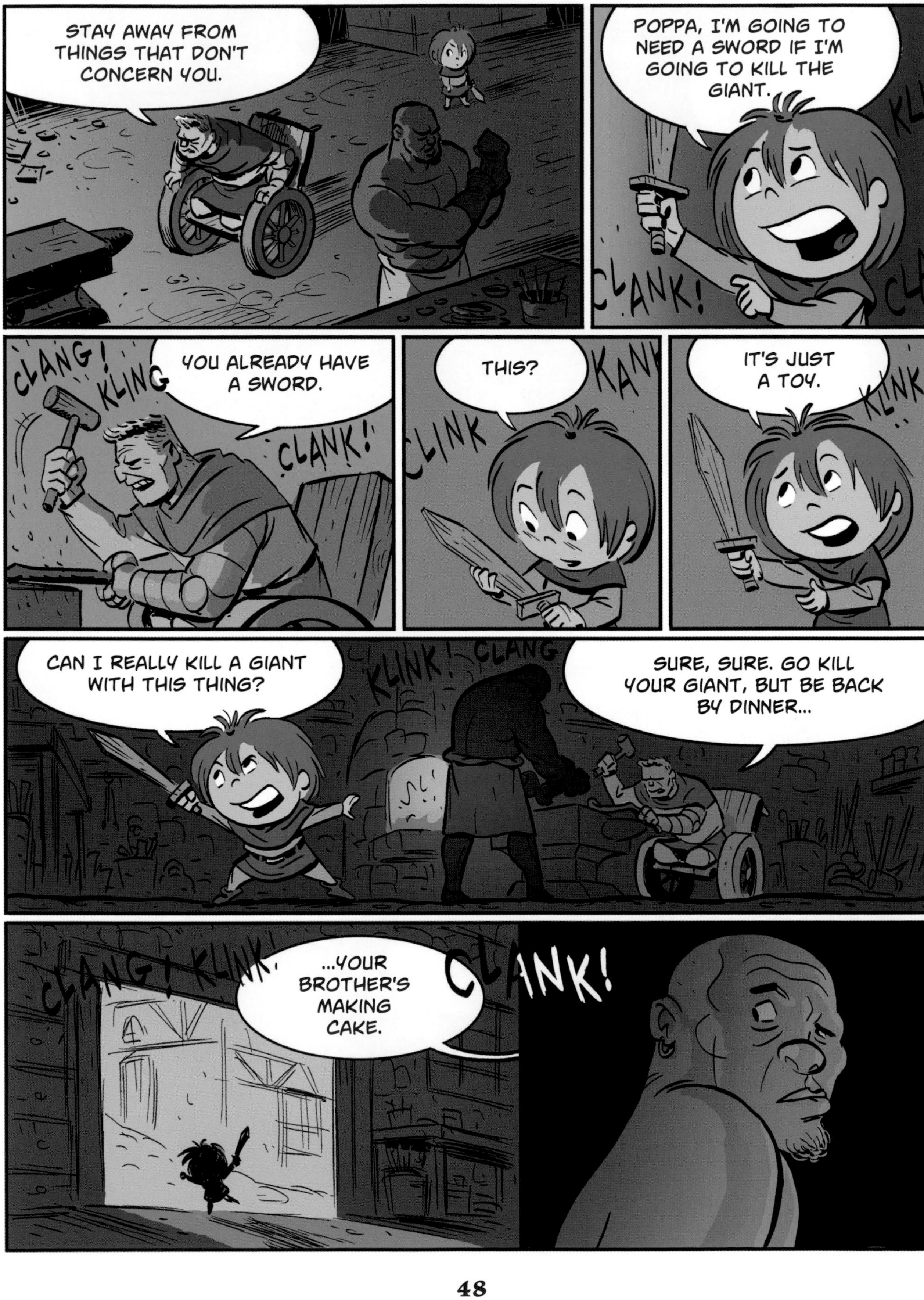
STAY AWAY FROM THINGS THAT DON'T CONCERN YOU.
POPPA, I'M GOING TO NEED A SWORD IF I'M GOING TO KILL THE GIANT.
CLANK!
CLANG!
KLING
YOU ALREADY HAVE A SWORD.
CLANK!
THIS?
CLINK
IT'S JUST A TOY.
KLINK
CAN I REALLY KILL A GIANT WITH THIS THING?
KLINK!
CLANG
SURE, SURE. GO KILL YOUR GIANT, BUT BE BACK BY DINNER...
CLANG!
...YOUR BROTHER'S MAKING CAKE.
CLANK!

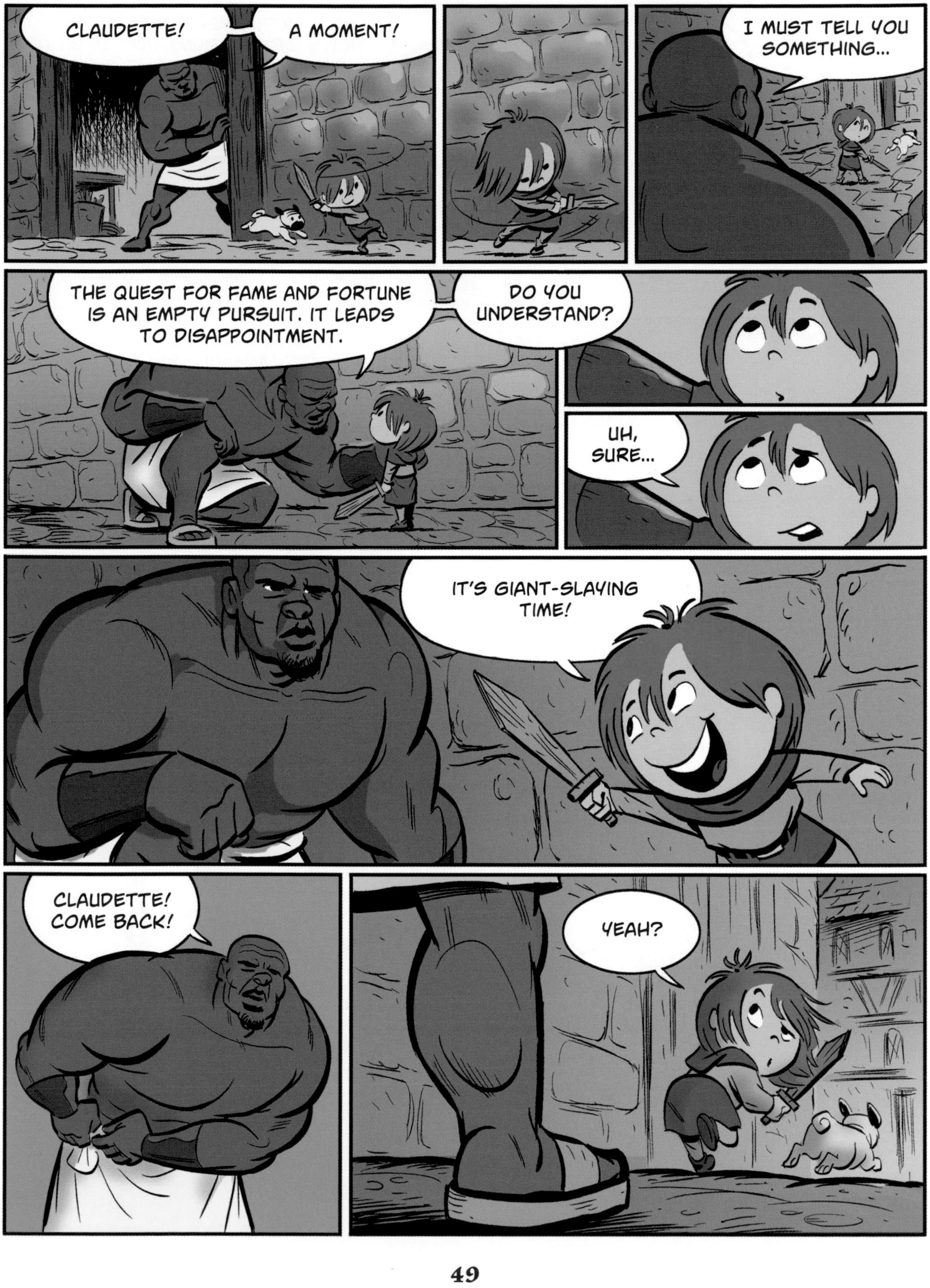
CLAUDETTE!
A MOMENT!
I MUST TELL YOU SOMETHING...
THE QUEST FOR FAME AND FORTUNE IS AN EMPTY PURSUIT. IT LEADS TO DISAPPOINTMENT.
DO YOU UNDERSTAND?
UH, SURE...
IT'S GIANT-SLAYING TIME!
CLAUDETTE! COME BACK!
YEAH?

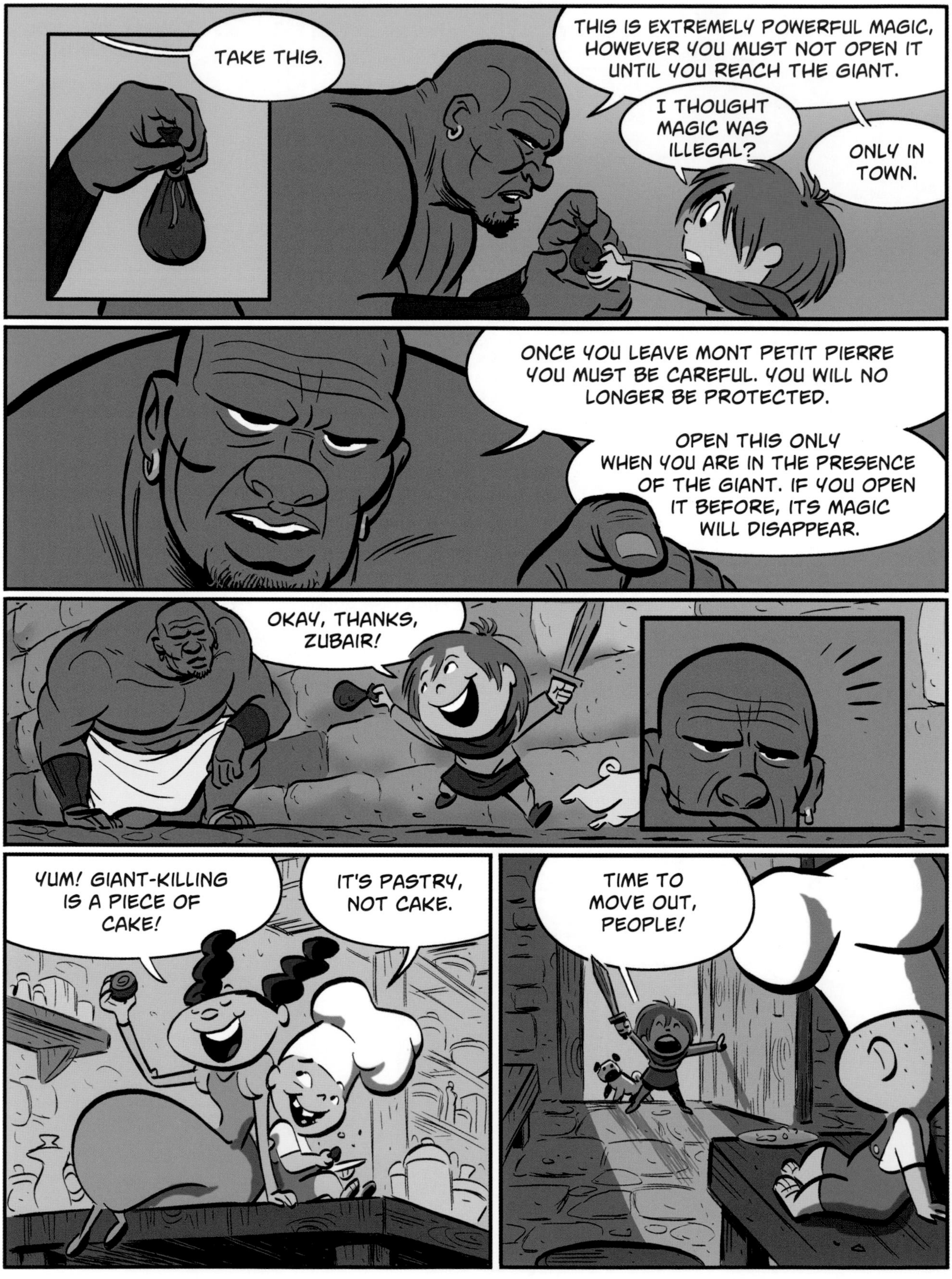
TAKE THIS.
THIS IS EXTREMELY POWERFUL MAGIC, HOWEVER YOU MUST NOT OPEN IT UNTIL YOU REACH THE GIANT.
I THOUGHT MAGIC WAS ILLEGAL?
ONLY IN TOWN.
ONCE YOU LEAVE MONT PETIT PIERRE YOU MUST BE CAREFUL. YOU WILL NO LONGER BE PROTECTED.
OPEN THIS ONLY WHEN YOU ARE IN THE PRESENCE OF THE GIANT. IF YOU OPEN IT BEFORE, ITS MAGIC WILL DISAPPEAR.
OKAY, THANKS, ZUBAIR!
YUM! GIANT-KILLING IS A PIECE OF CAKE!
IT'S PASTRY, NOT CAKE.
TIME TO MOVE OUT, PEOPLE!

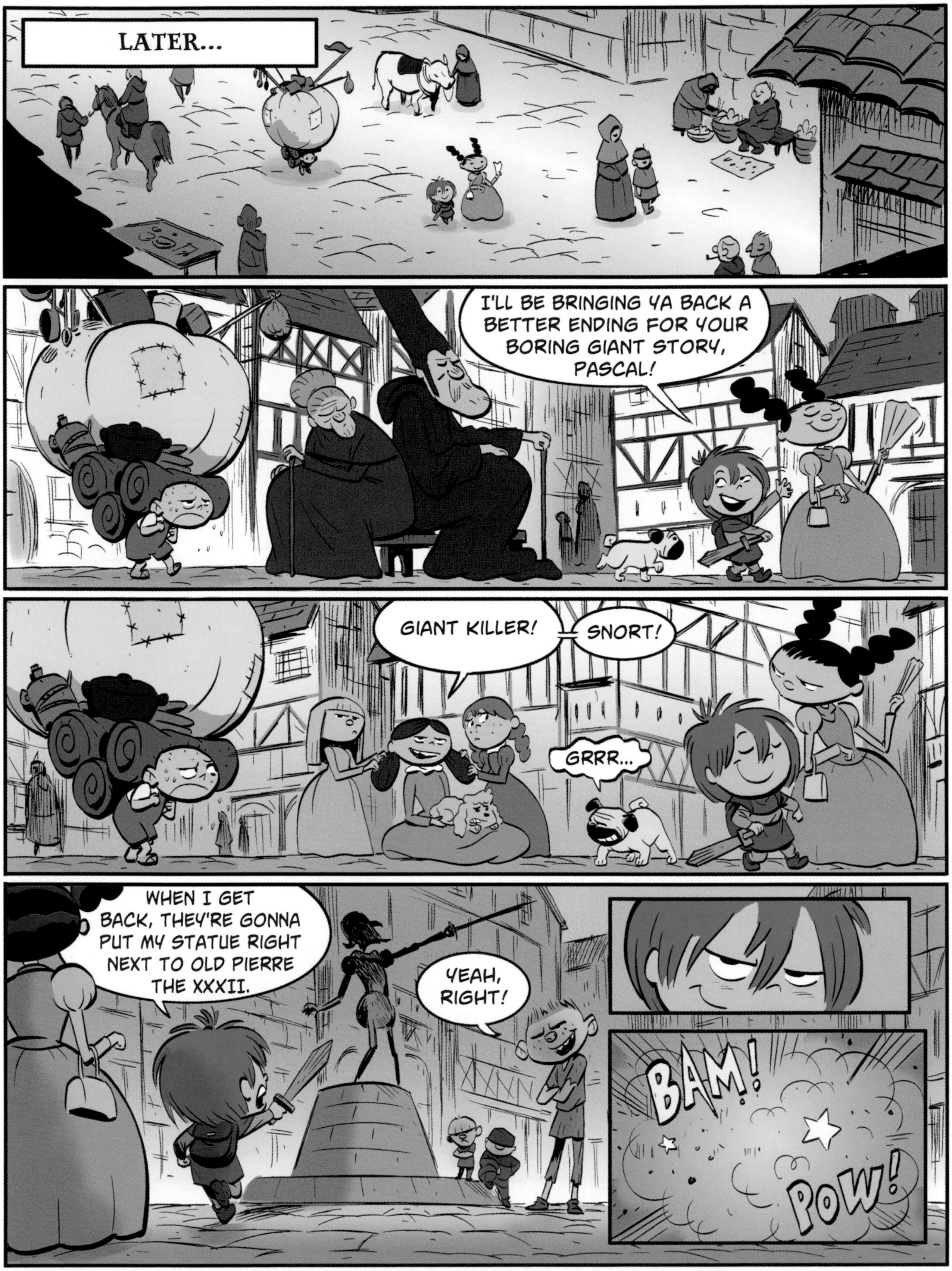
LATER...
I'LL BE BRINGING YA BACK A BETTER ENDING FOR YOUR BORING GIANT STORY, PASCAL!
GIANT KILLER!
SNORT!
GRRR...
WHEN I GET BACK, THEY'RE GONNA PUT MY STATUE RIGHT NEXT TO OLD PIERRE THE XXXII.
YEAH, RIGHT!
BAM!
POW!

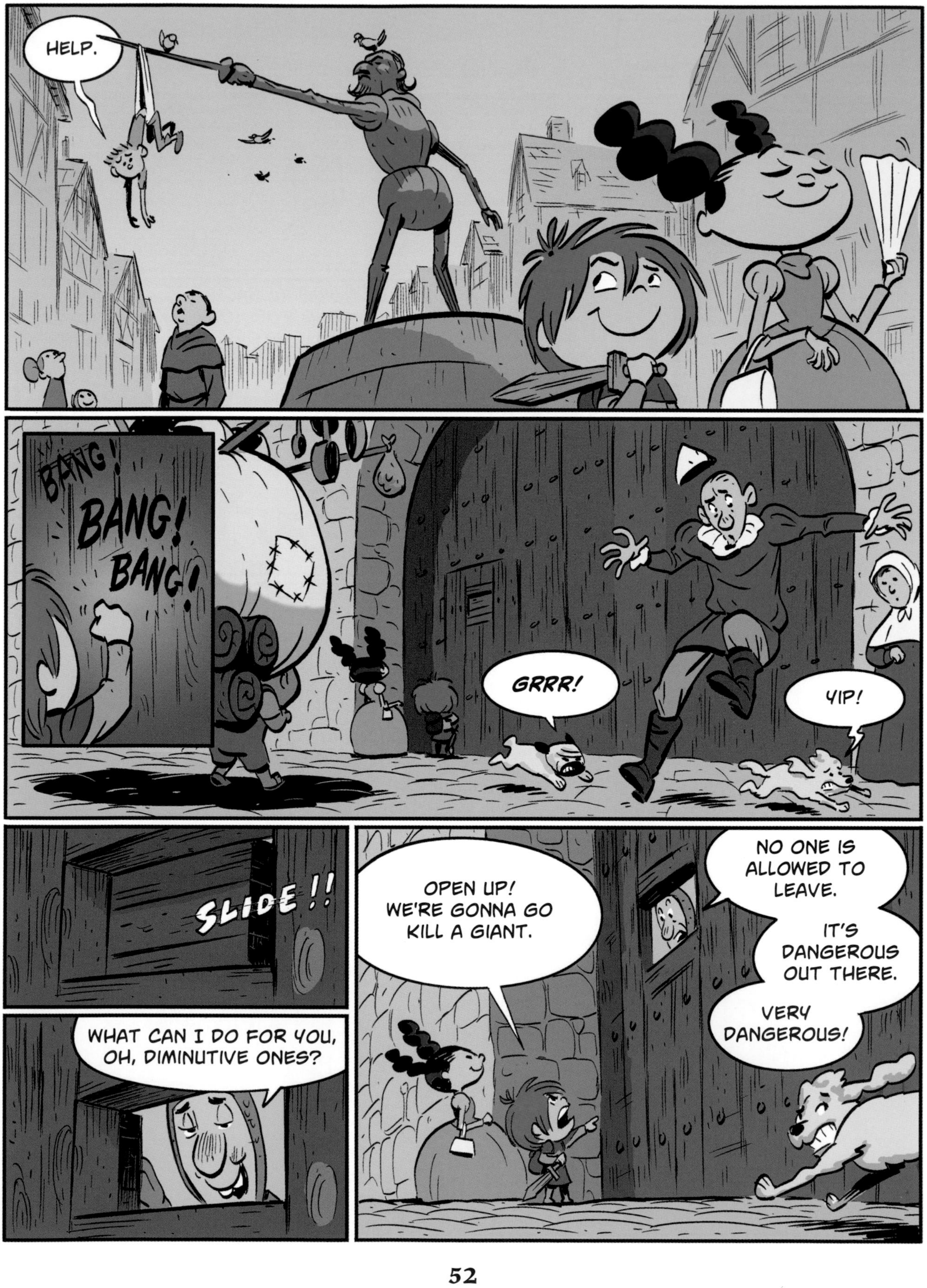
HELP.
BANG!
BANG!
BANG!
GRRR!
YIP!
SLIDE!!
WHAT CAN I DO FOR YOU, OH, DIMINUTIVE ONES?
OPEN UP! WE'RE GONNA GO KILL A GIANT.
NO ONE IS ALLOWED TO LEAVE.
IT'S DANGEROUS OUT THERE.
VERY DANGEROUS!

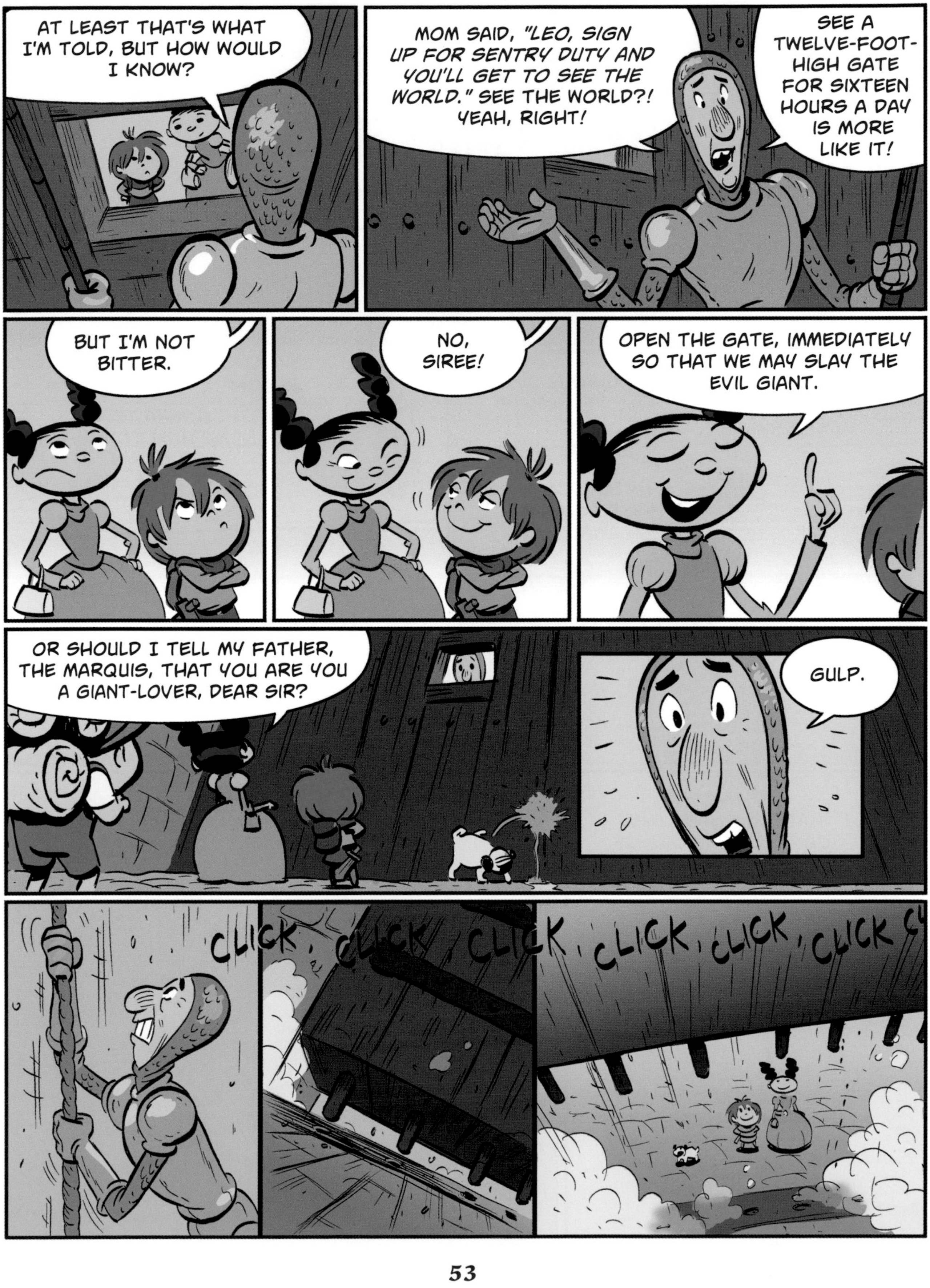

AT LEAST THAT'S WHAT I'M TOLD, BUT HOW WOULD I KNOW?
MOM SAID, "LEO, SIGN UP FOR SENTRY DUTY AND YOU'LL GET TO SEE THE WORLD." SEE THE WORLD?! YEAH, RIGHT!
SEE A TWELVE-FOOT-HIGH GATE FOR SIXTEEN HOURS A DAY IS MORE LIKE IT!
BUT I'M NOT BITTER.
NO, SIREE!
OPEN THE GATE, IMMEDIATELY SO THAT WE MAY SLAY THE EVIL GIANT.
OR SHOULD I TELL MY FATHER, THE MARQUIS, THAT YOU ARE YOU A GIANT-LOVER, DEAR SIR?
GULP.
CLICK, CLICK, CLICK, CLICK, CLICK, CLICK

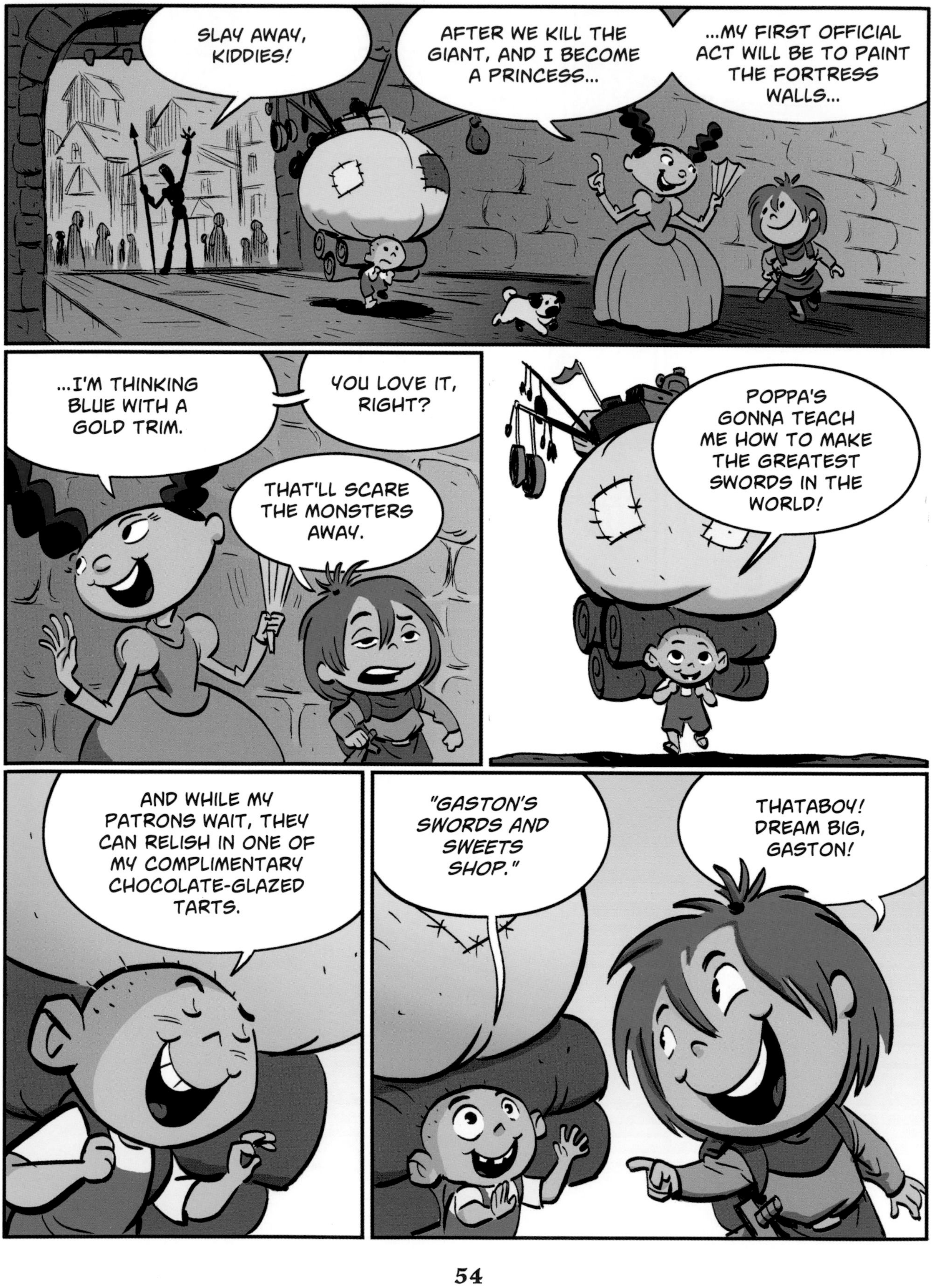
SLAY AWAY, KIDDIES!
AFTER WE KILL THE GIANT, AND I BECOME A PRINCESS...
...MY FIRST OFFICIAL ACT WILL BE TO PAINT THE FORTRESS WALLS...
...I'M THINKING BLUE WITH A GOLD TRIM.
YOU LOVE IT, RIGHT?
THAT'LL SCARE THE MONSTERS AWAY.
POPPA'S GONNA TEACH ME HOW TO MAKE THE GREATEST SWORDS IN THE WORLD!
AND WHILE MY PATRONS WAIT, THEY CAN RELISH IN ONE OF MY COMPLIMENTARY CHOCOLATE-GLAZED TARTS.
"GASTON'S SWORDS AND SWEETS SHOP."
THATABOY! DREAM BIG, GASTON!

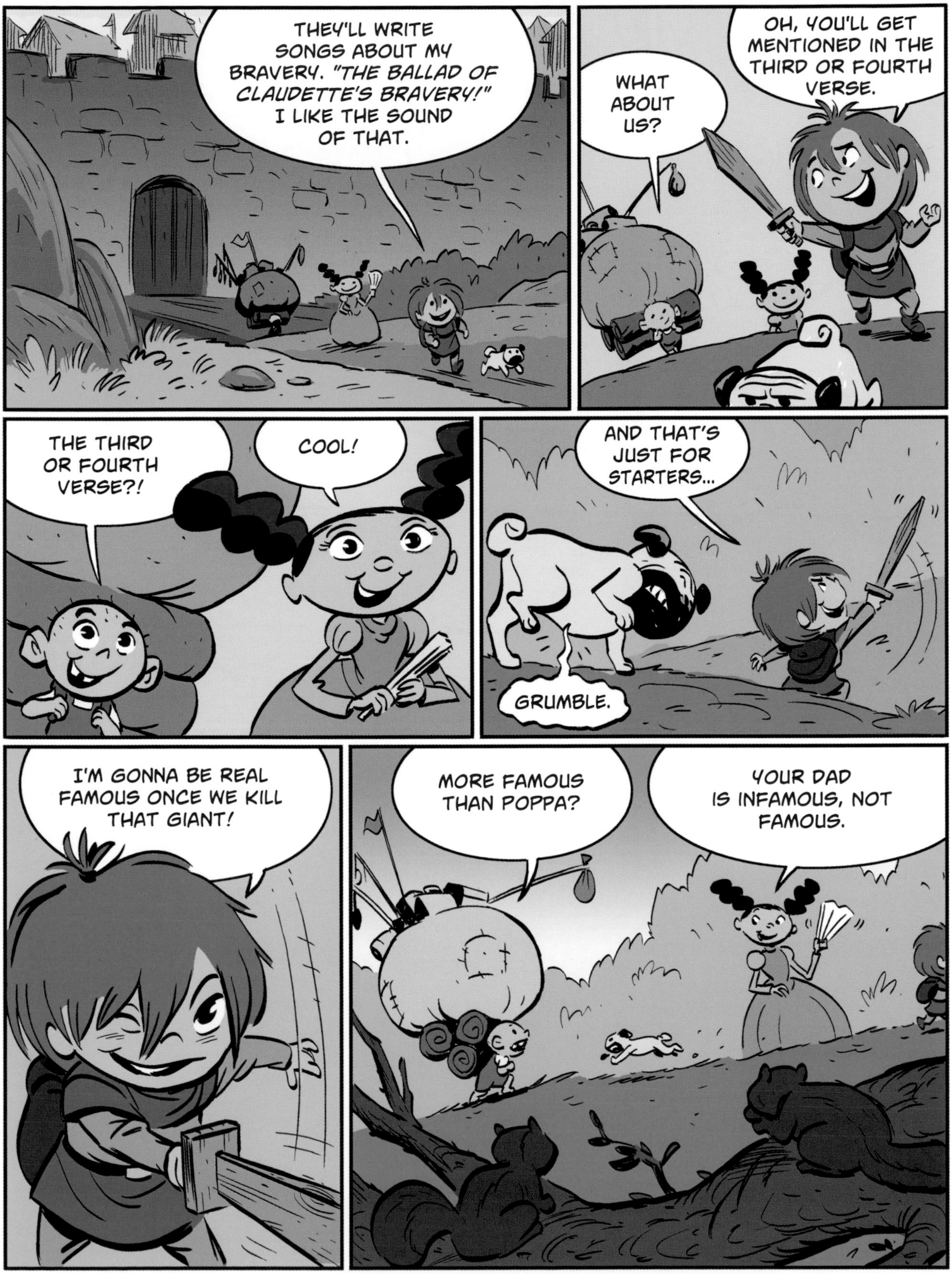
THEY'LL WRITE SONGS ABOUT MY BRAVERY. "THE BALLAD OF CLAUDETTE'S BRAVERY!" I LIKE THE SOUND OF THAT.
WHAT ABOUT US?
OH, YOU'LL GET MENTIONED IN THE THIRD OR FOURTH VERSE.
THE THIRD OR FOURTH VERSE?!
COOL!
AND THAT'S JUST FOR STARTERS...
GRUMBLE.
I'M GONNA BE REAL FAMOUS ONCE WE KILL THAT GIANT!
MORE FAMOUS THAN POPPA?
YOUR DAD IS INFAMOUS, NOT FAMOUS.

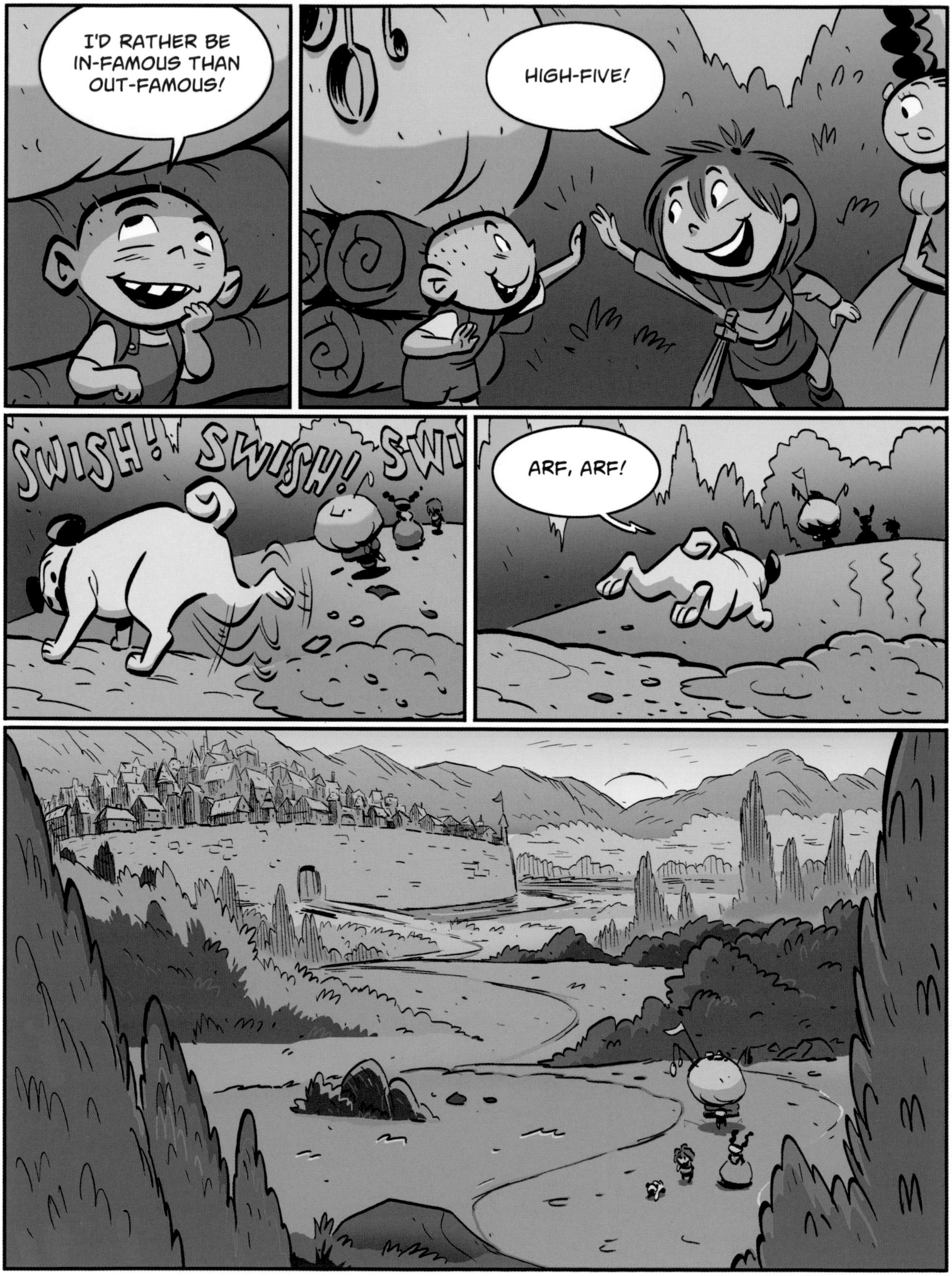
I'D RATHER BE IN-FAMOUS THAN OUT-FAMOUS!
HIGH-FIVE!
SWISH! SWISH! SWI
ARF, ARF!

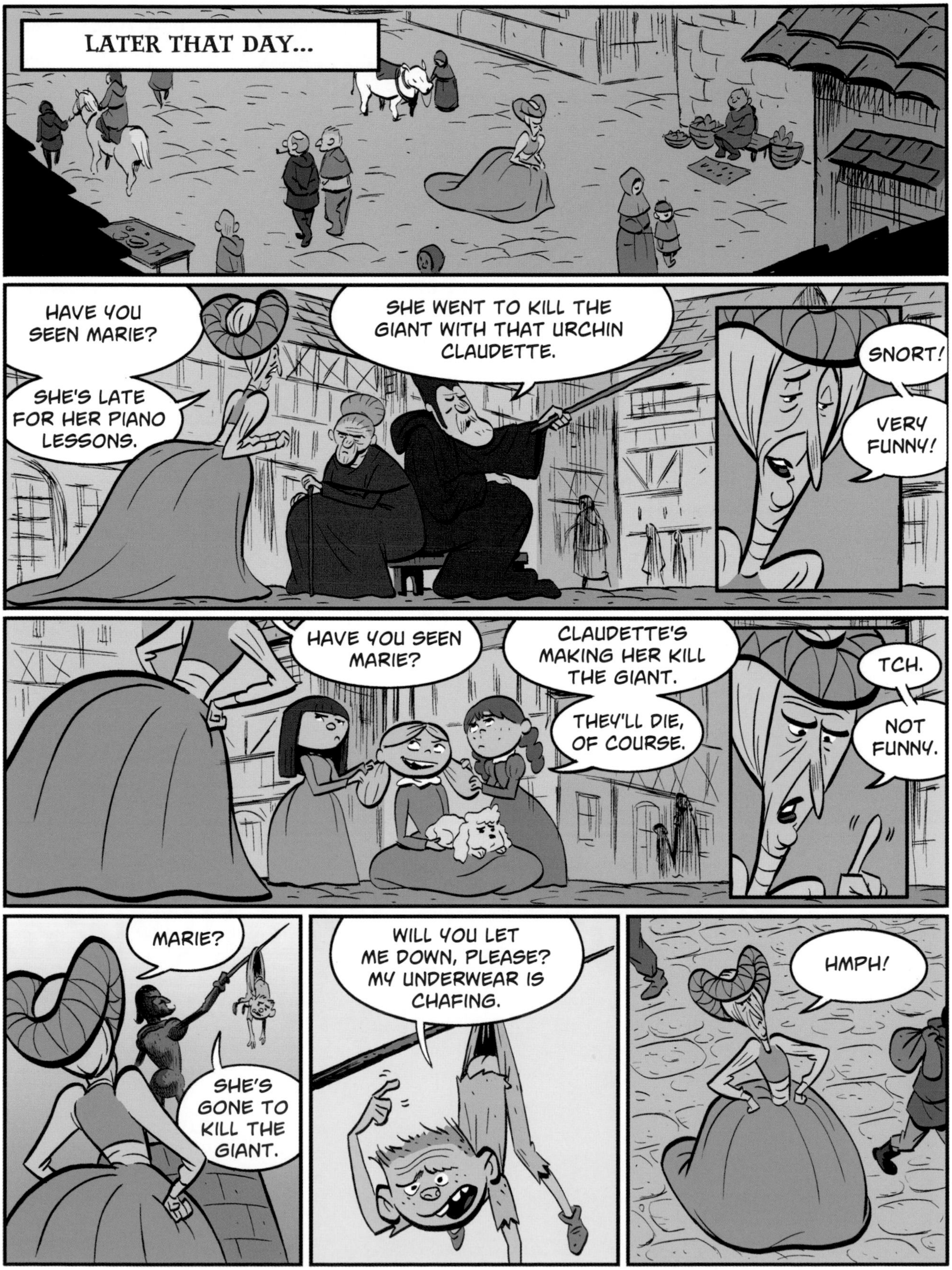
LATER THAT DAY...
HAVE YOU SEEN MARIE?
SHE'S LATE FOR HER PIANO LESSONS.
SHE WENT TO KILL THE GIANT WITH THAT URCHIN CLAUDETTE.
SNORT!
VERY FUNNY!
HAVE YOU SEEN MARIE?
CLAUDETTE'S MAKING HER KILL THE GIANT.
THEY'LL DIE, OF COURSE.
TCH.
NOT FUNNY.
MARIE?
SHE'S GONE TO KILL THE GIANT.
WILL YOU LET ME DOWN, PLEASE? MY UNDERWEAR IS CHAFING.
HMPH!

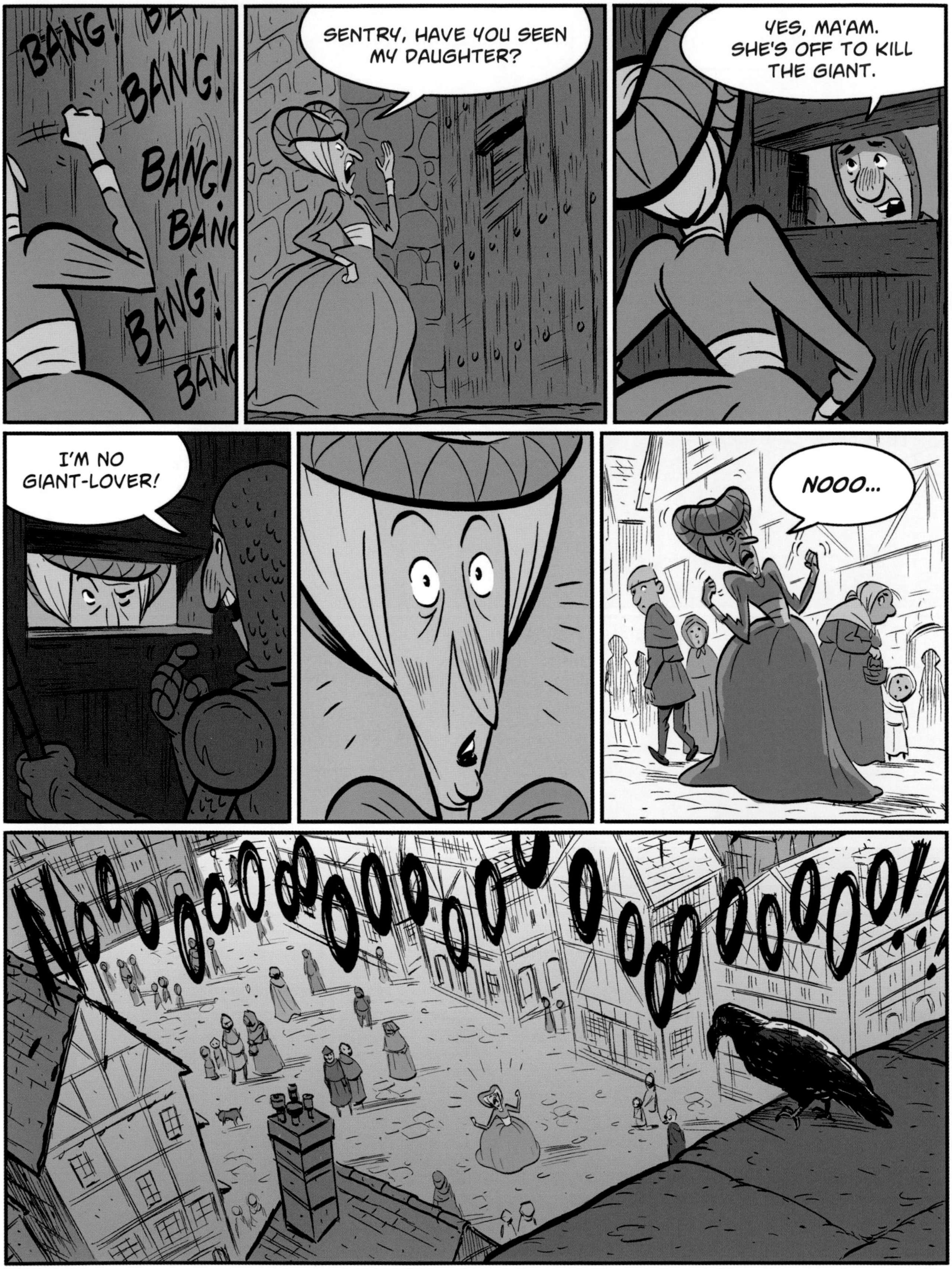
BANG! BA
BANG!
BANG!
BANG
BANG!
BANG
SENTRY, HAVE YOU SEEN MY DAUGHTER?
YES, MA'AM. SHE'S OFF TO KILL THE GIANT.
I'M NO GIANT-LOVER!
NOOO...
NOOOOOOOOOOOOOOOOOOOOOOOOOO!!!

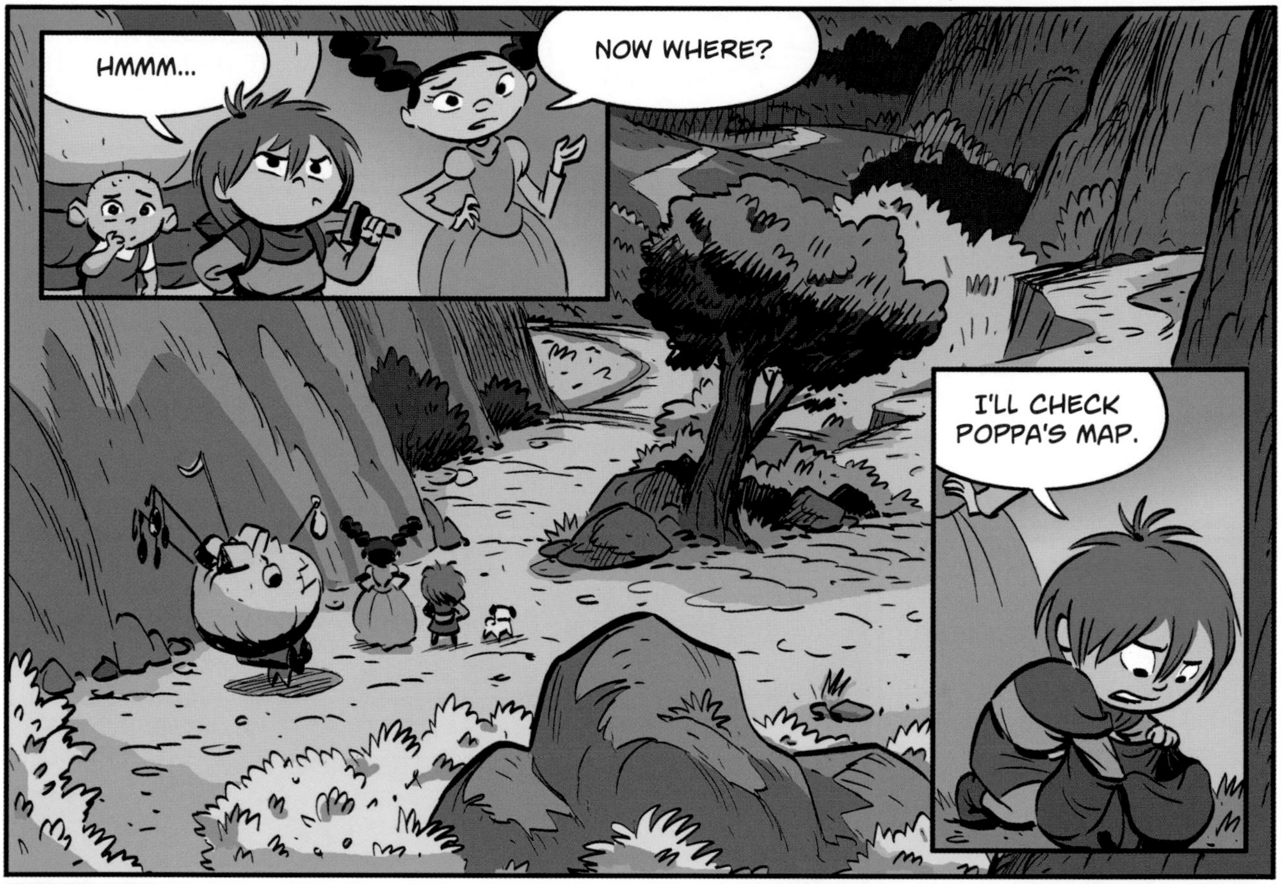
HMMM...
NOW WHERE?
I'LL CHECK POPPA'S MAP.

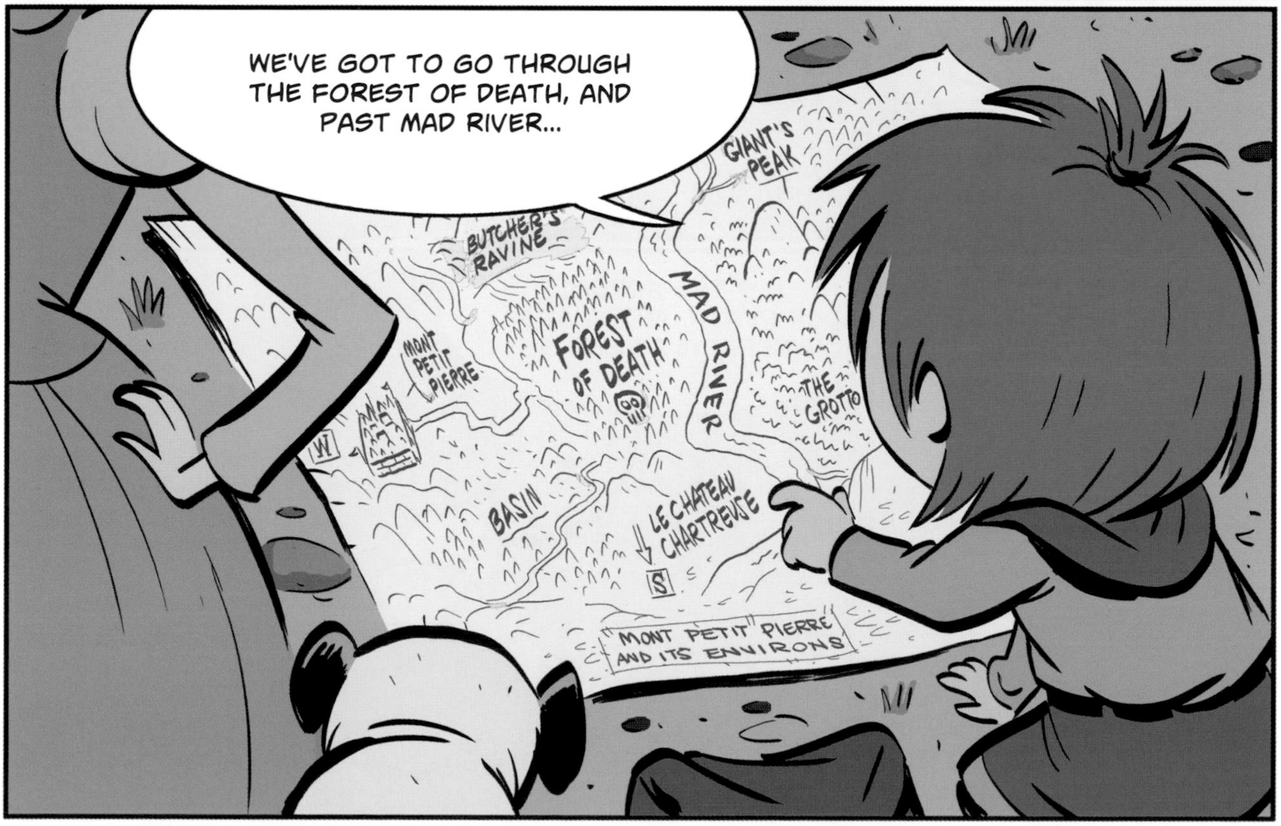
WE'VE GOT TO GO THROUGH THE FOREST OF DEATH, AND PAST MAD RIVER...
GIANT'S PEAK
BUTCHER'S RAVINE
MAD RIVER
MONT PETIT PIERRE
FOREST OF DEATH
THE GROTTO
W
BASIN
LE CHATEAU CHARTREUSE
S
MONT PETIT PIERRE AND ITS ENVIRONS

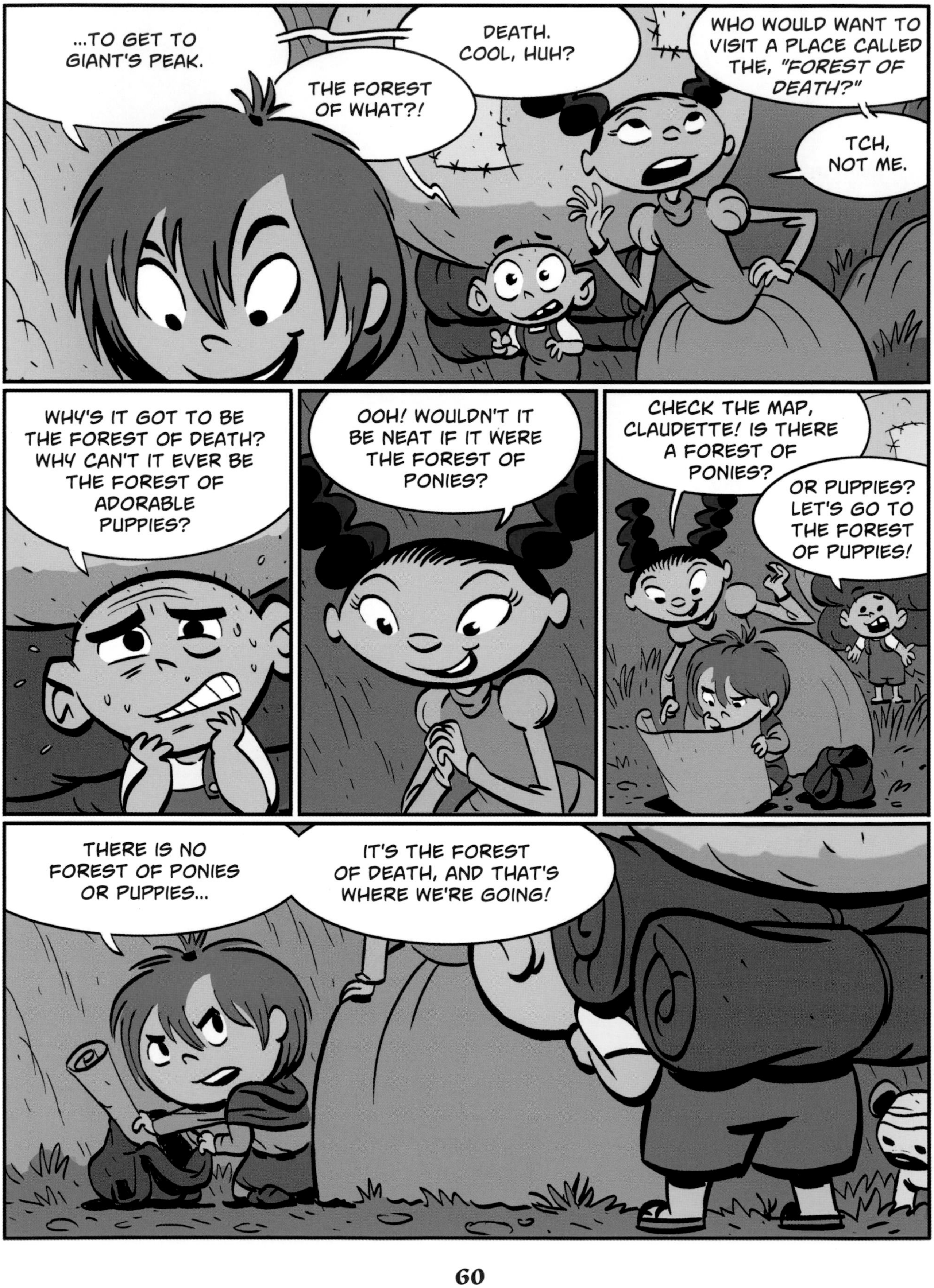
...TO GET TO GIANT'S PEAK.
THE FOREST OF WHAT?!
DEATH. COOL, HUH?
WHO WOULD WANT TO VISIT A PLACE CALLED THE, "FOREST OF DEATH?"
TCH, NOT ME.
WHY'S IT GOT TO BE THE FOREST OF DEATH? WHY CAN'T IT EVER BE THE FOREST OF ADORABLE PUPPIES?
OOH! WOULDN'T IT BE NEAT IF IT WERE THE FOREST OF PONIES?
CHECK THE MAP, CLAUDETTE! IS THERE A FOREST OF PONIES?
OR PUPPIES? LET'S GO TO THE FOREST OF PUPPIES!
THERE IS NO FOREST OF PONIES OR PUPPIES...
IT'S THE FOREST OF DEATH, AND THAT'S WHERE WE'RE GOING!

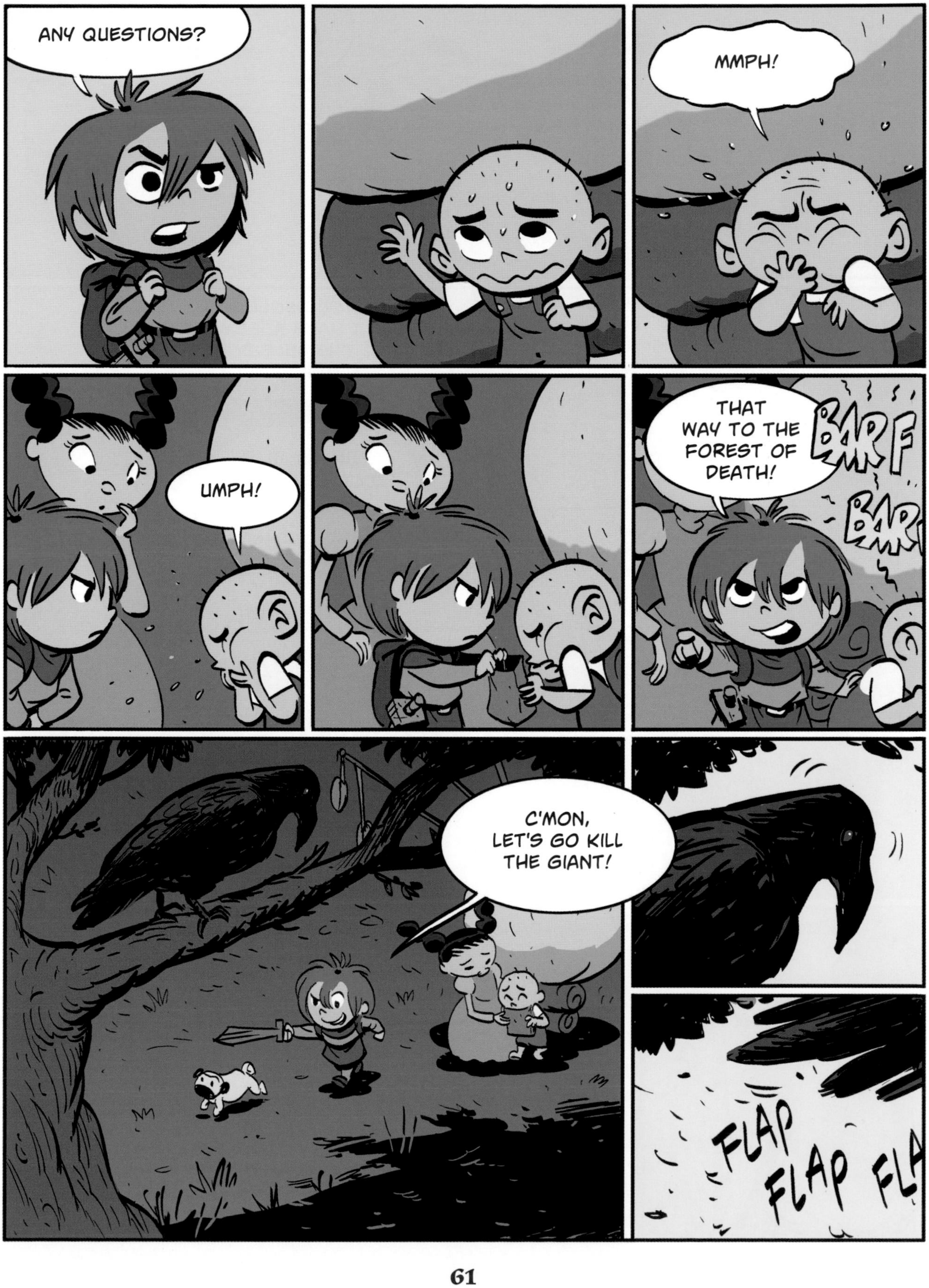
ANY QUESTIONS?
MMPH!
UMPH!
THAT WAY TO THE FOREST OF DEATH!
BARF
BAR
C'MON, LET'S GO KILL THE GIANT!
FLAP
FLAP
FLA

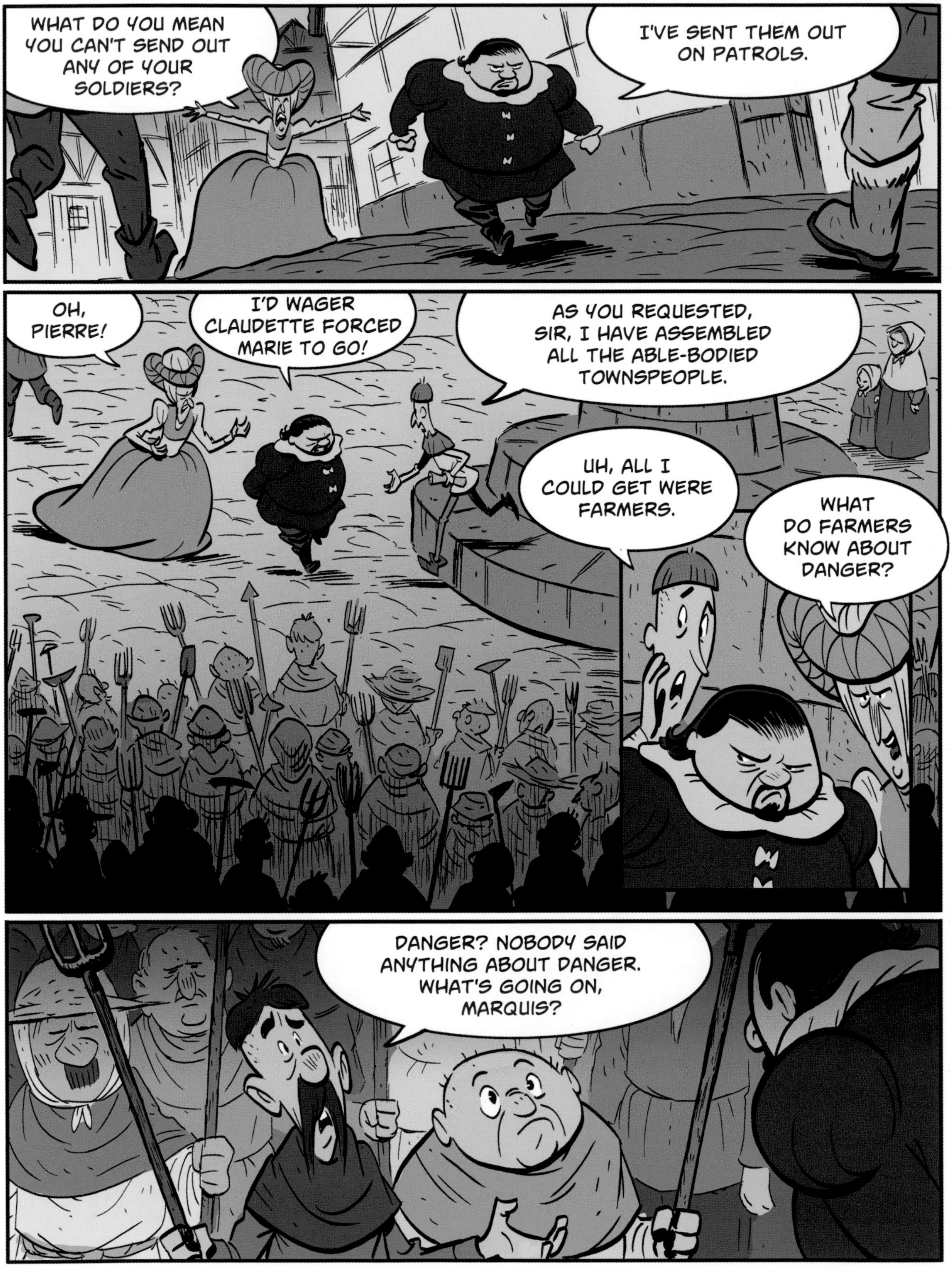
WHAT DO YOU MEAN YOU CAN'T SEND OUT ANY OF YOUR SOLDIERS?
I'VE SENT THEM OUT ON PATROLS.
OH, PIERRE!
I'D WAGER CLAUDETTE FORCED MARIE TO GO!
AS YOU REQUESTED, SIR, I HAVE ASSEMBLED ALL THE ABLE-BODIED TOWNSPEOPLE.
UH, ALL I COULD GET WERE FARMERS.
WHAT DO FARMERS KNOW ABOUT DANGER?
DANGER? NOBODY SAID ANYTHING ABOUT DANGER. WHAT'S GOING ON, MARQUIS?

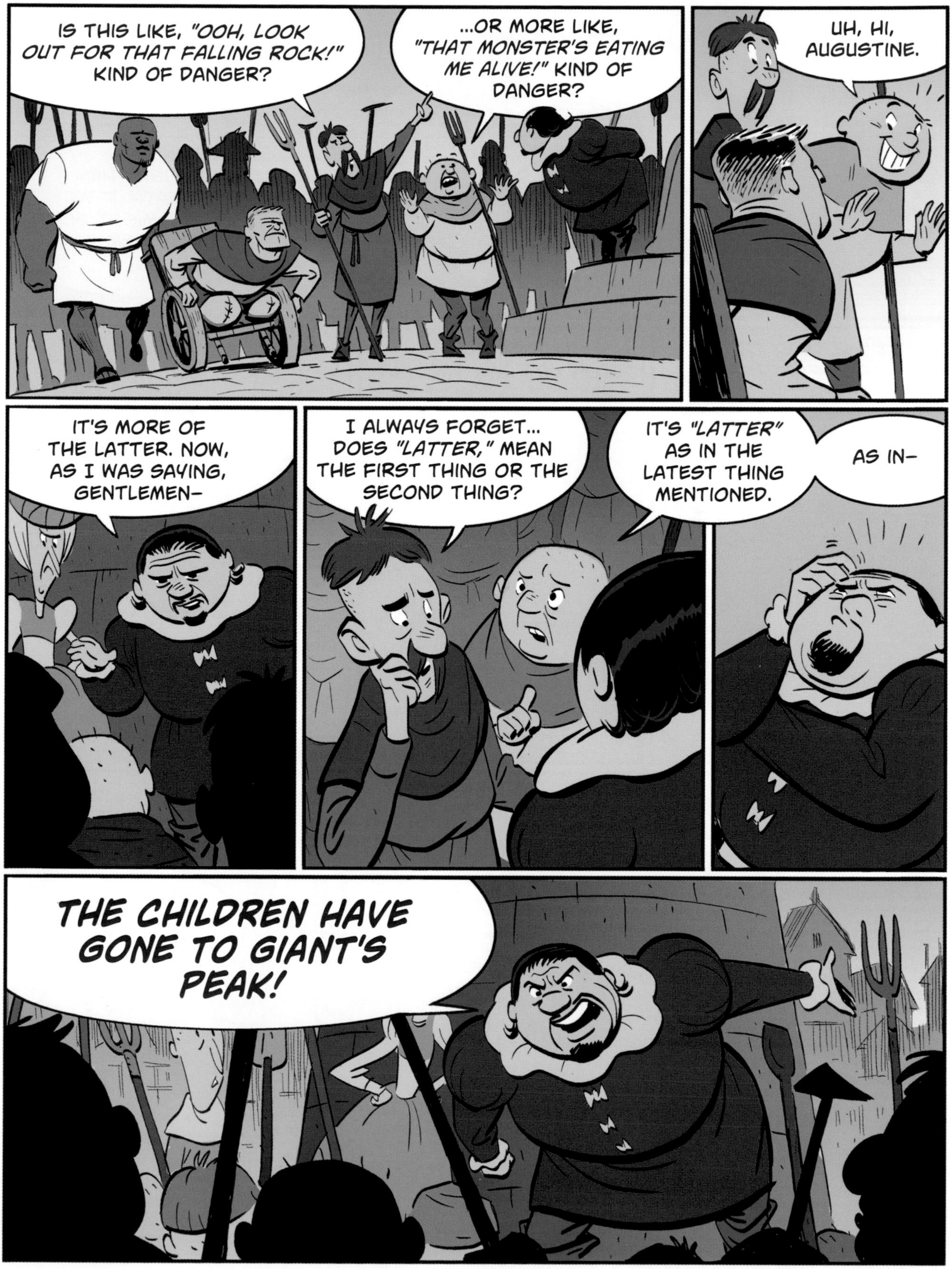
IS THIS LIKE, "OOH, LOOK OUT FOR THAT FALLING ROCK!" KIND OF DANGER?
...OR MORE LIKE, "THAT MONSTER'S EATING ME ALIVE!" KIND OF DANGER?
UH, HI, AUGUSTINE.
IT'S MORE OF THE LATTER. NOW, AS I WAS SAYING, GENTLEMEN–
I ALWAYS FORGET... DOES "LATTER," MEAN THE FIRST THING OR THE SECOND THING?
IT'S "LATTER" AS IN THE LATEST THING MENTIONED.
AS IN–
THE CHILDREN HAVE GONE TO GIANT'S PEAK!

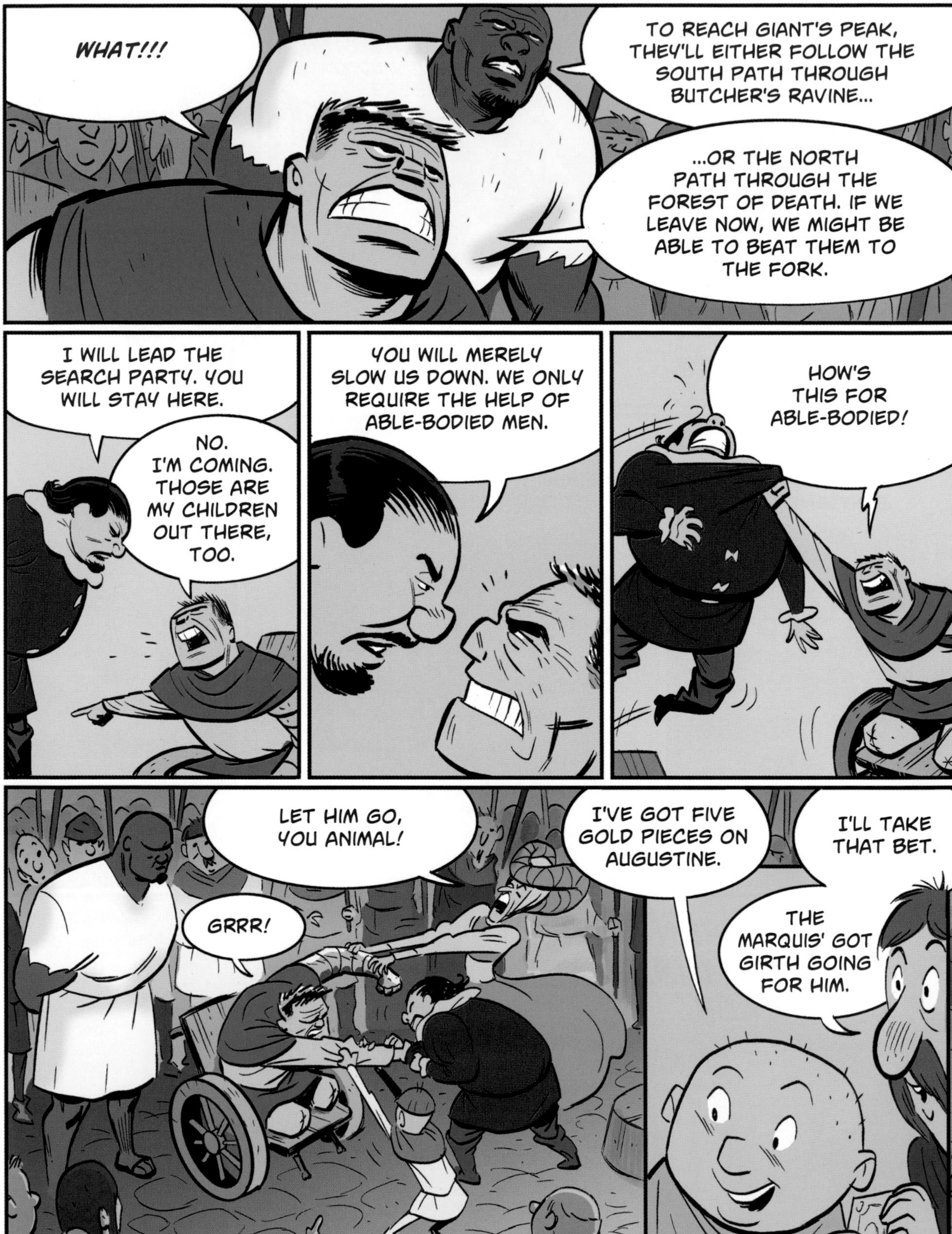
WHAT!!!
TO REACH GIANT'S PEAK, THEY'LL EITHER FOLLOW THE SOUTH PATH THROUGH BUTCHER'S RAVINE...
...OR THE NORTH PATH THROUGH THE FOREST OF DEATH. IF WE LEAVE NOW, WE MIGHT BE ABLE TO BEAT THEM TO THE FORK.
I WILL LEAD THE SEARCH PARTY. YOU WILL STAY HERE.
NO. I'M COMING. THOSE ARE MY CHILDREN OUT THERE, TOO.
YOU WILL MERELY SLOW US DOWN. WE ONLY REQUIRE THE HELP OF ABLE-BODIED MEN.
HOW'S THIS FOR ABLE-BODIED!
LET HIM GO, YOU ANIMAL!
GRRR!
I'VE GOT FIVE GOLD PIECES ON AUGUSTINE.
I'LL TAKE THAT BET.
THE MARQUIS' GOT GIRTH GOING FOR HIM.

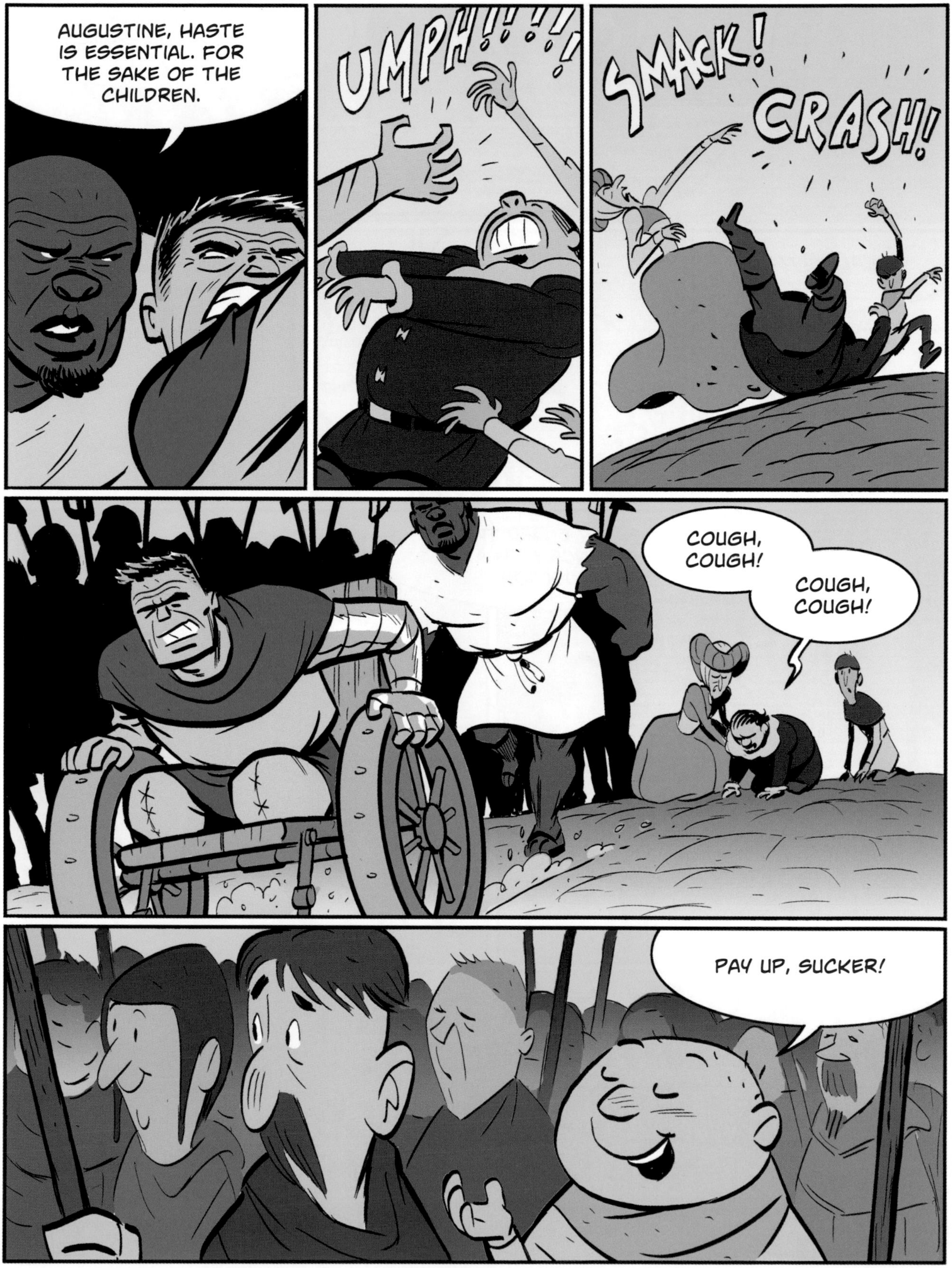
AUGUSTINE, HASTE IS ESSENTIAL. FOR THE SAKE OF THE CHILDREN.
UMPH!!!!!!
SMACK!
CRASH!
COUGH, COUGH!
COUGH, COUGH!
PAY UP, SUCKER!

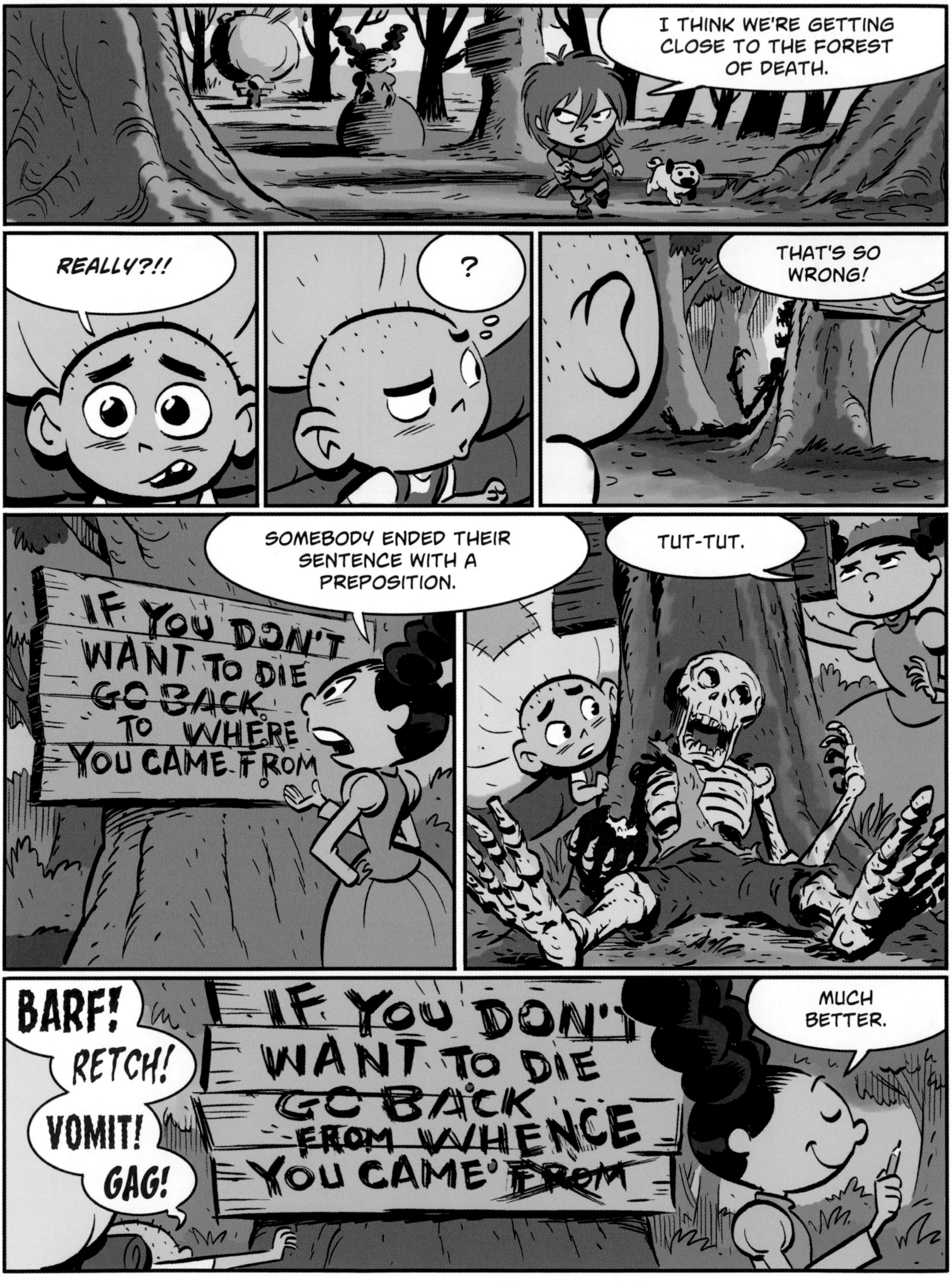
I THINK WE'RE GETTING CLOSE TO THE FOREST OF DEATH.
REALLY?!!
?
THAT'S SO WRONG!
SOMEBODY ENDED THEIR SENTENCE WITH A PREPOSITION.
IF YOU DON'T WANT TO DIE GO BACK TO WHERE YOU CAME FROM
TUT-TUT.
BARF!
RETCH!
VOMIT!
GAG!
IF YOU DON'T WANT TO DIE GO BACK FROM WHENCE YOU CAME FROM
MUCH BETTER.

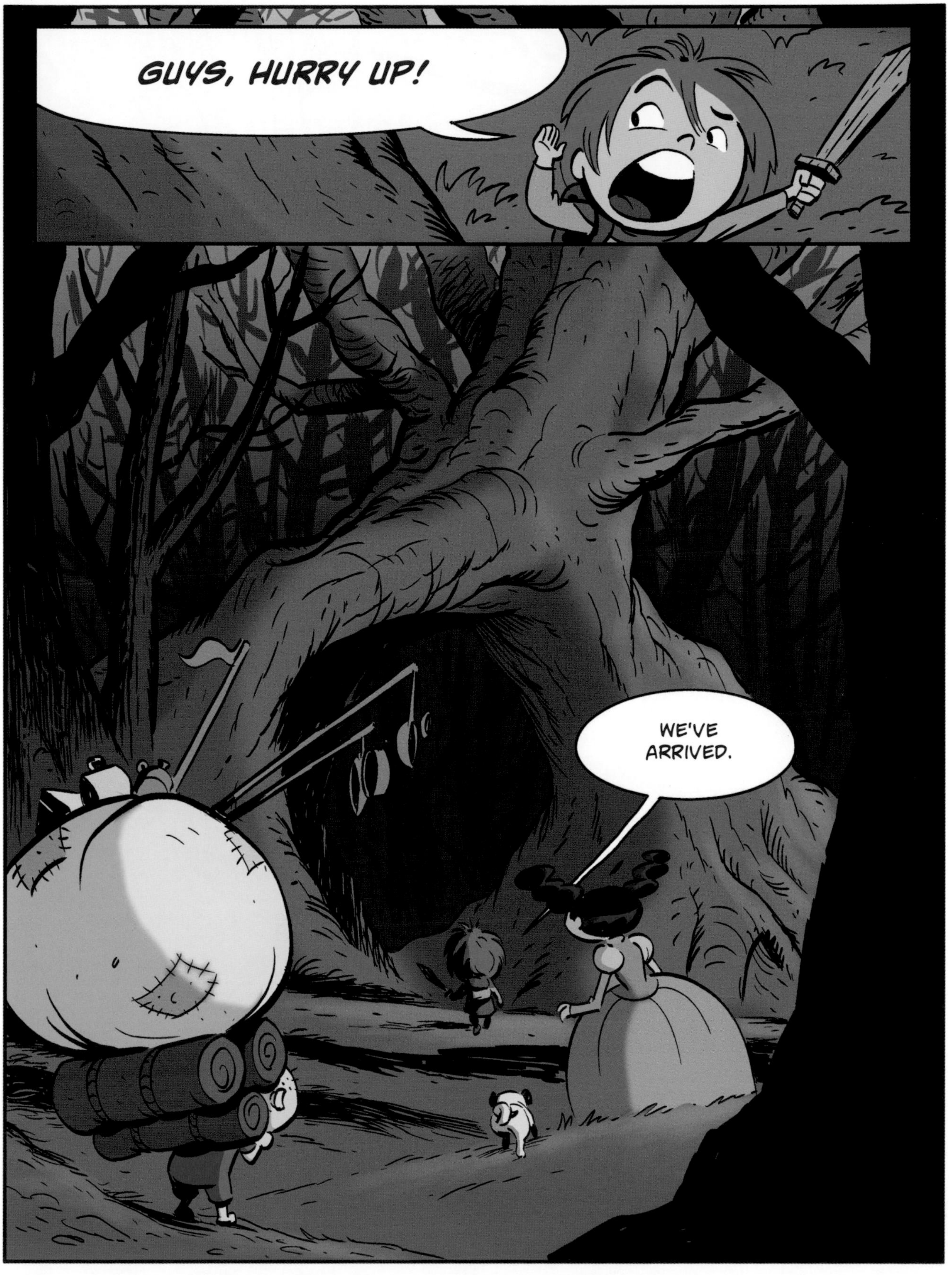
GUYS, HURRY UP!
WE'VE ARRIVED.

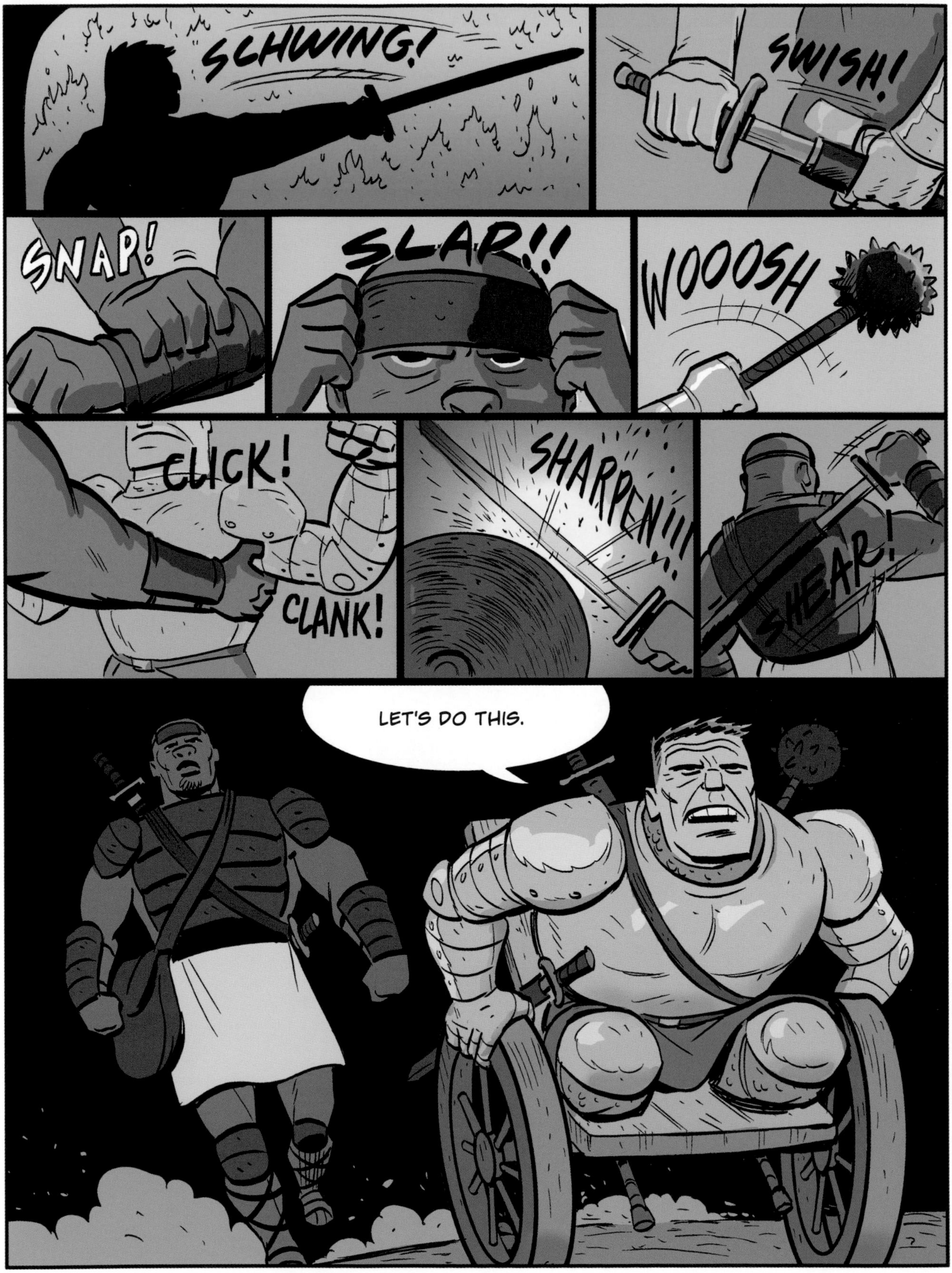
SCHWING!
SWISH!
SNAP!
SLAP!!
WOOOSH
CLICK!
CLANK!
SHARPEN!!!!
SHEAR!
LET'S DO THIS.

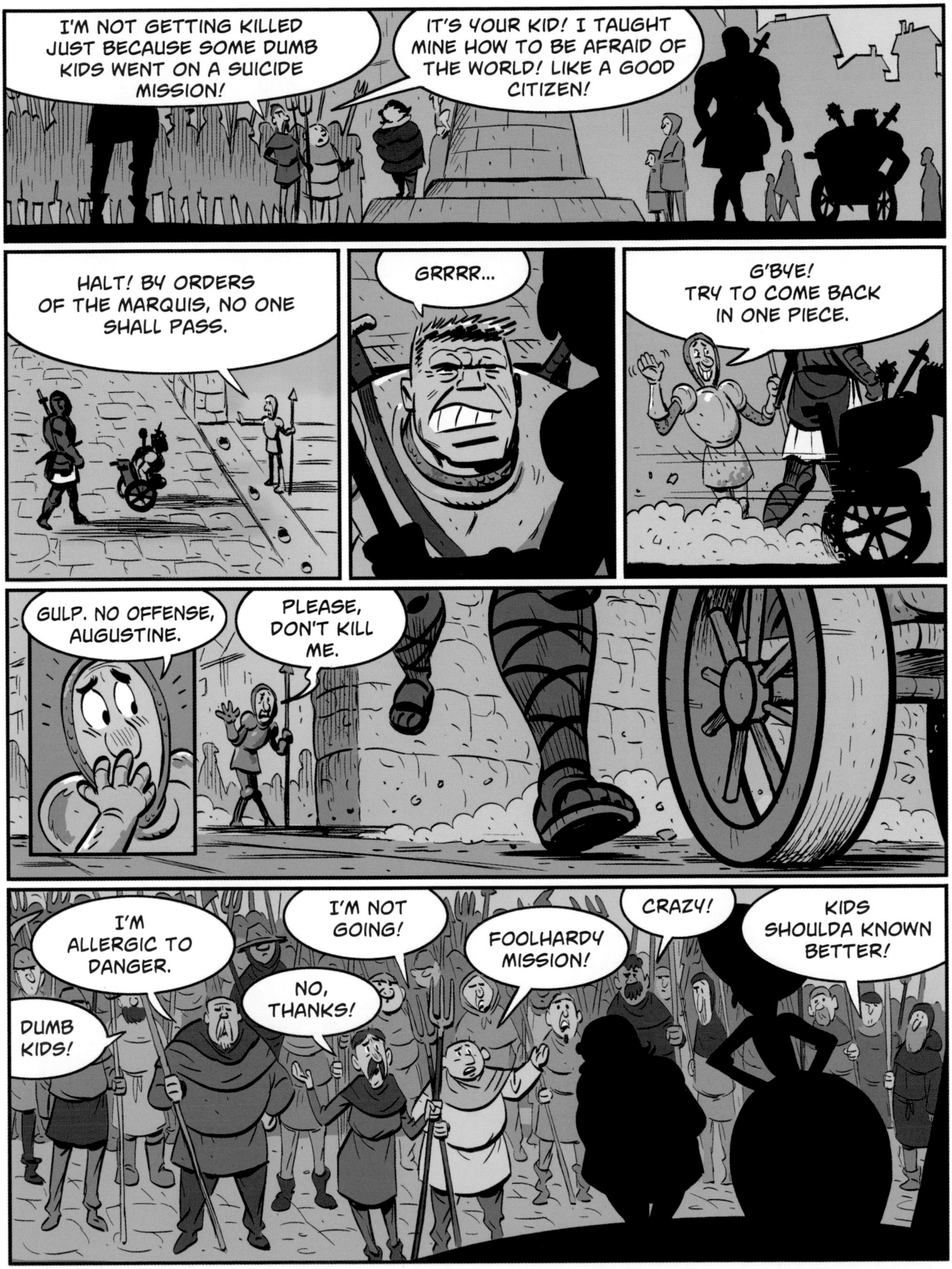
I'M NOT GETTING KILLED JUST BECAUSE SOME DUMB KIDS WENT ON A SUICIDE MISSION!
IT'S YOUR KID! I TAUGHT MINE HOW TO BE AFRAID OF THE WORLD! LIKE A GOOD CITIZEN!
HALT! BY ORDERS OF THE MARQUIS, NO ONE SHALL PASS.
GRRRR...
G'BYE! TRY TO COME BACK IN ONE PIECE.
GULP. NO OFFENSE, AUGUSTINE.
PLEASE, DON'T KILL ME.
I'M ALLERGIC TO DANGER.
I'M NOT GOING!
FOOLHARDY MISSION!
CRAZY!
KIDS SHOULDA KNOWN BETTER!
NO, THANKS!
DUMB KIDS!

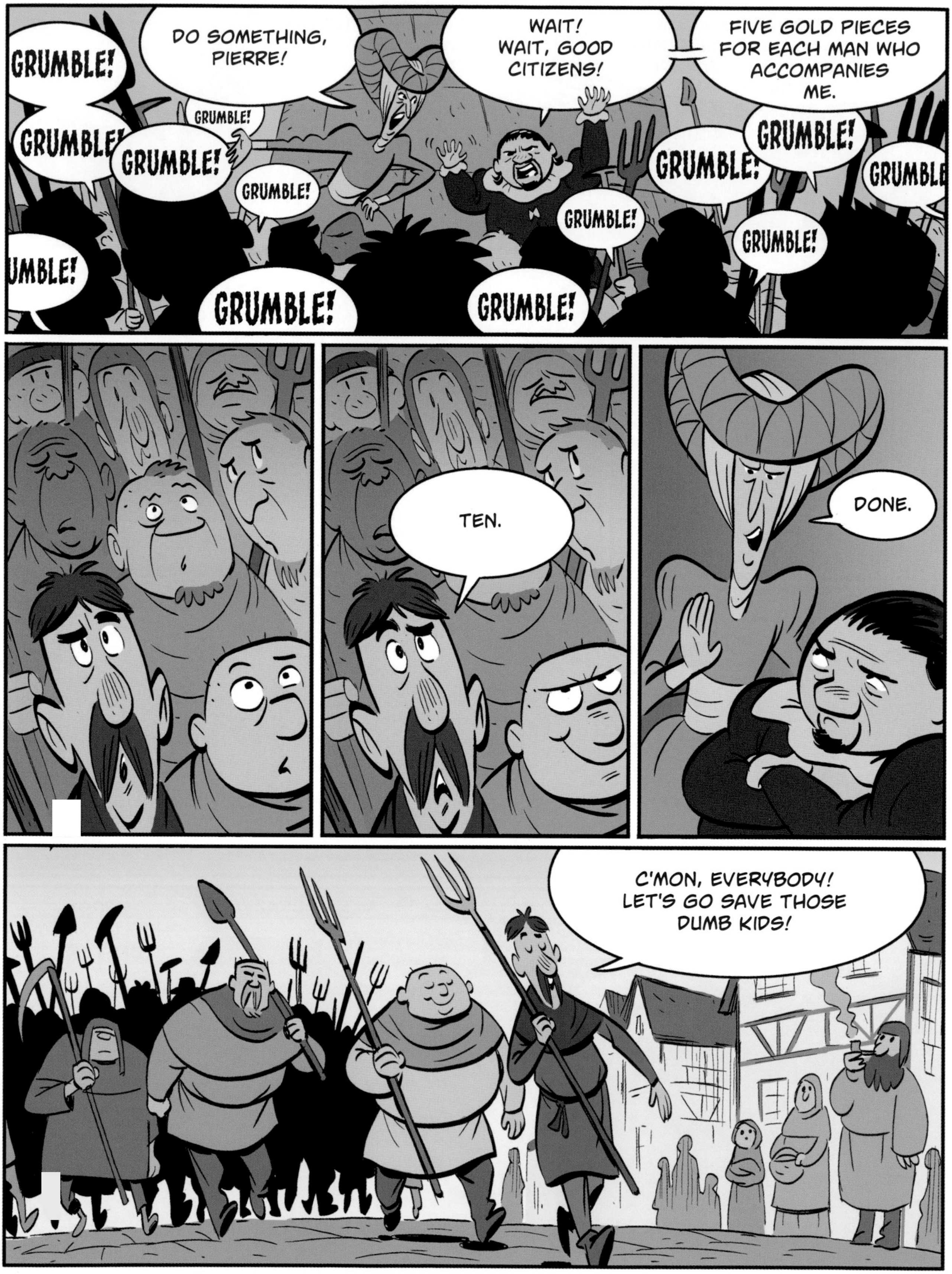
GRUMBLE!
DO SOMETHING, PIERRE!
GRUMBLE!
GRUMBLE!
GRUMBLE!
GRUMBLE!
WAIT! WAIT, GOOD CITIZENS!
FIVE GOLD PIECES FOR EACH MAN WHO ACCOMPANIES ME.
GRUMBLE!
GRUMBLE!
GRUMBLE!
GRUMBLE!
GRUMBLE!
GRUMBLE!
GRUMBLE!
TEN.
DONE.
C'MON, EVERYBODY! LET'S GO SAVE THOSE DUMB KIDS!

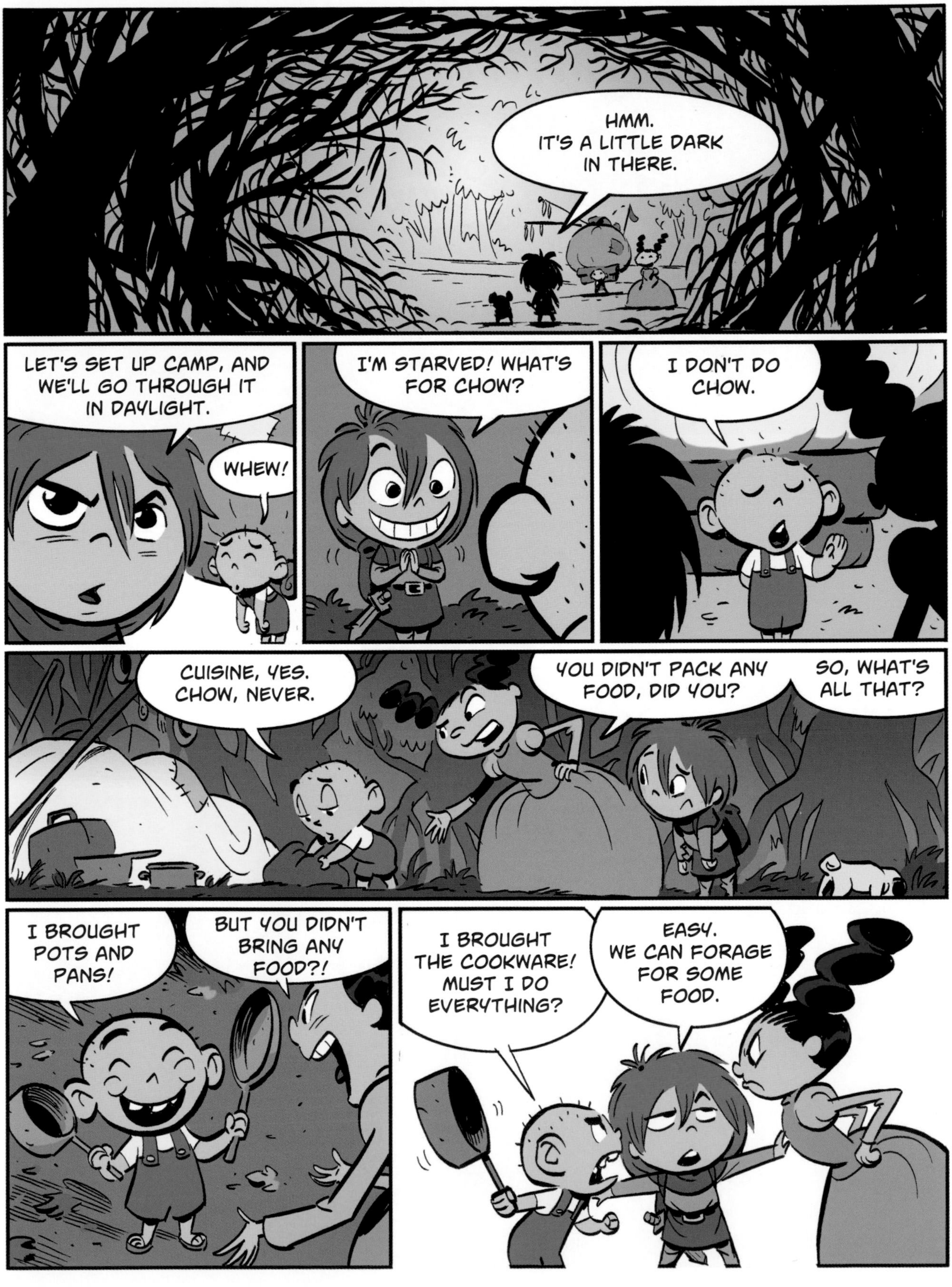
HMM.
IT'S A LITTLE DARK
IN THERE.
LET'S SET UP CAMP, AND WE'LL GO THROUGH IT IN DAYLIGHT.
WHEW!
I'M STARVED! WHAT'S FOR CHOW?
I DON'T DO CHOW.
CUISINE, YES. CHOW, NEVER.
YOU DIDN'T PACK ANY FOOD, DID YOU?
SO, WHAT'S ALL THAT?
I BROUGHT POTS AND PANS!
BUT YOU DIDN'T BRING ANY FOOD?!
I BROUGHT THE COOKWARE! MUST I DO EVERYTHING?
EASY. WE CAN FORAGE FOR SOME FOOD.

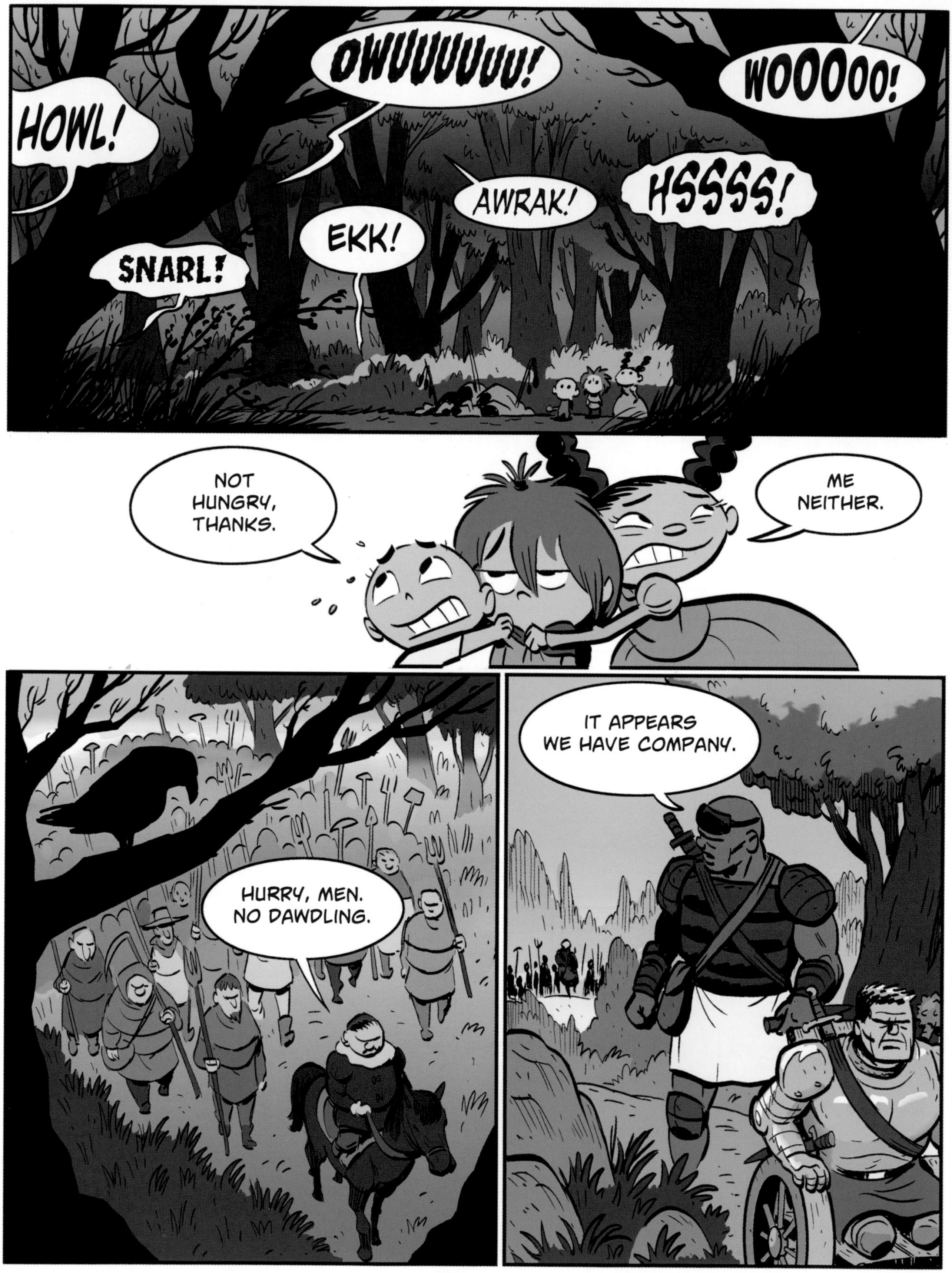
HOWL!
OWUUUUUUU!
WOOOOO!
SNARL!
EKK!
AWRAK!
HSSSS!
NOT HUNGRY, THANKS.
ME NEITHER.
HURRY, MEN. NO DAWDLING.
IT APPEARS WE HAVE COMPANY.

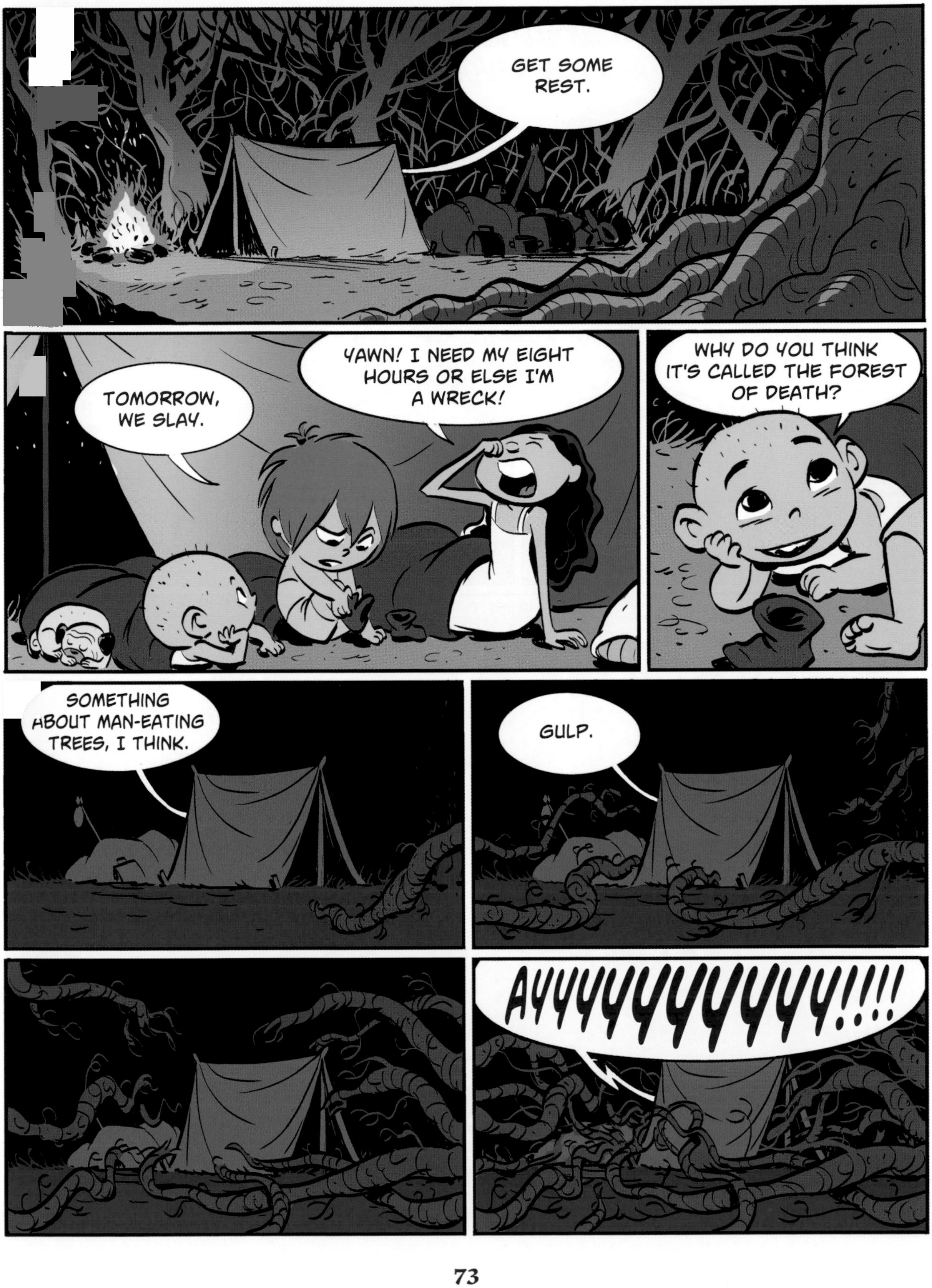
GET SOME REST.
TOMORROW, WE SLAY.
YAWN! I NEED MY EIGHT HOURS OR ELSE I'M A WRECK!
WHY DO YOU THINK IT'S CALLED THE FOREST OF DEATH?
SOMETHING ABOUT MAN-EATING TREES, I THINK.
GULP.
AYYYYYYYYYYY!!!!

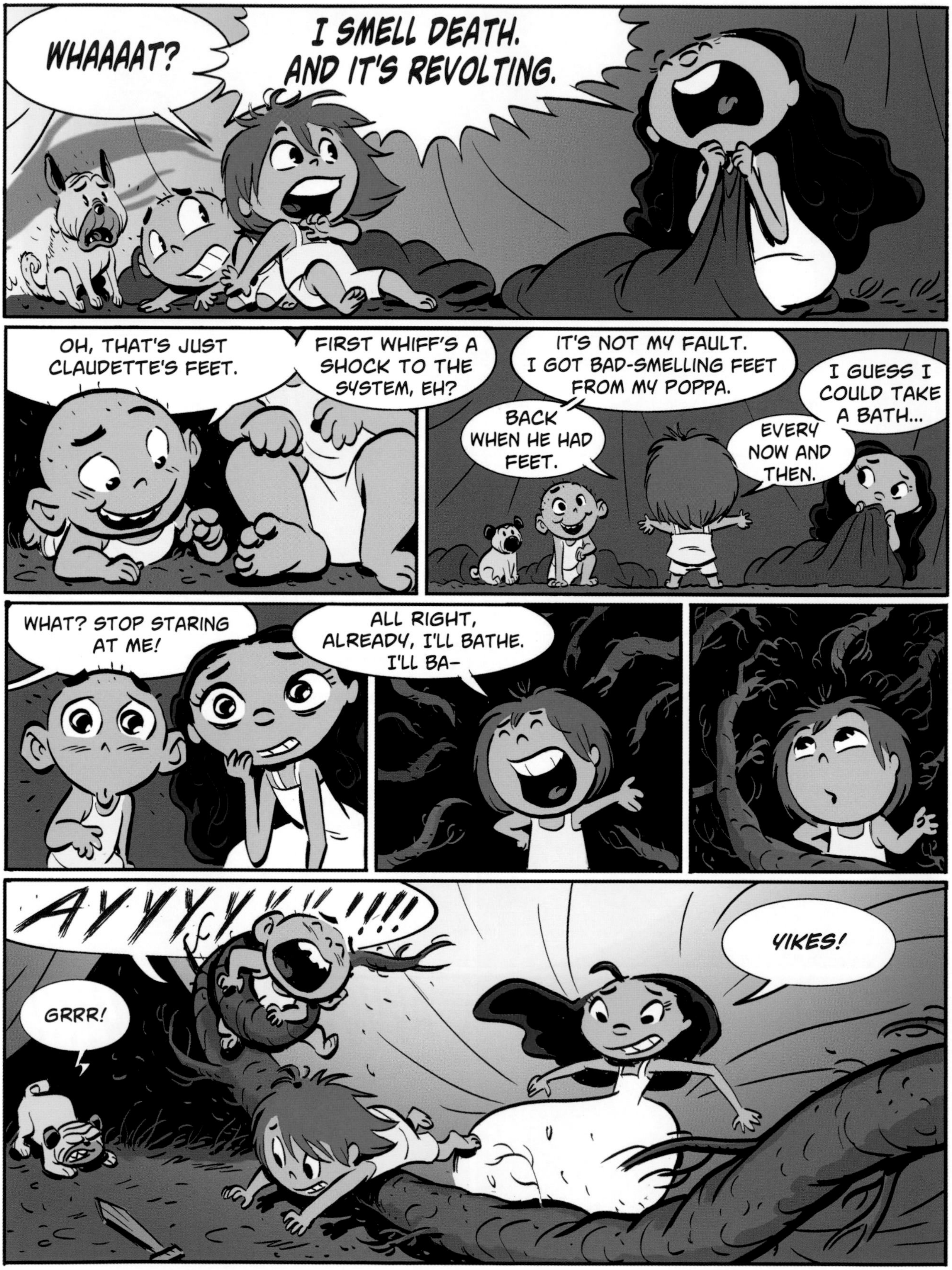
WHAAAAT?
I SMELL DEATH. AND IT'S REVOLTING.
OH, THAT'S JUST CLAUDETTE'S FEET.
FIRST WHIFF'S A SHOCK TO THE SYSTEM, EH?
IT'S NOT MY FAULT. I GOT BAD-SMELLING FEET FROM MY POPPA.
BACK WHEN HE HAD FEET.
I GUESS I COULD TAKE A BATH...
EVERY NOW AND THEN.
WHAT? STOP STARING AT ME!
ALL RIGHT, ALREADY, I'LL BATHE. I'LL BA-
AYYYY!!!!
YIKES!
GRRR!

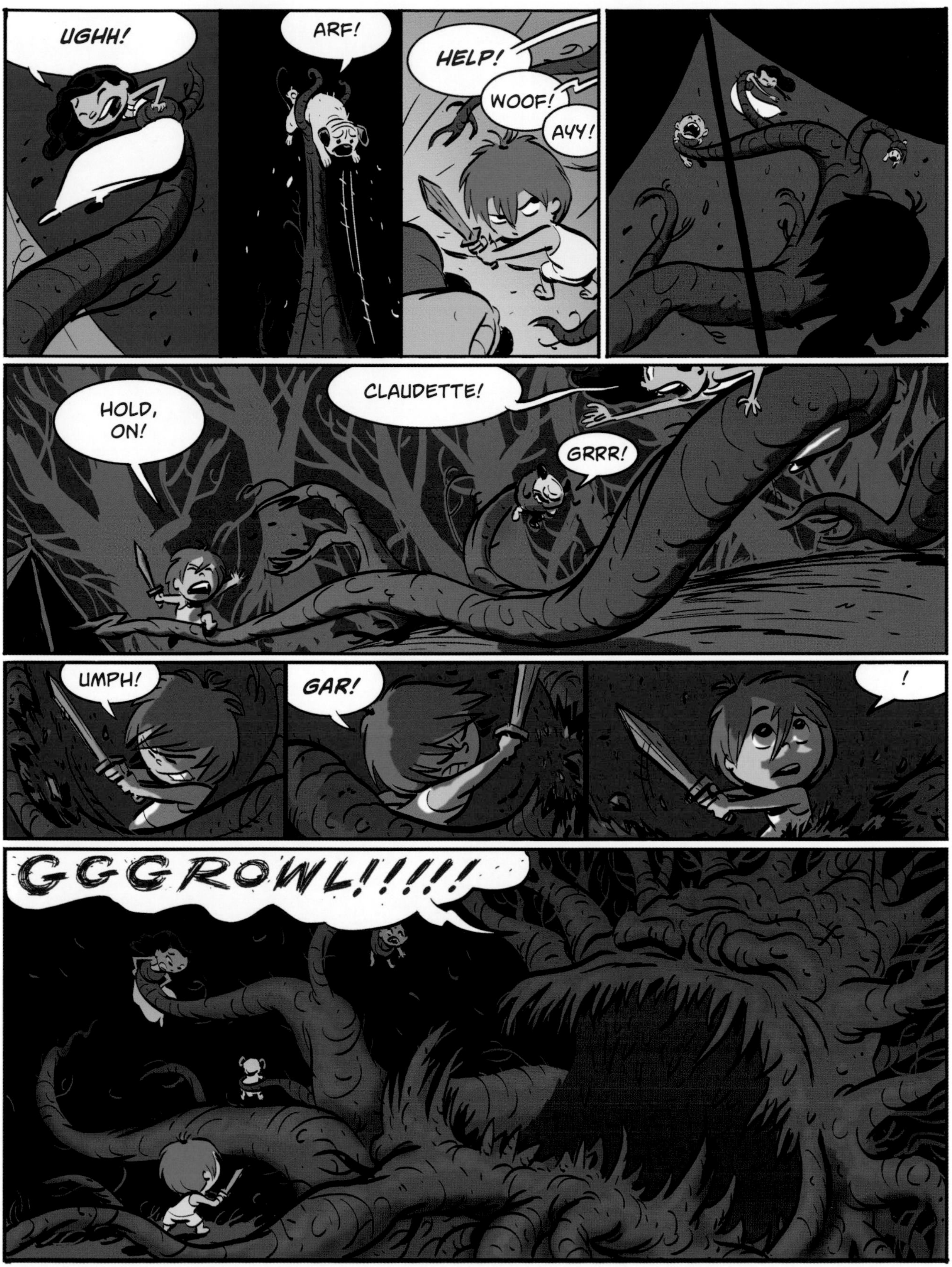
UGHH!
ARF!
HELP!
WOOF!
AYY!
HOLD, ON!
CLAUDETTE!
GRRR!
UMPH!
GAR!
!
GGGROWL!!!!!

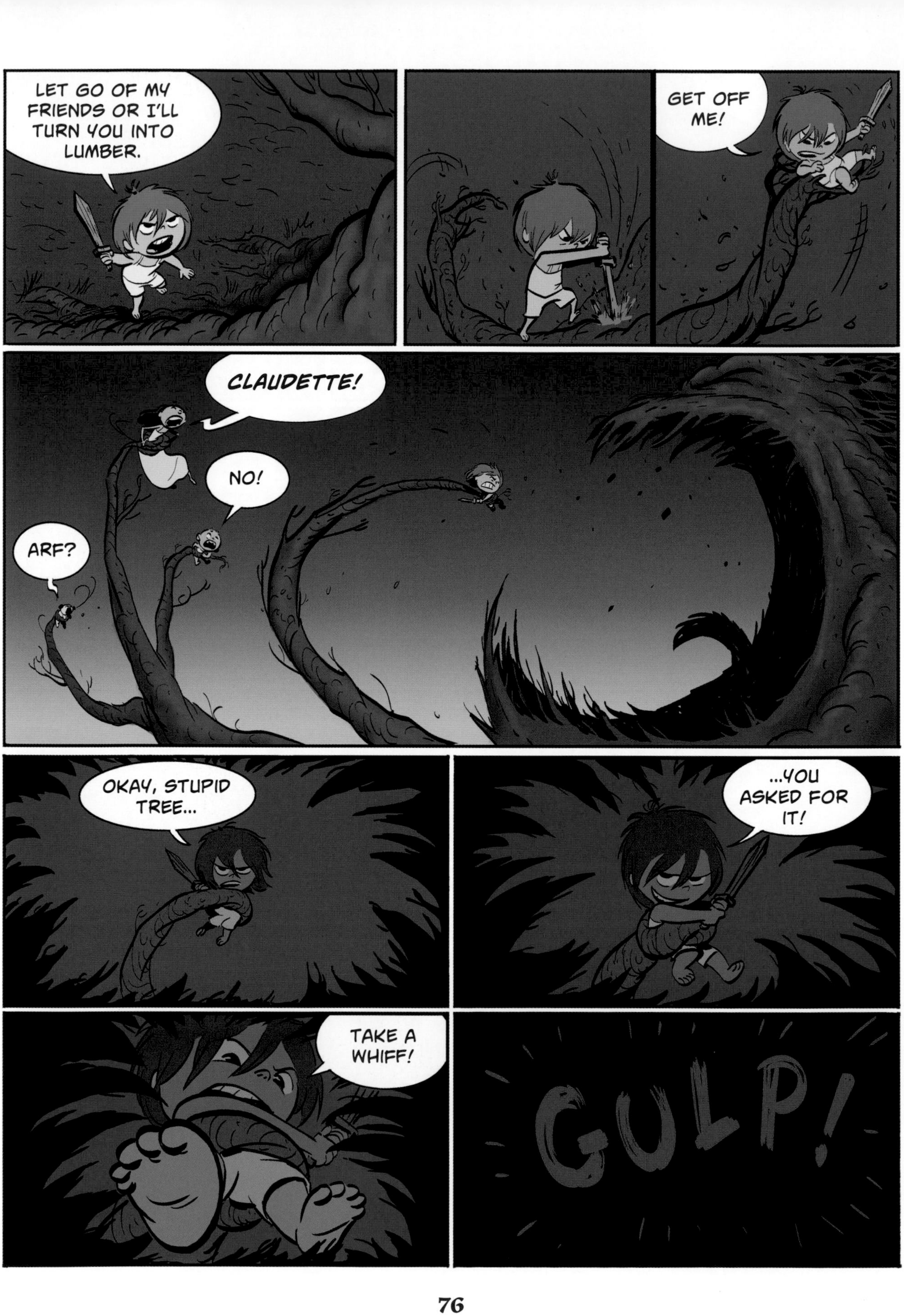
LET GO OF MY FRIENDS OR I'LL TURN YOU INTO LUMBER.
GET OFF ME!
CLAUDETTE!
NO!
ARF?
OKAY, STUPID TREE...
...YOU ASKED FOR IT!
TAKE A WHIFF!
GULP!

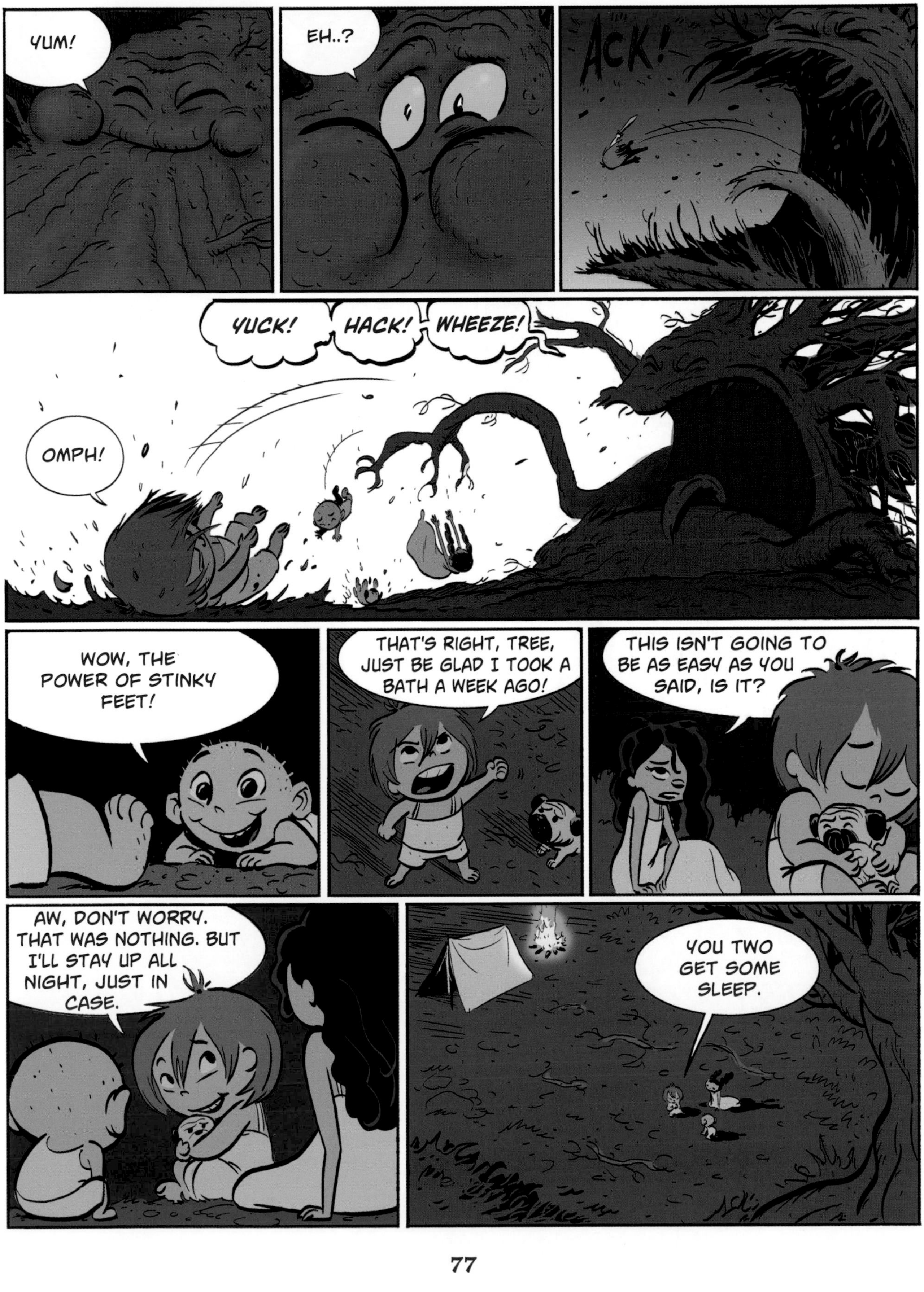
YUM!
EH..?
ACK!
YUCK! HACK! WHEEZE!
OMPH!
WOW, THE POWER OF STINKY FEET!
THAT'S RIGHT, TREE, JUST BE GLAD I TOOK A BATH A WEEK AGO!
THIS ISN'T GOING TO BE AS EASY AS YOU SAID, IS IT?
AW, DON'T WORRY. THAT WAS NOTHING. BUT I'LL STAY UP ALL NIGHT, JUST IN CASE.
YOU TWO GET SOME SLEEP.

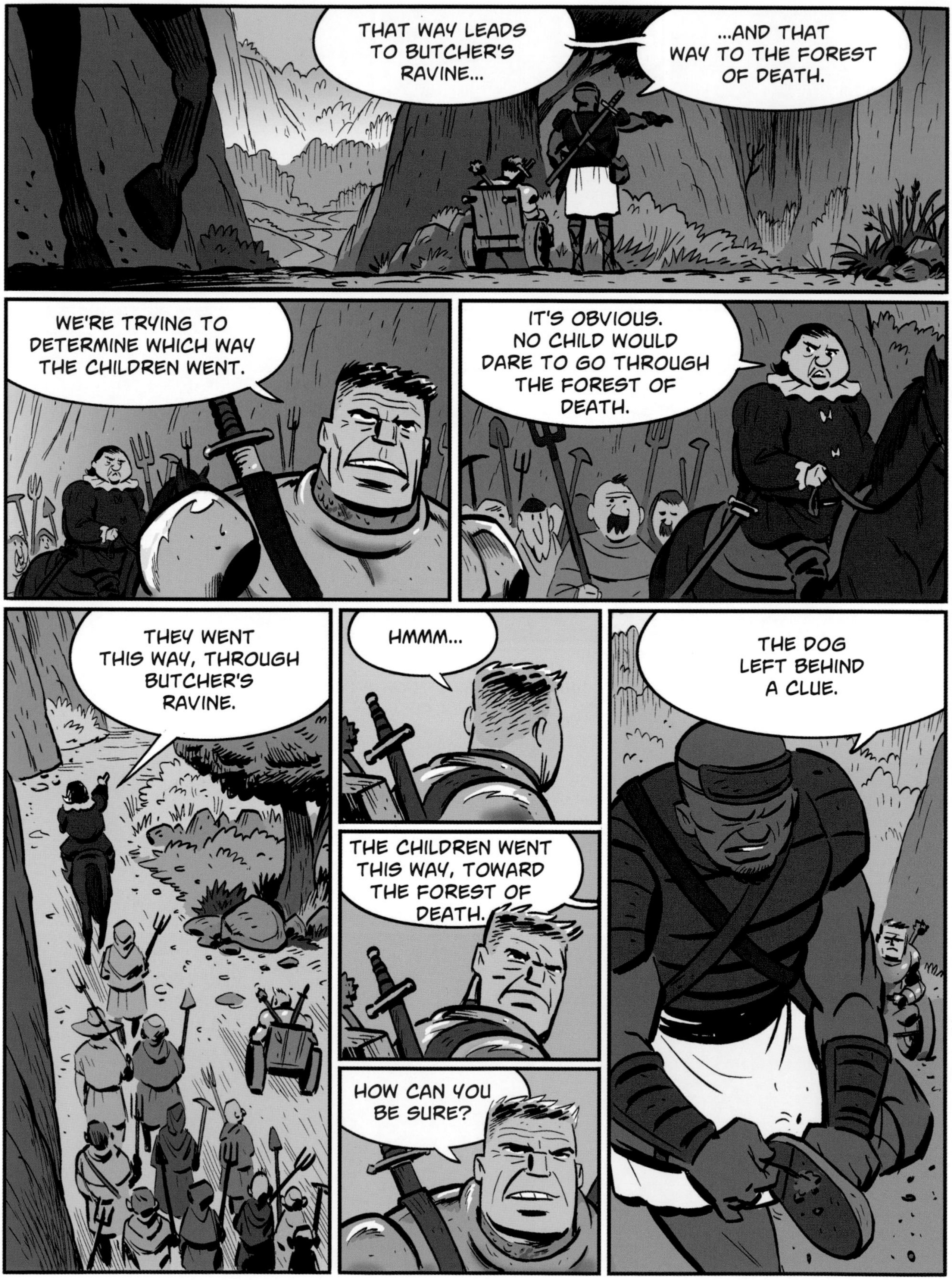
THAT WAY LEADS TO BUTCHER'S RAVINE...
...AND THAT WAY TO THE FOREST OF DEATH.
WE'RE TRYING TO DETERMINE WHICH WAY THE CHILDREN WENT.
IT'S OBVIOUS. NO CHILD WOULD DARE TO GO THROUGH THE FOREST OF DEATH.
THEY WENT THIS WAY, THROUGH BUTCHER'S RAVINE.
HMMM...
THE CHILDREN WENT THIS WAY, TOWARD THE FOREST OF DEATH.
HOW CAN YOU BE SURE?
THE DOG LEFT BEHIND A CLUE.

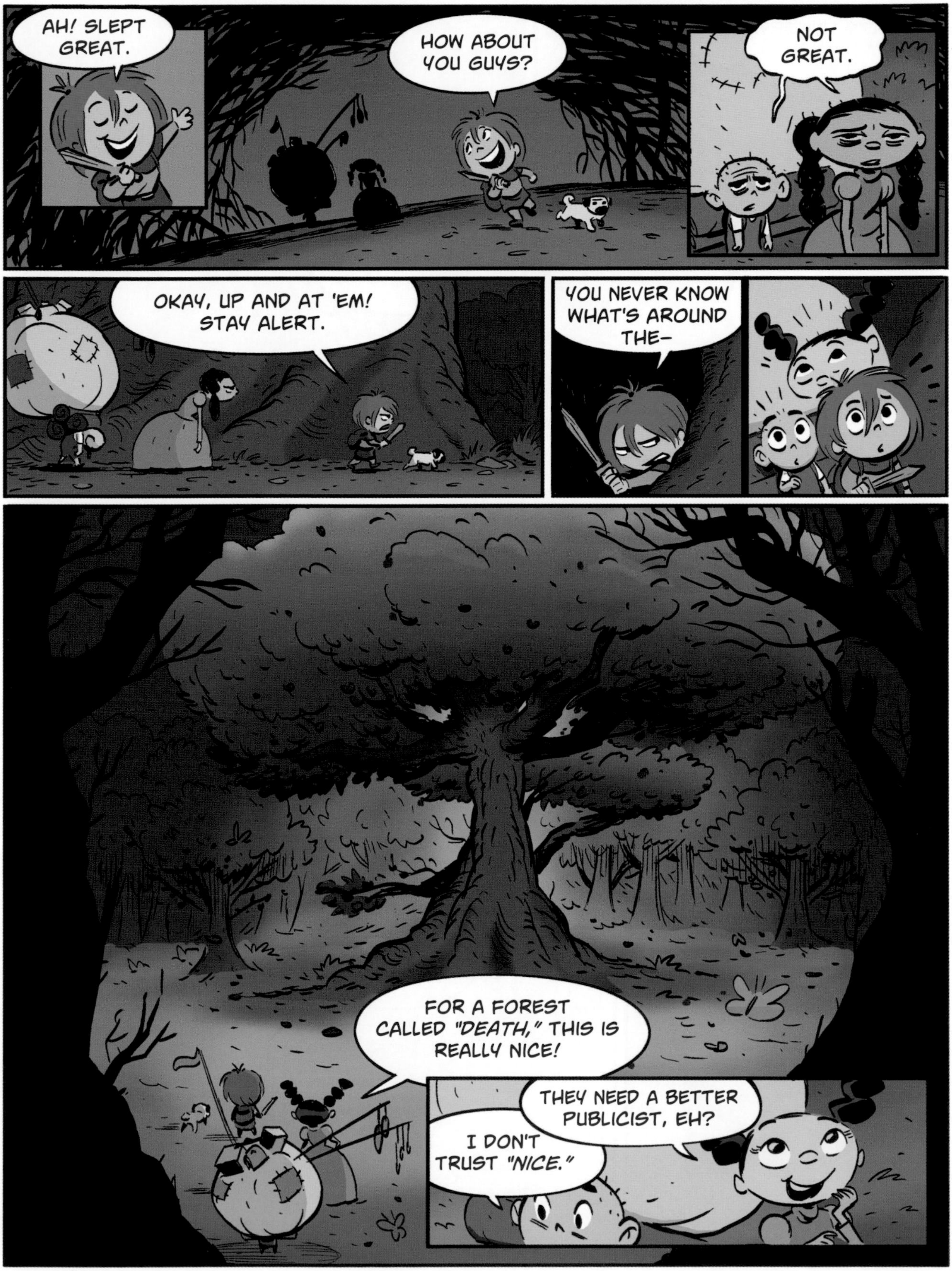
AH! SLEPT GREAT.
HOW ABOUT YOU GUYS?
NOT GREAT.
OKAY, UP AND AT 'EM! STAY ALERT.
YOU NEVER KNOW WHAT'S AROUND THE–
FOR A FOREST CALLED "DEATH," THIS IS REALLY NICE!
THEY NEED A BETTER PUBLICIST, EH?
I DON'T TRUST "NICE."

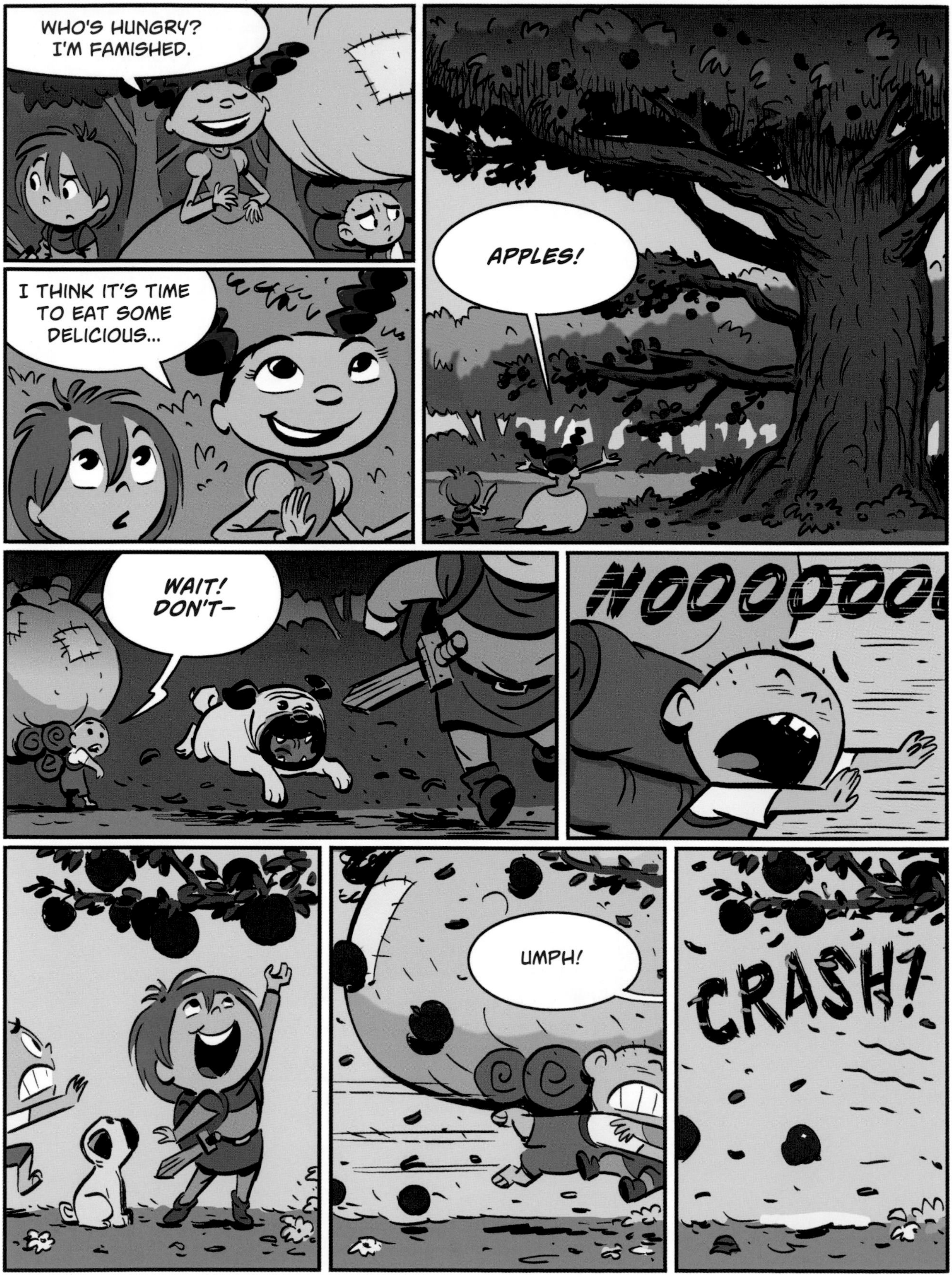
WHO'S HUNGRY? I'M FAMISHED.
I THINK IT'S TIME TO EAT SOME DELICIOUS...
APPLES!
WAIT! DON'T–
NOOOOOOO
UMPH!
CRASH!

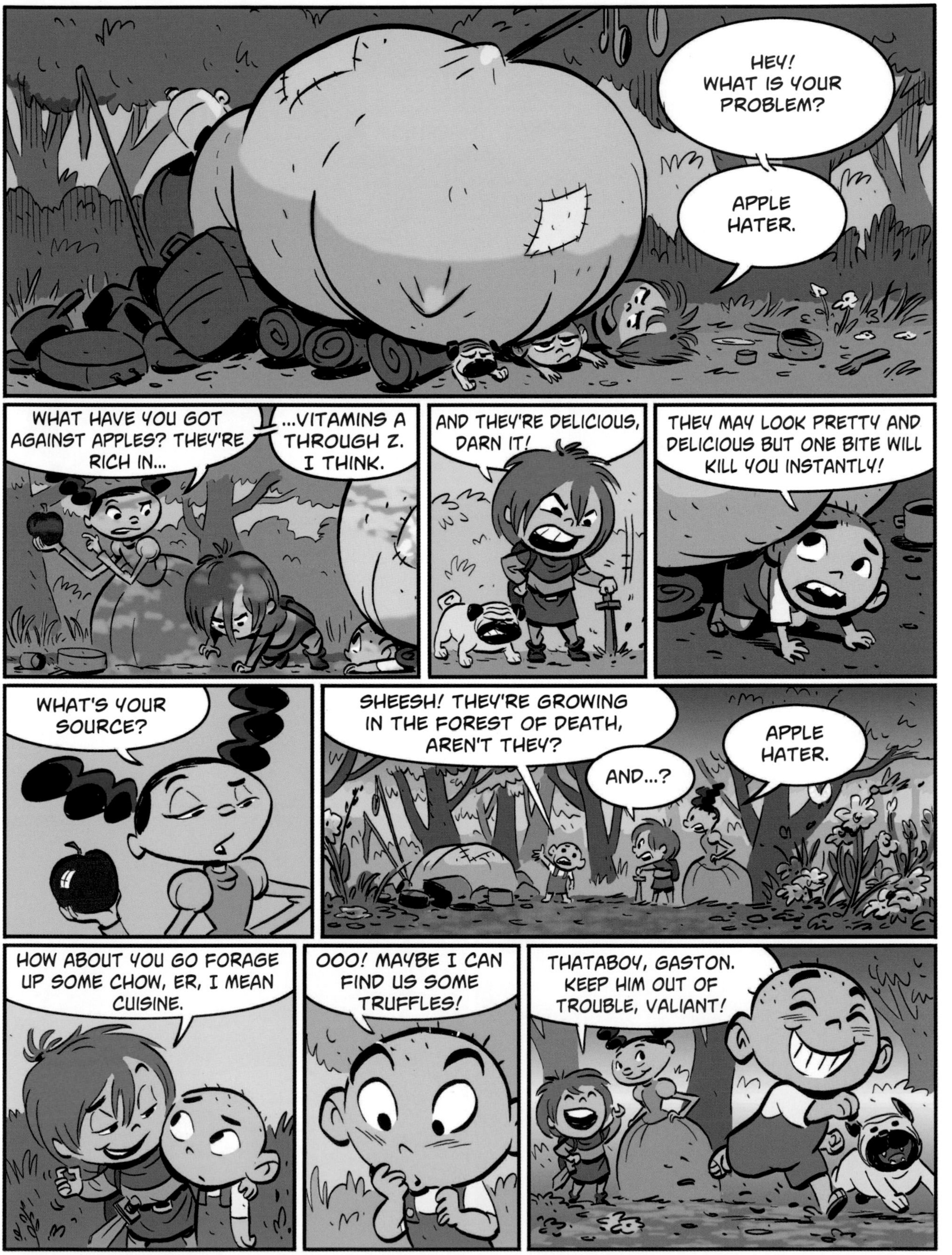

HEY! WHAT IS YOUR PROBLEM?
APPLE HATER.
WHAT HAVE YOU GOT AGAINST APPLES? THEY'RE RICH IN...
...VITAMINS A THROUGH Z. I THINK.
AND THEY'RE DELICIOUS, DARN IT!
THEY MAY LOOK PRETTY AND DELICIOUS BUT ONE BITE WILL KILL YOU INSTANTLY!
WHAT'S YOUR SOURCE?
SHEESH! THEY'RE GROWING IN THE FOREST OF DEATH, AREN'T THEY?
AND...?
APPLE HATER.
HOW ABOUT YOU GO FORAGE UP SOME CHOW, ER, I MEAN CUISINE.
OOO! MAYBE I CAN FIND US SOME TRUFFLES!
THATABOY, GASTON. KEEP HIM OUT OF TROUBLE, VALIANT!

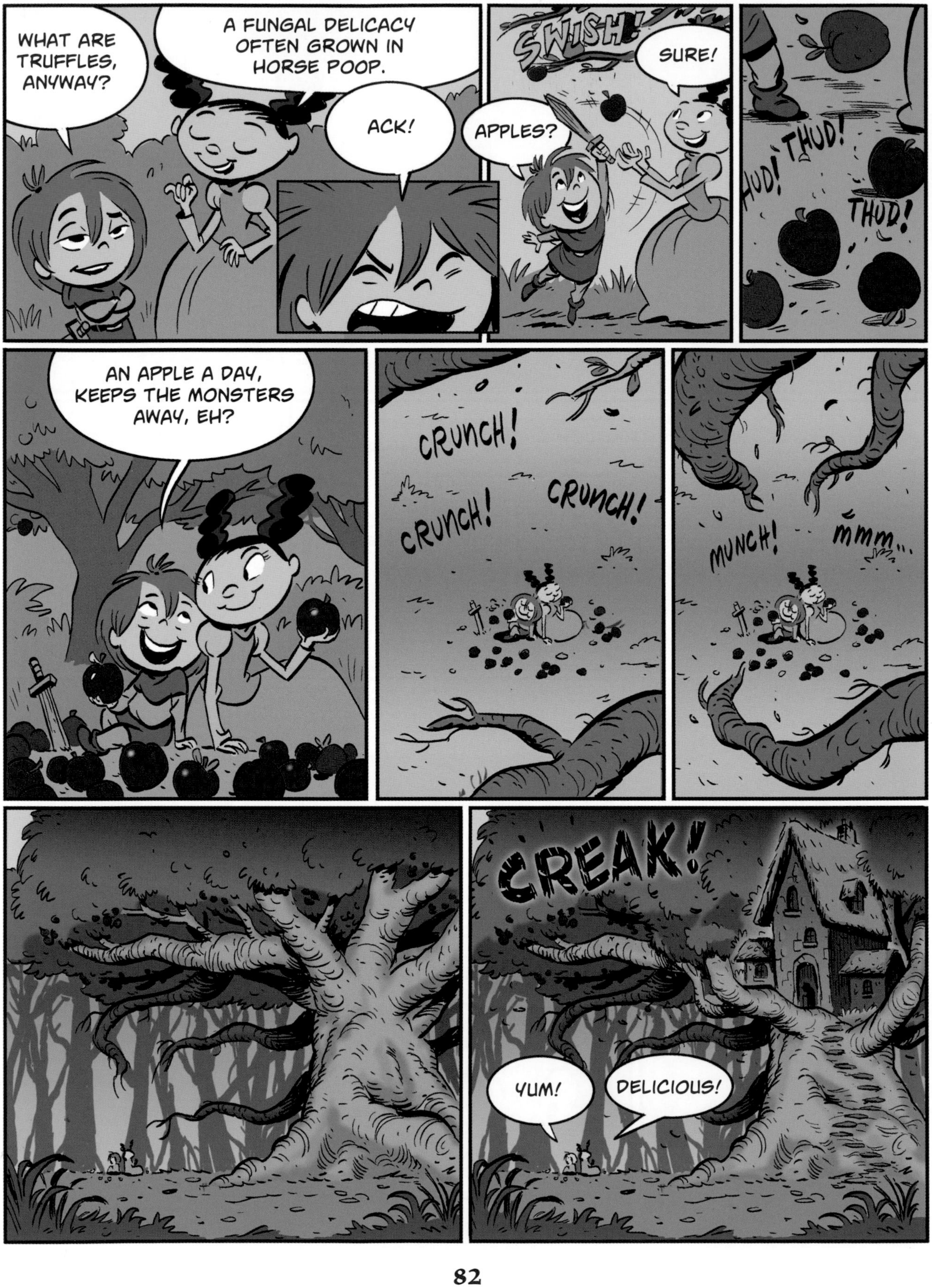
WHAT ARE TRUFFLES, ANYWAY?
A FUNGAL DELICACY OFTEN GROWN IN HORSE POOP.
ACK!
SWISH!
APPLES?
SURE!
THUD!
THUD!
THUD!
AN APPLE A DAY, KEEPS THE MONSTERS AWAY, EH?
CRUNCH!
CRUNCH!
CRUNCH!
MUNCH!
MMM...
CREAK!
YUM!
DELICIOUS!

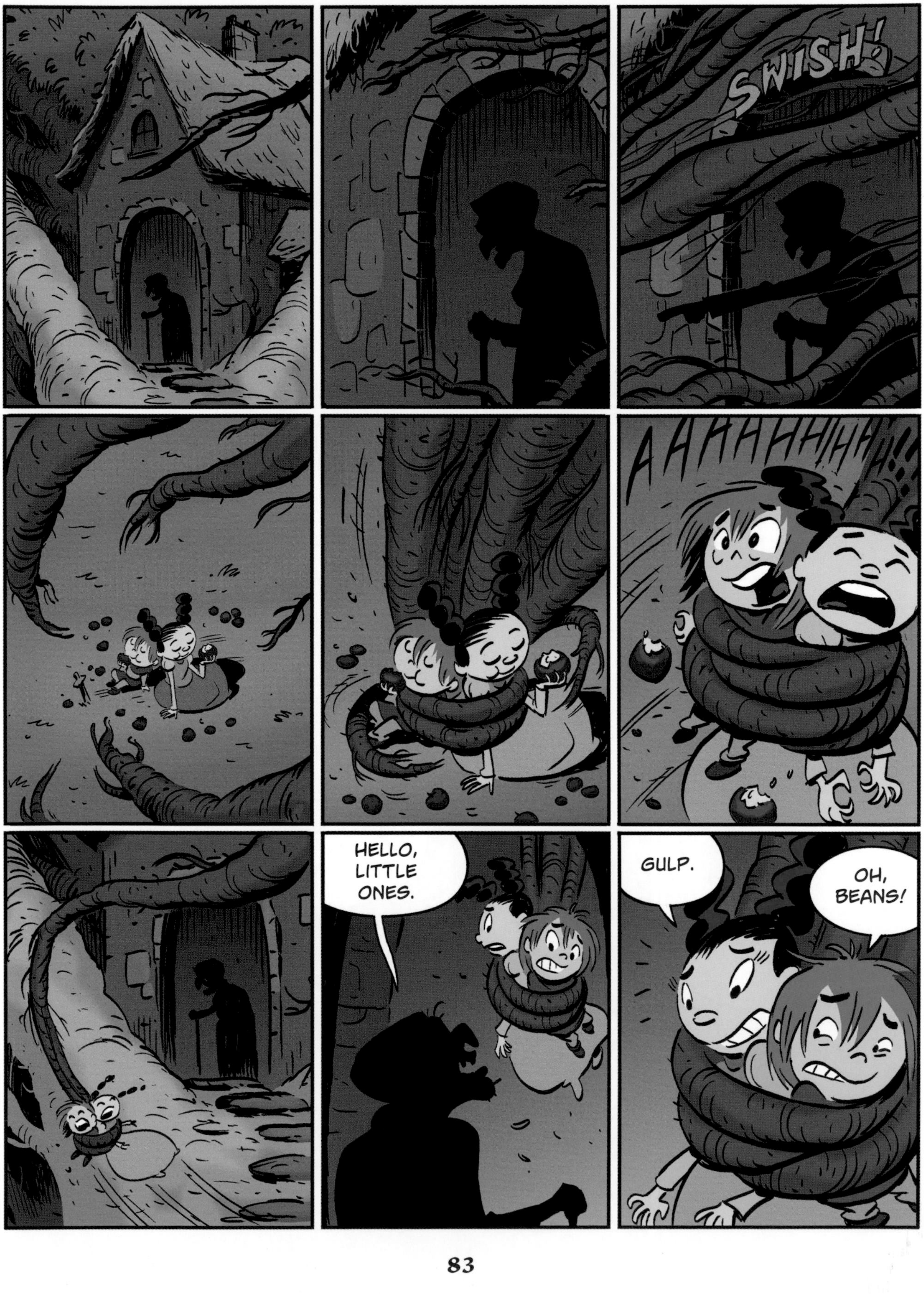
SWISH!
AAAHHHHH!!
HELLO, LITTLE ONES.
GULP.
OH, BEANS!

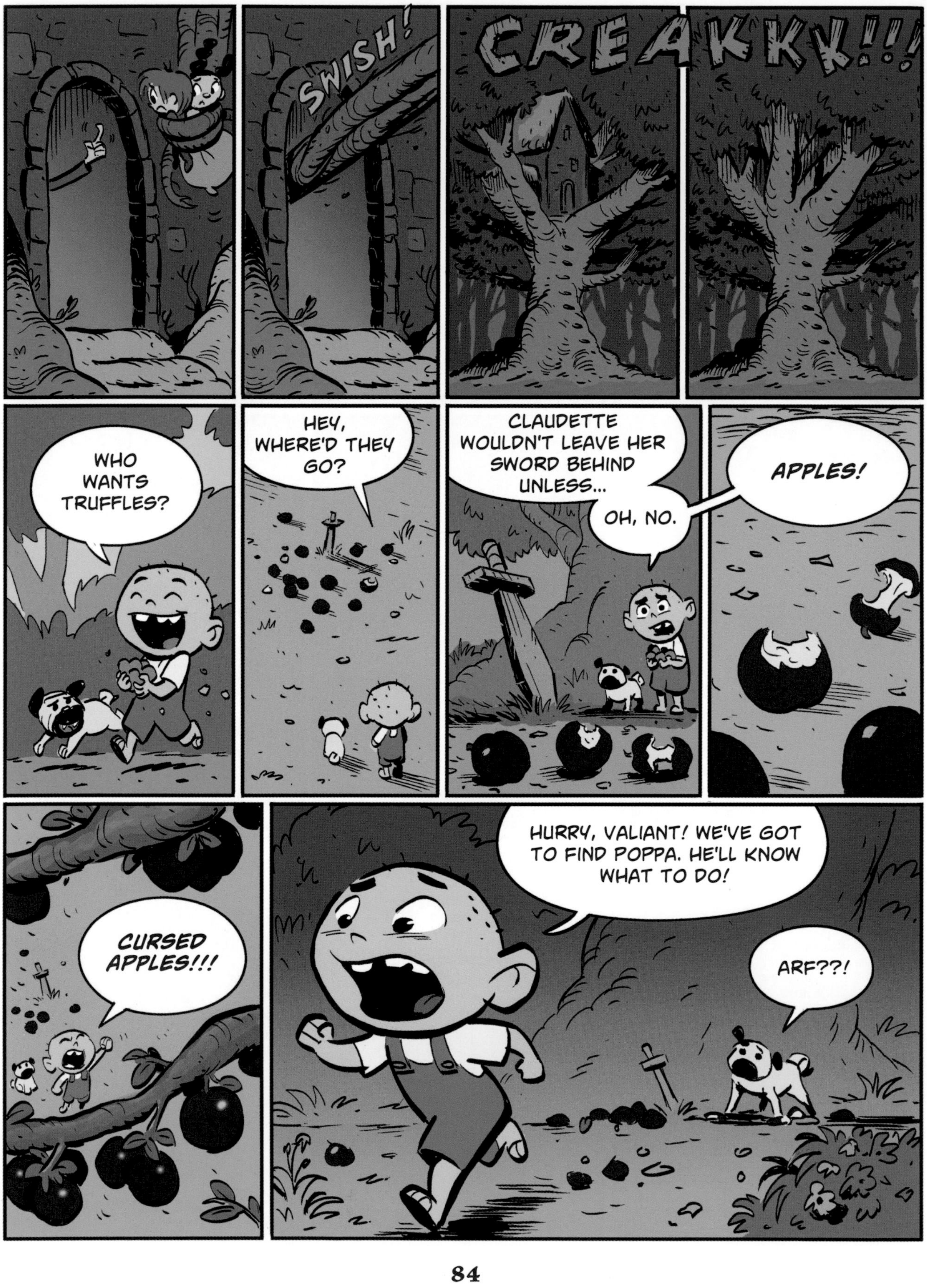
SWISH!
CREAKKK!!!
WHO WANTS TRUFFLES?
HEY, WHERE'D THEY GO?
CLAUDETTE WOULDN'T LEAVE HER SWORD BEHIND UNLESS...
OH, NO.
APPLES!
CURSED APPLES!!!
HURRY, VALIANT! WE'VE GOT TO FIND POPPA. HE'LL KNOW WHAT TO DO!
ARF??!

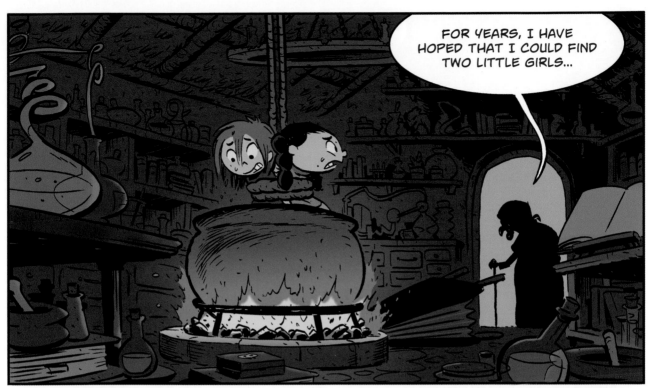

FOR YEARS, I HAVE HOPED THAT I COULD FIND TWO LITTLE GIRLS...

...SO I COULD MAKE THE POTION TO REVERSE THE CURSE THAT TURNED ME INTO...

THE APPLE HAG!

"...BRING TWO LITTLE GIRLS TO A BOIL, MIX WITH SUGAR-FREE EYE OF NEWT, WOOL OF BAT, TONGUE OF DOG, AND BASIL."

IS BOILING US REALLY NECESSARY?

YES, SWEET ONE. I'M GOING TO BOIL YOU, BLEND YOU...

...AND THEN I'M GOING TO EAT YOU!

GULP.

I WAS ONCE THE MAIDEN OF THE FOREST. THE MOST BEAUTIFUL WOMAN THIS SIDE OF THE MOUNTAIN.

BUT I DISPLEASED THE MOST POWERFUL WIZARD OF MONT PETIT PIERRE...

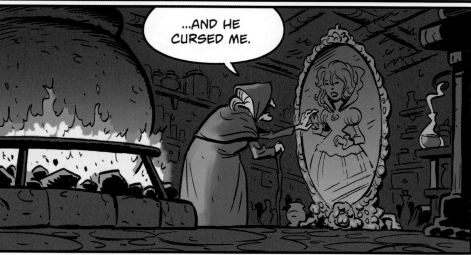

...AND HE CURSED ME.

SHE'S CRAZY. MONT PETIT DOESN'T HAVE ANY WIZARDS!

THIS MIRROR IS THE ONLY MEMORY I HAVE OF THE...

...BEAUTIFUL MAIDEN I ONCE WAS.

MAYBE ON THE INSIDE...

WHAT DID YOU SAY, LITTLE GIRL?

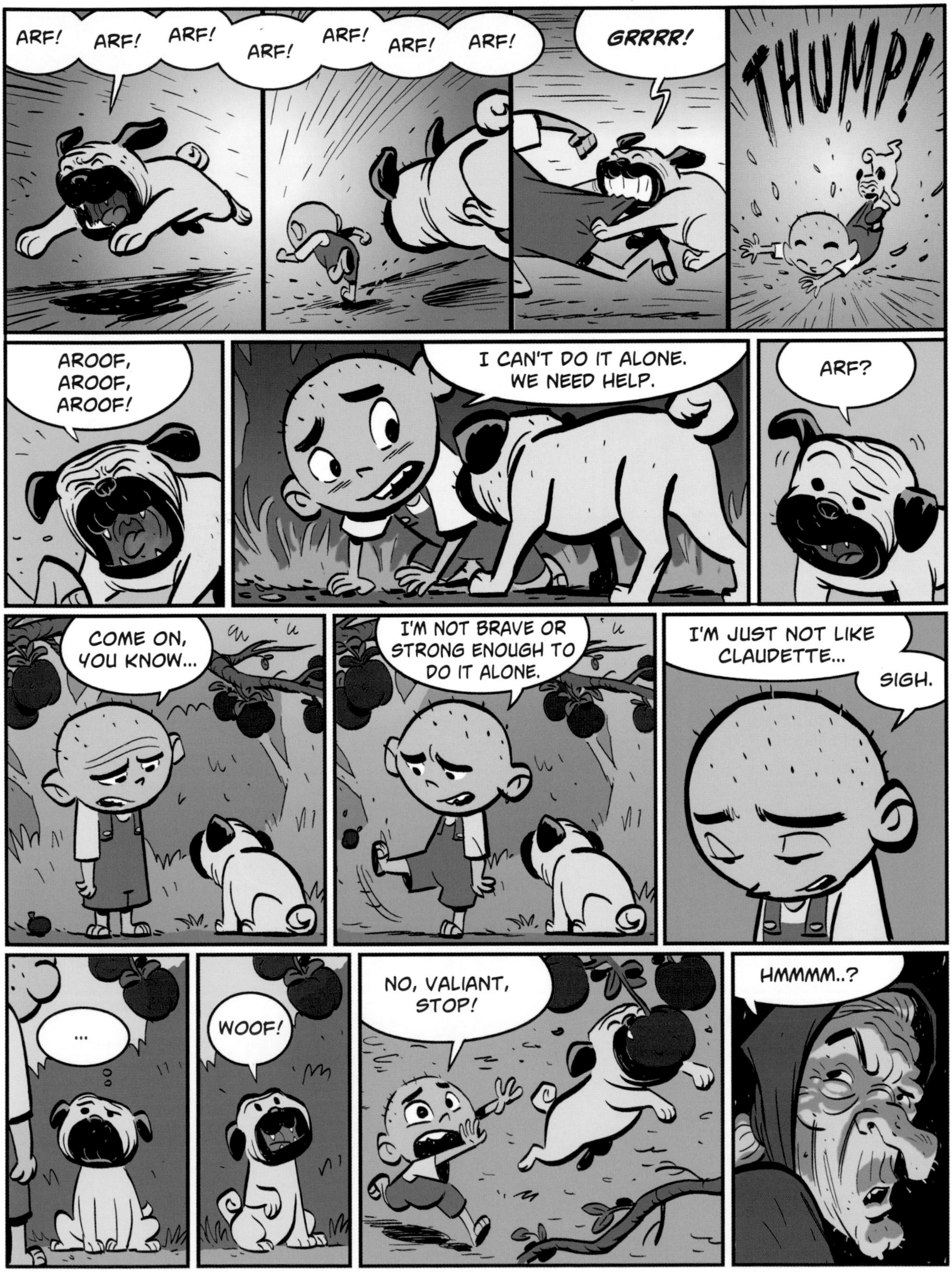
ARF! ARF! ARF! ARF! ARF! ARF! ARF!
GRRRR!
THUMP!
AROOF, AROOF, AROOF!
I CAN'T DO IT ALONE. WE NEED HELP.
ARF?
COME ON, YOU KNOW...
I'M NOT BRAVE OR STRONG ENOUGH TO DO IT ALONE.
I'M JUST NOT LIKE CLAUDETTE...
SIGH.
...
WOOF!
NO, VALIANT, STOP!
HMMMM..?

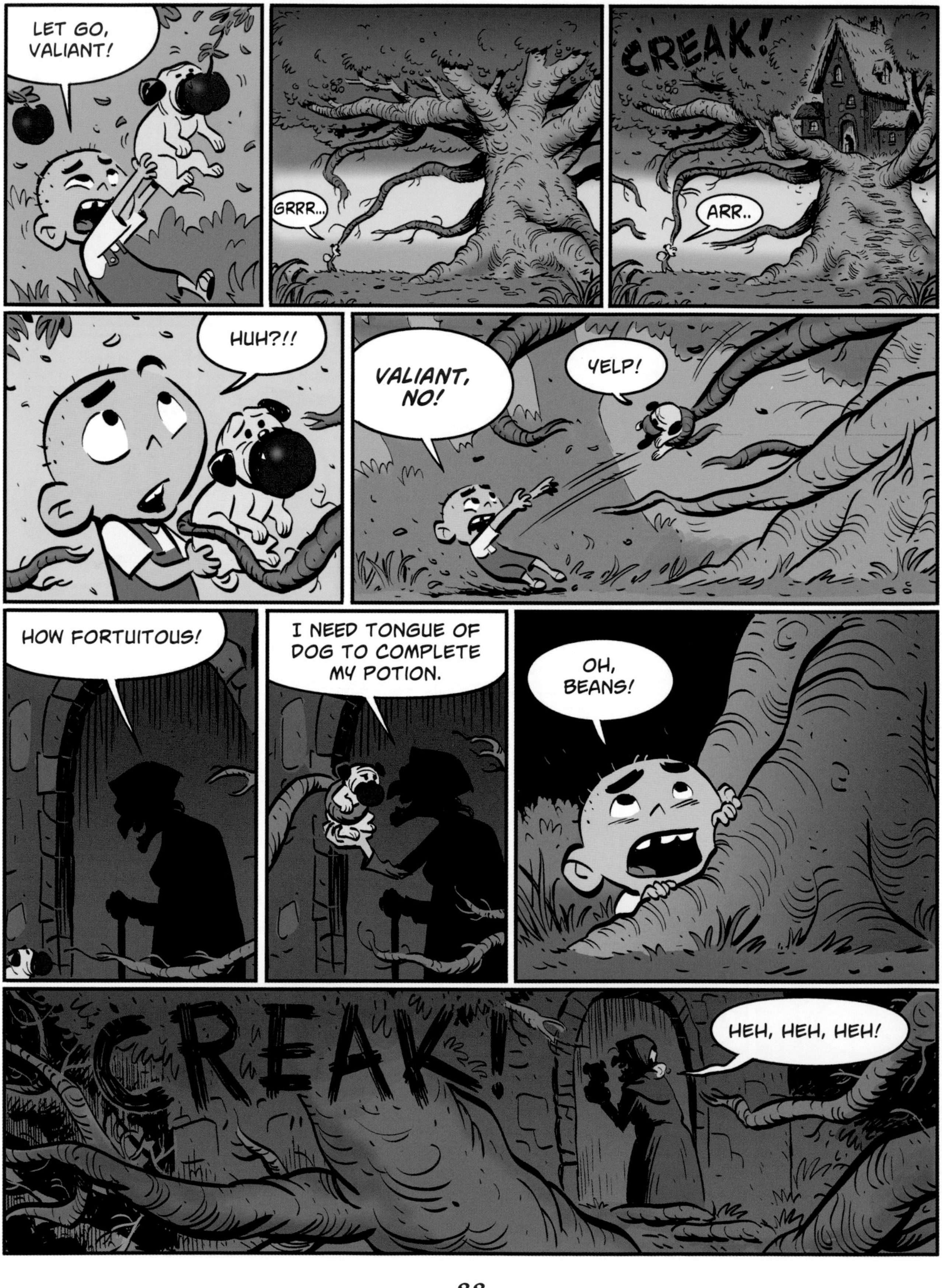
LET GO, VALIANT!
GRRR...
CREAK!
ARR..
HUH?!!
VALIANT, NO!
YELP!
HOW FORTUITOUS!
I NEED TONGUE OF DOG TO COMPLETE MY POTION.
OH, BEANS!
CREAK!
HEH, HEH, HEH!

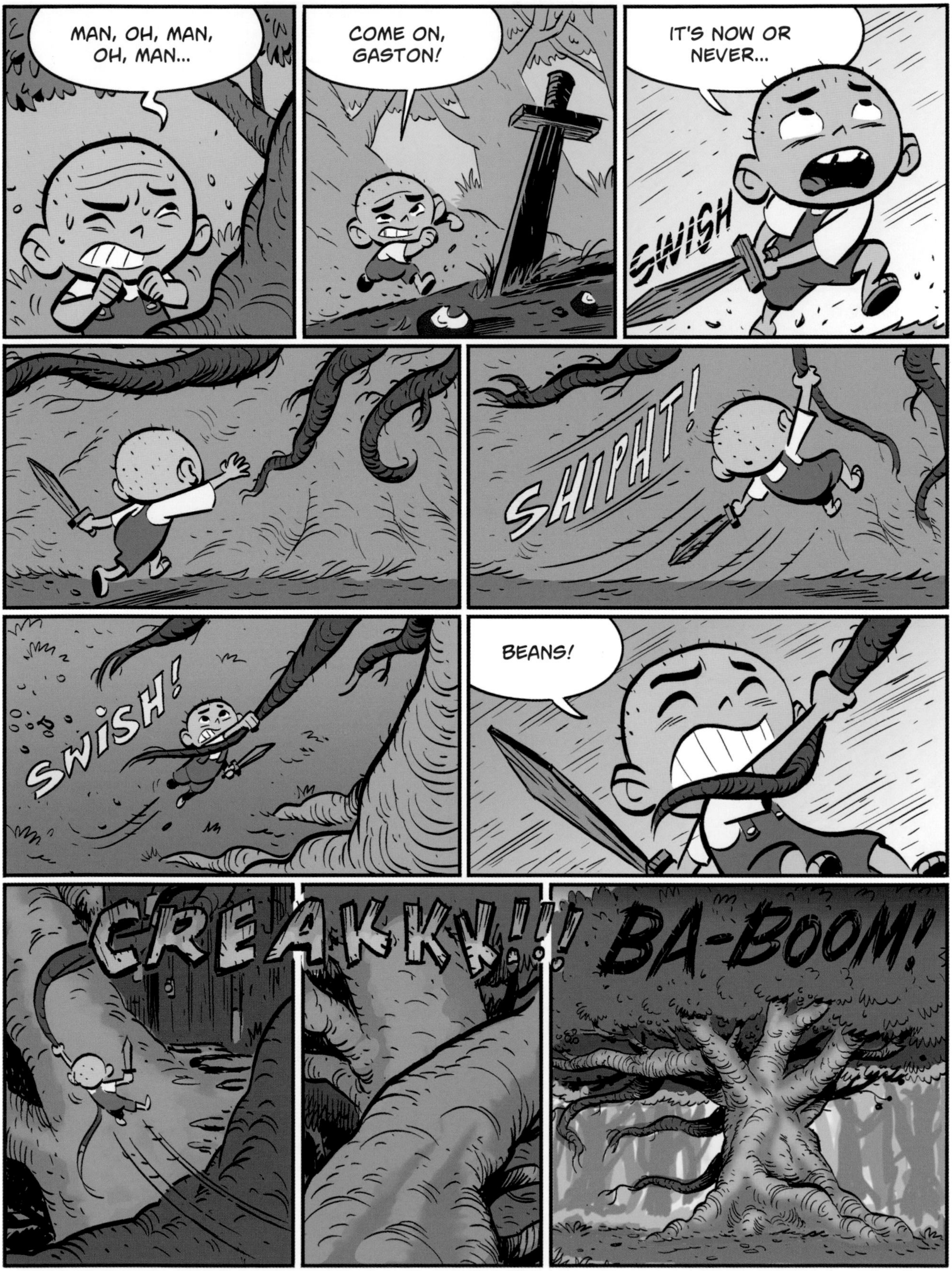
MAN, OH, MAN, OH, MAN...
COME ON, GASTON!
IT'S NOW OR NEVER...
SWISH
SHIPHT!
SWISH!
BEANS!
CREAKK!!!
BA-BOOM!

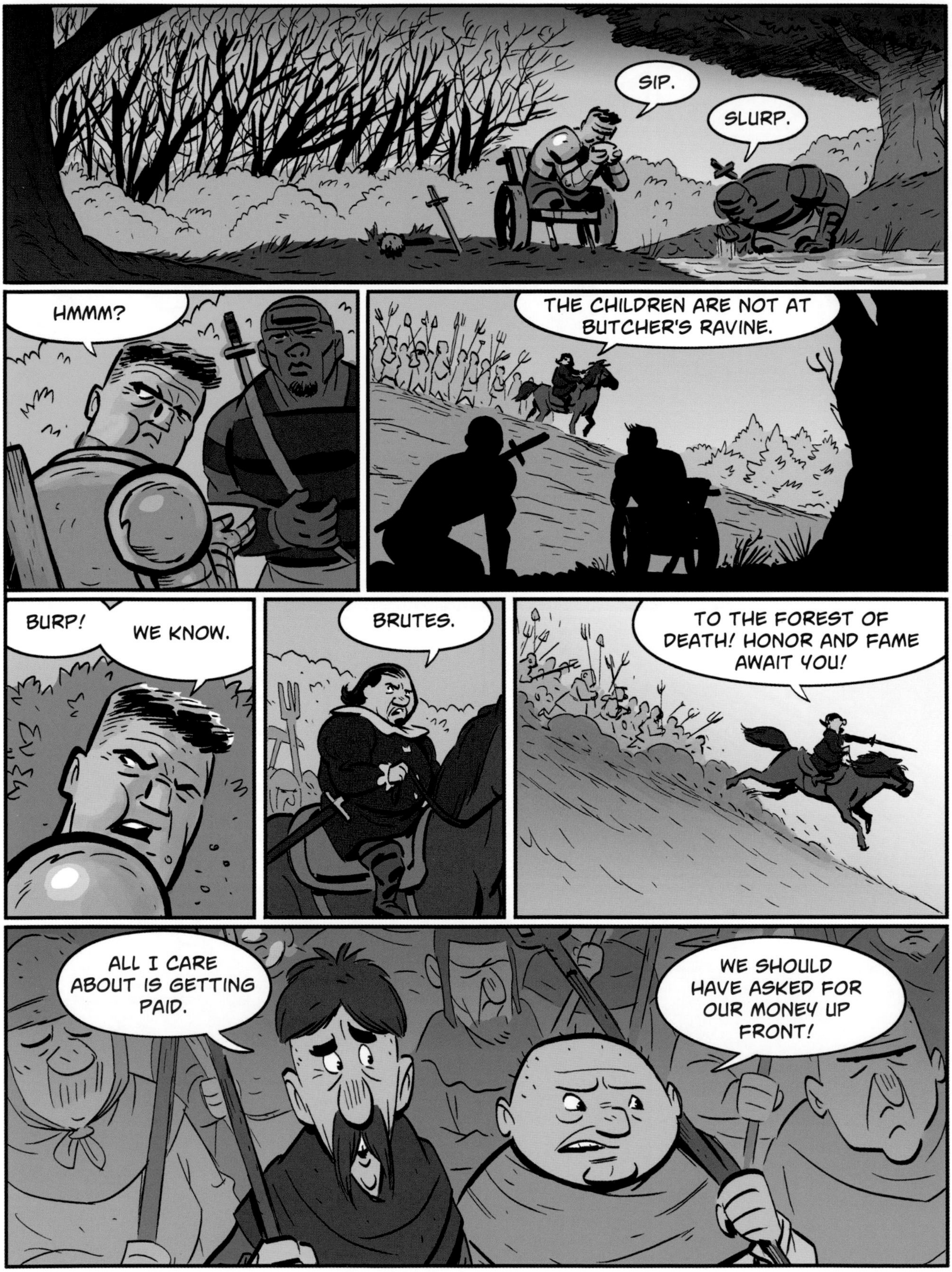
SIP.
SLURP.
HMMM?
THE CHILDREN ARE NOT AT BUTCHER'S RAVINE.
BURP!
WE KNOW.
BRUTES.
TO THE FOREST OF DEATH! HONOR AND FAME AWAIT YOU!
ALL I CARE ABOUT IS GETTING PAID.
WE SHOULD HAVE ASKED FOR OUR MONEY UP FRONT!

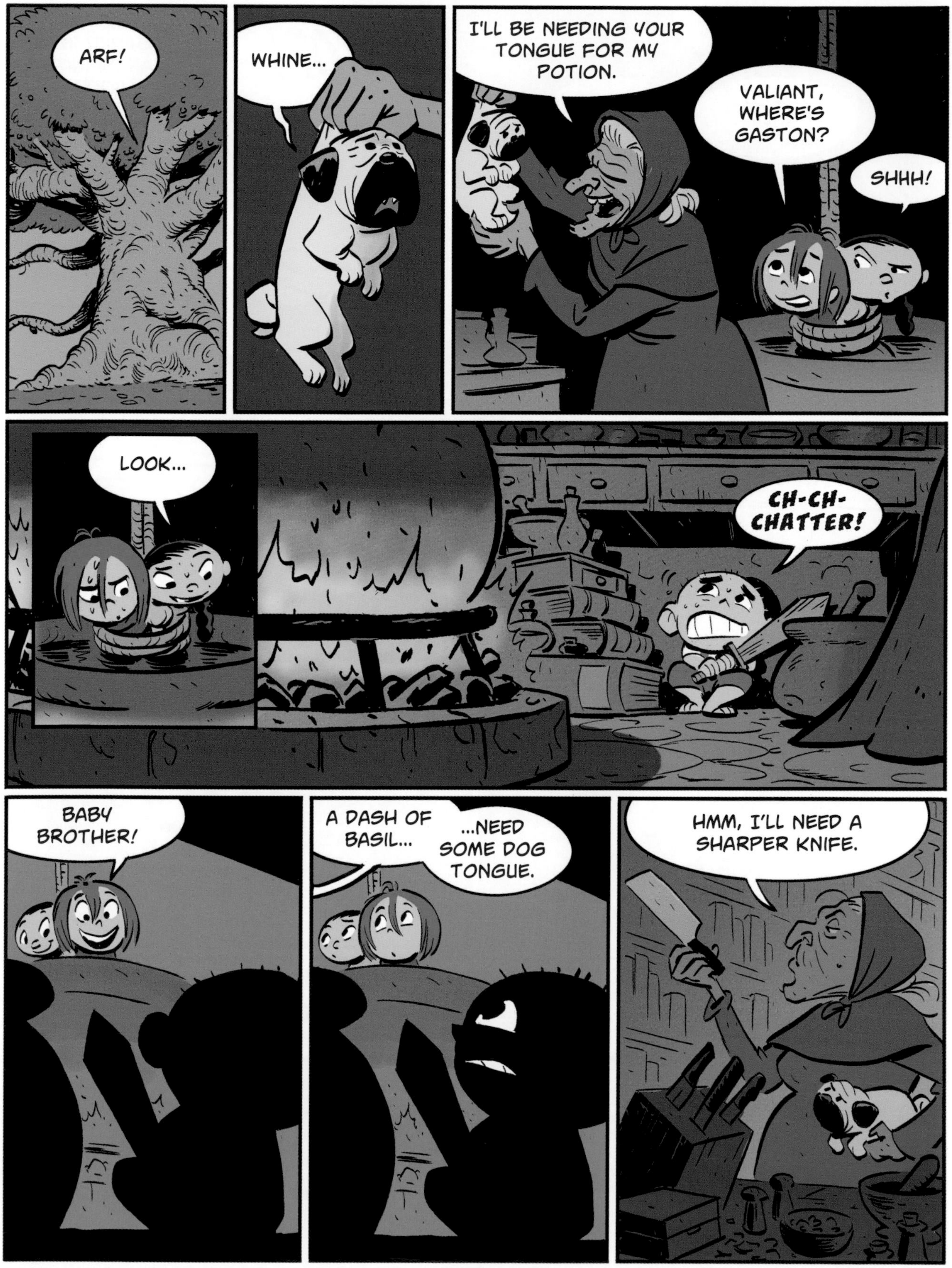
ARF!
WHINE...
I'LL BE NEEDING YOUR TONGUE FOR MY POTION.
VALIANT, WHERE'S GASTON?
SHHH!
LOOK...
CH-CH-CHATTER!
BABY BROTHER!
A DASH OF BASIL...
...NEED SOME DOG TONGUE.
HMM, I'LL NEED A SHARPER KNIFE.

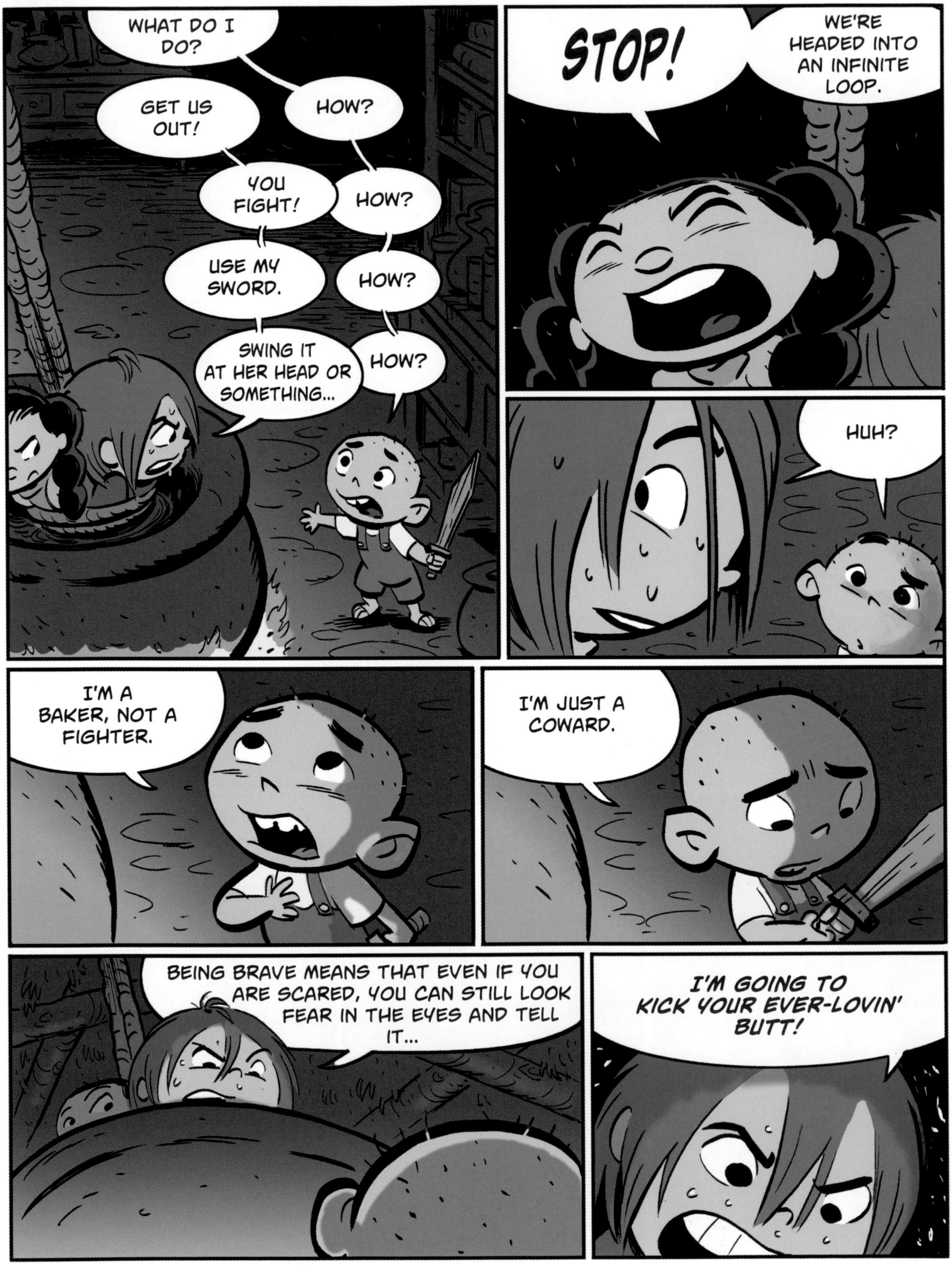
WHAT DO I DO?
GET US OUT!
HOW?
YOU FIGHT!
HOW?
USE MY SWORD.
HOW?
SWING IT AT HER HEAD OR SOMETHING...
HOW?
STOP!
WE'RE HEADED INTO AN INFINITE LOOP.
HUH?
I'M A BAKER, NOT A FIGHTER.
I'M JUST A COWARD.
BEING BRAVE MEANS THAT EVEN IF YOU ARE SCARED, YOU CAN STILL LOOK FEAR IN THE EYES AND TELL IT...
I'M GOING TO KICK YOUR EVER-LOVIN' BUTT!

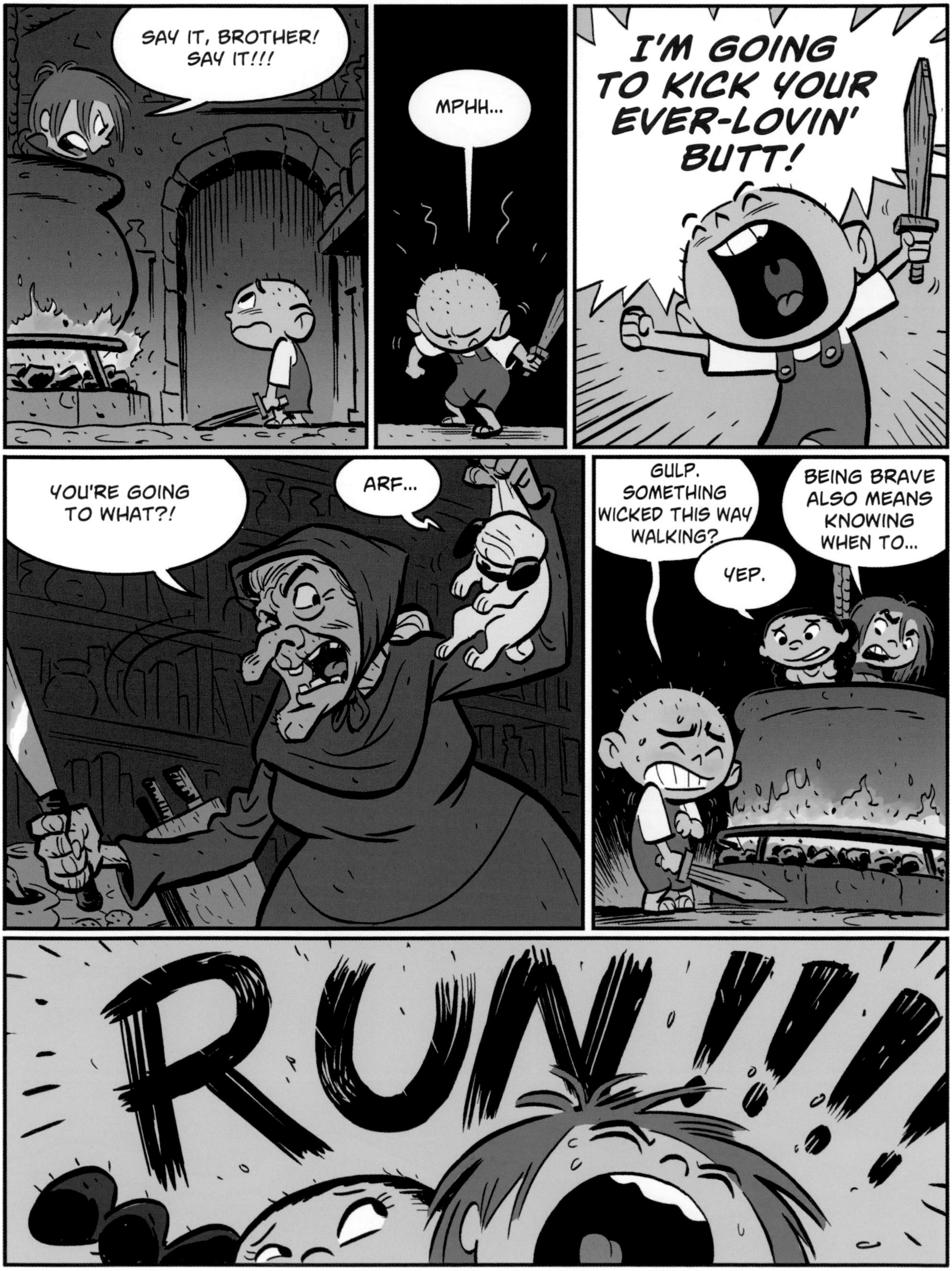
SAY IT, BROTHER! SAY IT!!!
MPHH...
I'M GOING TO KICK YOUR EVER-LOVIN' BUTT!
YOU'RE GOING TO WHAT?!
ARF...
GULP. SOMETHING WICKED THIS WAY WALKING?
YEP.
BEING BRAVE ALSO MEANS KNOWING WHEN TO...
RUN!!!

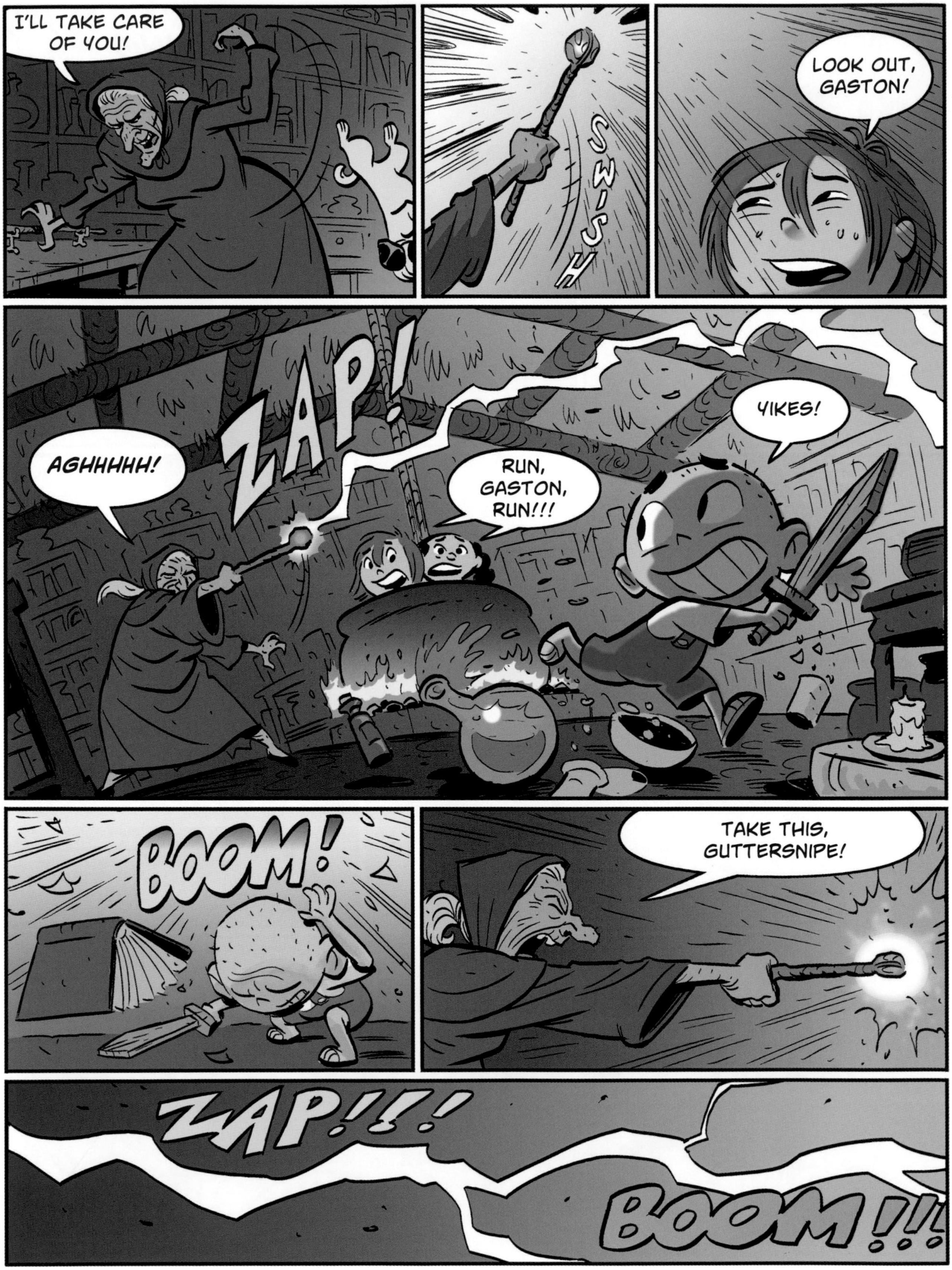
I'LL TAKE CARE OF YOU!
SWISH
LOOK OUT, GASTON!
ZAP!
AGHHHHH!
RUN, GASTON, RUN!!!
YIKES!
BOOM!
TAKE THIS, GUTTERSNIPE!
ZAP!!!
BOOM!!!

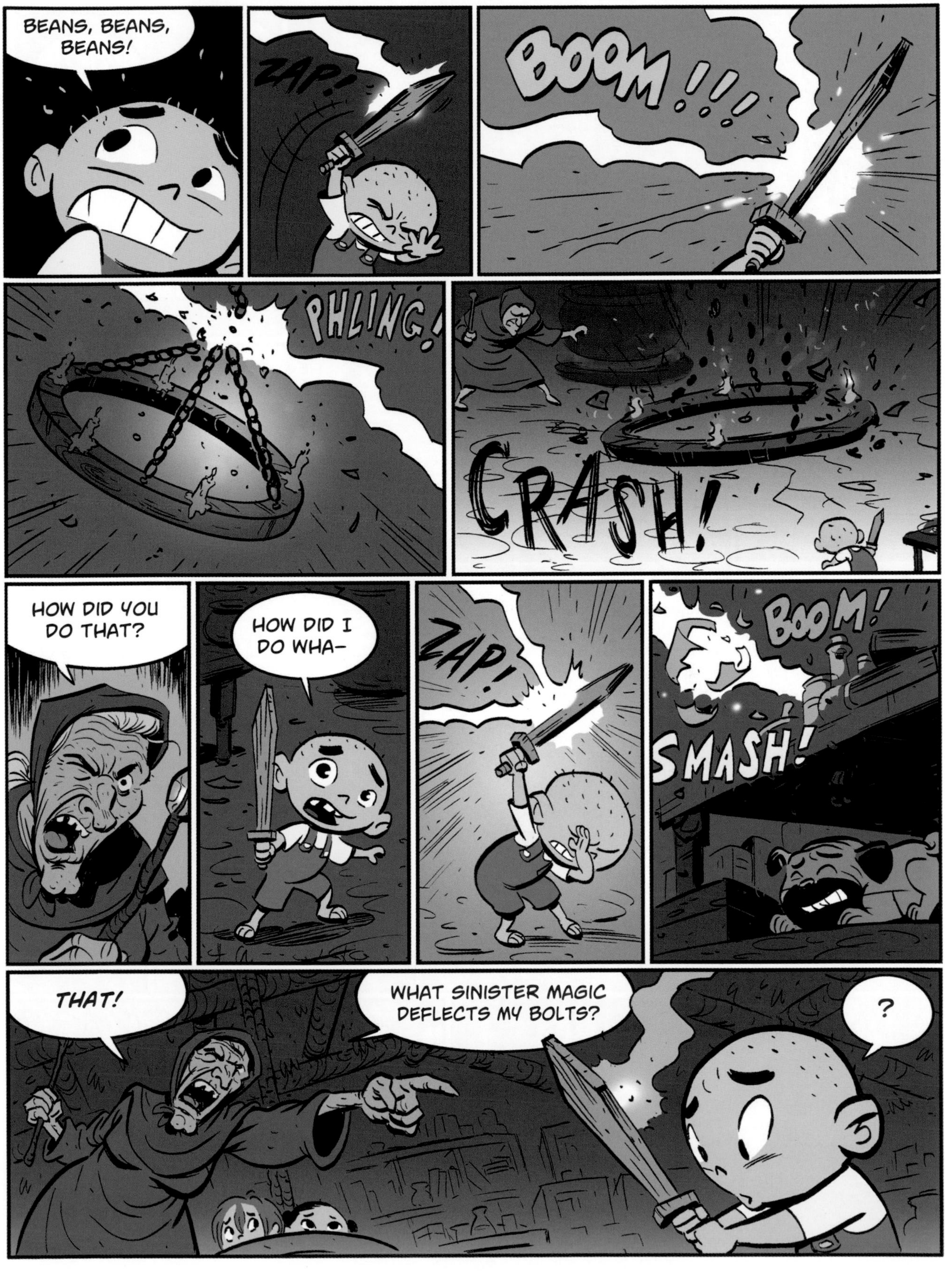
BEANS, BEANS, BEANS!
ZAP!
BOOM!!!!
PHLING!
CRASH!
HOW DID YOU DO THAT?
HOW DID I DO WHA–
ZAP!
BOOM!
SMASH!
THAT!
WHAT SINISTER MAGIC DEFLECTS MY BOLTS?
?

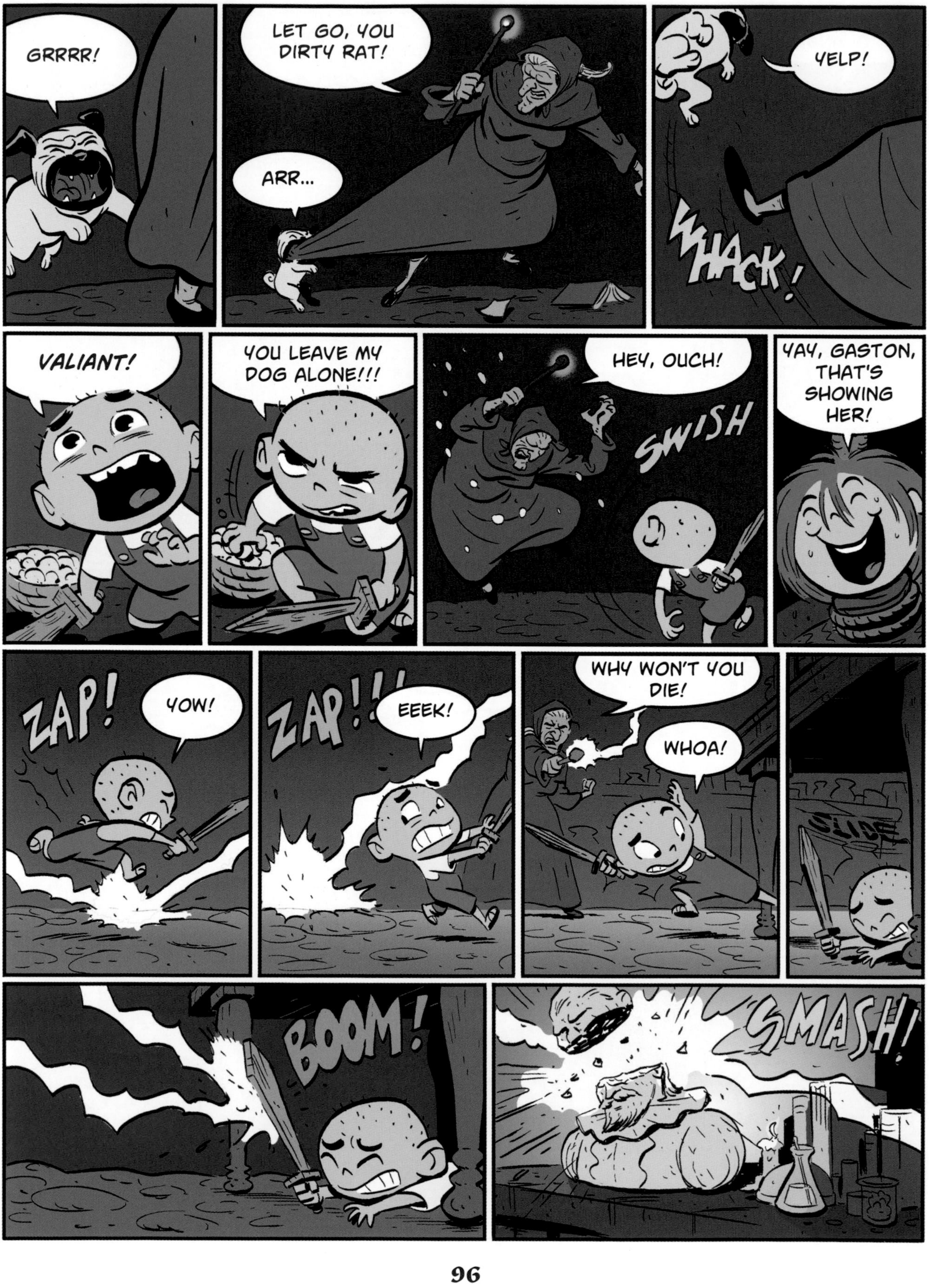
GRRRR!
LET GO, YOU DIRTY RAT!
ARR...
YELP!
WHACK!
VALIANT!
YOU LEAVE MY DOG ALONE!!!
HEY, OUCH!
SWISH
YAY, GASTON, THAT'S SHOWING HER!
ZAP!
YOW!
ZAP!!!
EEEK!
WHY WON'T YOU DIE!
WHOA!
SLIDE
BOOM!
SMASH!

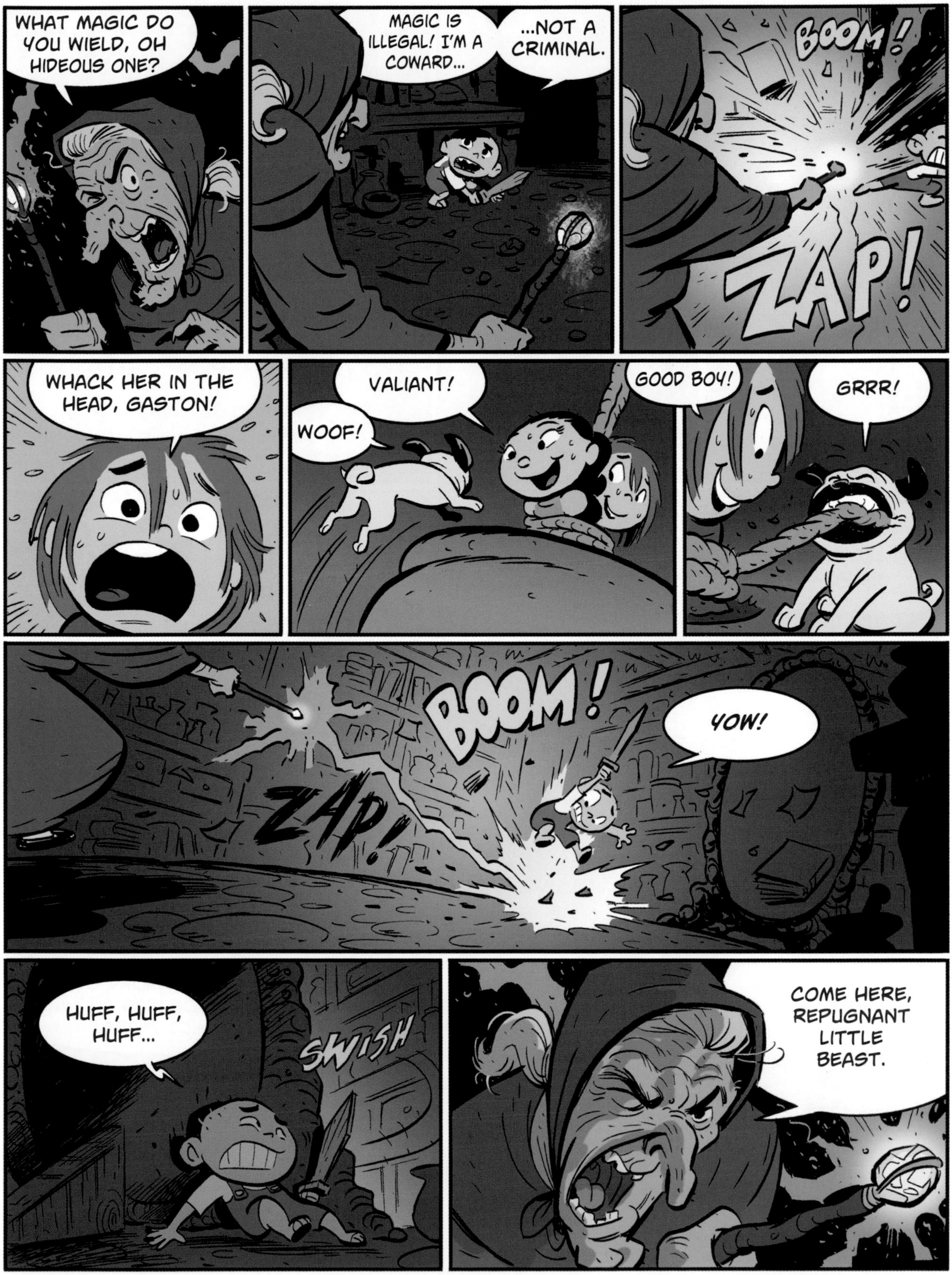
WHAT MAGIC DO YOU WIELD, OH HIDEOUS ONE?
MAGIC IS ILLEGAL! I'M A COWARD...
...NOT A CRIMINAL.
BOOM!
ZAP!
WHACK HER IN THE HEAD, GASTON!
VALIANT!
WOOF!
GOOD BOY!
GRRR!
BOOM!
YOW!
ZAP!
HUFF, HUFF, HUFF...
SWISH
COME HERE, REPUGNANT LITTLE BEAST.

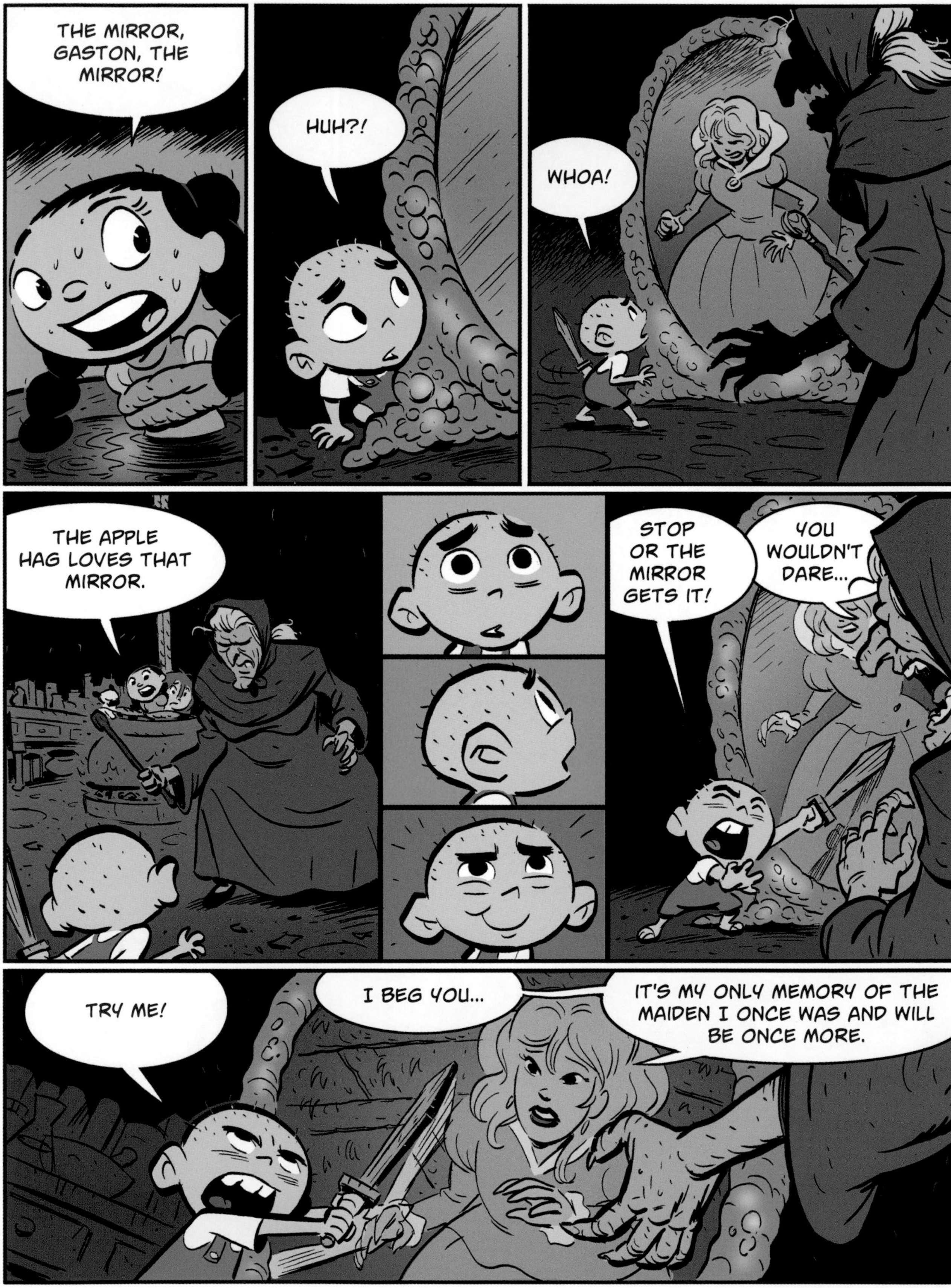
THE MIRROR, GASTON, THE MIRROR!
HUH?!
WHOA!
THE APPLE HAG LOVES THAT MIRROR.
STOP OR THE MIRROR GETS IT!
YOU WOULDN'T DARE...
TRY ME!
I BEG YOU...
IT'S MY ONLY MEMORY OF THE MAIDEN I ONCE WAS AND WILL BE ONCE MORE.

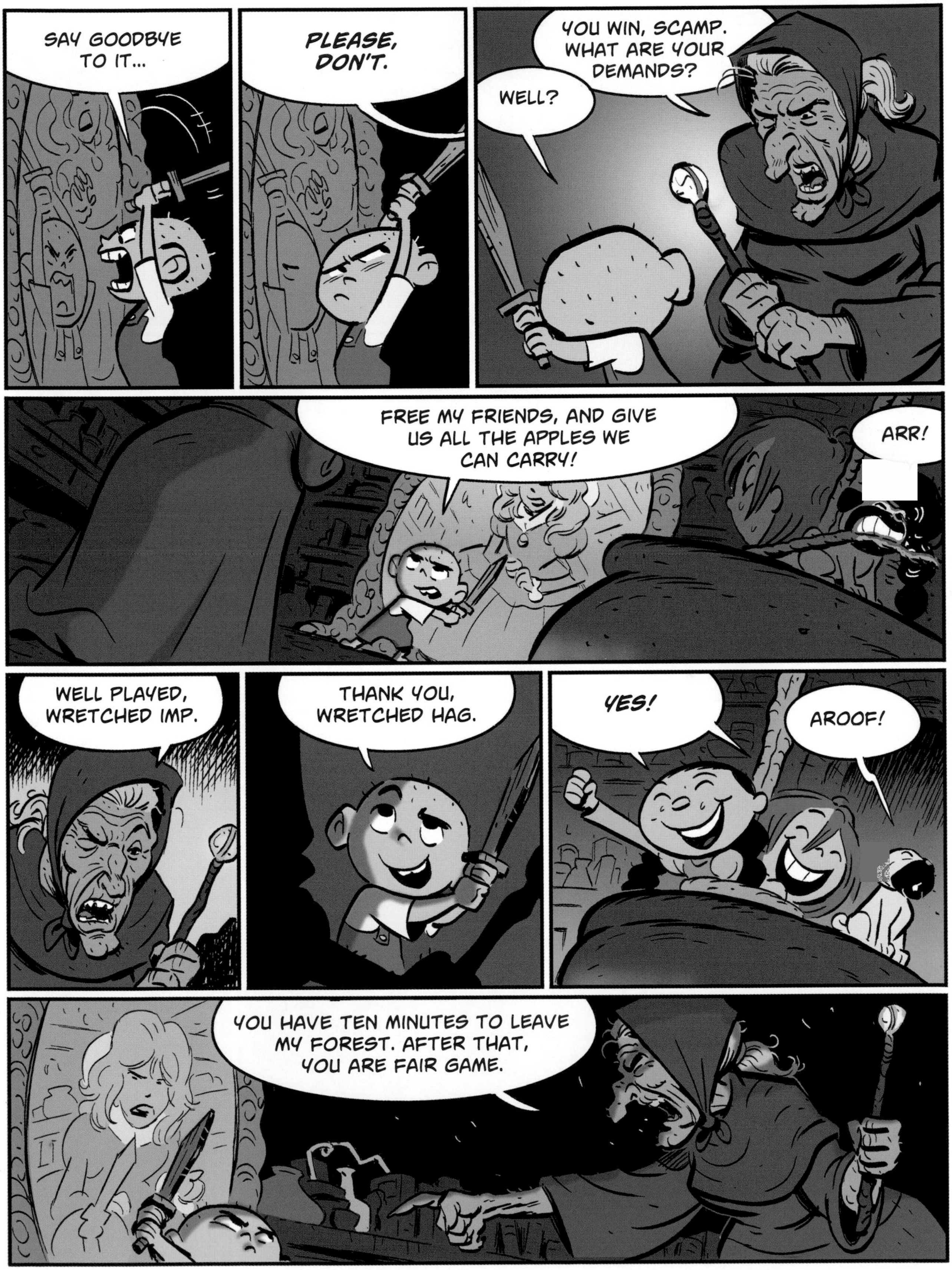
SAY GOODBYE TO IT...
PLEASE, DON'T.
WELL?
YOU WIN, SCAMP. WHAT ARE YOUR DEMANDS?
FREE MY FRIENDS, AND GIVE US ALL THE APPLES WE CAN CARRY!
ARR!
WELL PLAYED, WRETCHED IMP.
THANK YOU, WRETCHED HAG.
YES!
AROOF!
YOU HAVE TEN MINUTES TO LEAVE MY FOREST. AFTER THAT, YOU ARE FAIR GAME.

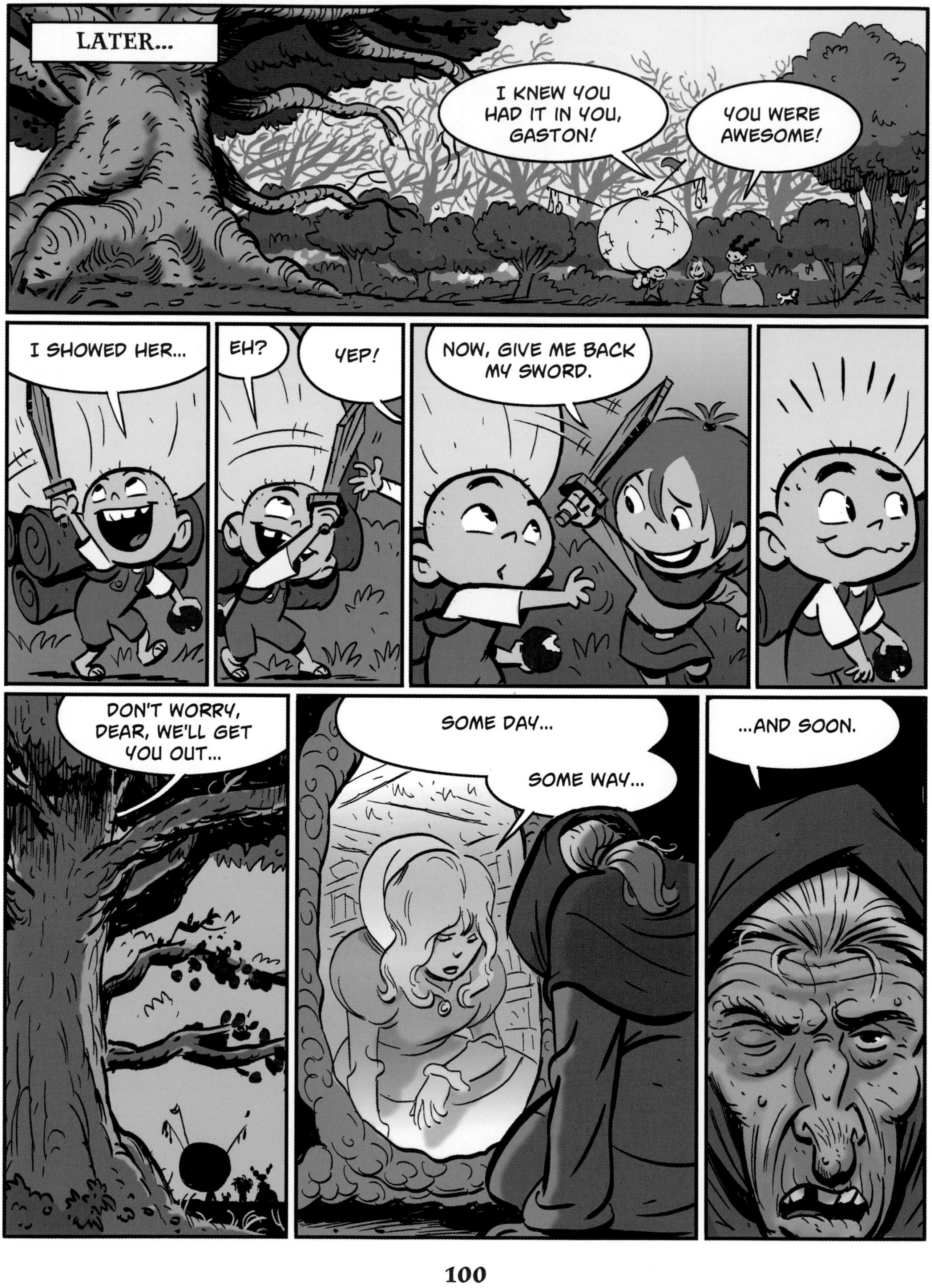
LATER...
I KNEW YOU HAD IT IN YOU, GASTON!
YOU WERE AWESOME!
I SHOWED HER...
EH?
YEP!
NOW, GIVE ME BACK MY SWORD.
DON'T WORRY, DEAR, WE'LL GET YOU OUT...
SOME DAY...
SOME WAY...
...AND SOON.

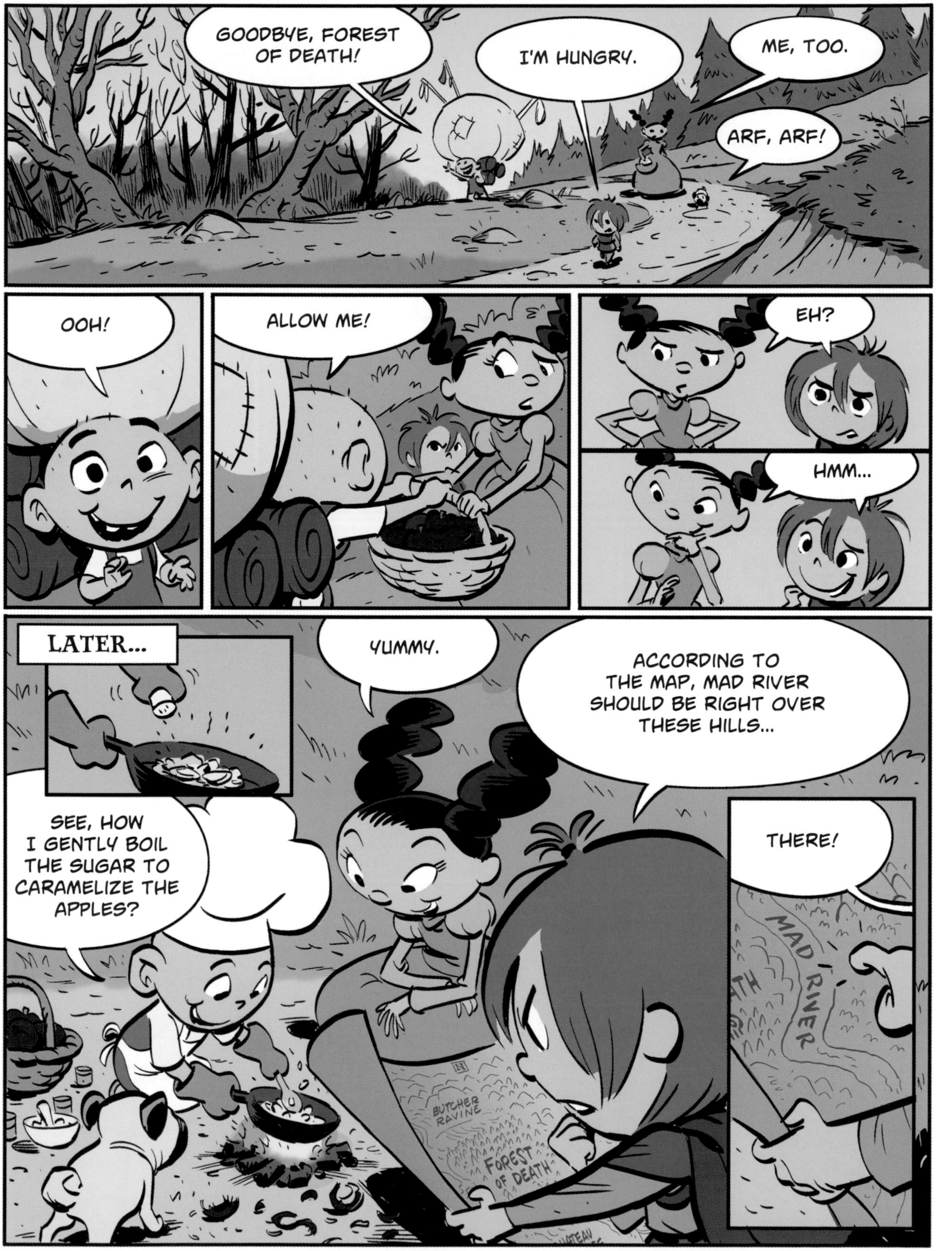
GOODBYE, FOREST OF DEATH!
I'M HUNGRY.
ME, TOO.
ARF, ARF!
OOH!
ALLOW ME!
EH?
HMM...
LATER...
YUMMY.
ACCORDING TO THE MAP, MAD RIVER SHOULD BE RIGHT OVER THESE HILLS...
SEE, HOW I GENTLY BOIL THE SUGAR TO CARAMELIZE THE APPLES?
THERE!
BUTCHER RAVINE
FOREST OF DEATH
MAD RIVER

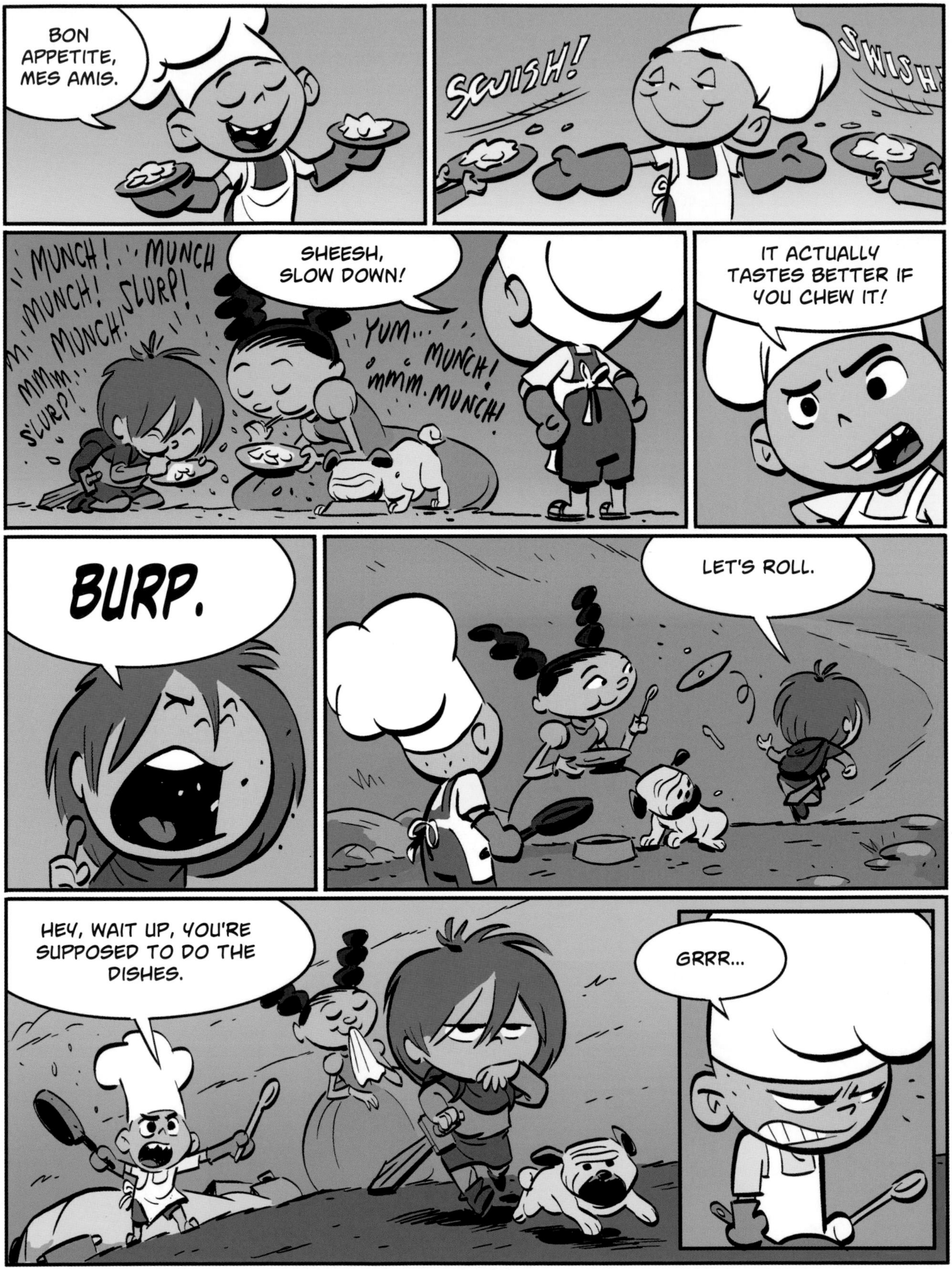
BON APPETITE, MES AMIS.
SWISH!
SWISH!
MUNCH! MUNCH
MUNCH! SLURP!
MUNCH!
MMM SLURP!
SHEESH, SLOW DOWN!
YUM...
MUNCH! MMM. MUNCH!
IT ACTUALLY TASTES BETTER IF YOU CHEW IT!
BURP.
LET'S ROLL.
HEY, WAIT UP, YOU'RE SUPPOSED TO DO THE DISHES.
GRRR...

MUCH LATER...

WOULD YOU LOOK AT THAT...

MAD RIVER!

C'MON!

IT DOESN'T LOOK THAT MAD TO ME.

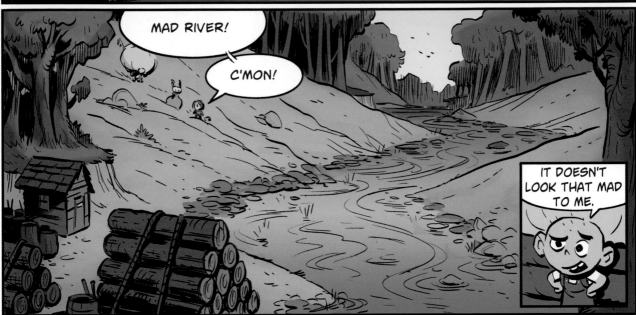

HEY, WHAT'S ALL THIS STUFF?

MY DAD SAYS THAT MONT PETIT PIERRE HAS BEEN...

...TRYING TO DAM THE RIVER FOR YEARS...

FLAMMABLE

BUT THE WORKERS KEEP DISAPPEARING.

EXPLOSIVE

EXPLOSI

I WONDER WHAT HAPPENED TO THEM?

GULP. I HAVE A HUNCH.

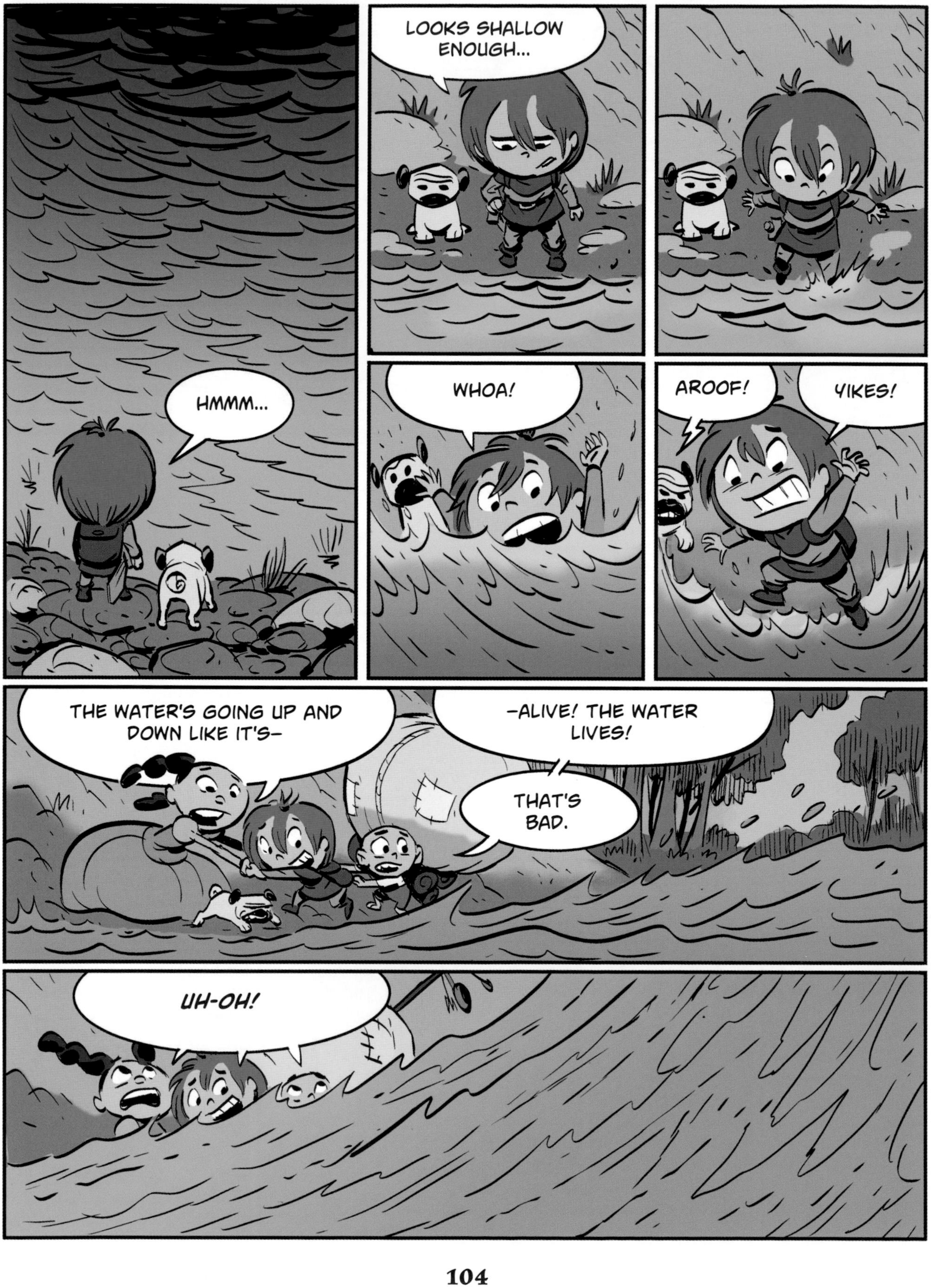
HMMM...
LOOKS SHALLOW ENOUGH...
WHOA!
AROOF!
YIKES!
THE WATER'S GOING UP AND DOWN LIKE IT'S–
–ALIVE! THE WATER LIVES!
THAT'S BAD.
UH-OH!

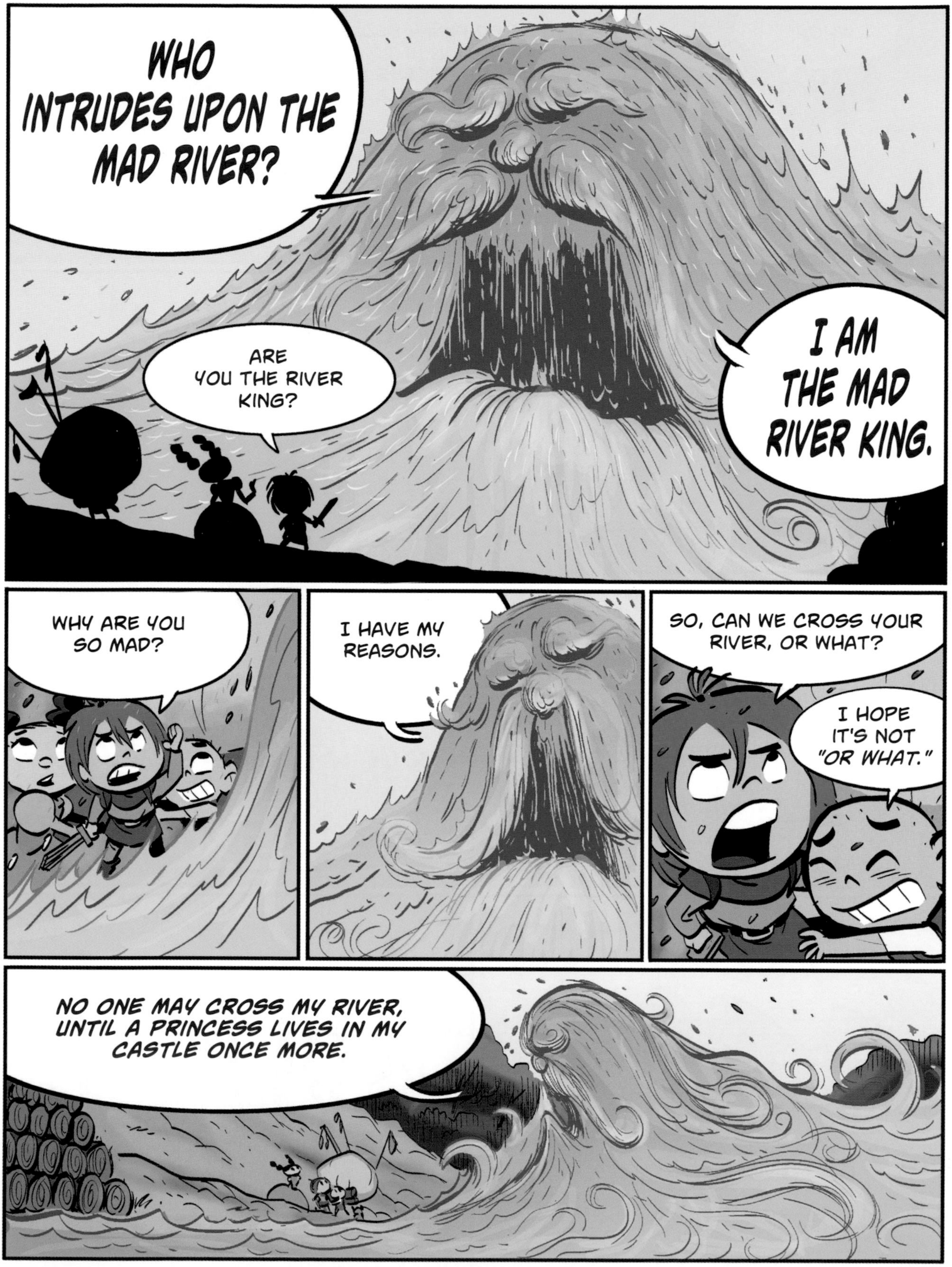
WHO INTRUDES UPON THE MAD RIVER?
ARE YOU THE RIVER KING?
I AM THE MAD RIVER KING.
WHY ARE YOU SO MAD?
I HAVE MY REASONS.
SO, CAN WE CROSS YOUR RIVER, OR WHAT?
I HOPE IT'S NOT "OR WHAT."
NO ONE MAY CROSS MY RIVER, UNTIL A PRINCESS LIVES IN MY CASTLE ONCE MORE.

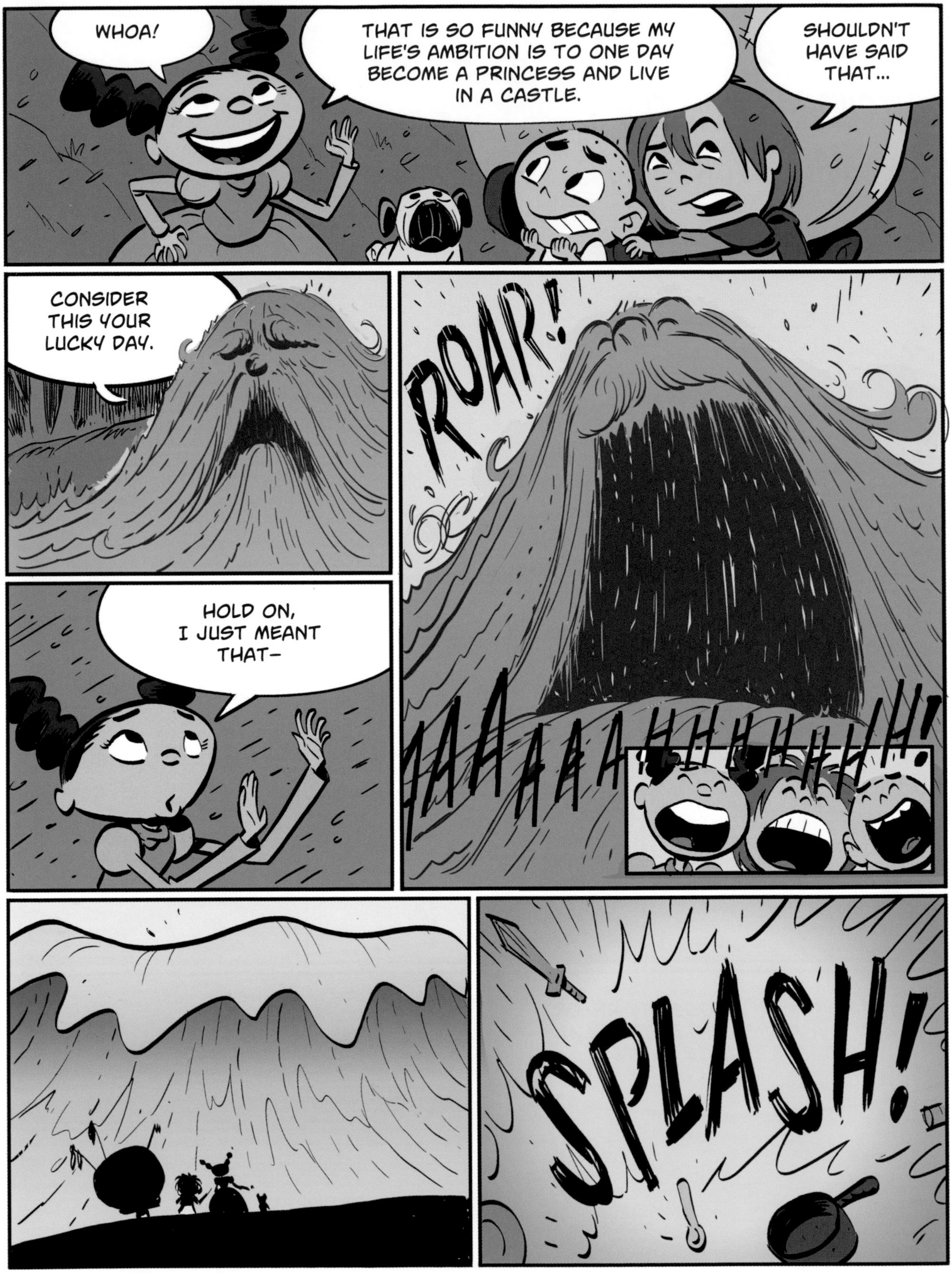
WHOA!
THAT IS SO FUNNY BECAUSE MY LIFE'S AMBITION IS TO ONE DAY BECOME A PRINCESS AND LIVE IN A CASTLE.
SHOULDN'T HAVE SAID THAT...
CONSIDER THIS YOUR LUCKY DAY.
ROAR!
HOLD ON, I JUST MEANT THAT–
AAAAAAAHHHHHHHH!
SPLASH!

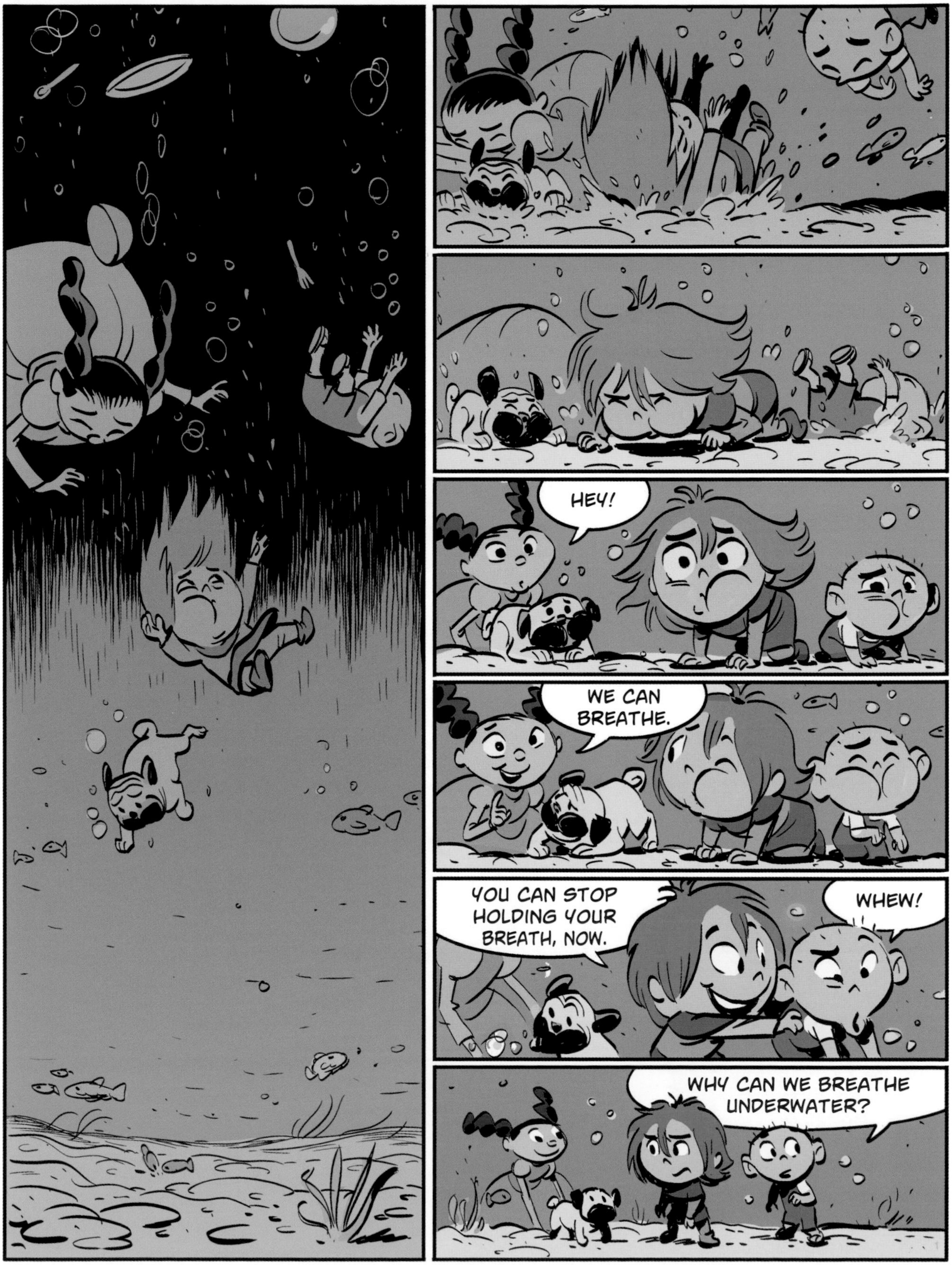
HEY!
WE CAN BREATHE.
YOU CAN STOP HOLDING YOUR BREATH, NOW.
WHEW!
WHY CAN WE BREATHE UNDERWATER?

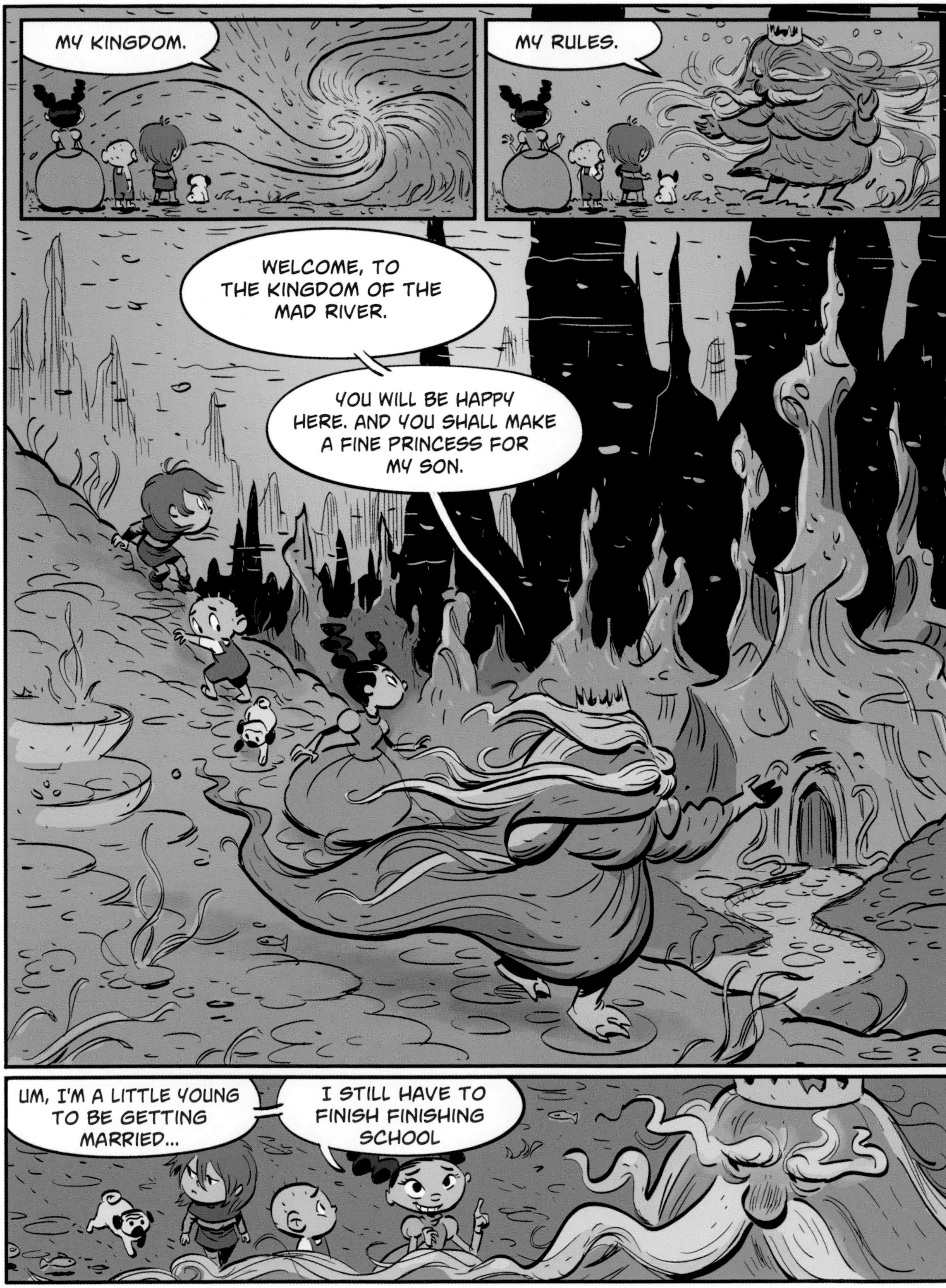
MY KINGDOM.
MY RULES.
WELCOME, TO THE KINGDOM OF THE MAD RIVER.
YOU WILL BE HAPPY HERE. AND YOU SHALL MAKE A FINE PRINCESS FOR MY SON.
UM, I'M A LITTLE YOUNG TO BE GETTING MARRIED...
I STILL HAVE TO FINISH FINISHING SCHOOL

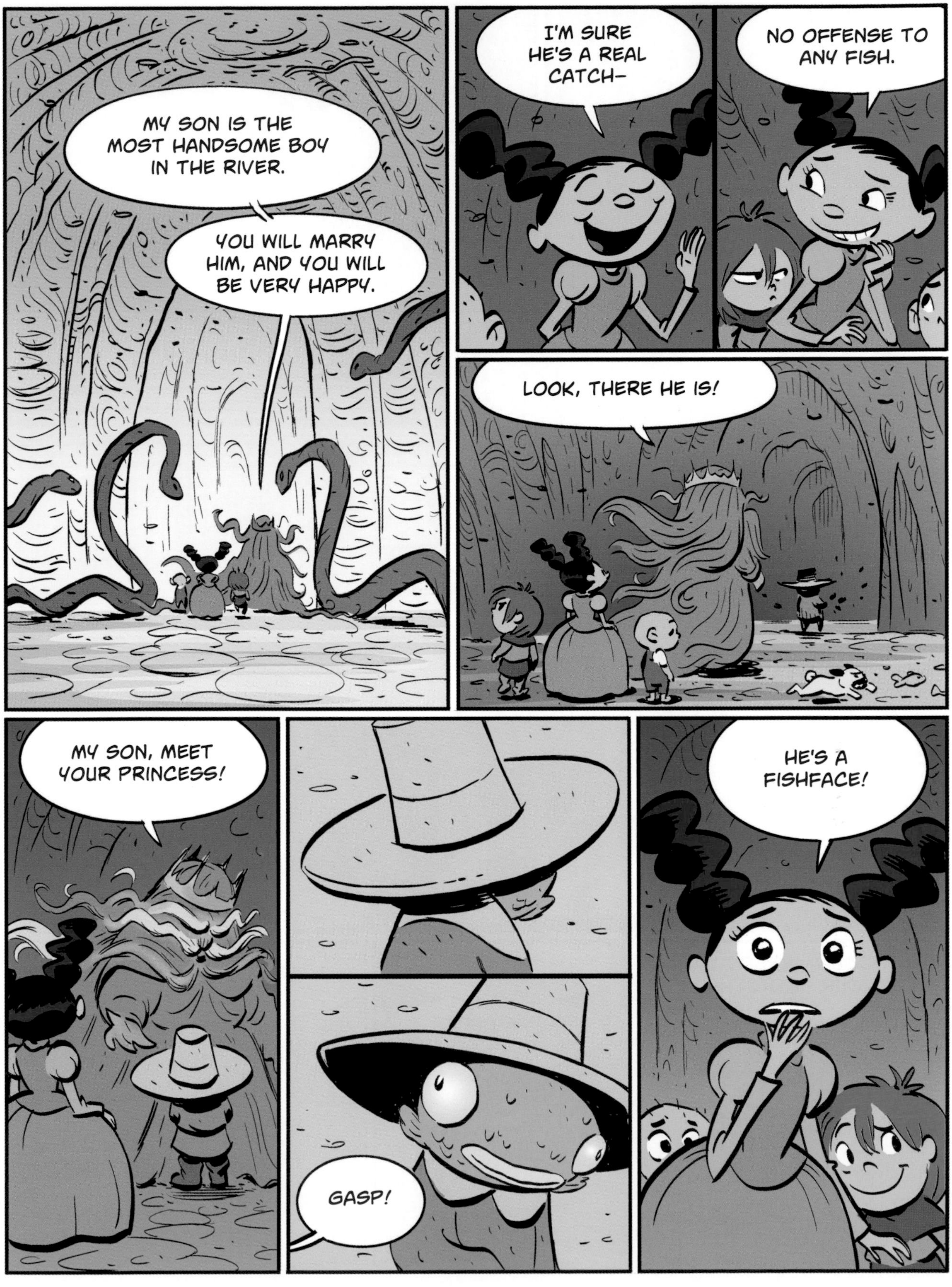
MY SON IS THE MOST HANDSOME BOY IN THE RIVER.
YOU WILL MARRY HIM, AND YOU WILL BE VERY HAPPY.
I'M SURE HE'S A REAL CATCH–
NO OFFENSE TO ANY FISH.
LOOK, THERE HE IS!
MY SON, MEET YOUR PRINCESS!
GASP!
HE'S A FISHFACE!

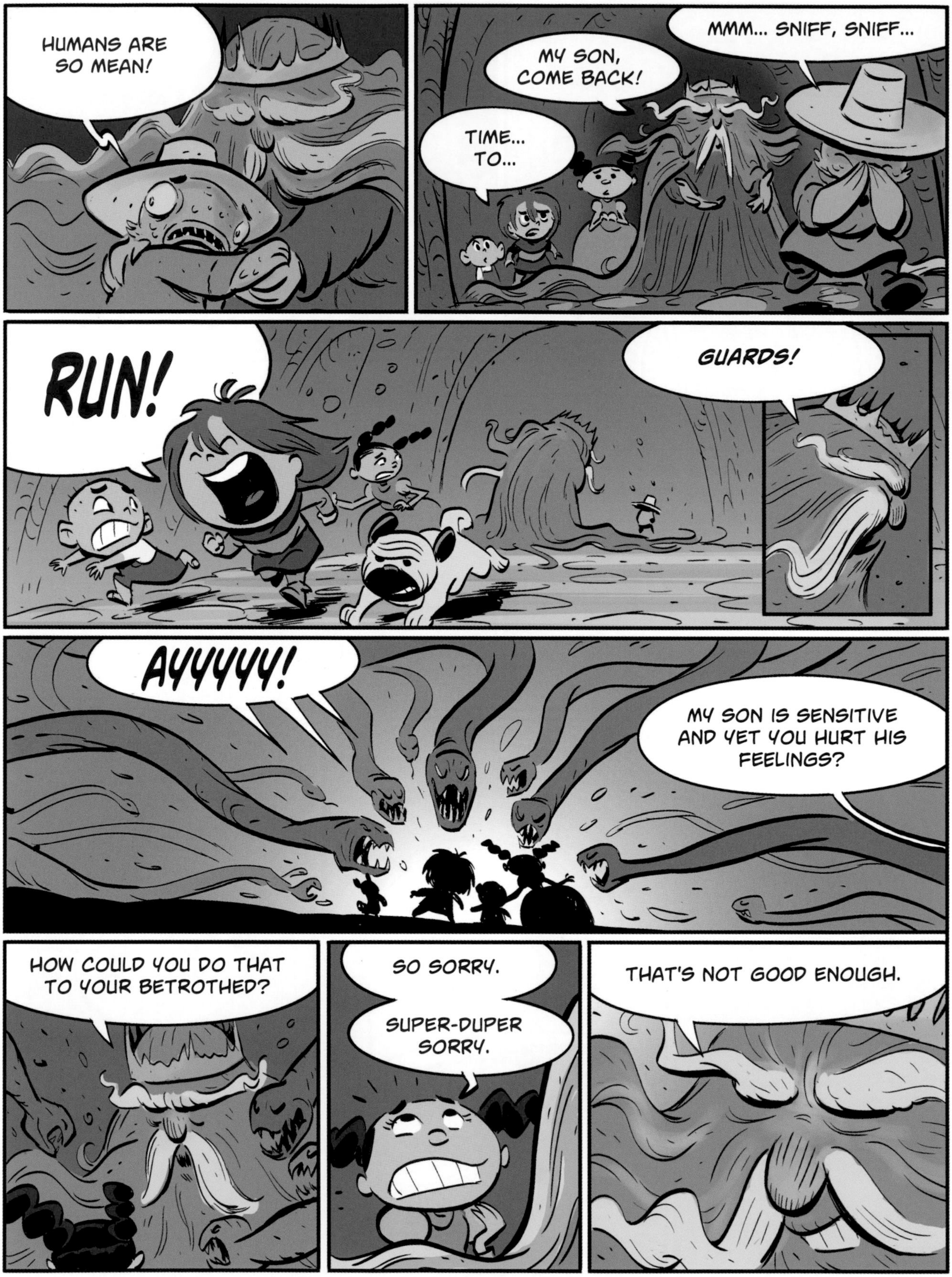
HUMANS ARE SO MEAN!
MY SON, COME BACK!
MMM... SNIFF, SNIFF...
TIME... TO...
RUN!
GUARDS!
AYYYYY!
MY SON IS SENSITIVE AND YET YOU HURT HIS FEELINGS?
HOW COULD YOU DO THAT TO YOUR BETROTHED?
SO SORRY.
SUPER-DUPER SORRY.
THAT'S NOT GOOD ENOUGH.

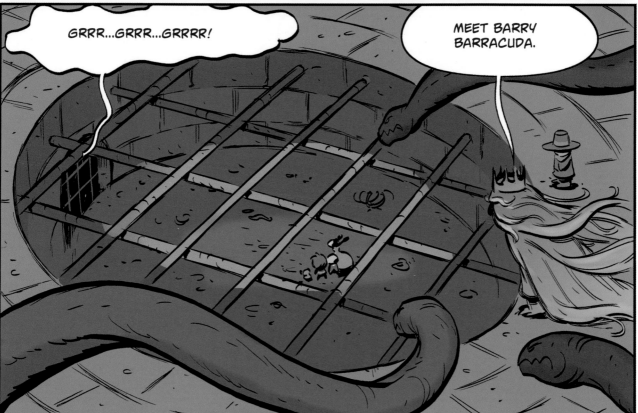

GRRR...GRRR...GRRRR!

MEET BARRY BARRACUDA.

SNARL!!!!

I CAN TAKE HIM!

I THINK.

GRRRR

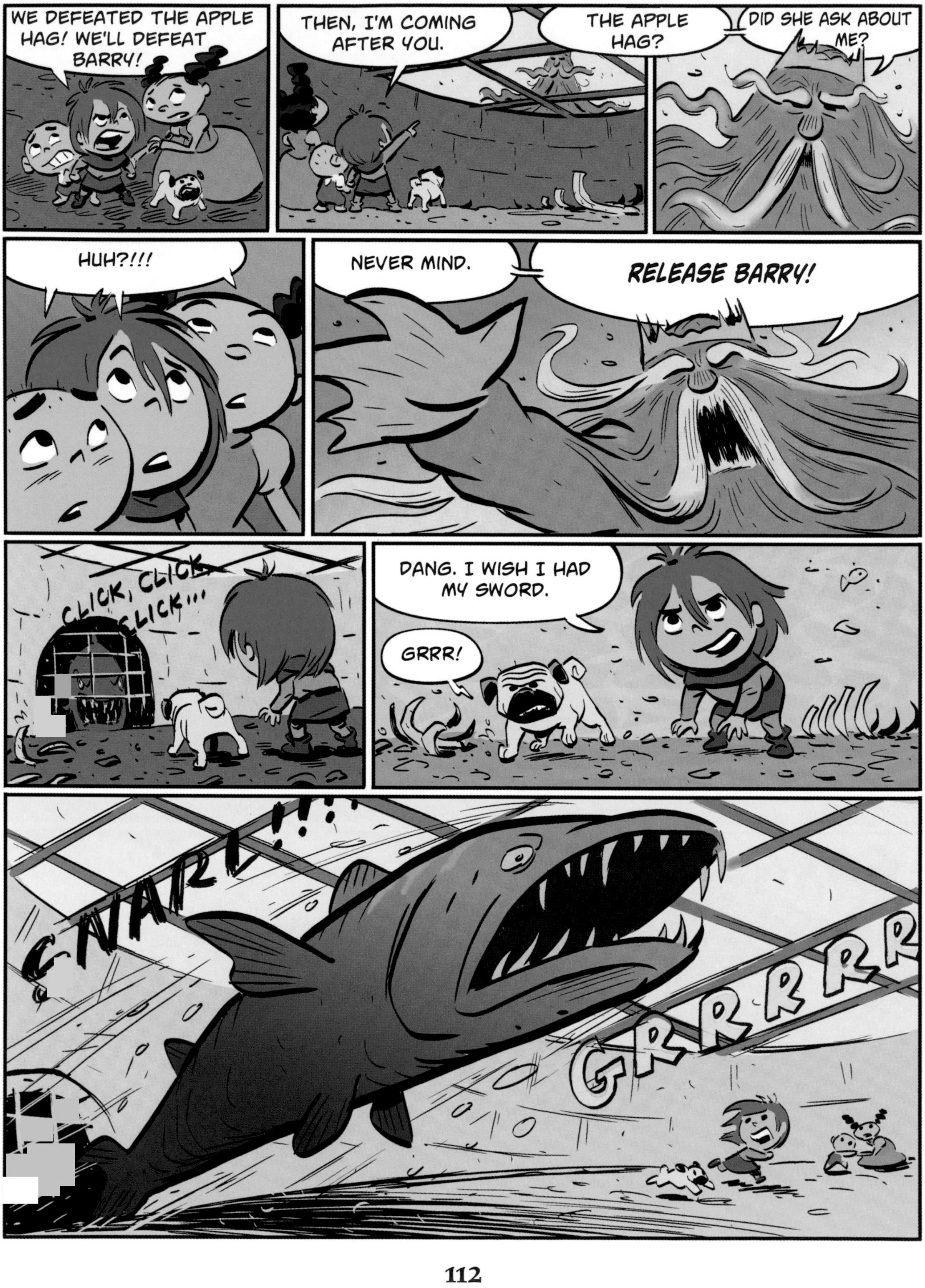
WE DEFEATED THE APPLE HAG! WE'LL DEFEAT BARRY!
THEN, I'M COMING AFTER YOU.
THE APPLE HAG?
DID SHE ASK ABOUT ME?
HUH?!!!
NEVER MIND.
RELEASE BARRY!
CLICK, CLICK, CLICK...
DANG. I WISH I HAD MY SWORD.
GRRR!
GNARL!!!
GRRRRRR

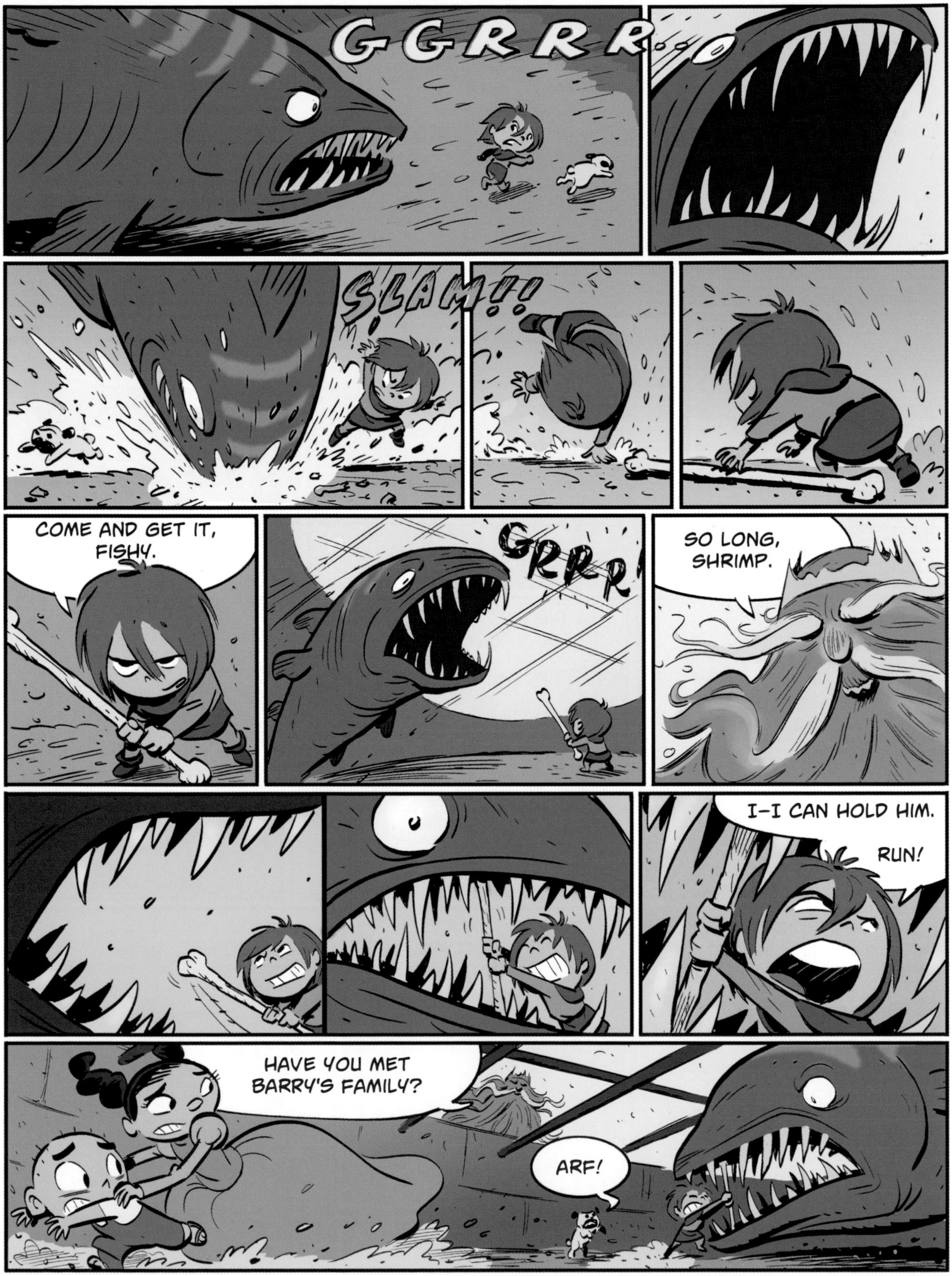
GGRRRR
SLAM!!
COME AND GET IT, FISHY.
GRRR
SO LONG, SHRIMP.
I-I CAN HOLD HIM.
RUN!
HAVE YOU MET BARRY'S FAMILY?
ARF!

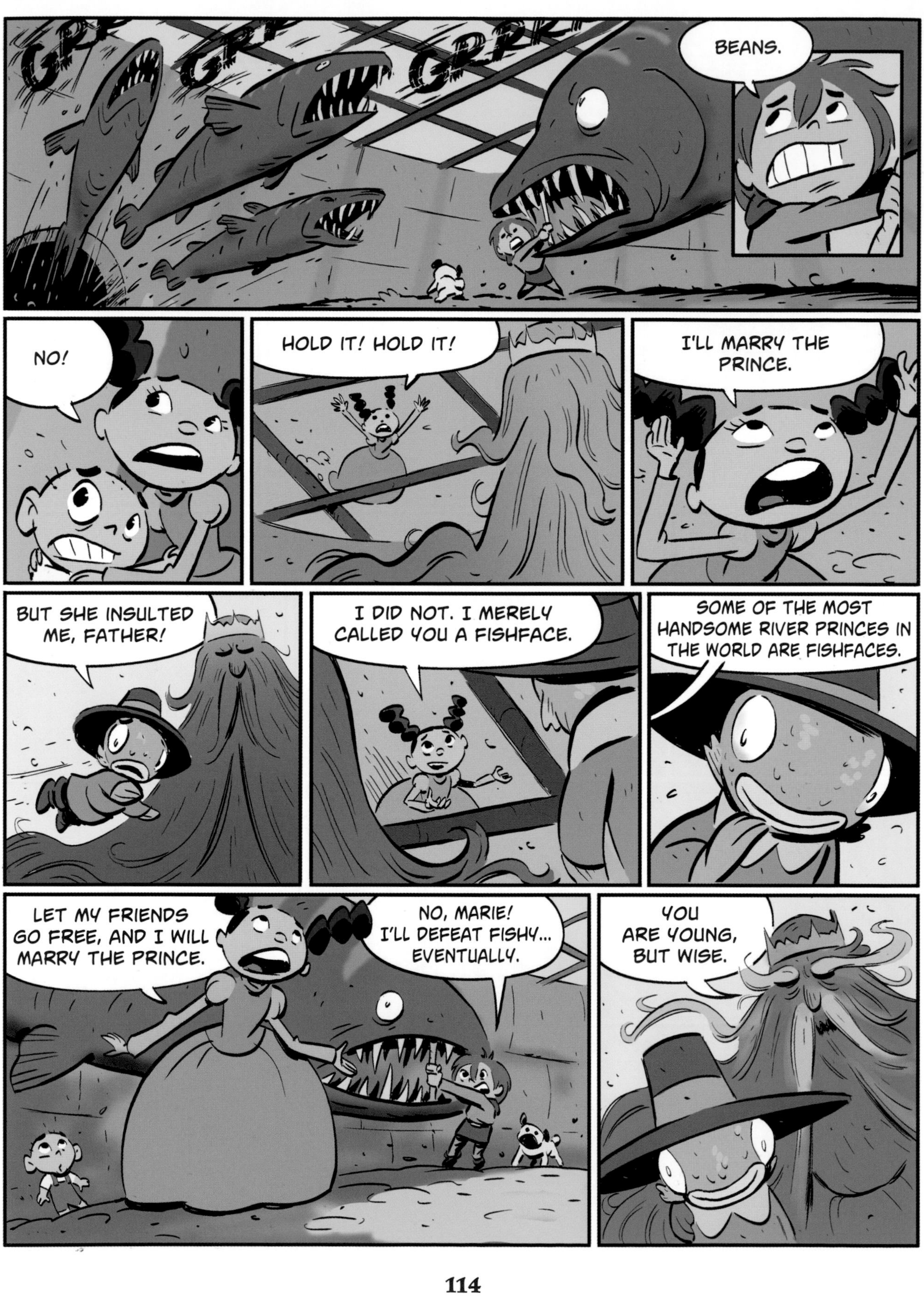
GRR GRR GRRR
BEANS.
NO!
HOLD IT! HOLD IT!
I'LL MARRY THE PRINCE.
BUT SHE INSULTED ME, FATHER!
I DID NOT. I MERELY CALLED YOU A FISHFACE.
SOME OF THE MOST HANDSOME RIVER PRINCES IN THE WORLD ARE FISHFACES.
LET MY FRIENDS GO FREE, AND I WILL MARRY THE PRINCE.
NO, MARIE! I'LL DEFEAT FISHY... EVENTUALLY.
YOU ARE YOUNG, BUT WISE.

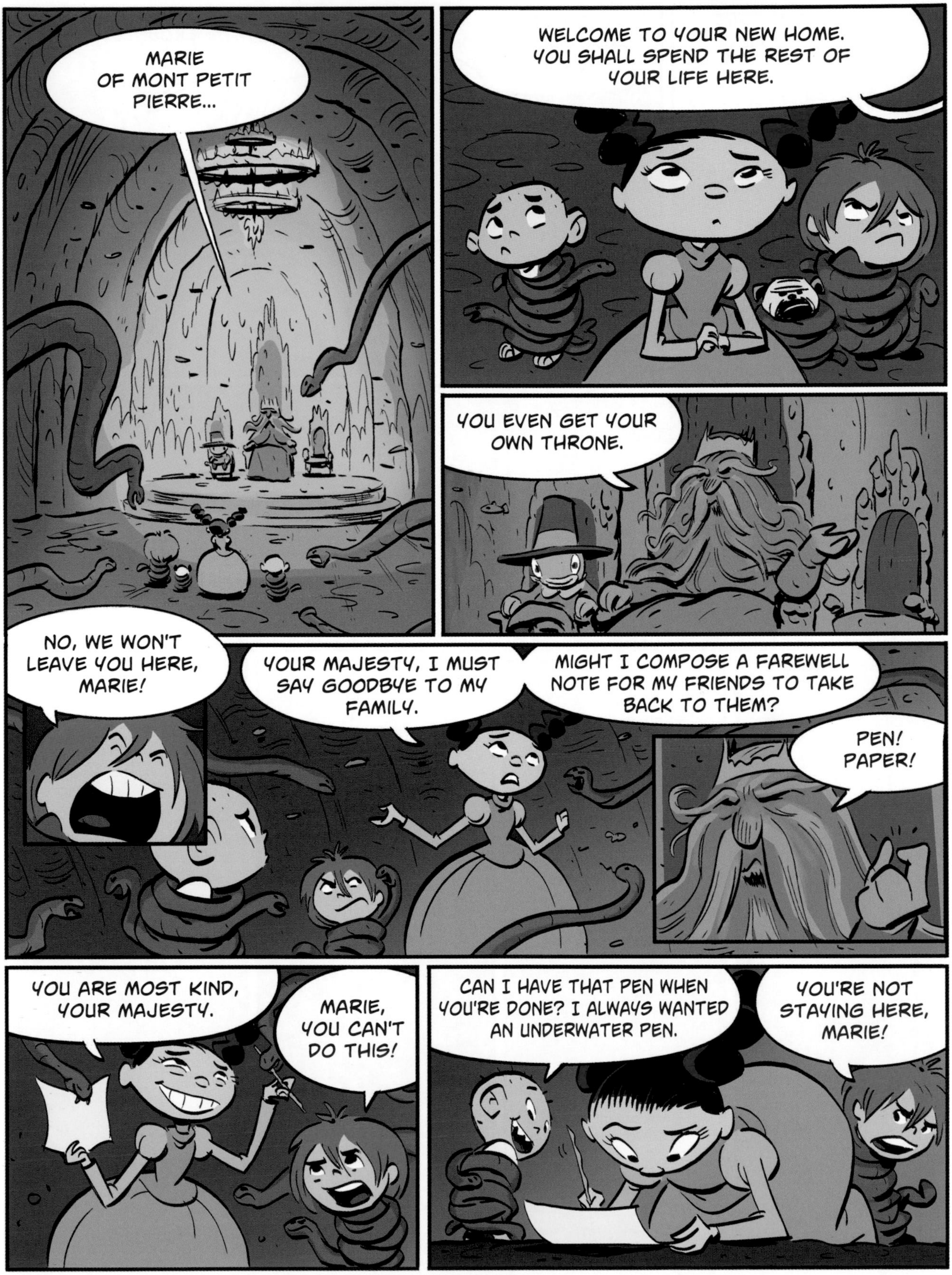

MARIE OF MONT PETIT PIERRE...
WELCOME TO YOUR NEW HOME. YOU SHALL SPEND THE REST OF YOUR LIFE HERE.
YOU EVEN GET YOUR OWN THRONE.
NO, WE WON'T LEAVE YOU HERE, MARIE!
YOUR MAJESTY, I MUST SAY GOODBYE TO MY FAMILY.
MIGHT I COMPOSE A FAREWELL NOTE FOR MY FRIENDS TO TAKE BACK TO THEM?
PEN! PAPER!
YOU ARE MOST KIND, YOUR MAJESTY.
MARIE, YOU CAN'T DO THIS!
CAN I HAVE THAT PEN WHEN YOU'RE DONE? I ALWAYS WANTED AN UNDERWATER PEN.
YOU'RE NOT STAYING HERE, MARIE!

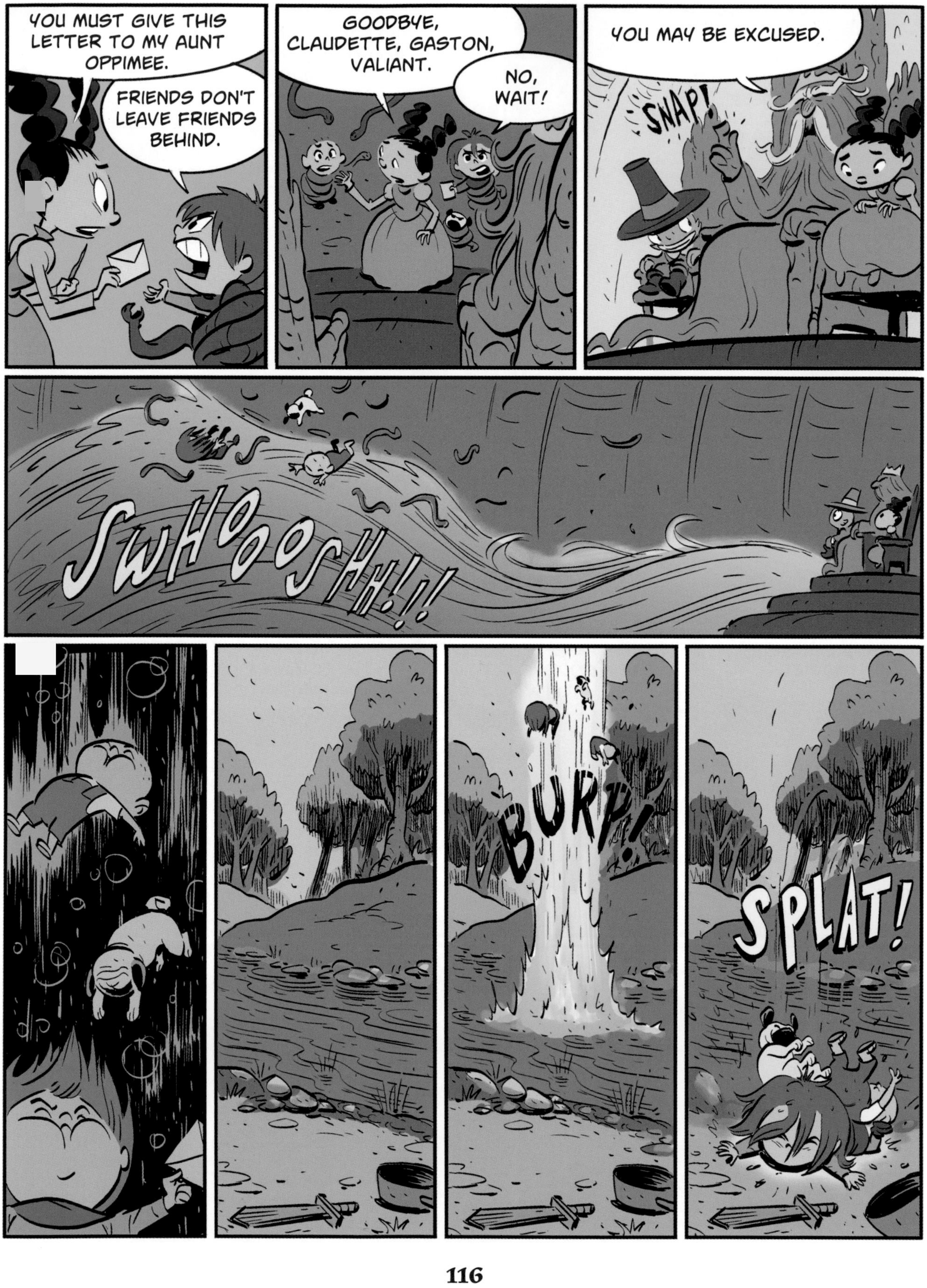
YOU MUST GIVE THIS LETTER TO MY AUNT OPPIMEE.
FRIENDS DON'T LEAVE FRIENDS BEHIND.
GOODBYE, CLAUDETTE, GASTON, VALIANT.
NO, WAIT!
YOU MAY BE EXCUSED.
SNAP!
SWHOOOSHH!!!
BURP!
SPLAT!

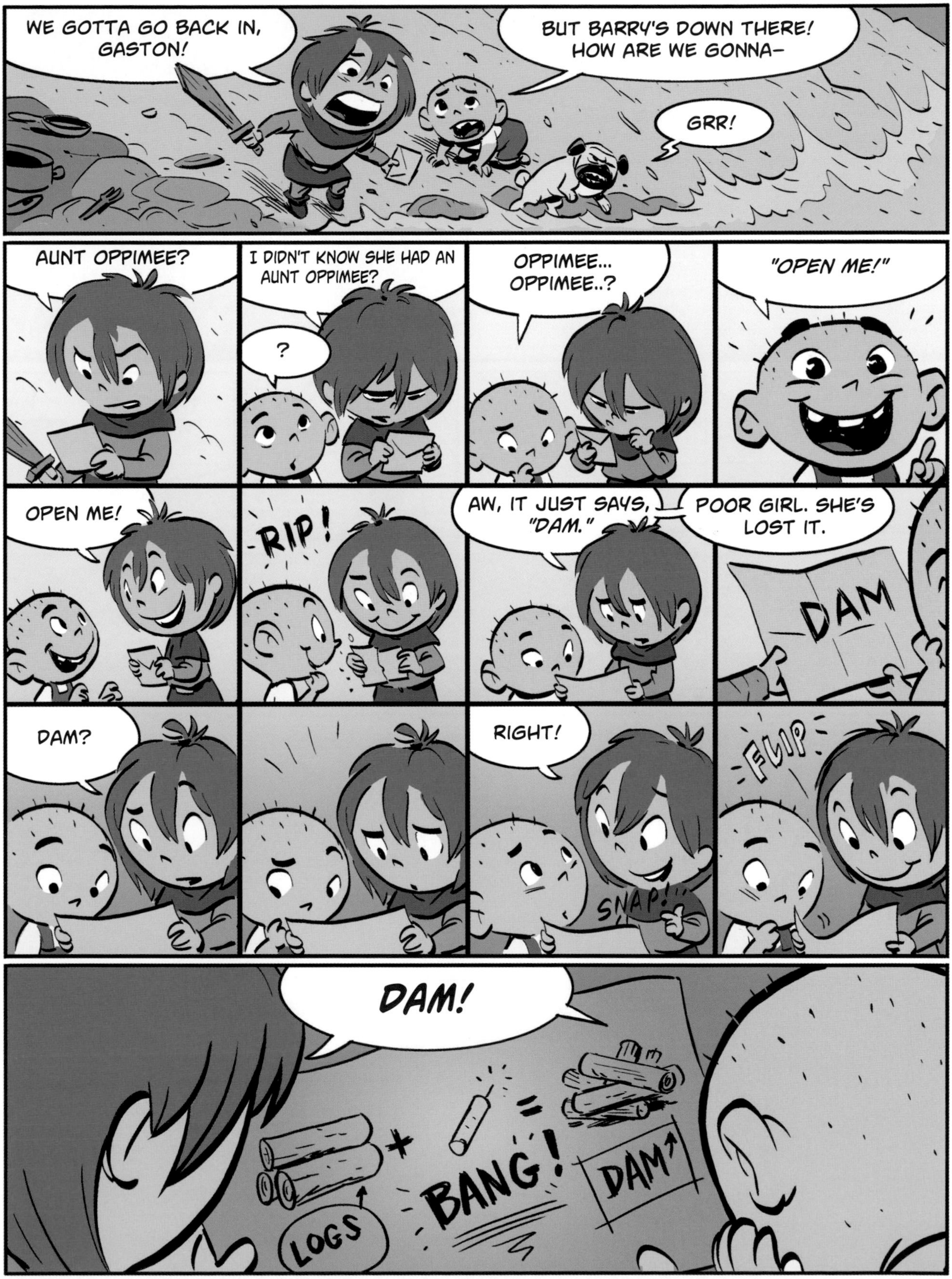

WE GOTTA GO BACK IN, GASTON!
BUT BARRY'S DOWN THERE! HOW ARE WE GONNA–
GRR!
AUNT OPPIMEE?
I DIDN'T KNOW SHE HAD AN AUNT OPPIMEE?
?
OPPIMEE... OPPIMEE..?
"OPEN ME!"
OPEN ME!
RIP!
AW, IT JUST SAYS, "DAM."
POOR GIRL. SHE'S LOST IT.
DAM
DAM?
RIGHT!
SNAP!
FLIP
DAM!
LOGS
BANG!
DAM

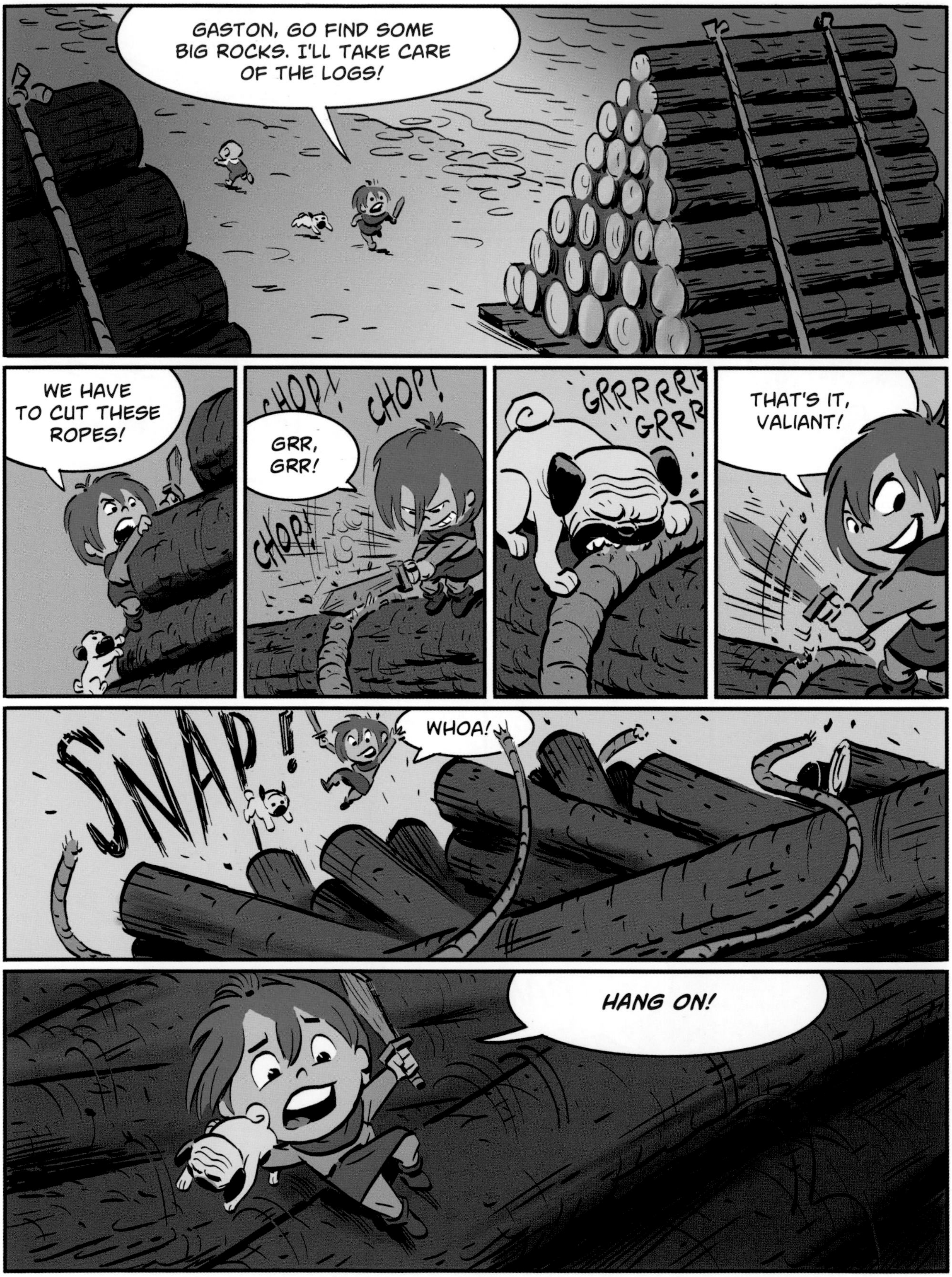
GASTON, GO FIND SOME BIG ROCKS. I'LL TAKE CARE OF THE LOGS!
WE HAVE TO CUT THESE ROPES!
CHOP! CHOP!
GRR, GRR!
CHOP!
GRRRRR GRRR
THAT'S IT, VALIANT!
SNAP!
WHOA!
HANG ON!

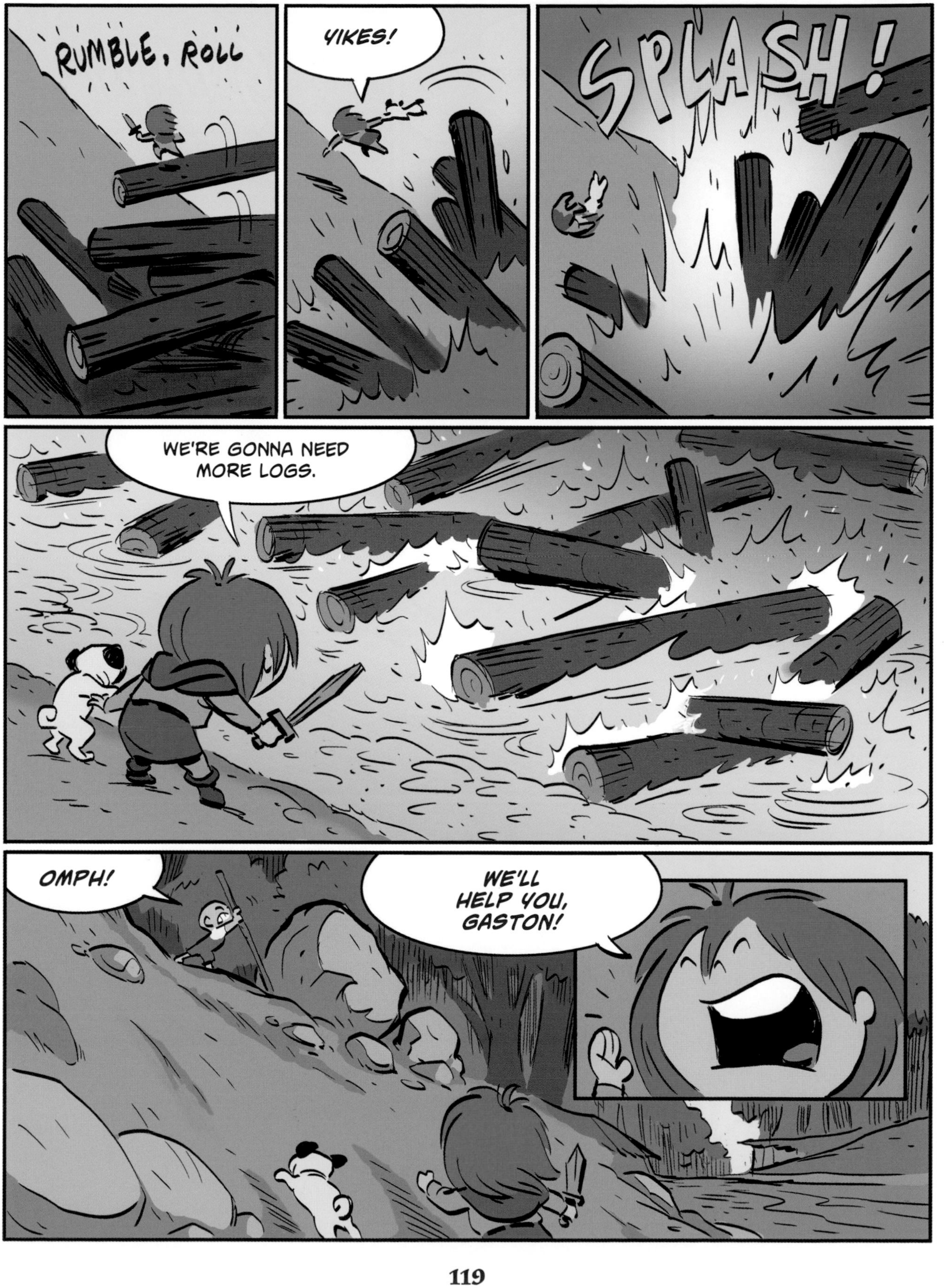
RUMBLE, ROLL
YIKES!
SPLASH!
WE'RE GONNA NEED MORE LOGS.
OMPH!
WE'LL HELP YOU, GASTON!

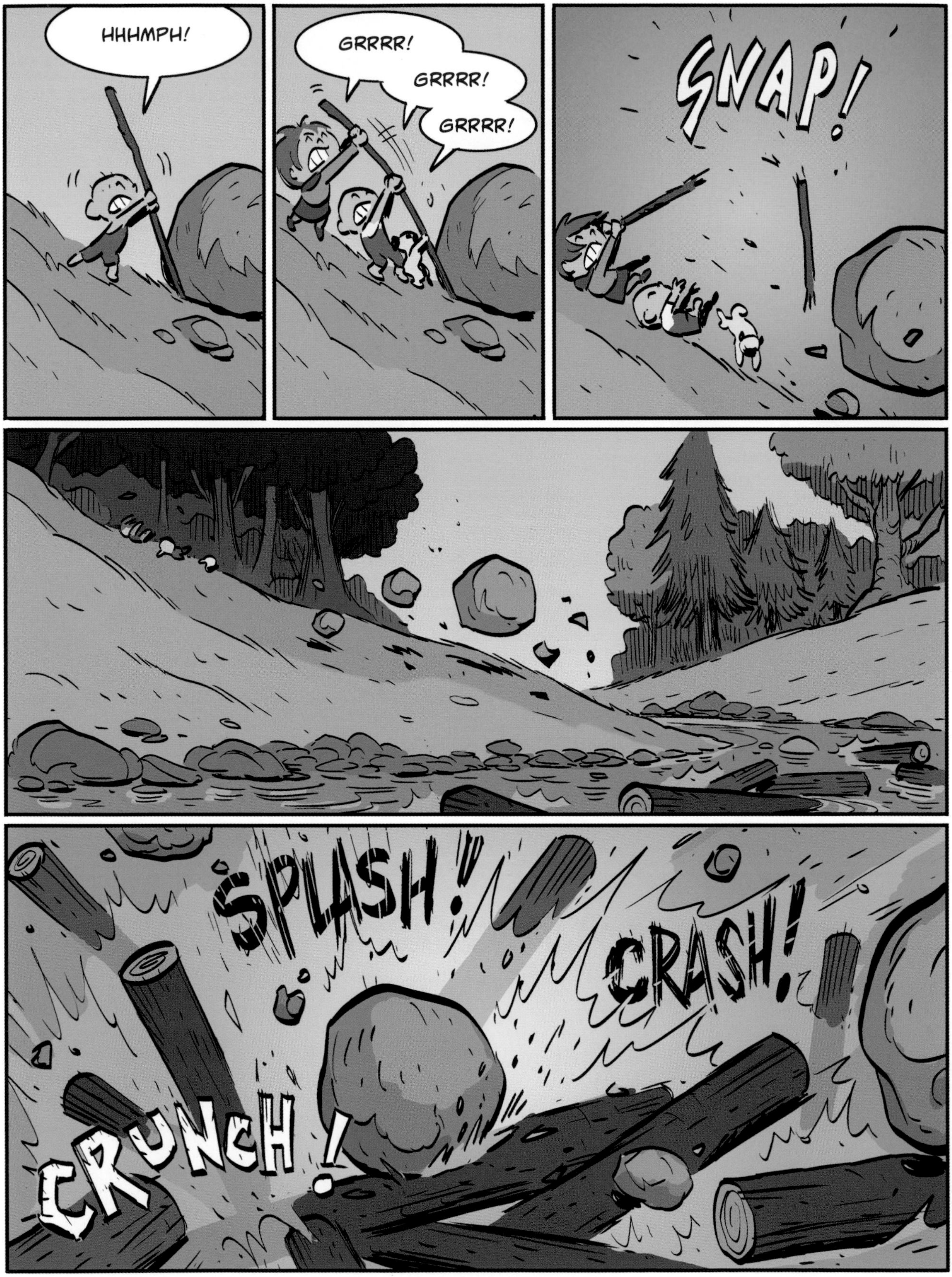
HHHMPH!
GRRRR!
GRRRR!
GRRRR!
SNAP!
SPLASH!
CRASH!
CRUNCH!

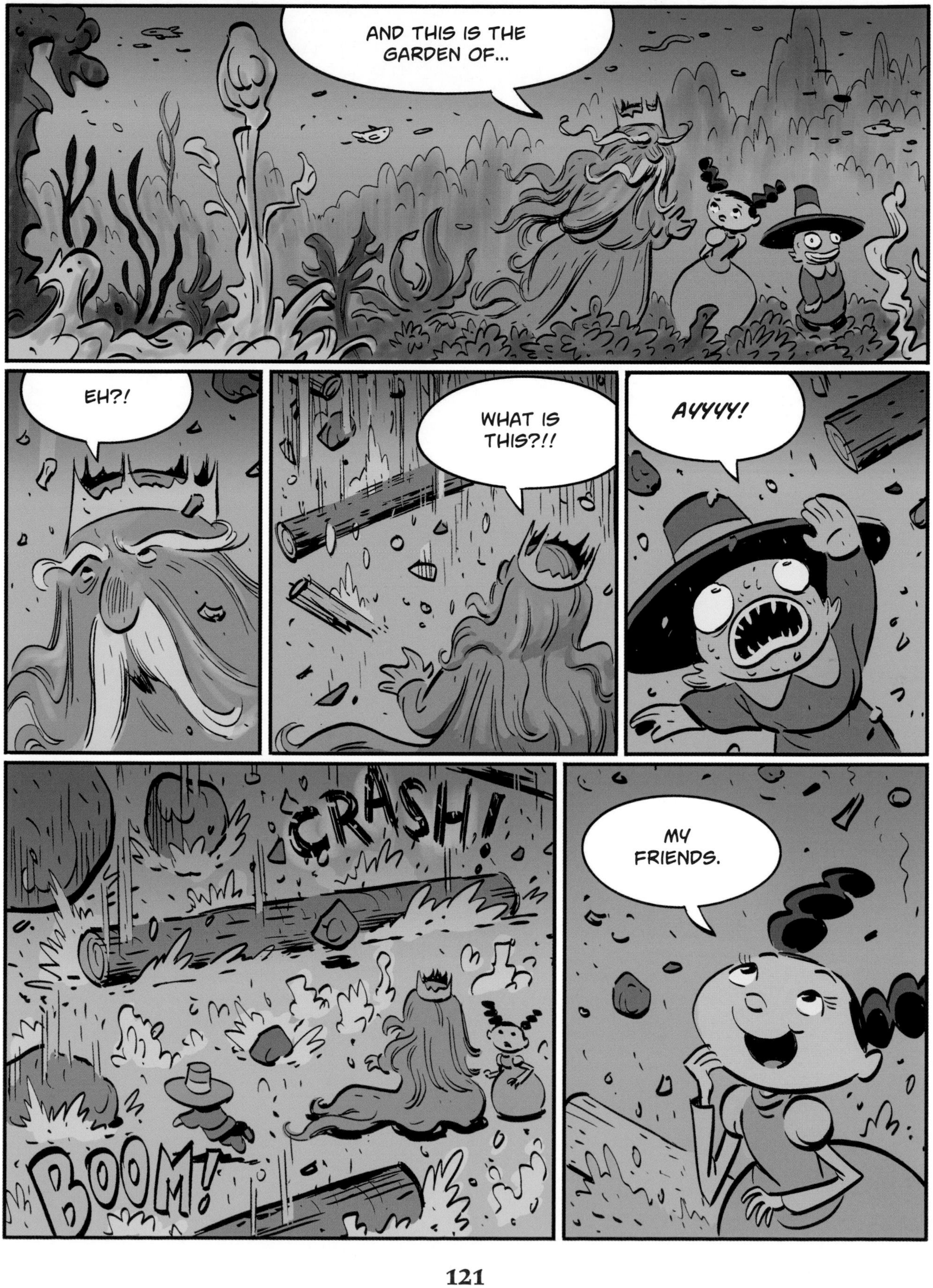
AND THIS IS THE GARDEN OF...
EH?!
WHAT IS THIS?!!
AYYYY!
CRASH!
BOOM!
MY FRIENDS.

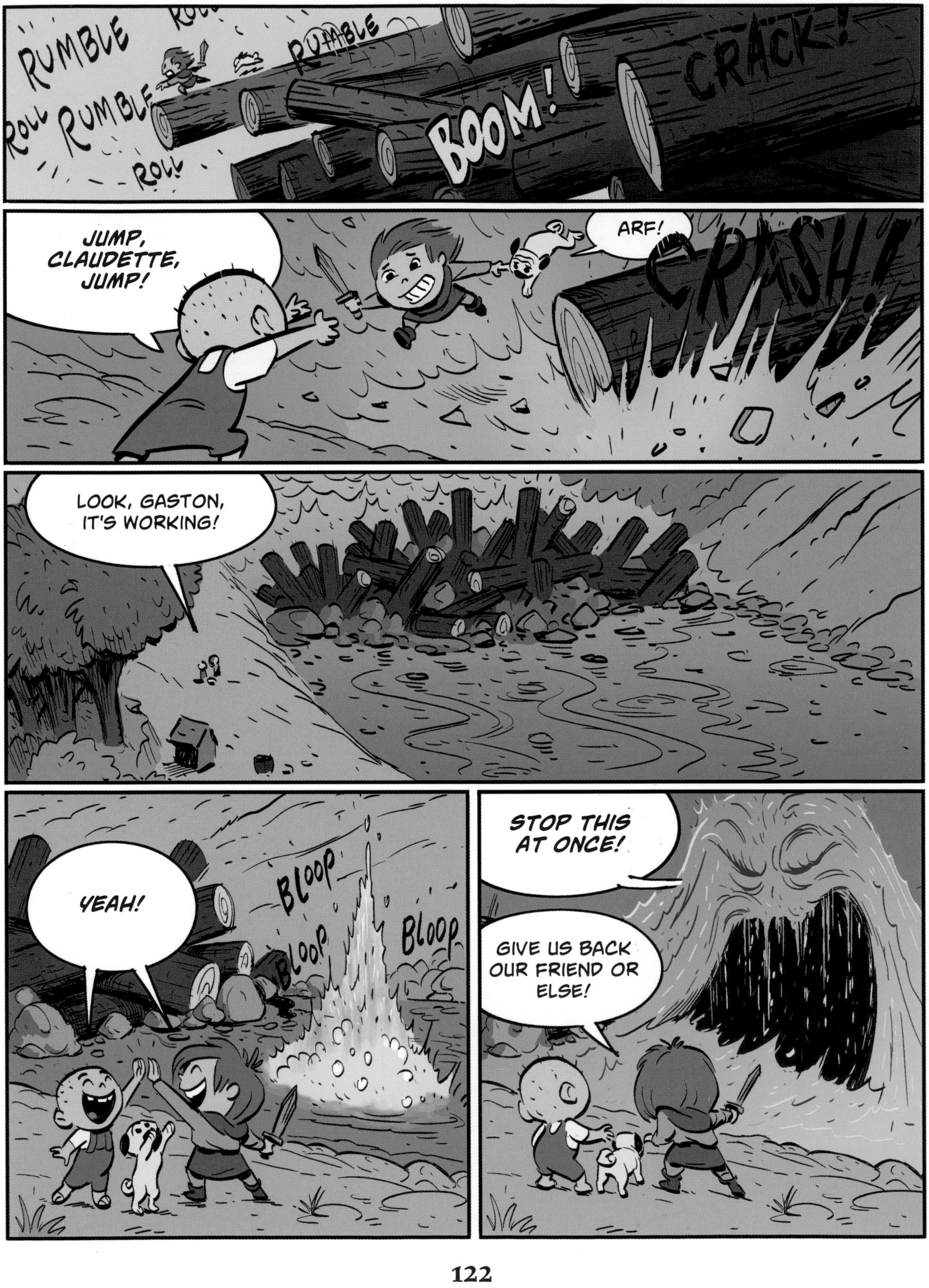
RUMBLE
ROLL
ROLL
RUMBLE
RUMBLE
ROLL
BOOM!
CRACK!
JUMP, CLAUDETTE, JUMP!
ARF!
CRASH!
LOOK, GASTON, IT'S WORKING!
YEAH!
BLOOP
BLOOP
BLOOP
STOP THIS AT ONCE!
GIVE US BACK OUR FRIEND OR ELSE!

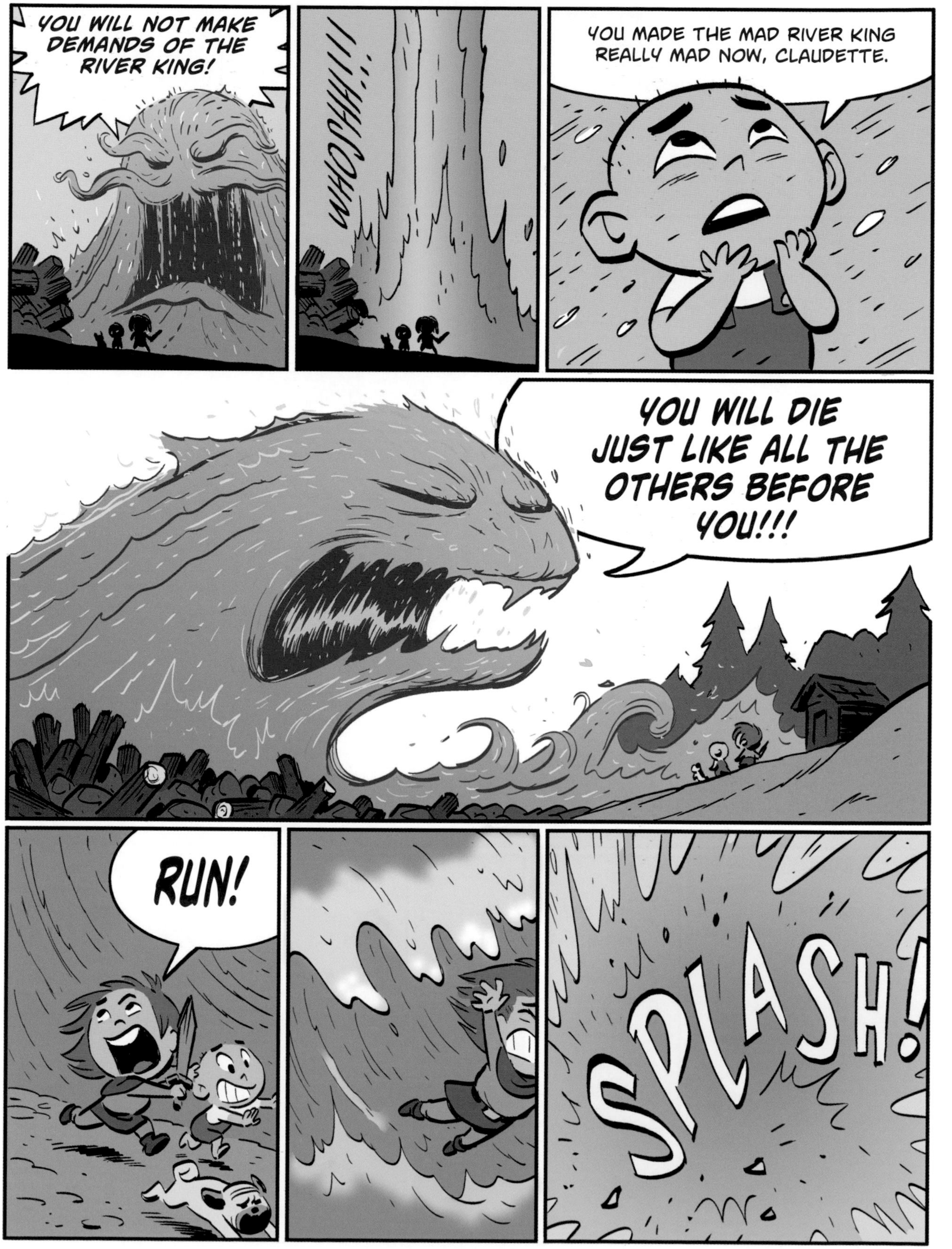
YOU WILL NOT MAKE DEMANDS OF THE RIVER KING!
WHOOSHH!!!
YOU MADE THE MAD RIVER KING REALLY MAD NOW, CLAUDETTE.
YOU WILL DIE JUST LIKE ALL THE OTHERS BEFORE YOU!!!
RUN!
SPLASH!

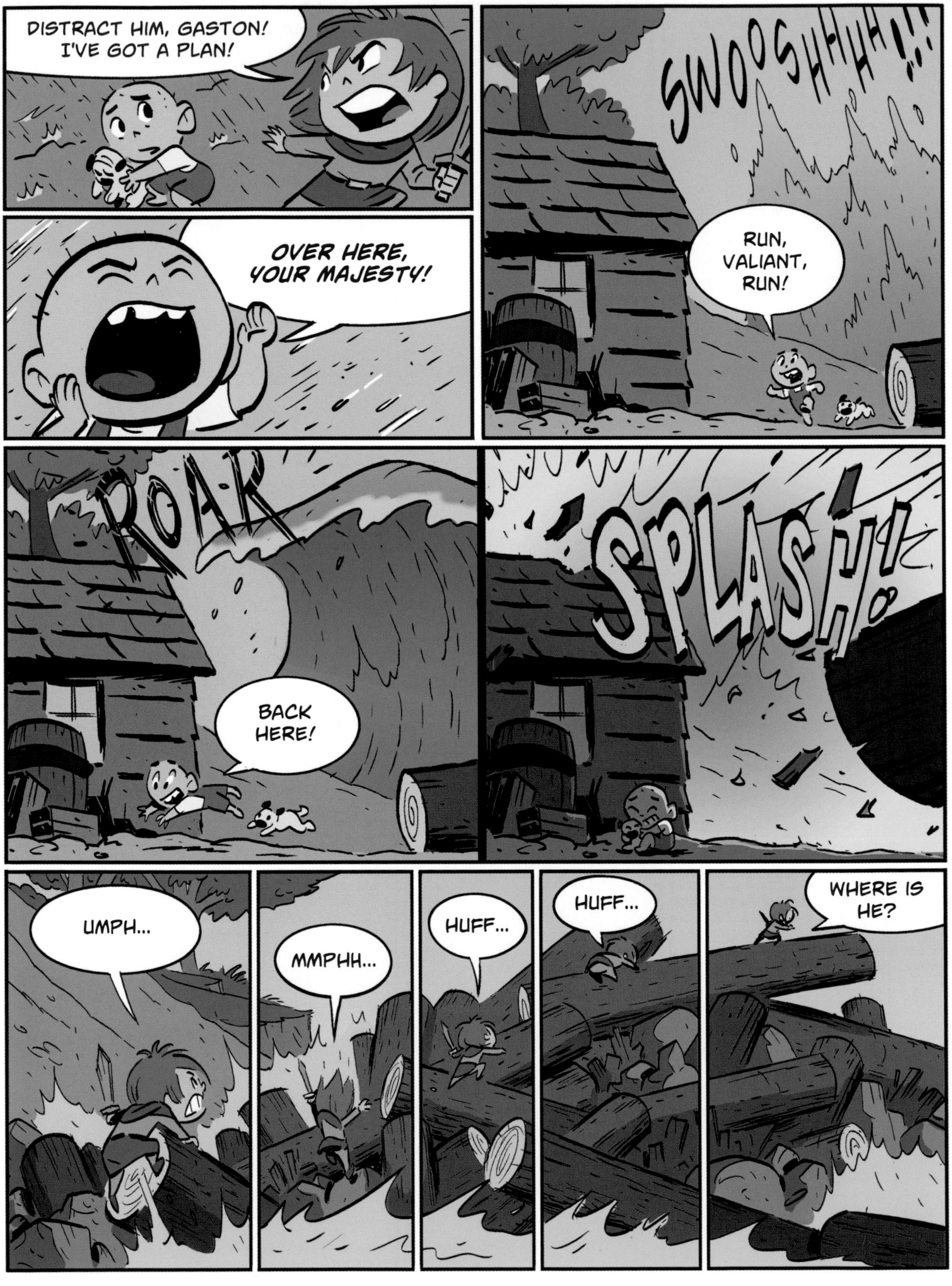
DISTRACT HIM, GASTON! I'VE GOT A PLAN!
OVER HERE, YOUR MAJESTY!
SWOOSHHHH!!!
RUN, VALIANT, RUN!
ROAR
BACK HERE!
SPLASH!
UMPH...
MMPHH...
HUFF...
HUFF...
WHERE IS HE?

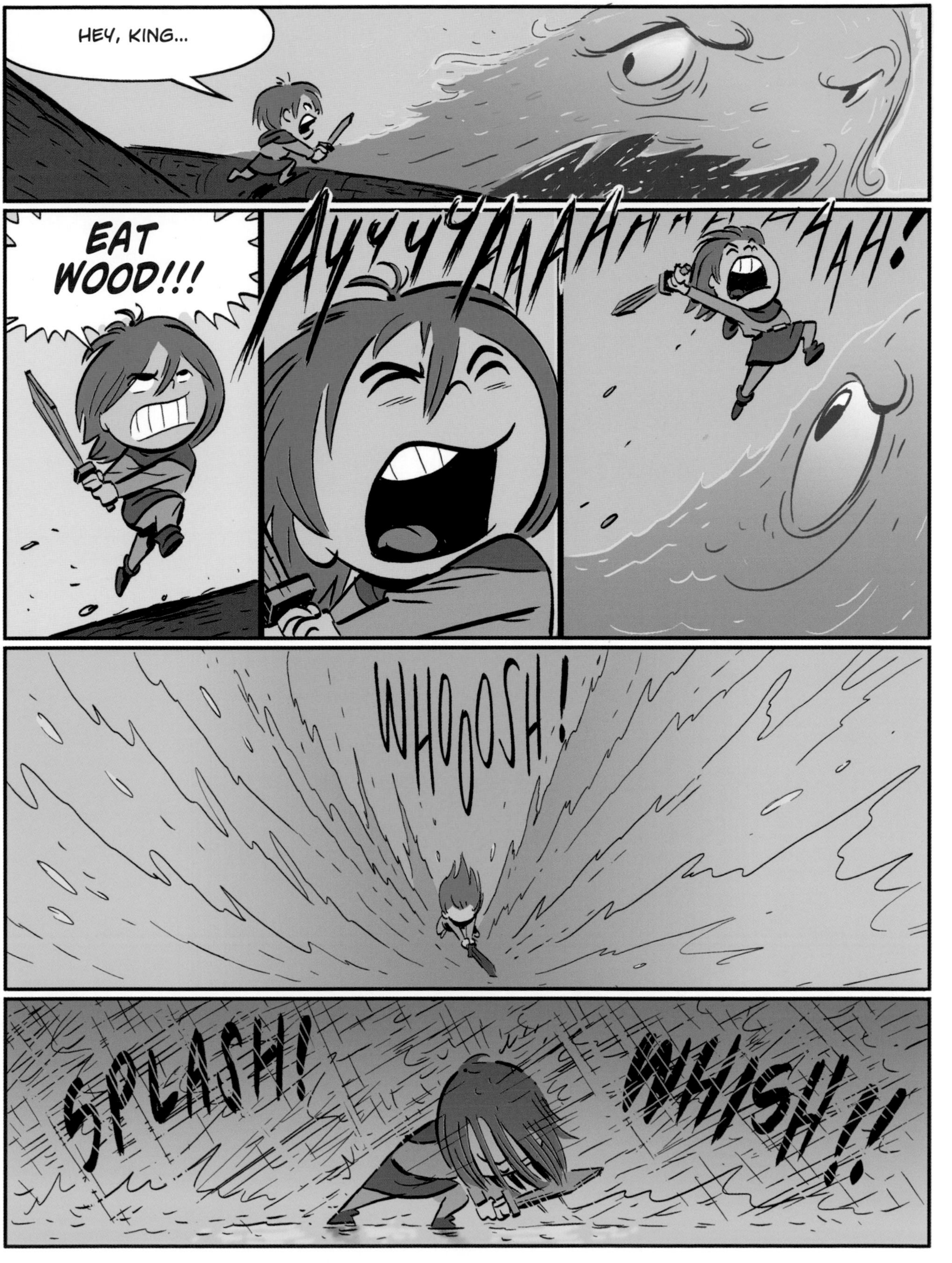
HEY, KING...
EAT WOOD!!!
AYYYYAAAAAAAAAAAAH!
WHOOOSH!
SPLASH!
WHISH!!

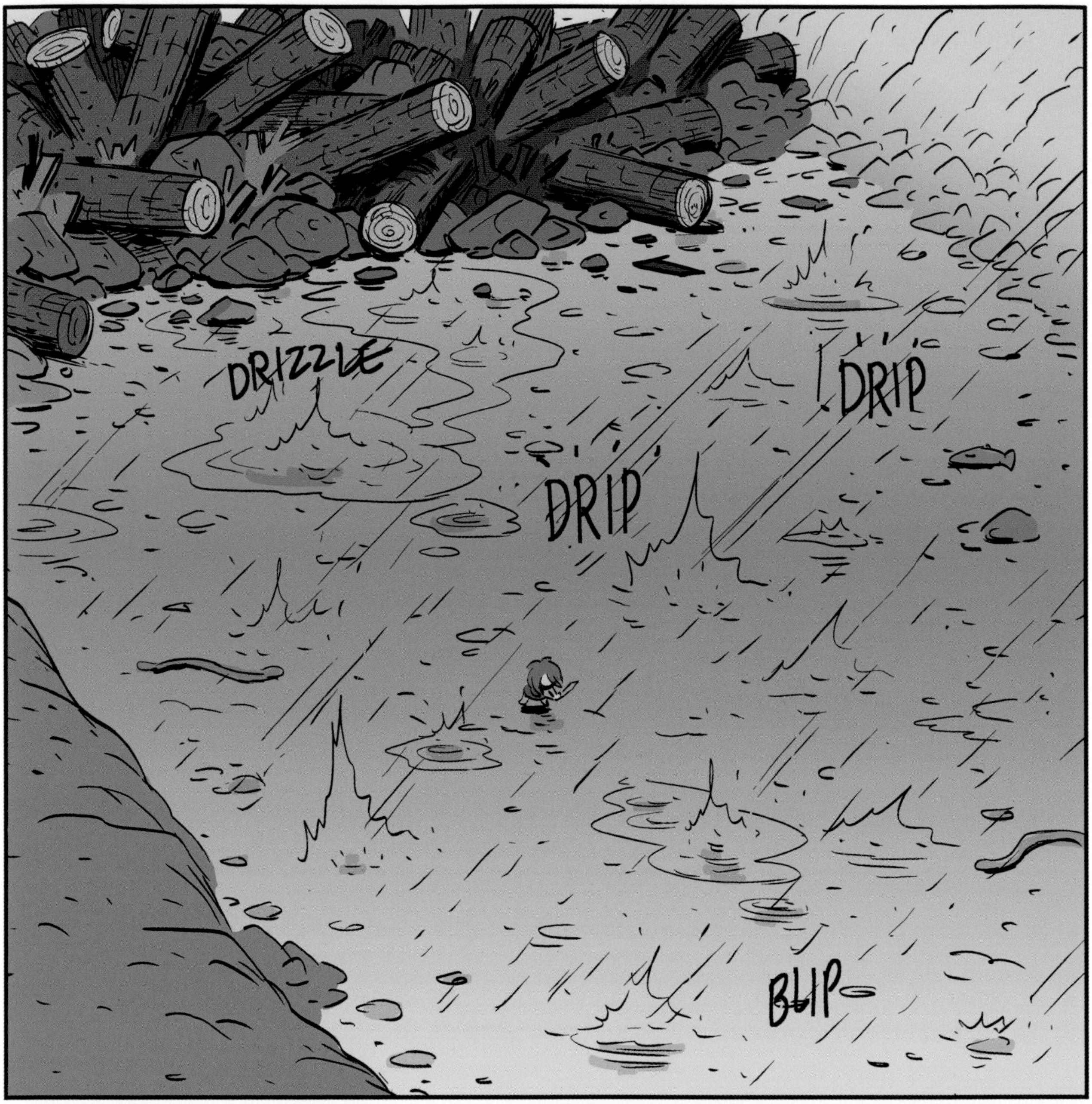
DRIZZLE
DRIP
DRIP
BLIP

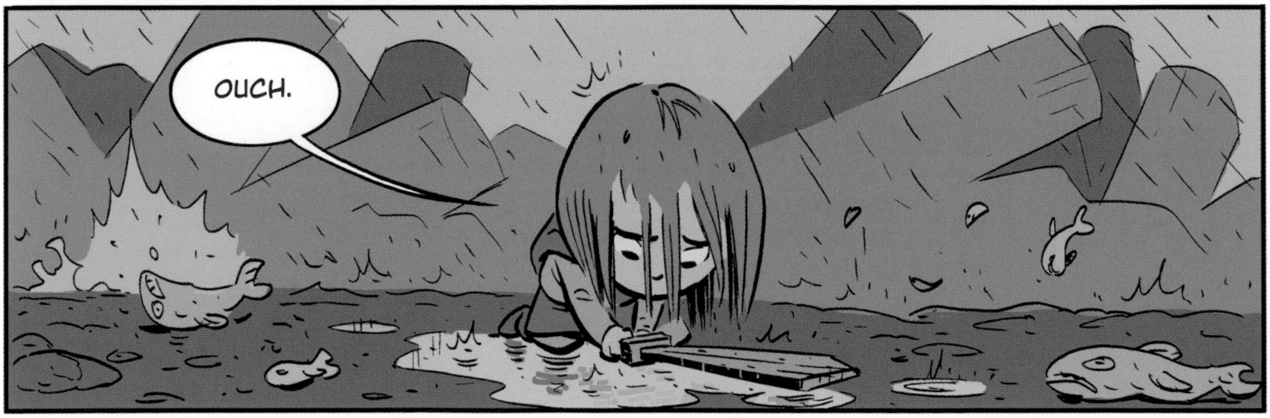
OUCH.

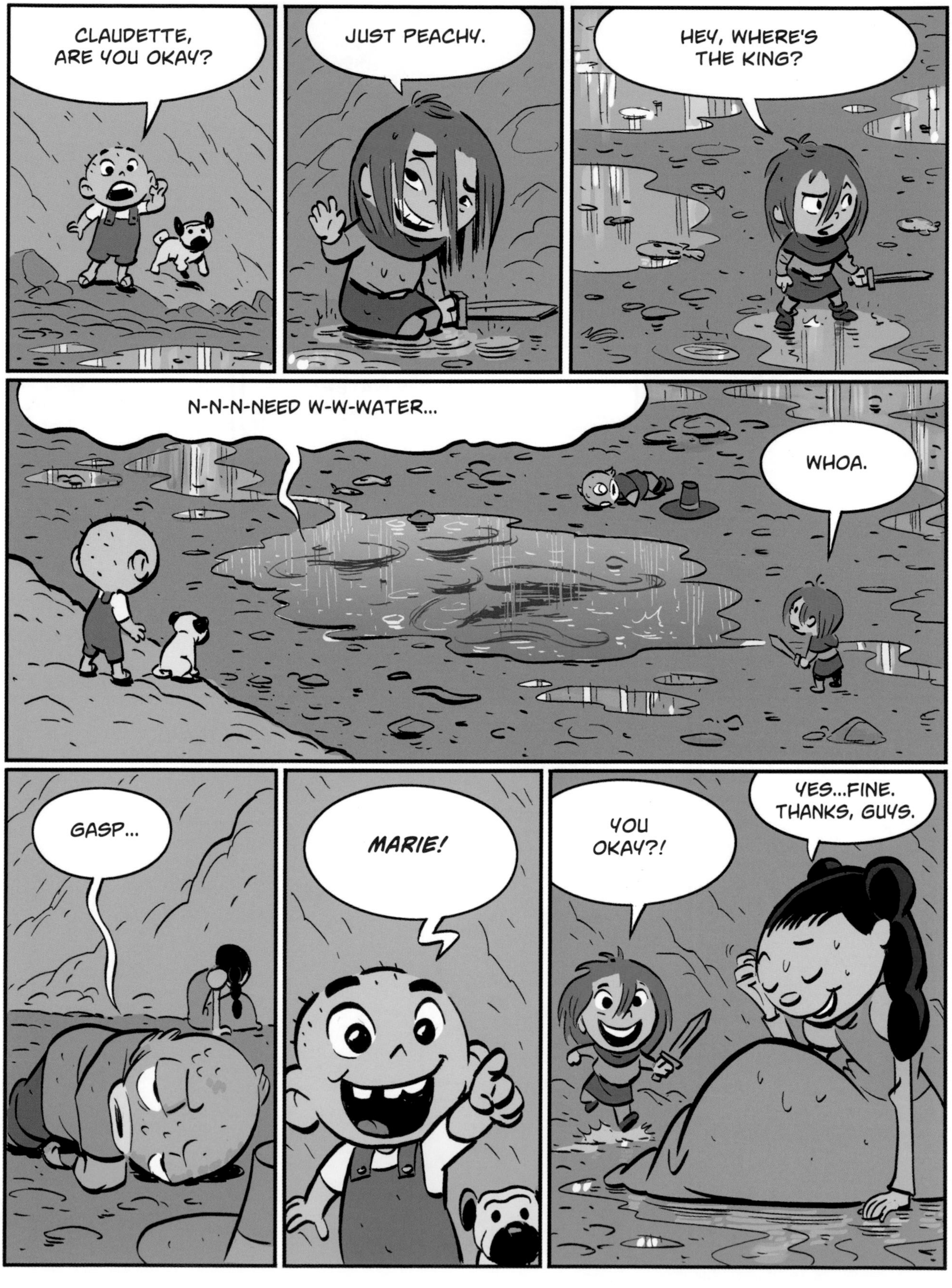
CLAUDETTE, ARE YOU OKAY?
JUST PEACHY.
HEY, WHERE'S THE KING?
N-N-N-NEED W-W-WATER...
WHOA.
GASP...
MARIE!
YOU OKAY?!
YES...FINE. THANKS, GUYS.

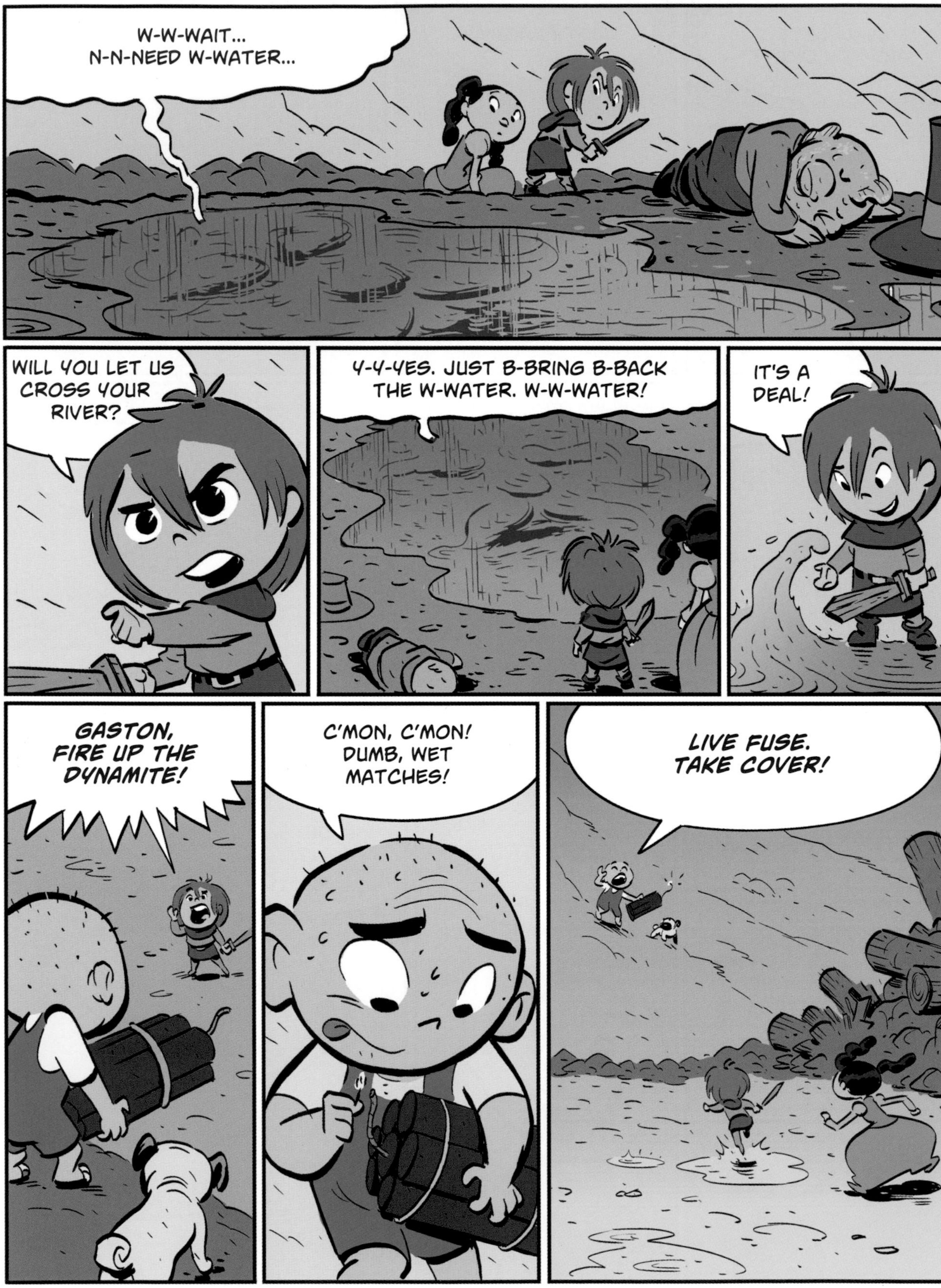
W-W-WAIT... N-N-NEED W-WATER...
WILL YOU LET US CROSS YOUR RIVER?
Y-Y-YES. JUST B-BRING B-BACK THE W-WATER. W-W-WATER!
IT'S A DEAL!
GASTON, FIRE UP THE DYNAMITE!
C'MON, C'MON! DUMB, WET MATCHES!
LIVE FUSE. TAKE COVER!

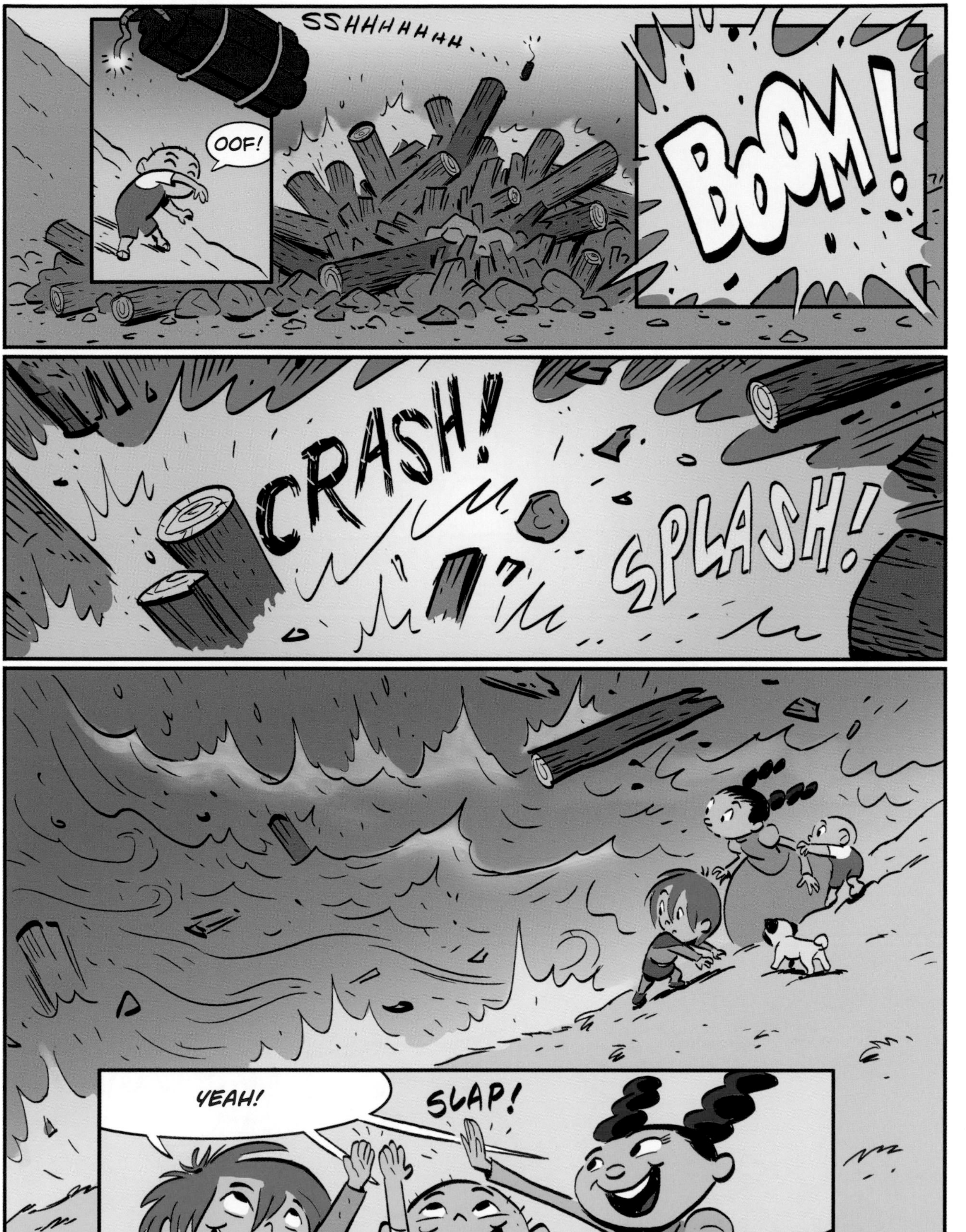
SSHHHHHHH...
OOF!
BOOM!
CRASH!
SPLASH!
YEAH!
SLAP!

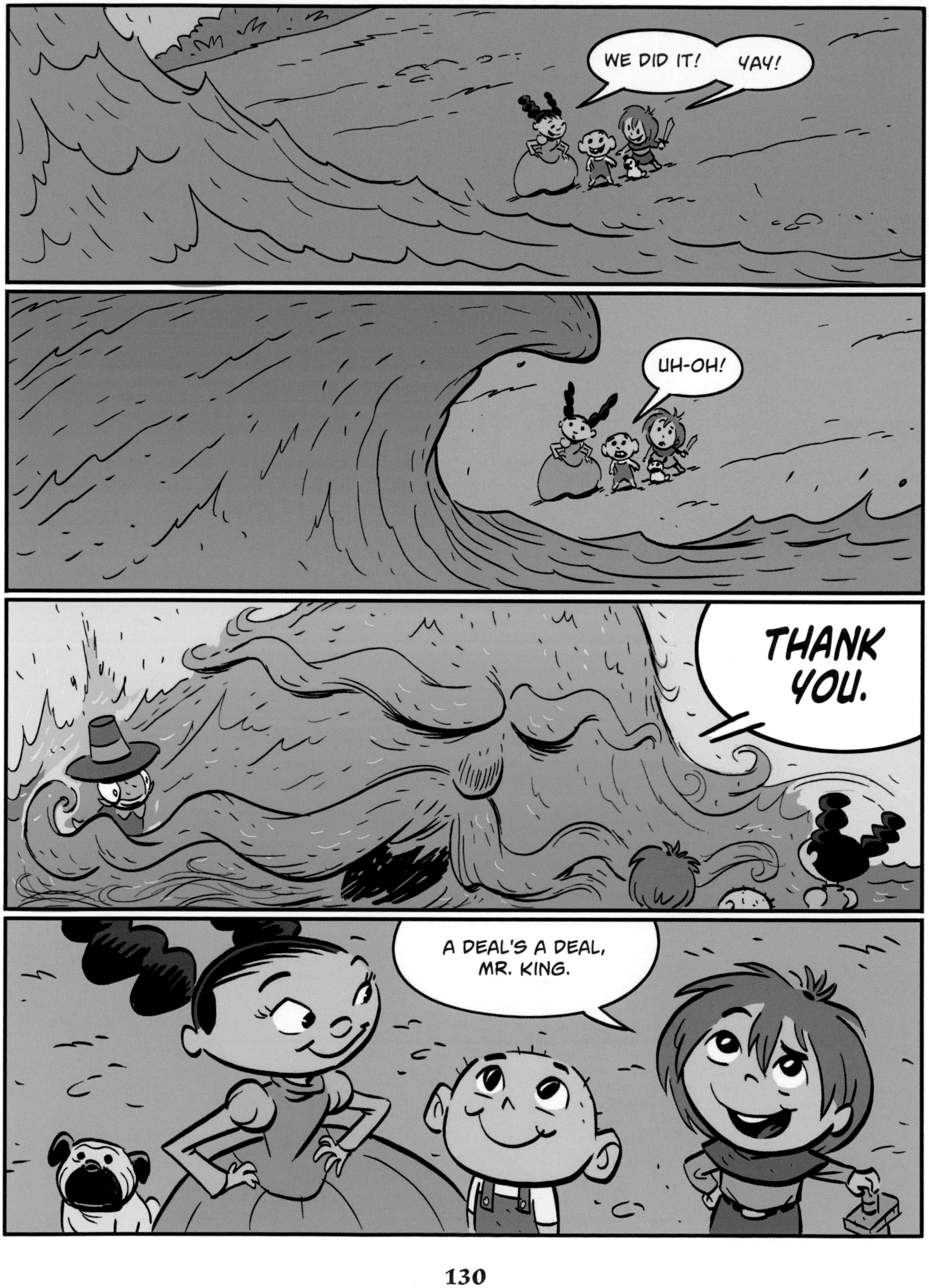
WE DID IT!
YAY!
UH-OH!
THANK YOU.
A DEAL'S A DEAL, MR. KING.

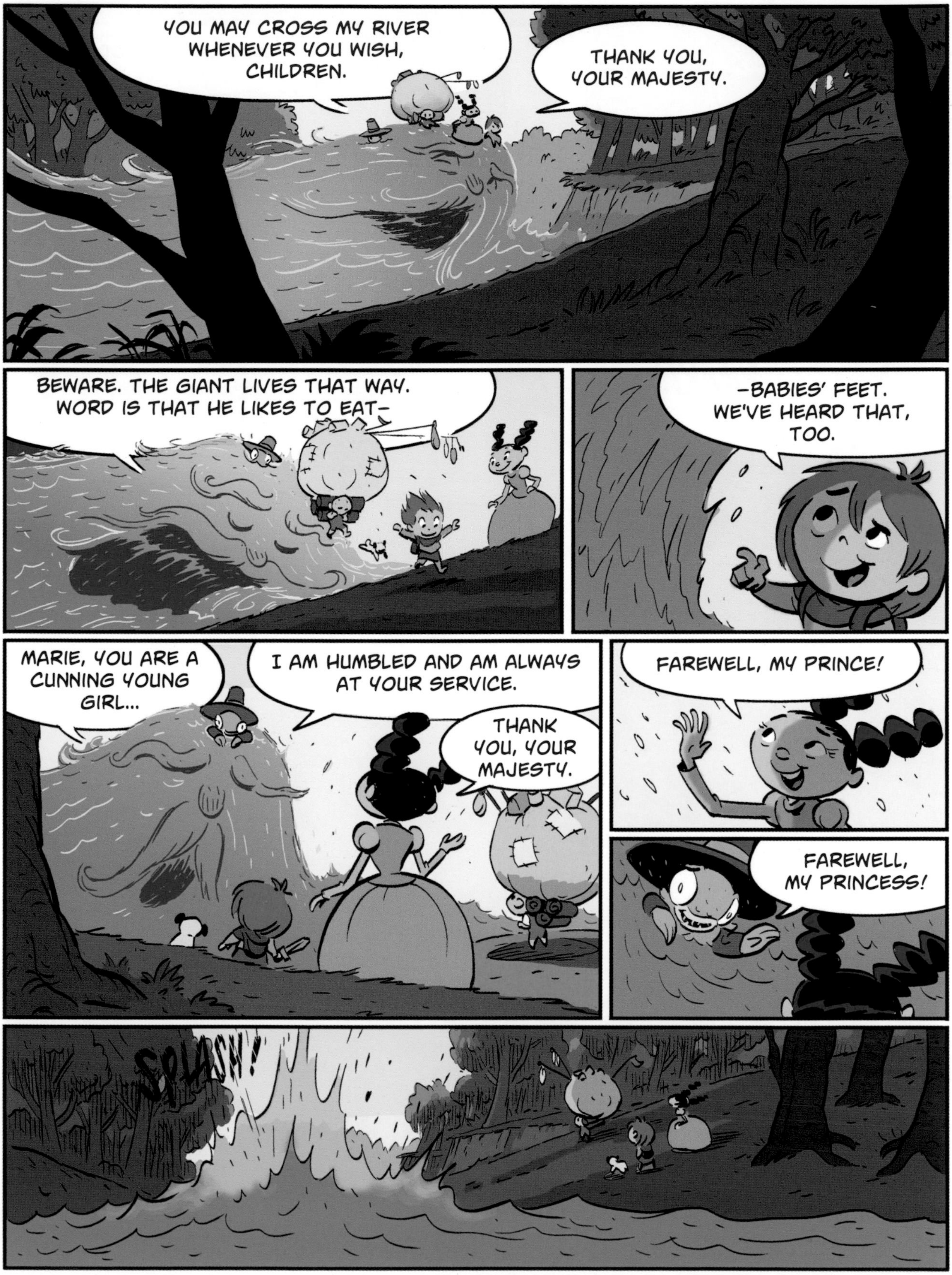
YOU MAY CROSS MY RIVER WHENEVER YOU WISH, CHILDREN.
THANK YOU, YOUR MAJESTY.
BEWARE. THE GIANT LIVES THAT WAY. WORD IS THAT HE LIKES TO EAT–
–BABIES' FEET. WE'VE HEARD THAT, TOO.
MARIE, YOU ARE A CUNNING YOUNG GIRL...
I AM HUMBLED AND AM ALWAYS AT YOUR SERVICE.
THANK YOU, YOUR MAJESTY.
FAREWELL, MY PRINCE!
FAREWELL, MY PRINCESS!
SPLASH!

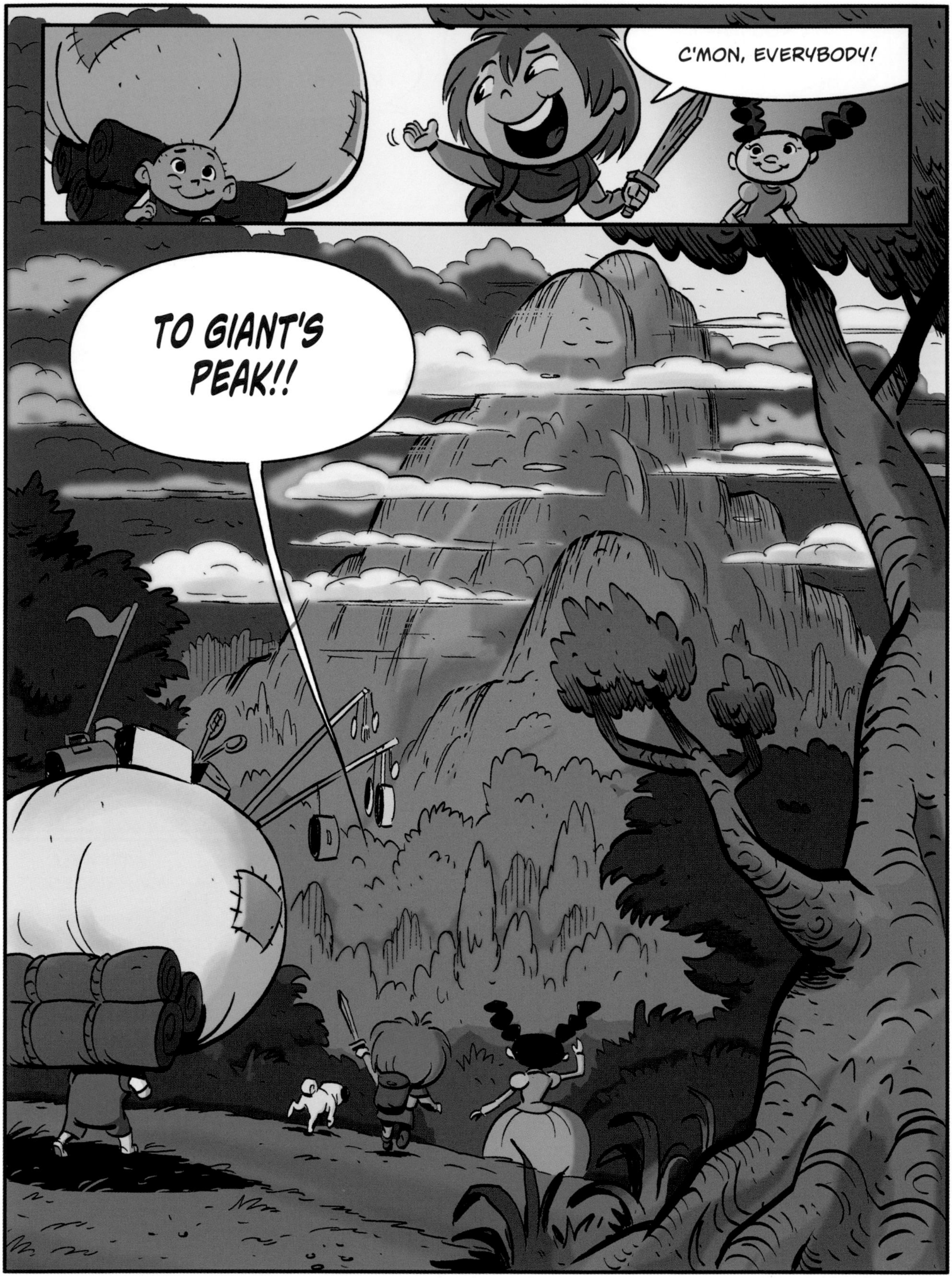
C'MON, EVERYBODY!
TO GIANT'S PEAK!!

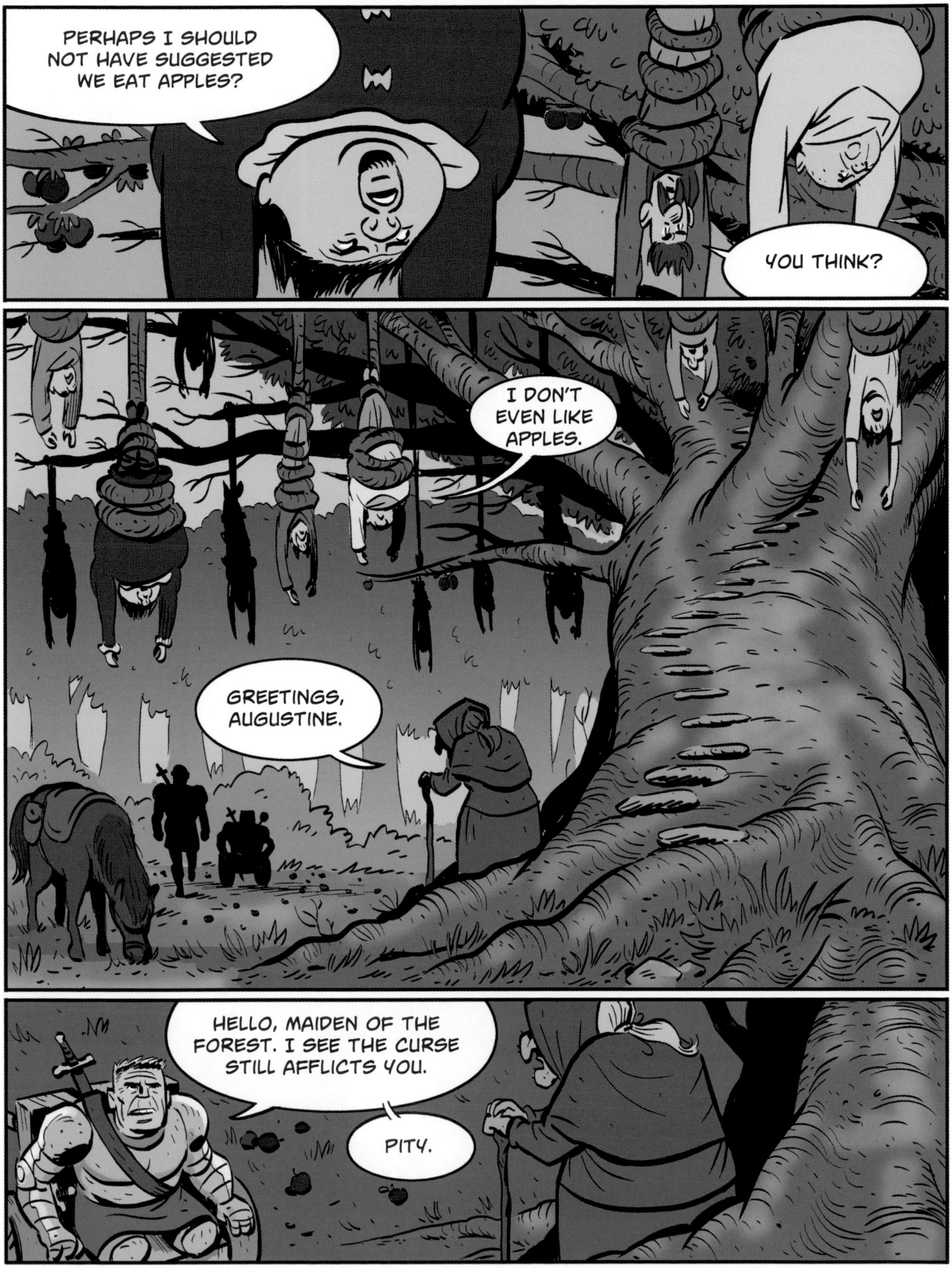
PERHAPS I SHOULD NOT HAVE SUGGESTED WE EAT APPLES?
YOU THINK?
I DON'T EVEN LIKE APPLES.
GREETINGS, AUGUSTINE.
HELLO, MAIDEN OF THE FOREST. I SEE THE CURSE STILL AFFLICTS YOU.
PITY.

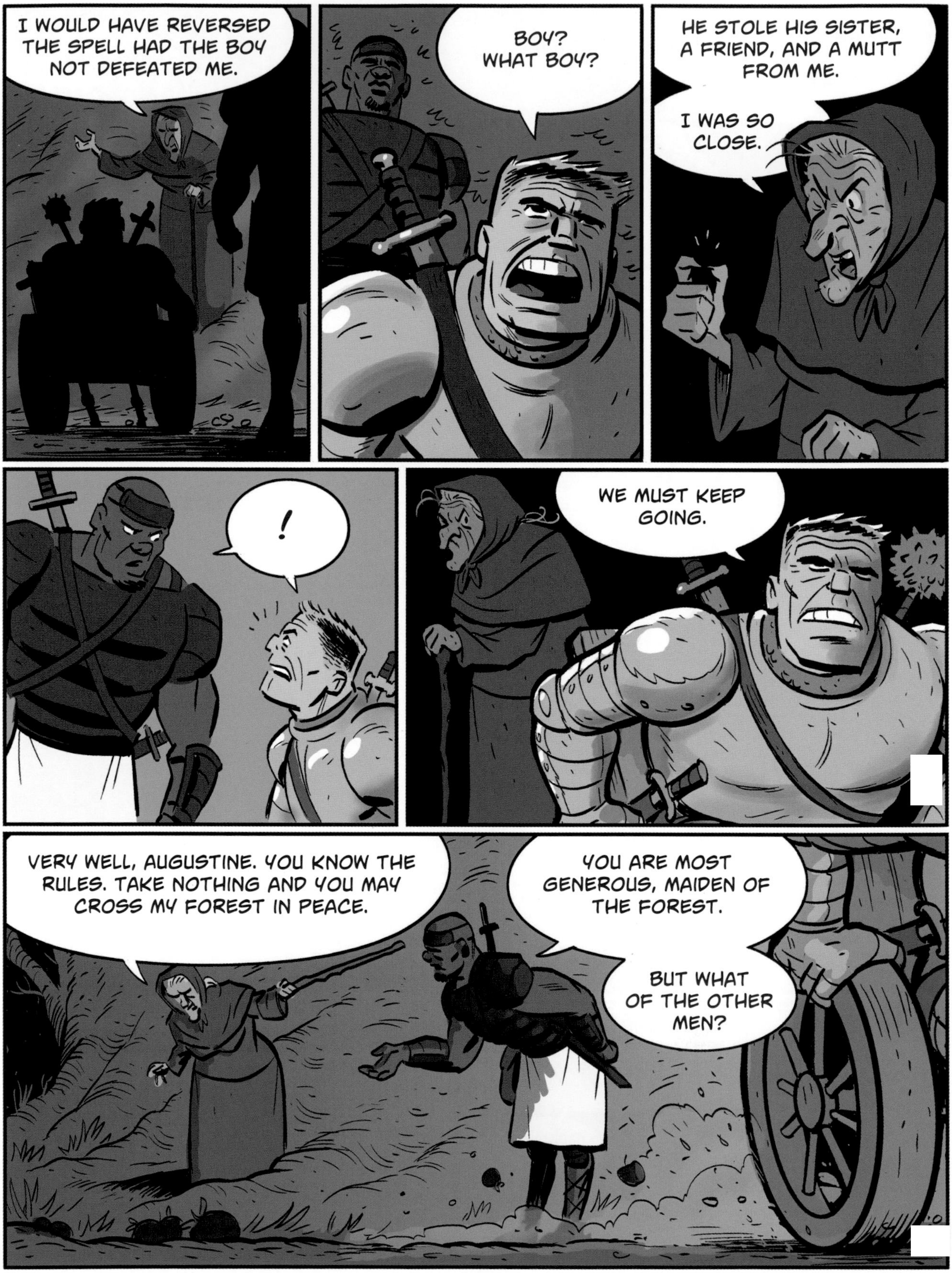

I WOULD HAVE REVERSED THE SPELL HAD THE BOY NOT DEFEATED ME.
BOY? WHAT BOY?
HE STOLE HIS SISTER, A FRIEND, AND A MUTT FROM ME.
I WAS SO CLOSE.
!
WE MUST KEEP GOING.
VERY WELL, AUGUSTINE. YOU KNOW THE RULES. TAKE NOTHING AND YOU MAY CROSS MY FOREST IN PEACE.
YOU ARE MOST GENEROUS, MAIDEN OF THE FOREST.
BUT WHAT OF THE OTHER MEN?

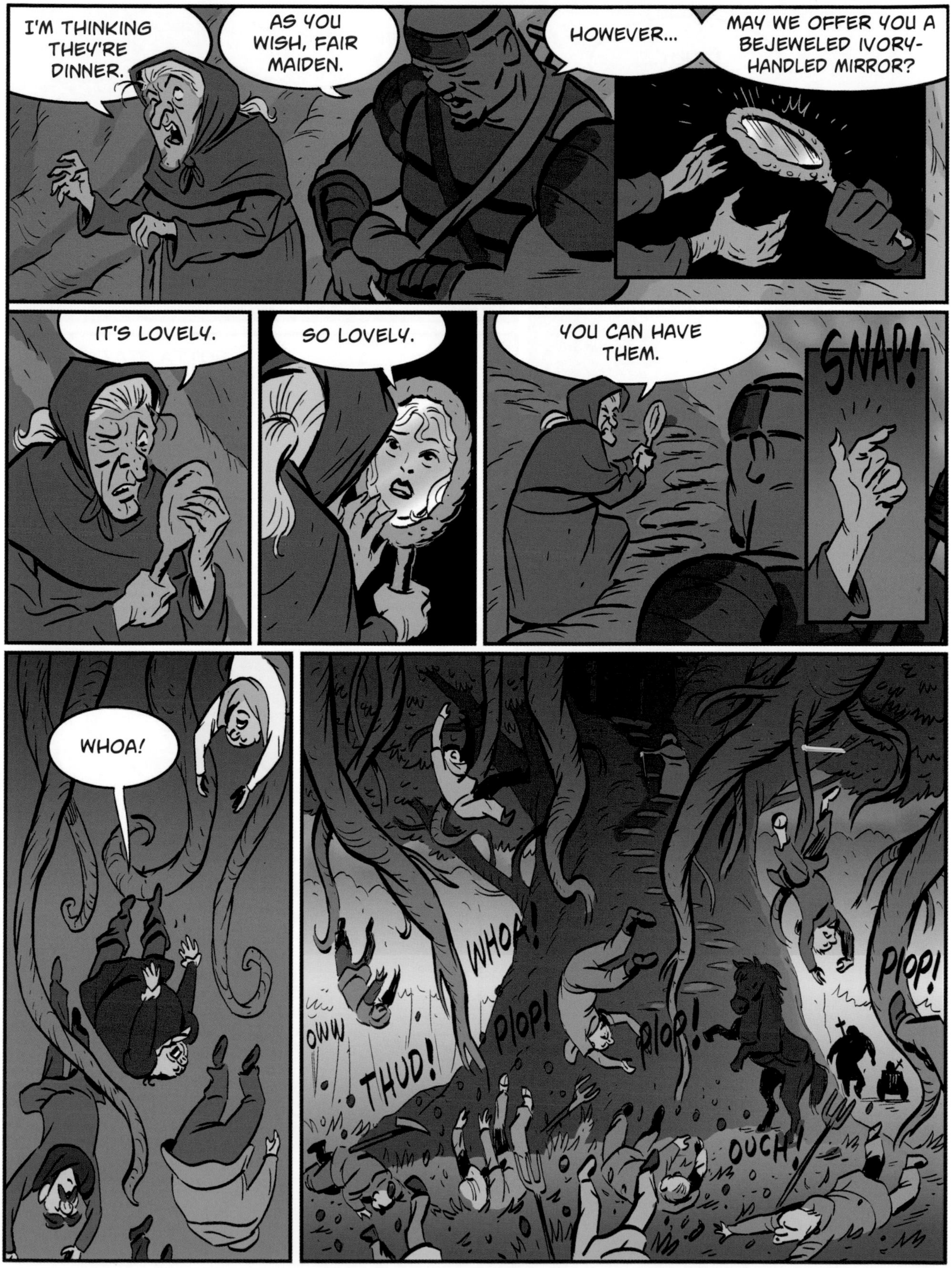
I'M THINKING THEY'RE DINNER.
AS YOU WISH, FAIR MAIDEN.
HOWEVER...
MAY WE OFFER YOU A BEJEWELED IVORY-HANDLED MIRROR?
IT'S LOVELY.
SO LOVELY.
YOU CAN HAVE THEM.
SNAP!
WHOA!
WHOA!
OWW
THUD!
PLOP!
PLOP!
PLOP!
OUCH!

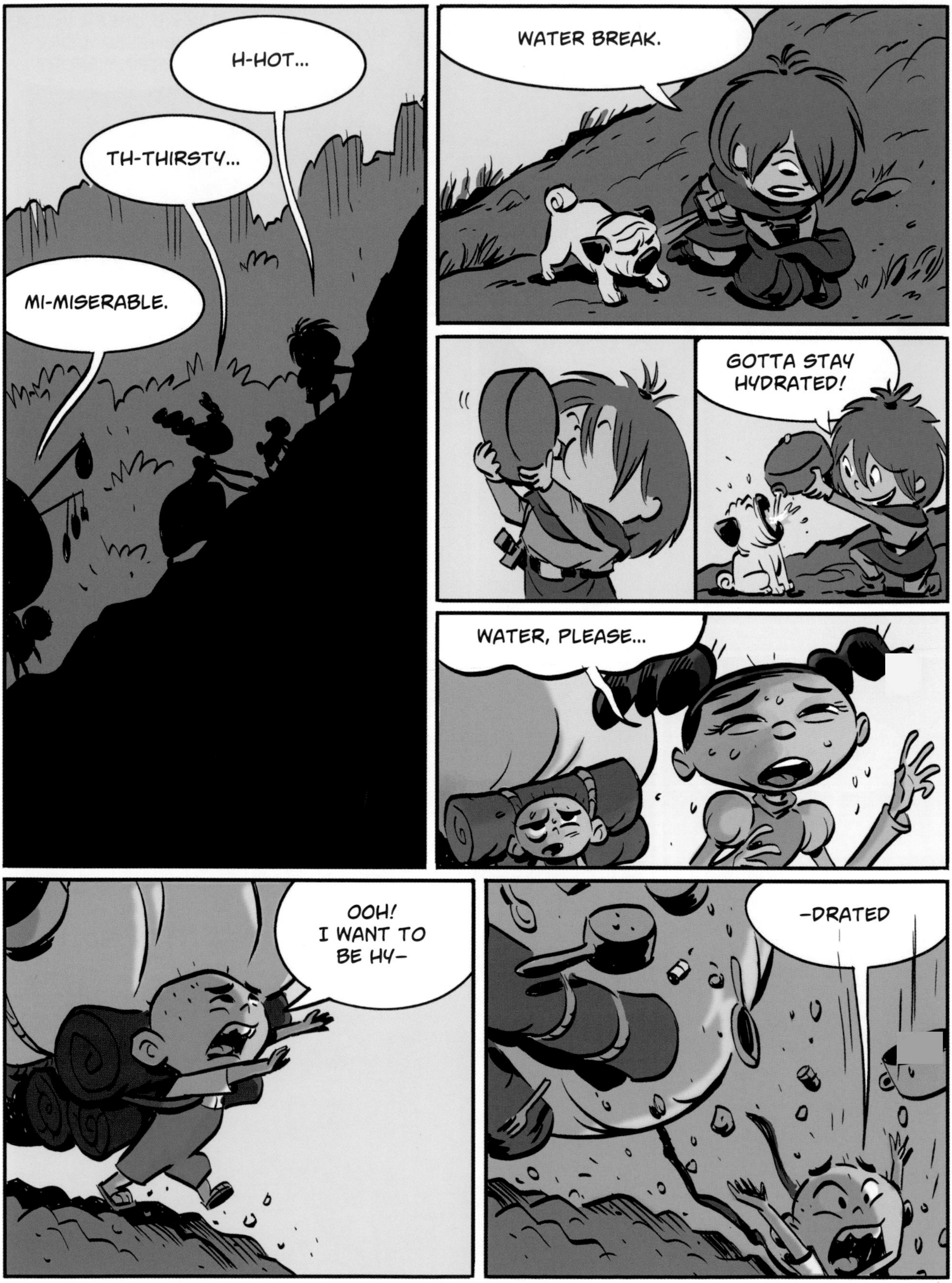
H-HOT...
TH-THIRSTY...
MI-MISERABLE.
WATER BREAK.
GOTTA STAY HYDRATED!
WATER, PLEASE...
OOH! I WANT TO BE HY-
-DRATED

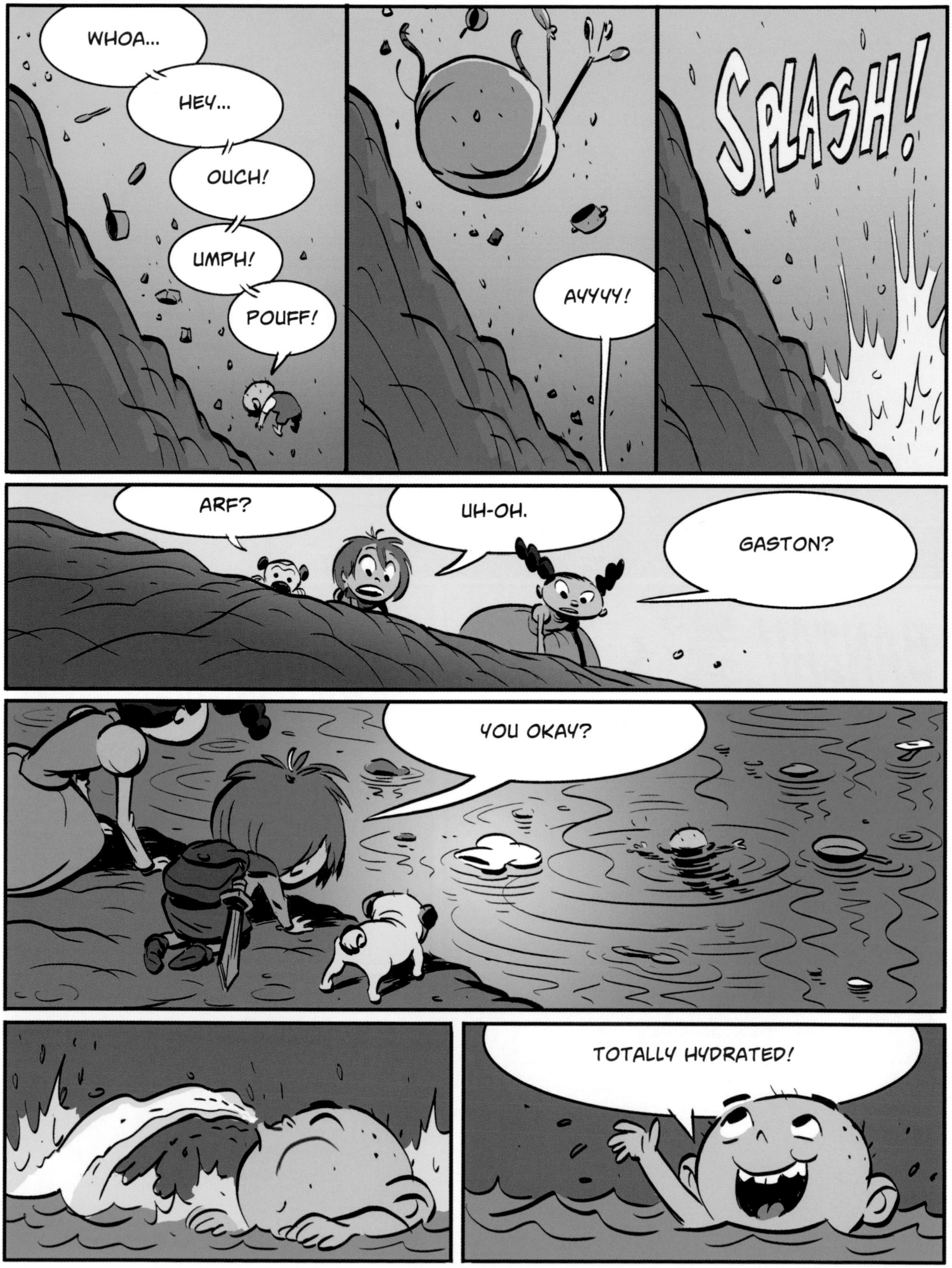
WHOA...
HEY...
OUCH!
UMPH!
POUFF!
AYYYY!
SPLASH!
ARF?
UH-OH.
GASTON?
YOU OKAY?
TOTALLY HYDRATED!

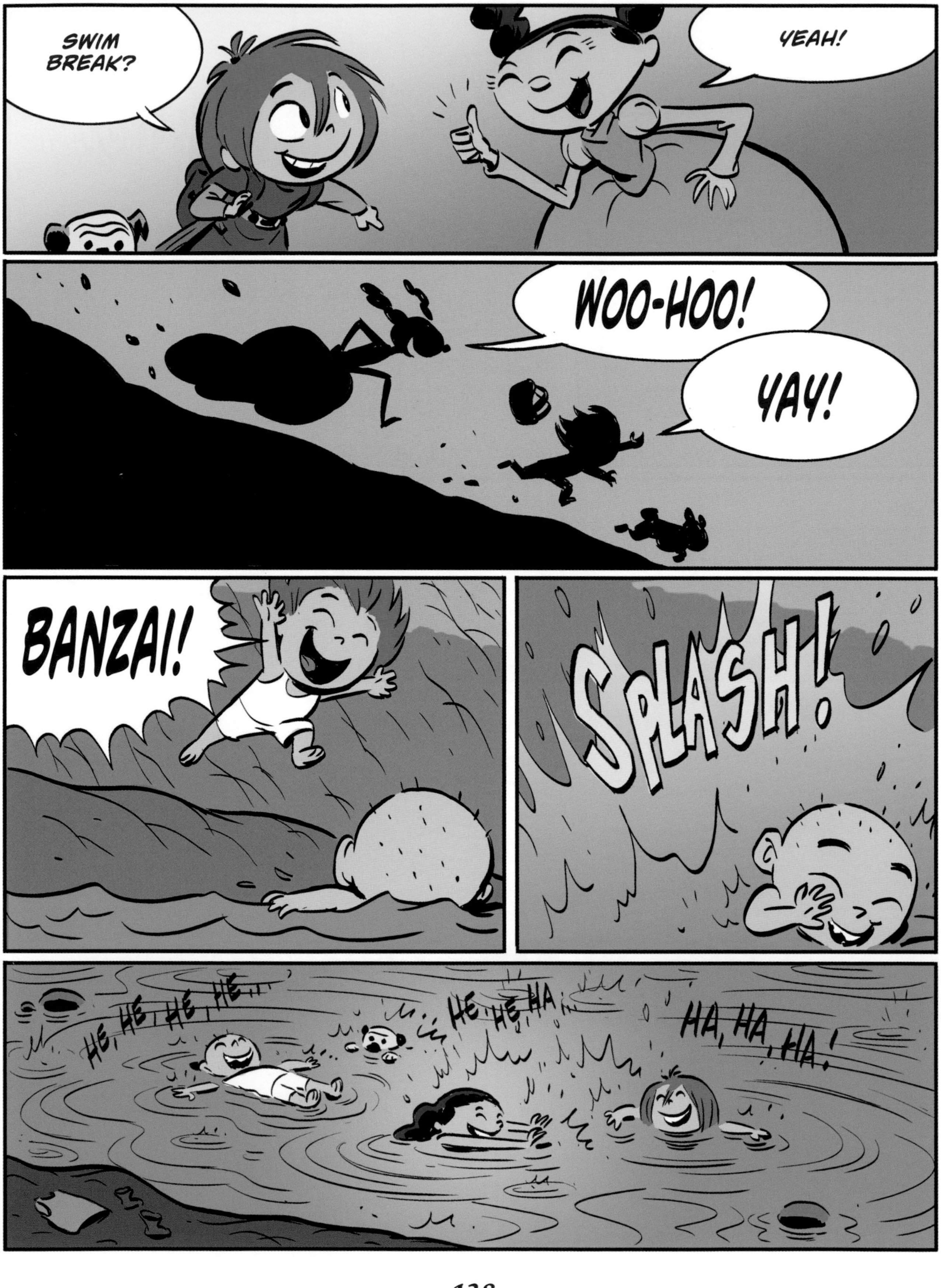
SWIM BREAK?
YEAH!
WOO-HOO!
YAY!
BANZAI!
SPLASH!
HE, HE, HE, HE...
HE HE HA...
HA, HA, HA!

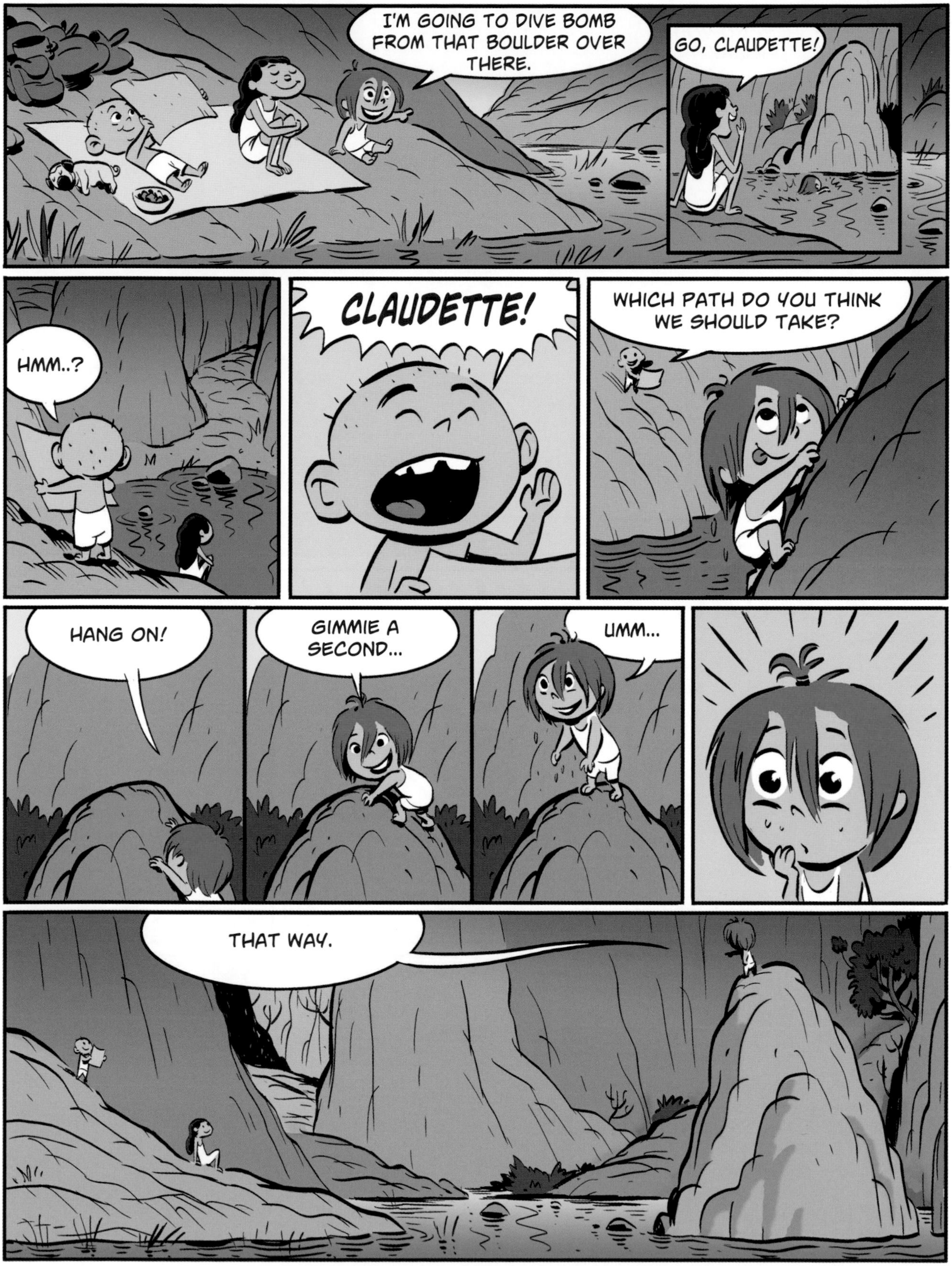
I'M GOING TO DIVE BOMB FROM THAT BOULDER OVER THERE.
GO, CLAUDETTE!
HMM..?
CLAUDETTE!
WHICH PATH DO YOU THINK WE SHOULD TAKE?
HANG ON!
GIMMIE A SECOND...
UMM...
THAT WAY.

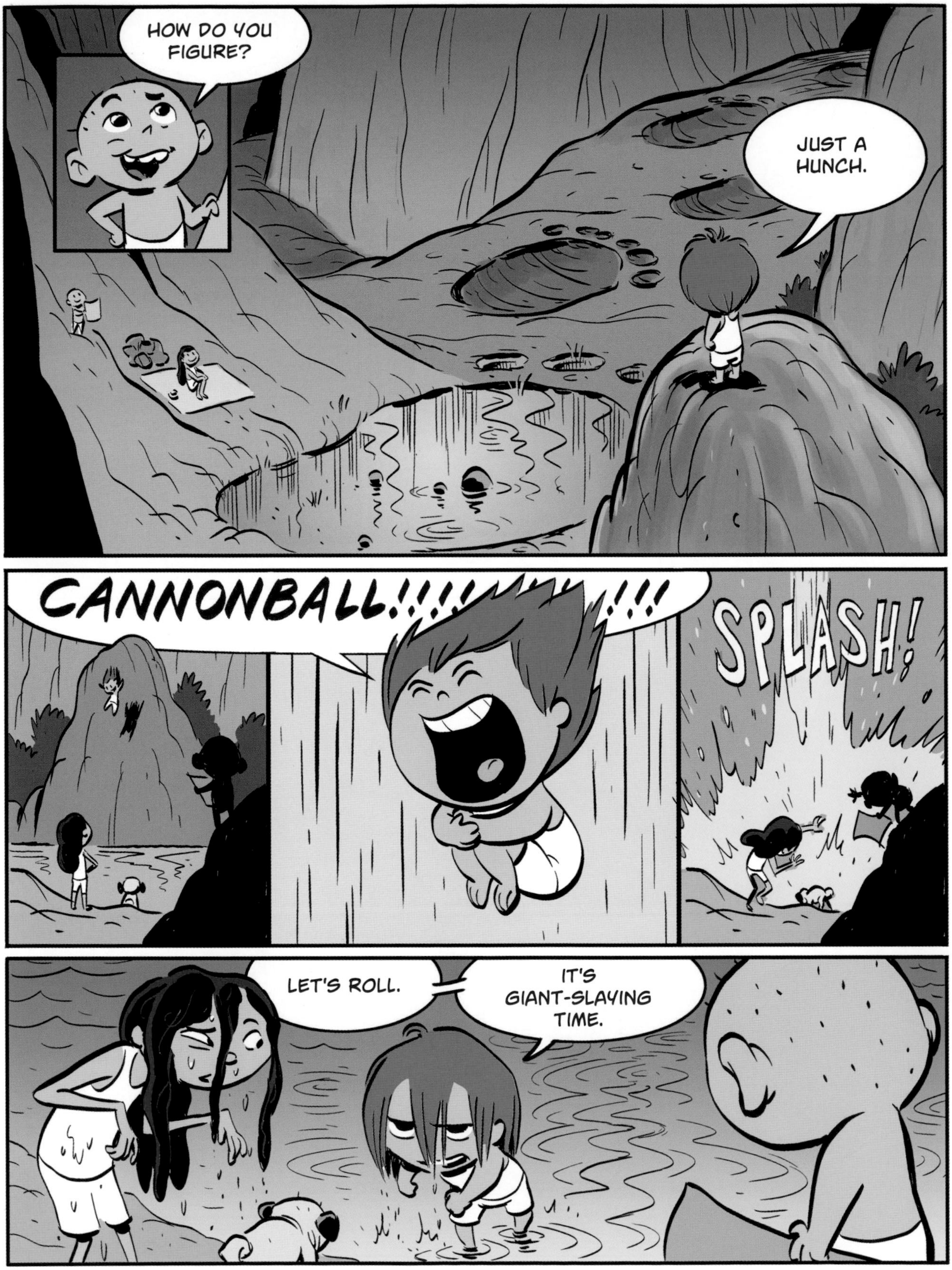
HOW DO YOU FIGURE?
JUST A HUNCH.
CANNONBALL!!!!!!!!
SPLASH!
LET'S ROLL.
IT'S GIANT-SLAYING TIME.

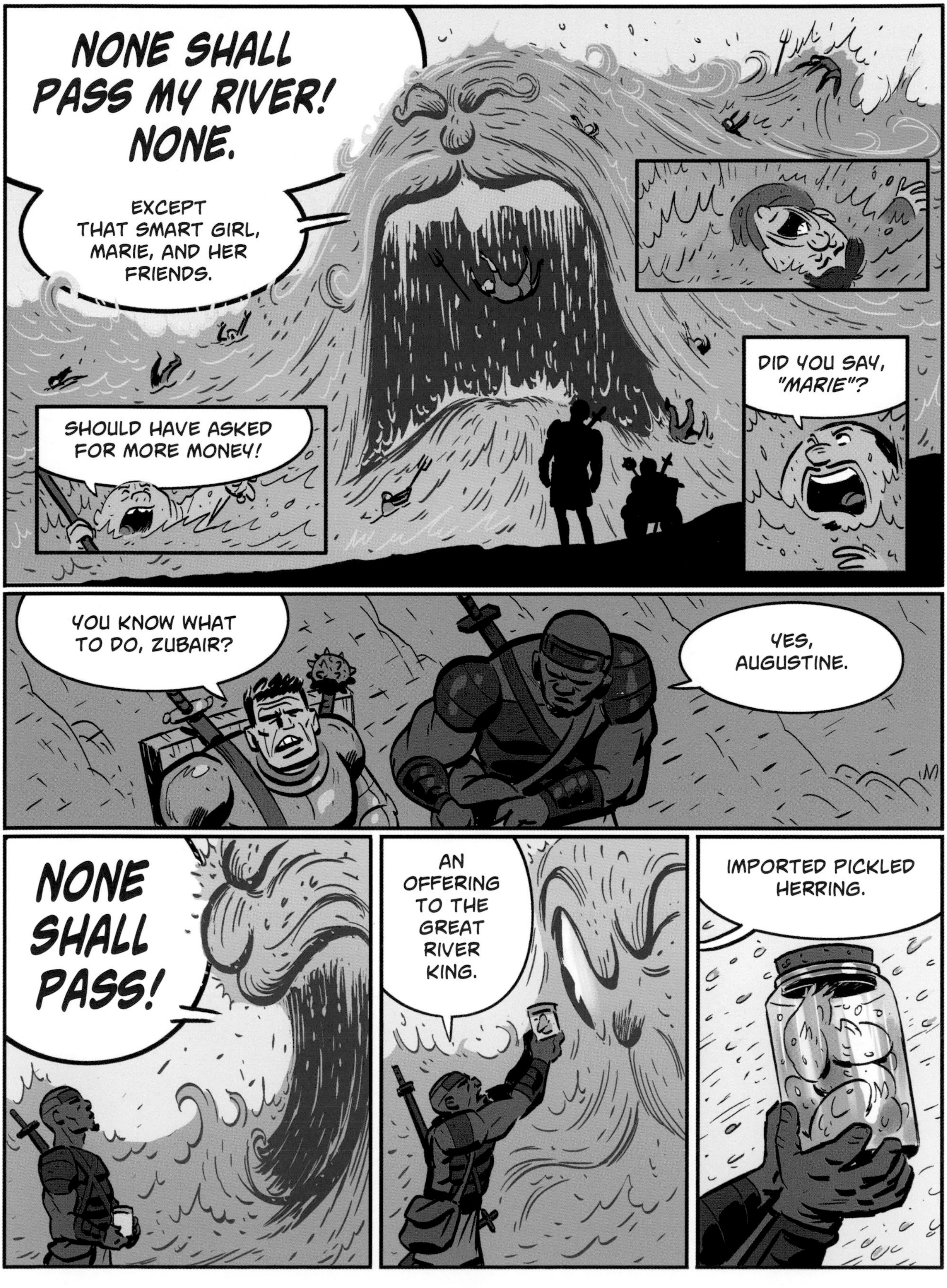
NONE SHALL PASS MY RIVER! NONE.
EXCEPT THAT SMART GIRL, MARIE, AND HER FRIENDS.
SHOULD HAVE ASKED FOR MORE MONEY!
DID YOU SAY, "MARIE"?
YOU KNOW WHAT TO DO, ZUBAIR?
YES, AUGUSTINE.
NONE SHALL PASS!
AN OFFERING TO THE GREAT RIVER KING.
IMPORTED PICKLED HERRING.

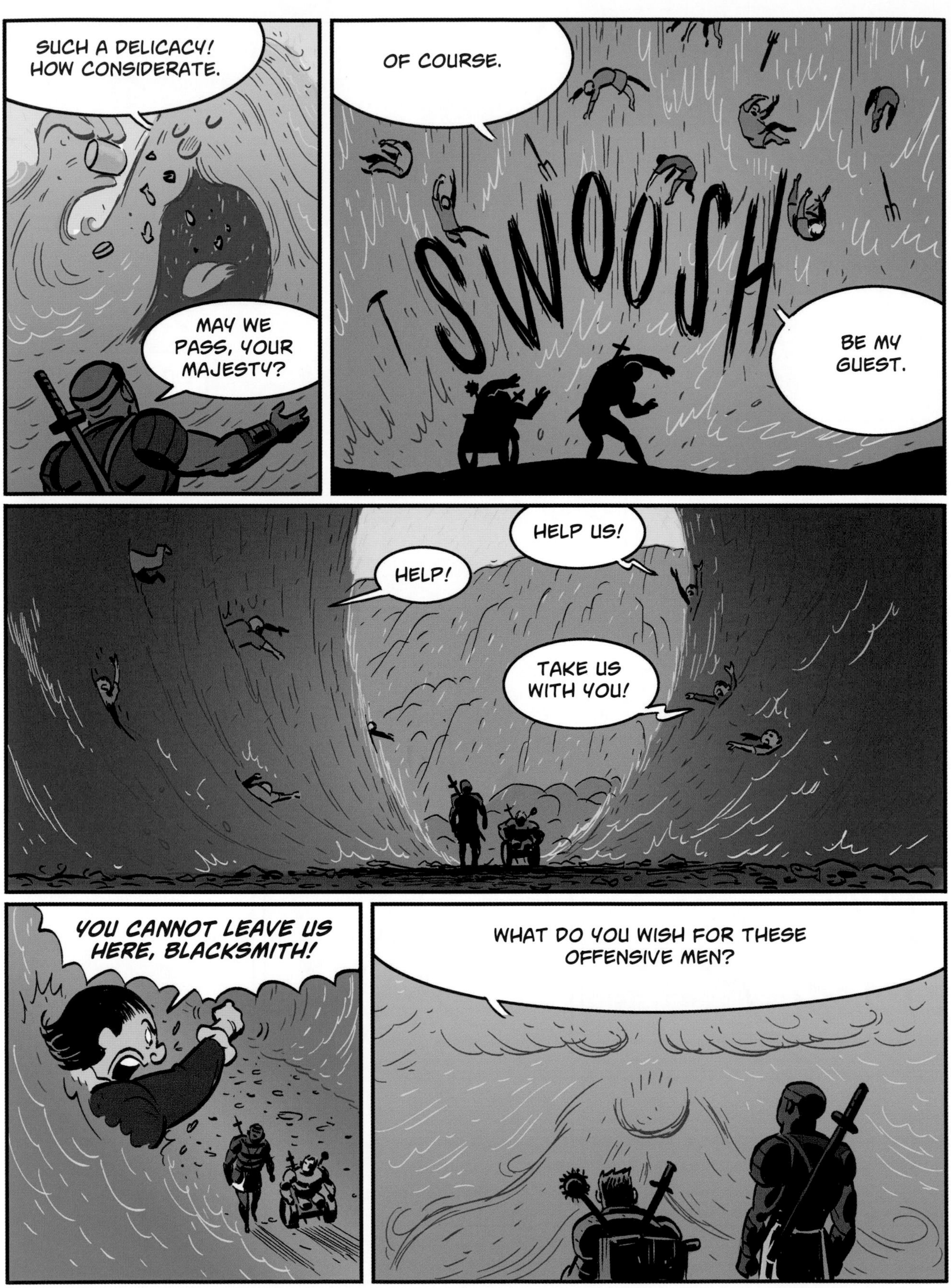
SUCH A DELICACY! HOW CONSIDERATE.
MAY WE PASS, YOUR MAJESTY?
OF COURSE.
SWOOSH
BE MY GUEST.
HELP US!
HELP!
TAKE US WITH YOU!
YOU CANNOT LEAVE US HERE, BLACKSMITH!
WHAT DO YOU WISH FOR THESE OFFENSIVE MEN?

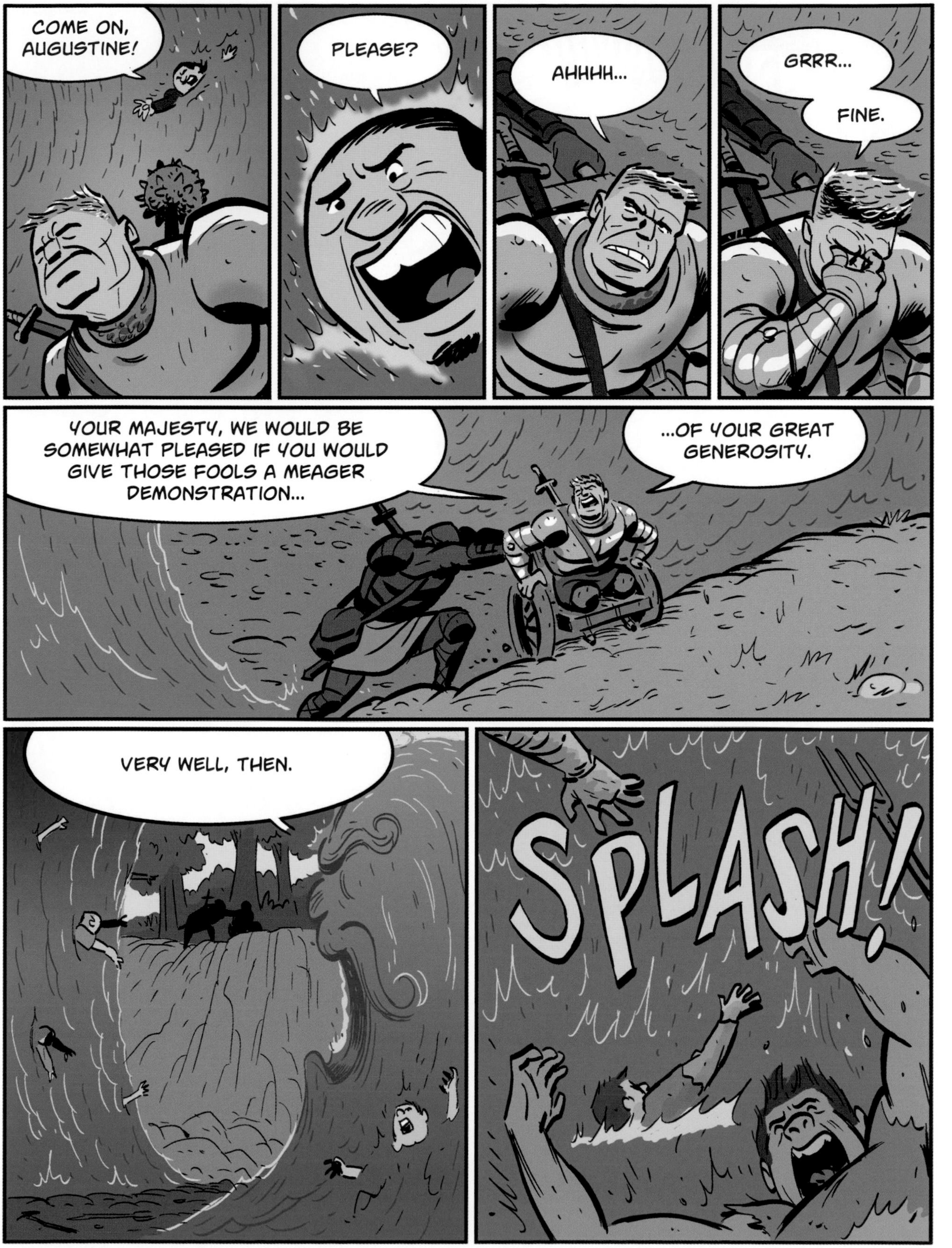
COME ON, AUGUSTINE!
PLEASE?
AHHHH...
GRRR...
FINE.
YOUR MAJESTY, WE WOULD BE SOMEWHAT PLEASED IF YOU WOULD GIVE THOSE FOOLS A MEAGER DEMONSTRATION...
...OF YOUR GREAT GENEROSITY.
VERY WELL, THEN.
SPLASH!

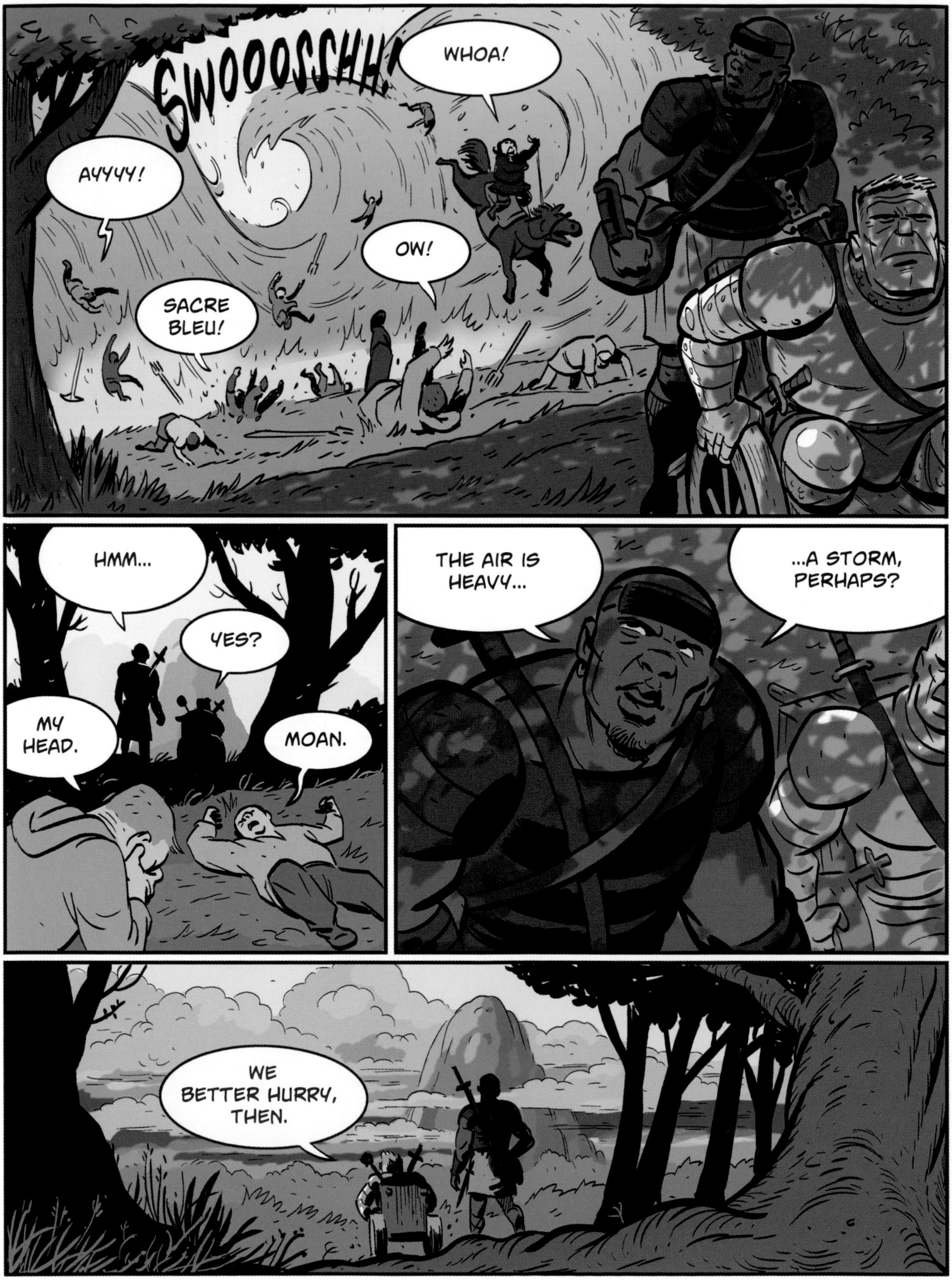
SWOOOSSHH!
AYYYY!
WHOA!
OW!
SACRE BLEU!
HMM...
YES?
MY HEAD.
MOAN.
THE AIR IS HEAVY...
...A STORM, PERHAPS?
WE BETTER HURRY, THEN.

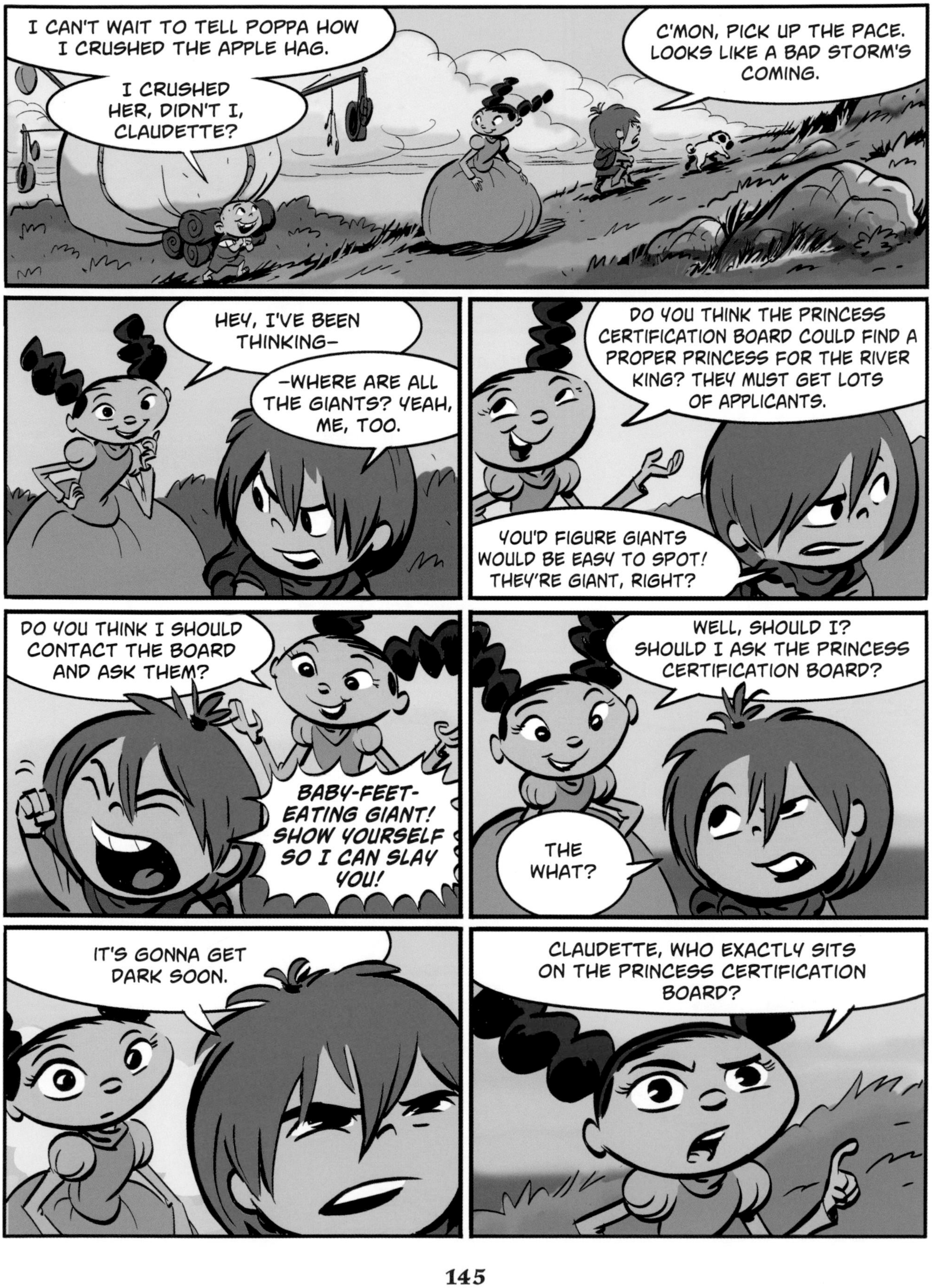

I CAN'T WAIT TO TELL POPPA HOW I CRUSHED THE APPLE HAG.
I CRUSHED HER, DIDN'T I, CLAUDETTE?
C'MON, PICK UP THE PACE. LOOKS LIKE A BAD STORM'S COMING.
HEY, I'VE BEEN THINKING–
–WHERE ARE ALL THE GIANTS? YEAH, ME, TOO.
DO YOU THINK THE PRINCESS CERTIFICATION BOARD COULD FIND A PROPER PRINCESS FOR THE RIVER KING? THEY MUST GET LOTS OF APPLICANTS.
YOU'D FIGURE GIANTS WOULD BE EASY TO SPOT! THEY'RE GIANT, RIGHT?
DO YOU THINK I SHOULD CONTACT THE BOARD AND ASK THEM?
BABY-FEET-EATING GIANT! SHOW YOURSELF SO I CAN SLAY YOU!
WELL, SHOULD I? SHOULD I ASK THE PRINCESS CERTIFICATION BOARD?
THE WHAT?
IT'S GONNA GET DARK SOON.
CLAUDETTE, WHO EXACTLY SITS ON THE PRINCESS CERTIFICATION BOARD?

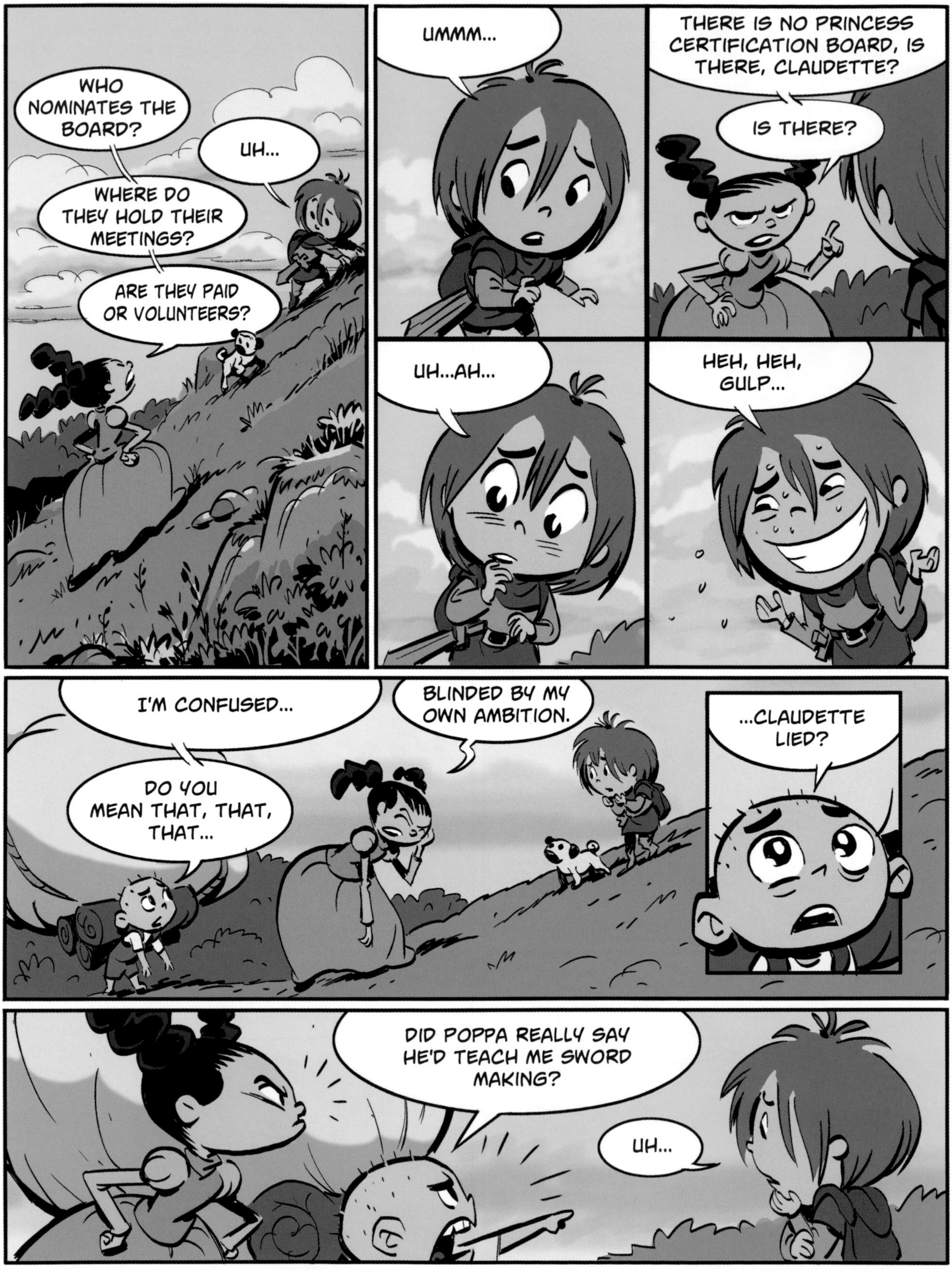
WHO NOMINATES THE BOARD?
UH...
WHERE DO THEY HOLD THEIR MEETINGS?
ARE THEY PAID OR VOLUNTEERS?
UMMM...
THERE IS NO PRINCESS CERTIFICATION BOARD, IS THERE, CLAUDETTE?
IS THERE?
UH...AH...
HEH, HEH, GULP...
I'M CONFUSED...
DO YOU MEAN THAT, THAT, THAT...
BLINDED BY MY OWN AMBITION.
...CLAUDETTE LIED?
DID POPPA REALLY SAY HE'D TEACH ME SWORD MAKING?
UH...

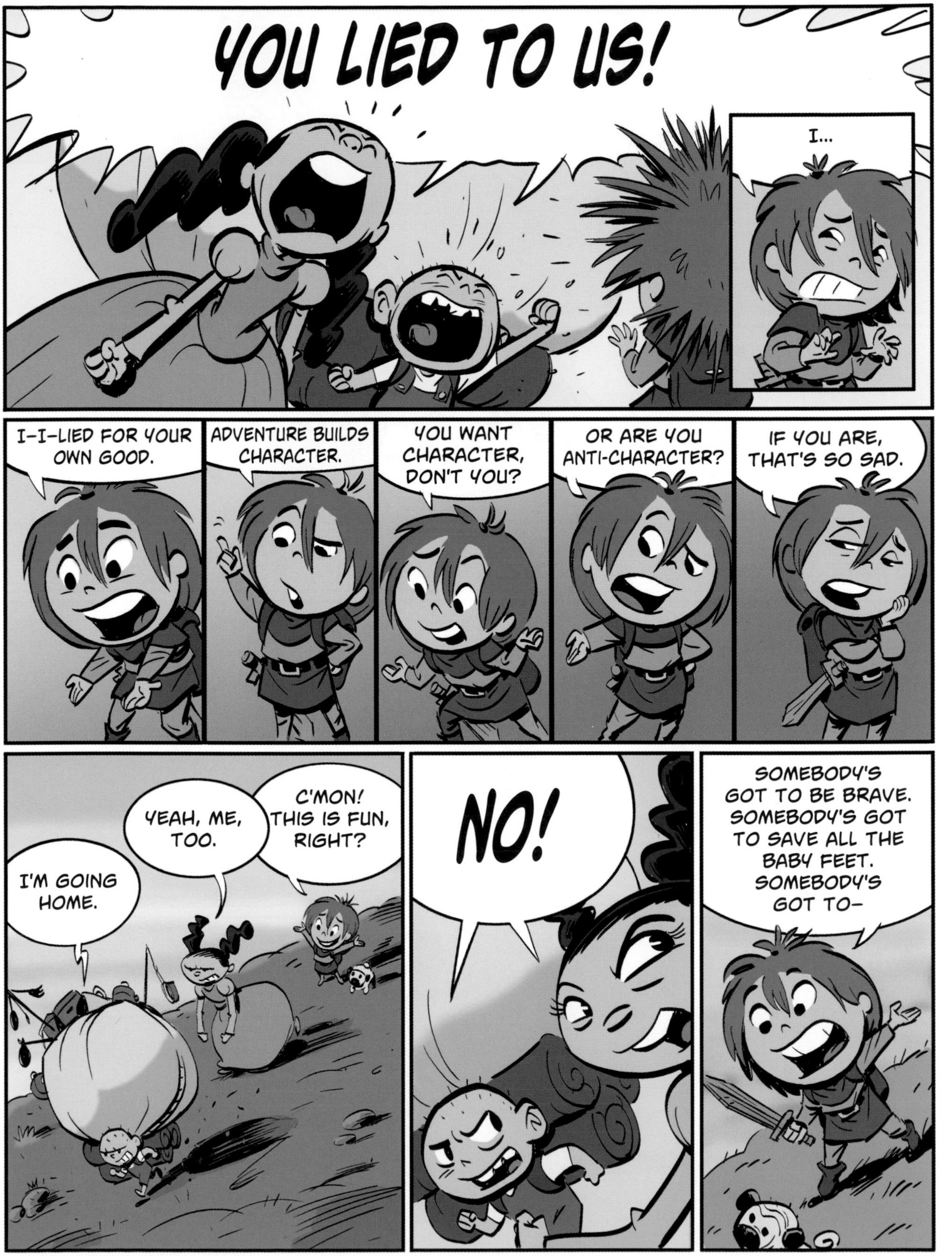
YOU LIED TO US!
I...
I-I-LIED FOR YOUR OWN GOOD.
ADVENTURE BUILDS CHARACTER.
YOU WANT CHARACTER, DON'T YOU?
OR ARE YOU ANTI-CHARACTER?
IF YOU ARE, THAT'S SO SAD.
I'M GOING HOME.
YEAH, ME, TOO.
C'MON! THIS IS FUN, RIGHT?
NO!
SOMEBODY'S GOT TO BE BRAVE. SOMEBODY'S GOT TO SAVE ALL THE BABY FEET. SOMEBODY'S GOT TO–

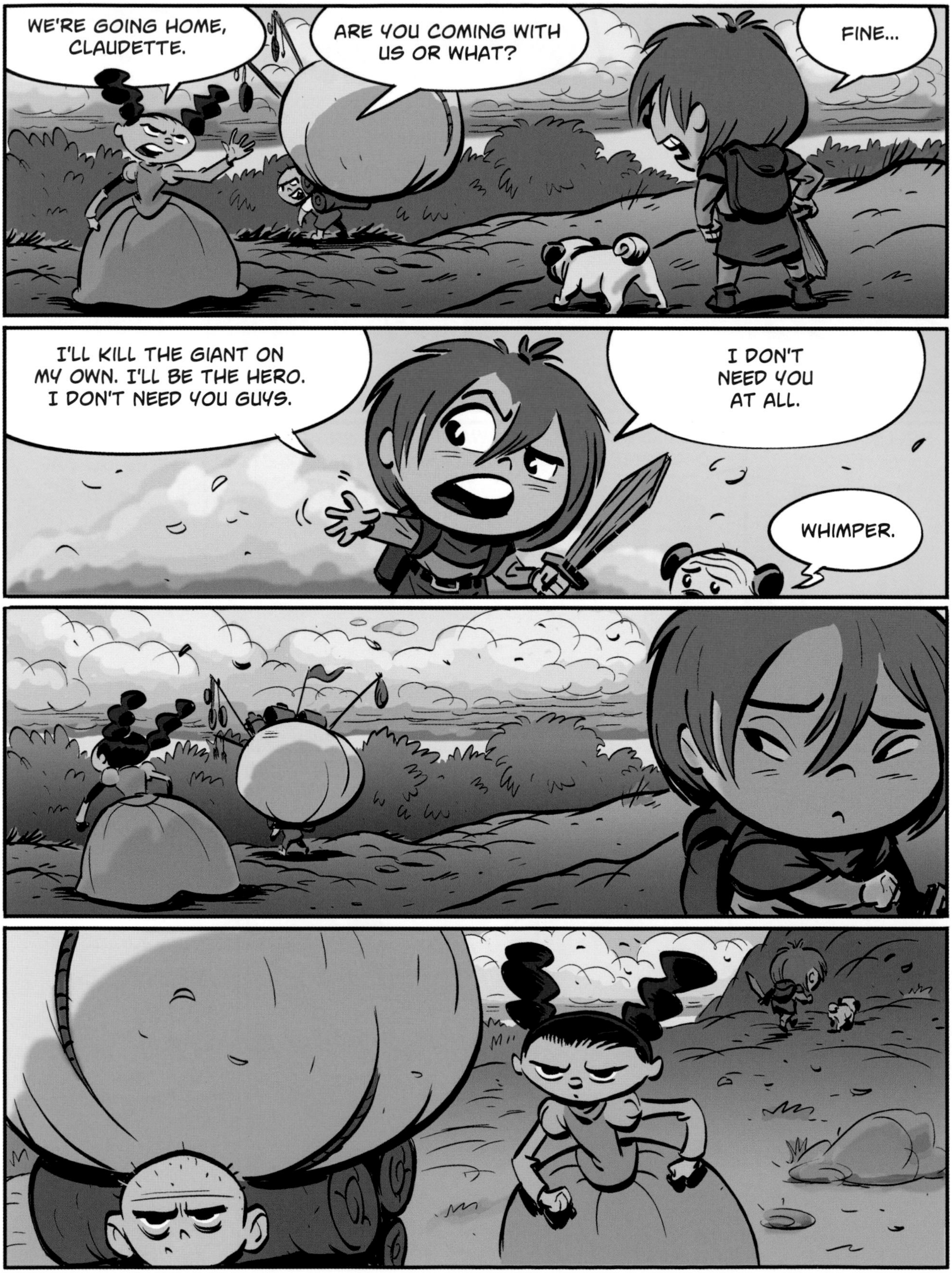
WE'RE GOING HOME, CLAUDETTE.
ARE YOU COMING WITH US OR WHAT?
FINE...
I'LL KILL THE GIANT ON MY OWN. I'LL BE THE HERO. I DON'T NEED YOU GUYS.
I DON'T NEED YOU AT ALL.
WHIMPER.

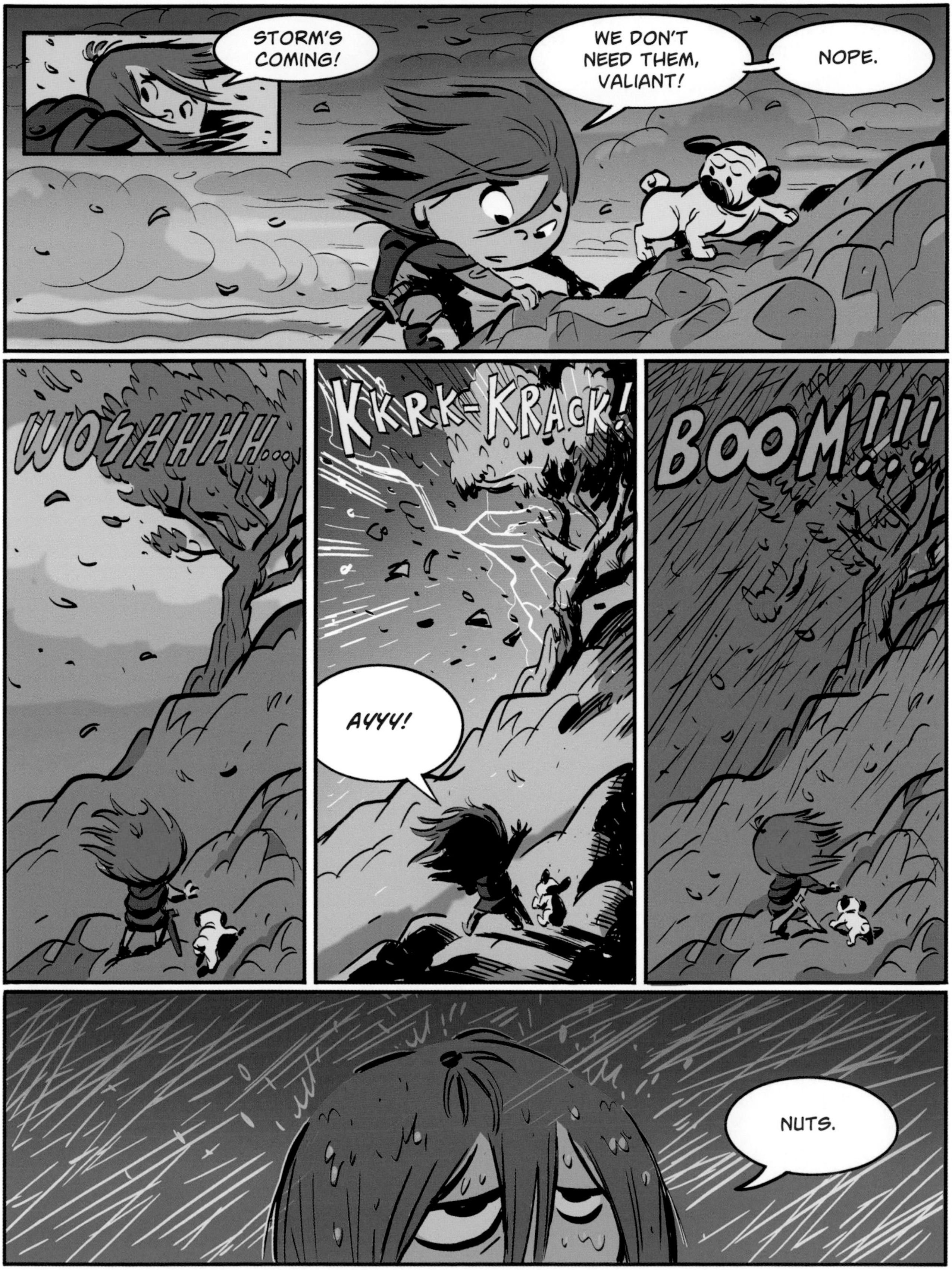
STORM'S COMING!
WE DON'T NEED THEM, VALIANT!
NOPE.
WOSHHHH...
KKRK-KRACK!
AYYY!
BOOM!!!...
NUTS.

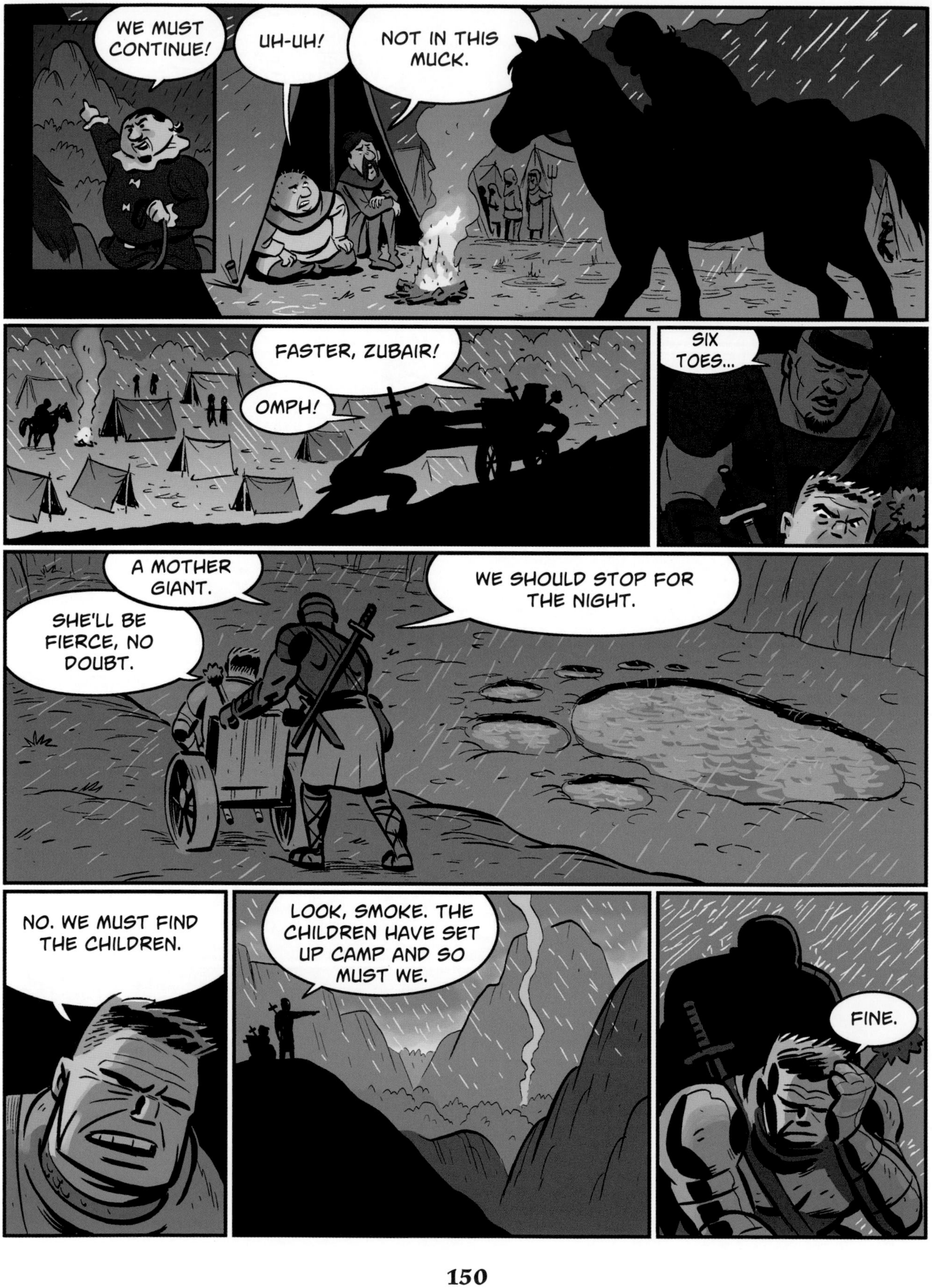
WE MUST CONTINUE!
UH-UH!
NOT IN THIS MUCK.
FASTER, ZUBAIR!
OMPH!
SIX TOES...
A MOTHER GIANT.
SHE'LL BE FIERCE, NO DOUBT.
WE SHOULD STOP FOR THE NIGHT.
NO. WE MUST FIND THE CHILDREN.
LOOK, SMOKE. THE CHILDREN HAVE SET UP CAMP AND SO MUST WE.
FINE.

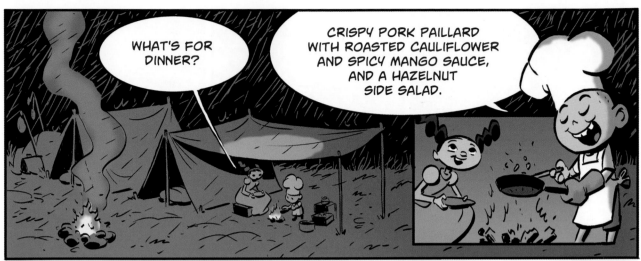

WHAT'S FOR DINNER?

CRISPY PORK PAILLARD WITH ROASTED CAULIFLOWER AND SPICY MANGO SAUCE, AND A HAZELNUT SIDE SALAD.

SORRY, I COULDN'T DO ANYTHING FANCY.

THANKS, GASTON.

I HOPE SHE'S OKAY.

ME, TOO.

I'M NOT SCARED.

I'M NOT SCARED.

NOT SCARED.

REALLY NOT SCARED.

ARF.

KRRR-AA

IC BOOM!

OH, BOY.

HUFF...HUFF!

UMPH!

UH!

GRRRR!

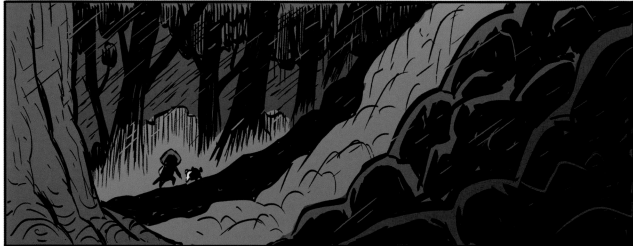

LOOK SHARP, VALIANT.

NOTHING TO BE SCARED OF!

NOTHING!

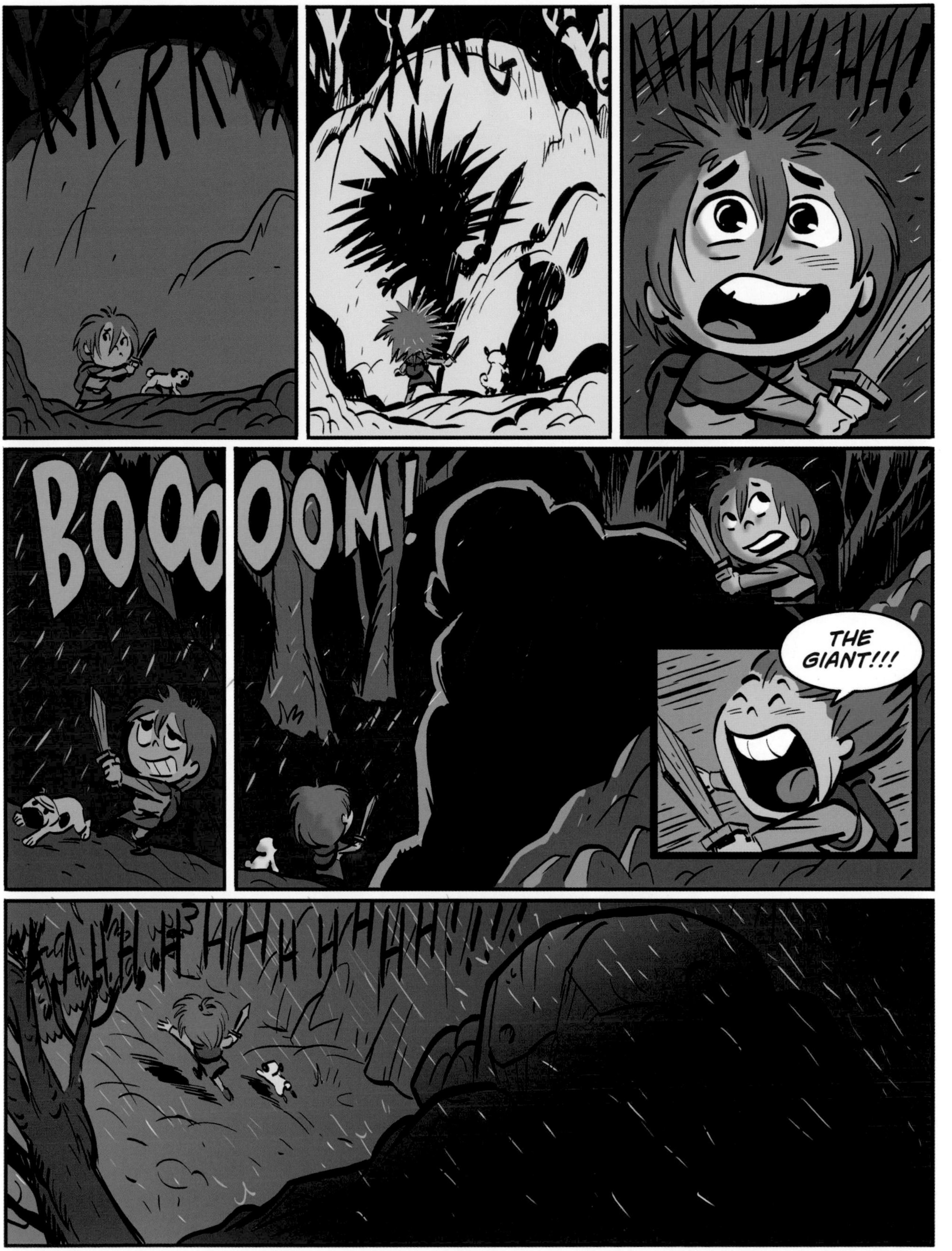
AHHHHHHHH!
BOOOOOM!
THE GIANT!!!
AAHHHHHHHHHHHH!!!

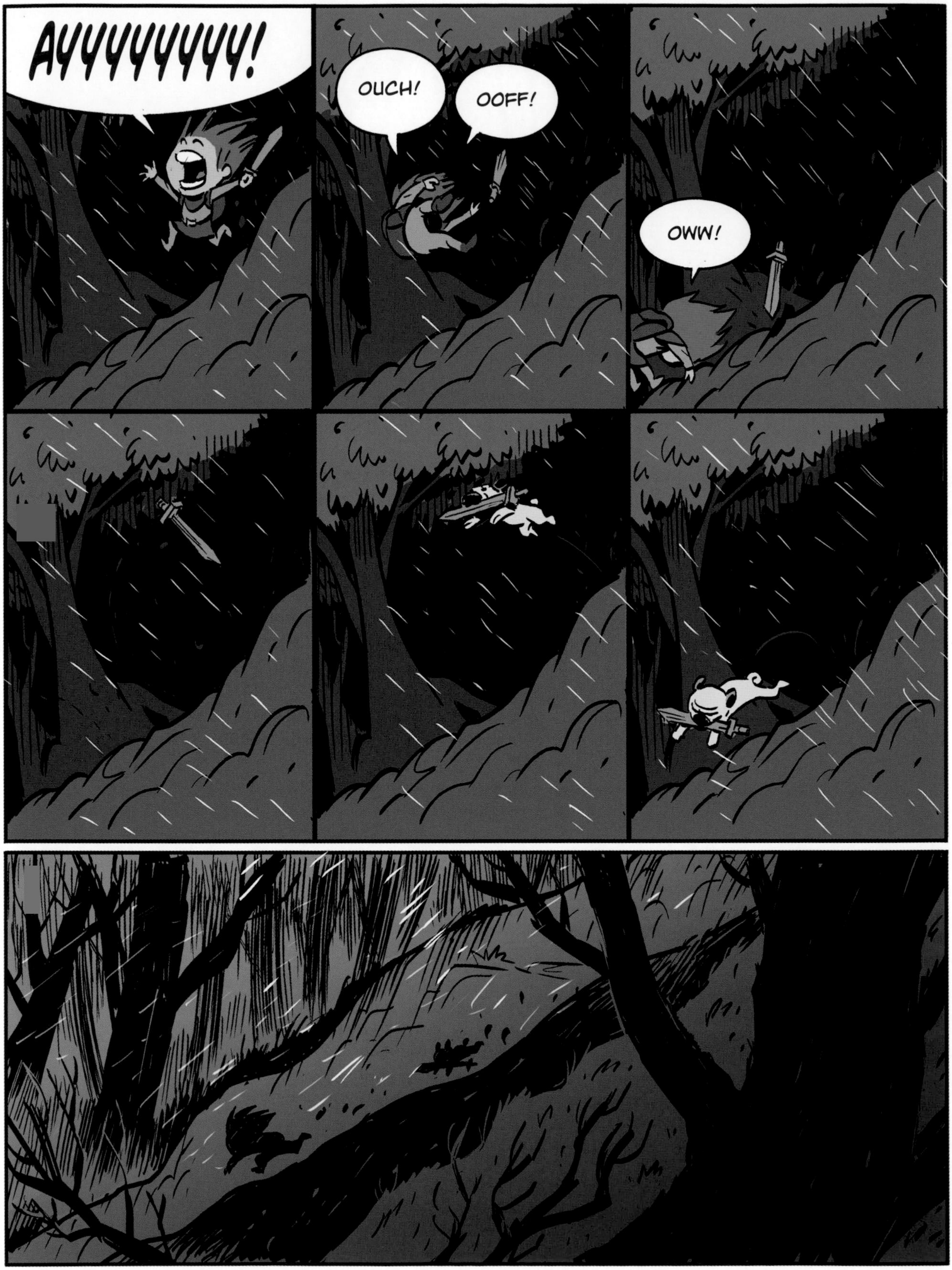
AYYYYYYYY!
OUCH!
OOFF!
OWW!

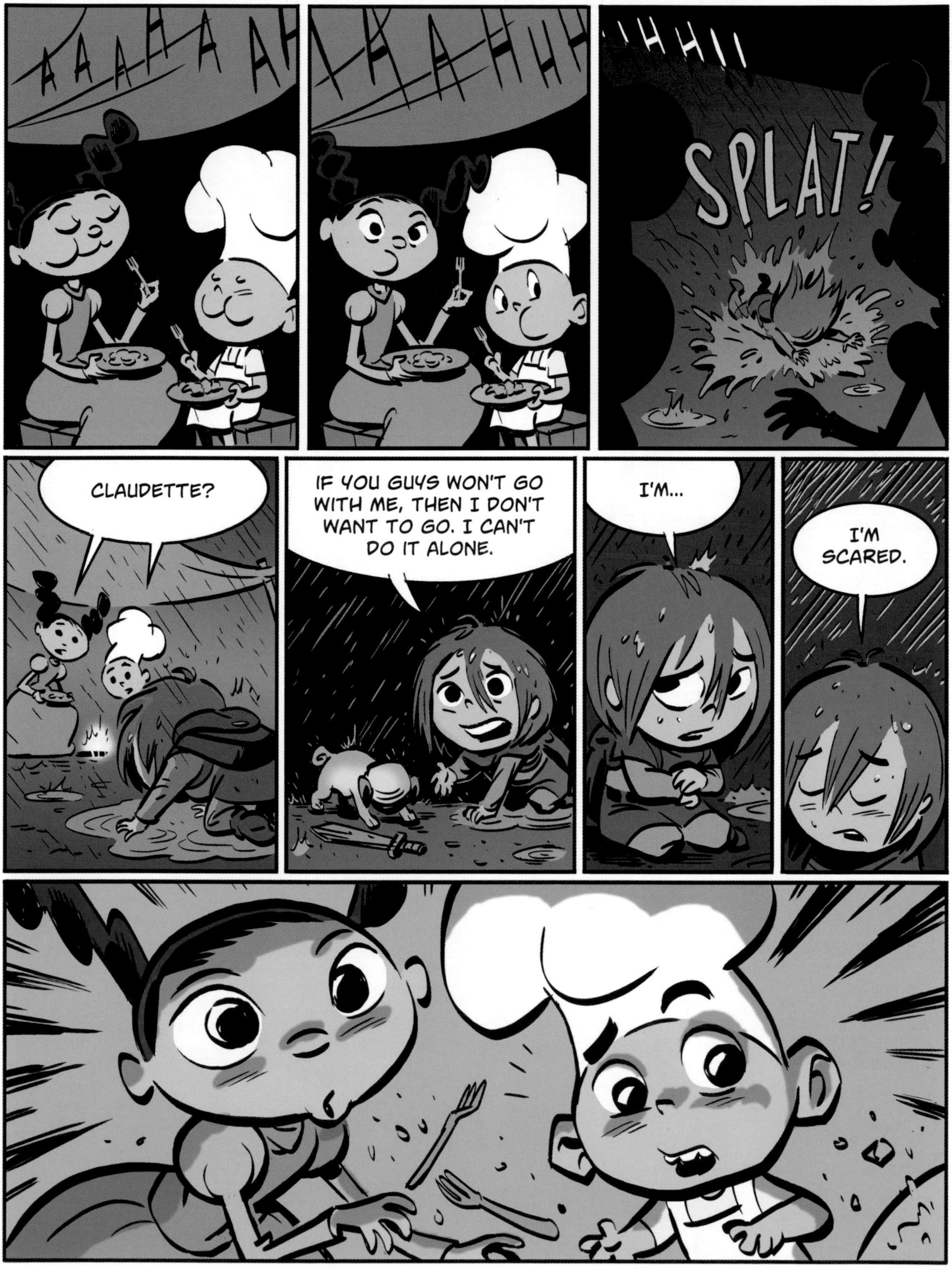
AAAAAH
AAAAHHH
HHHH!!
SPLAT!
CLAUDETTE?
IF YOU GUYS WON'T GO WITH ME, THEN I DON'T WANT TO GO. I CAN'T DO IT ALONE.
I'M...
I'M SCARED.

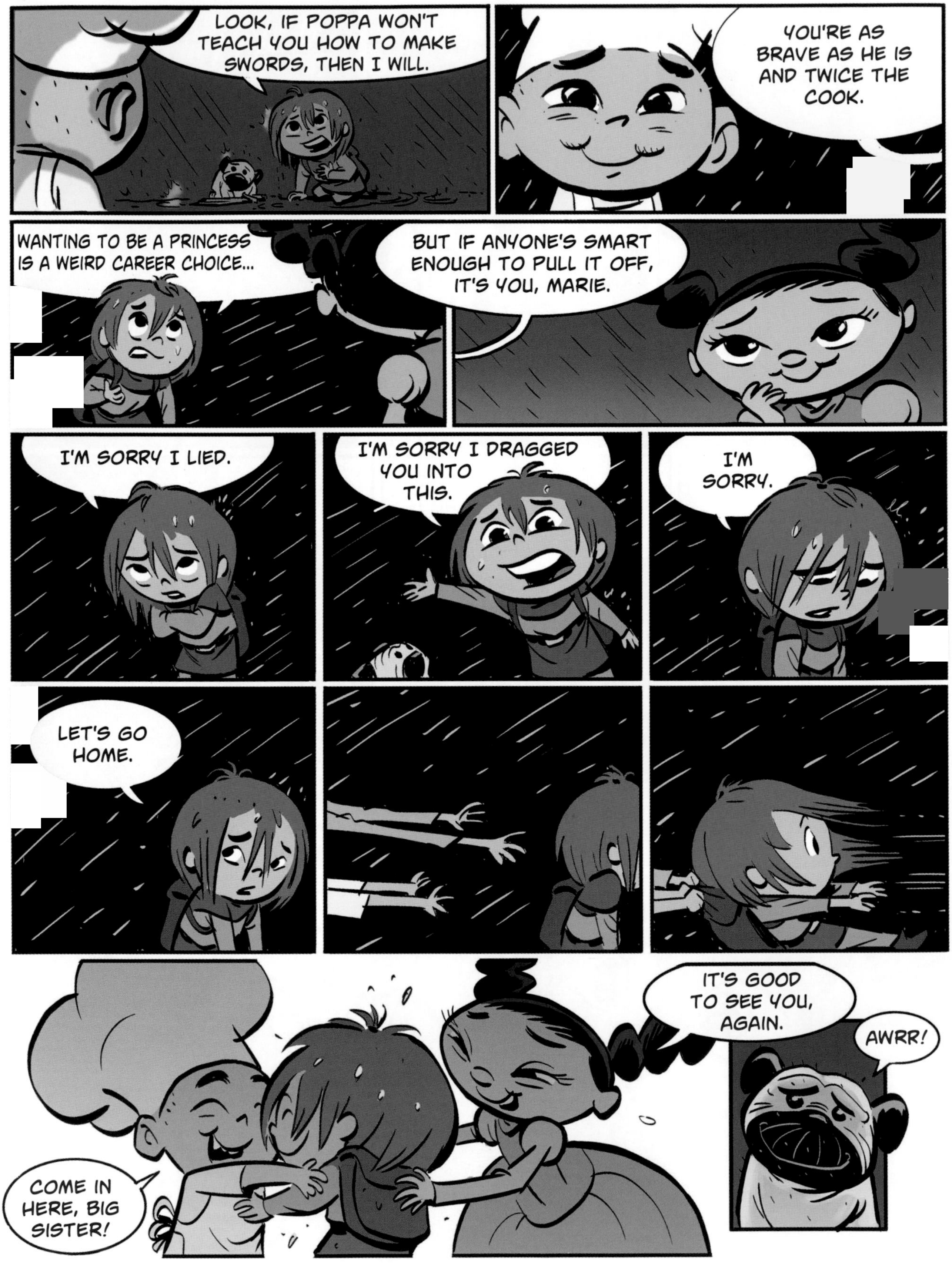
LOOK, IF POPPA WON'T TEACH YOU HOW TO MAKE SWORDS, THEN I WILL.
YOU'RE AS BRAVE AS HE IS AND TWICE THE COOK.
WANTING TO BE A PRINCESS IS A WEIRD CAREER CHOICE...
BUT IF ANYONE'S SMART ENOUGH TO PULL IT OFF, IT'S YOU, MARIE.
I'M SORRY I LIED.
I'M SORRY I DRAGGED YOU INTO THIS.
I'M SORRY.
LET'S GO HOME.
IT'S GOOD TO SEE YOU, AGAIN.
AWRR!
COME IN HERE, BIG SISTER!

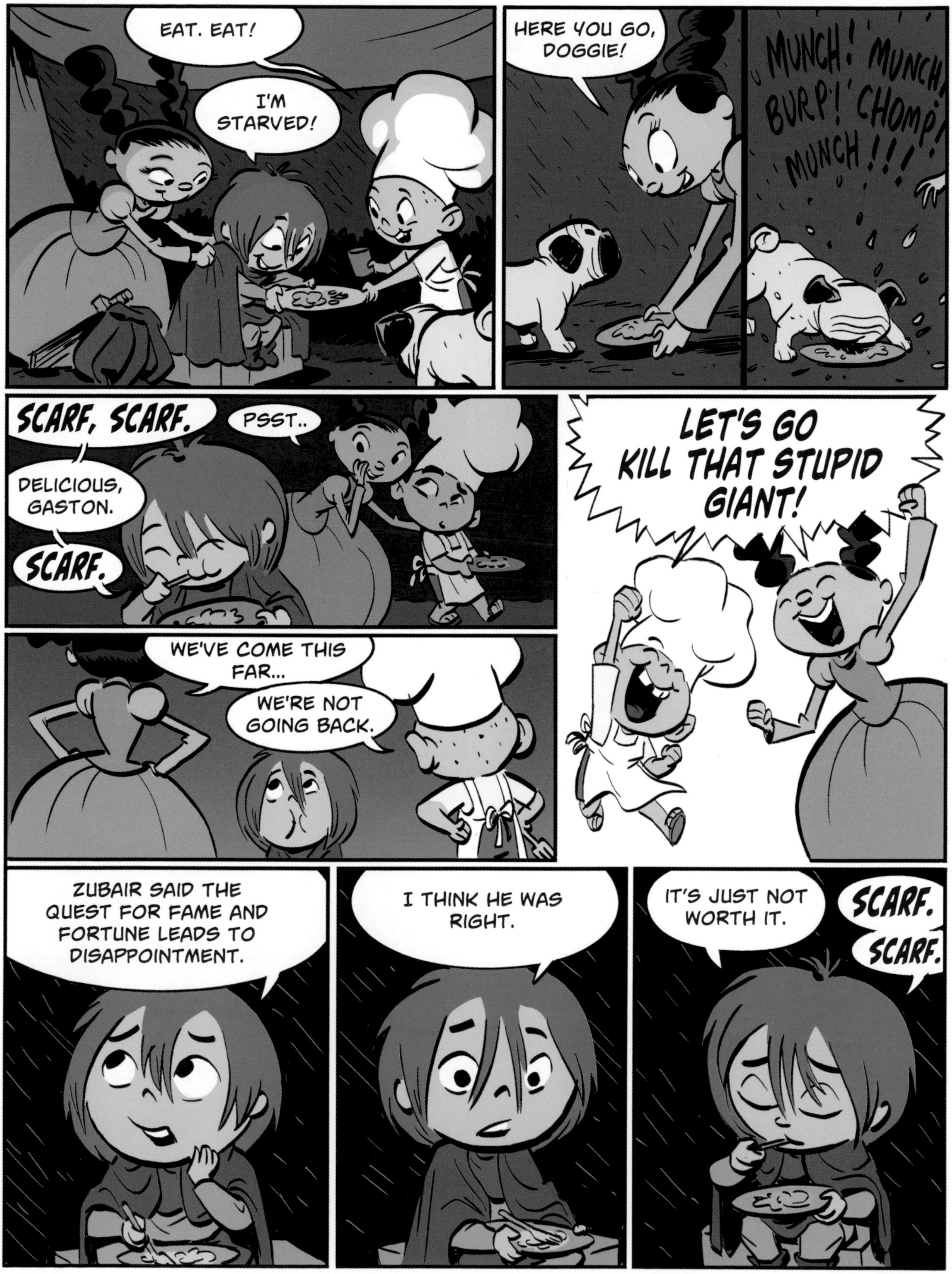
EAT. EAT!
I'M STARVED!
HERE YOU GO, DOGGIE!
MUNCH! MUNCH! BURP! CHOMP! MUNCH!!!
SCARF, SCARF.
DELICIOUS, GASTON.
SCARF.
PSST..
LET'S GO KILL THAT STUPID GIANT!
WE'VE COME THIS FAR...
WE'RE NOT GOING BACK.
ZUBAIR SAID THE QUEST FOR FAME AND FORTUNE LEADS TO DISAPPOINTMENT.
I THINK HE WAS RIGHT.
IT'S JUST NOT WORTH IT.
SCARF.
SCARF.

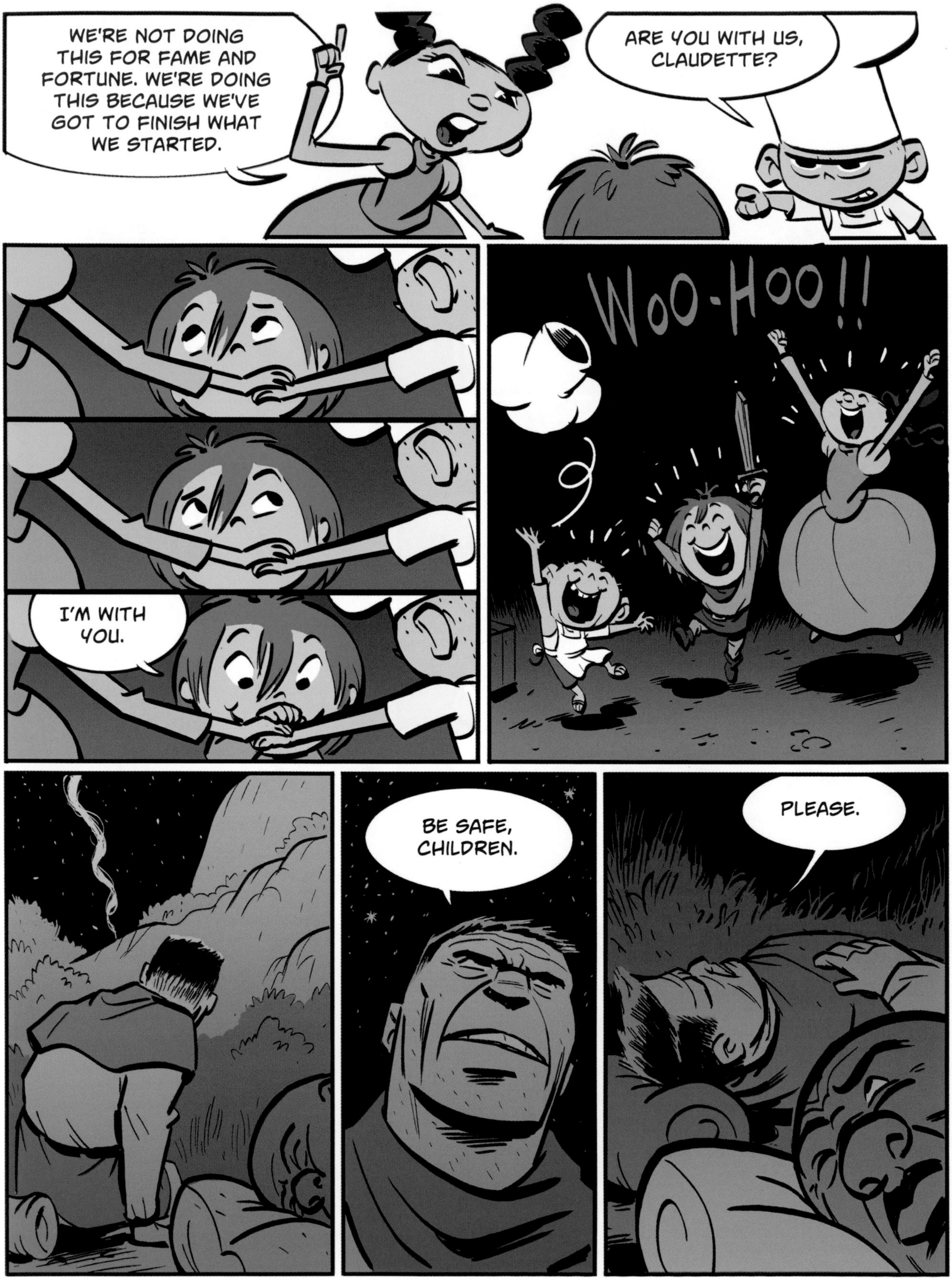
WE'RE NOT DOING THIS FOR FAME AND FORTUNE. WE'RE DOING THIS BECAUSE WE'VE GOT TO FINISH WHAT WE STARTED.
ARE YOU WITH US, CLAUDETTE?
I'M WITH YOU.
WOO-HOO!!
BE SAFE, CHILDREN.
PLEASE.

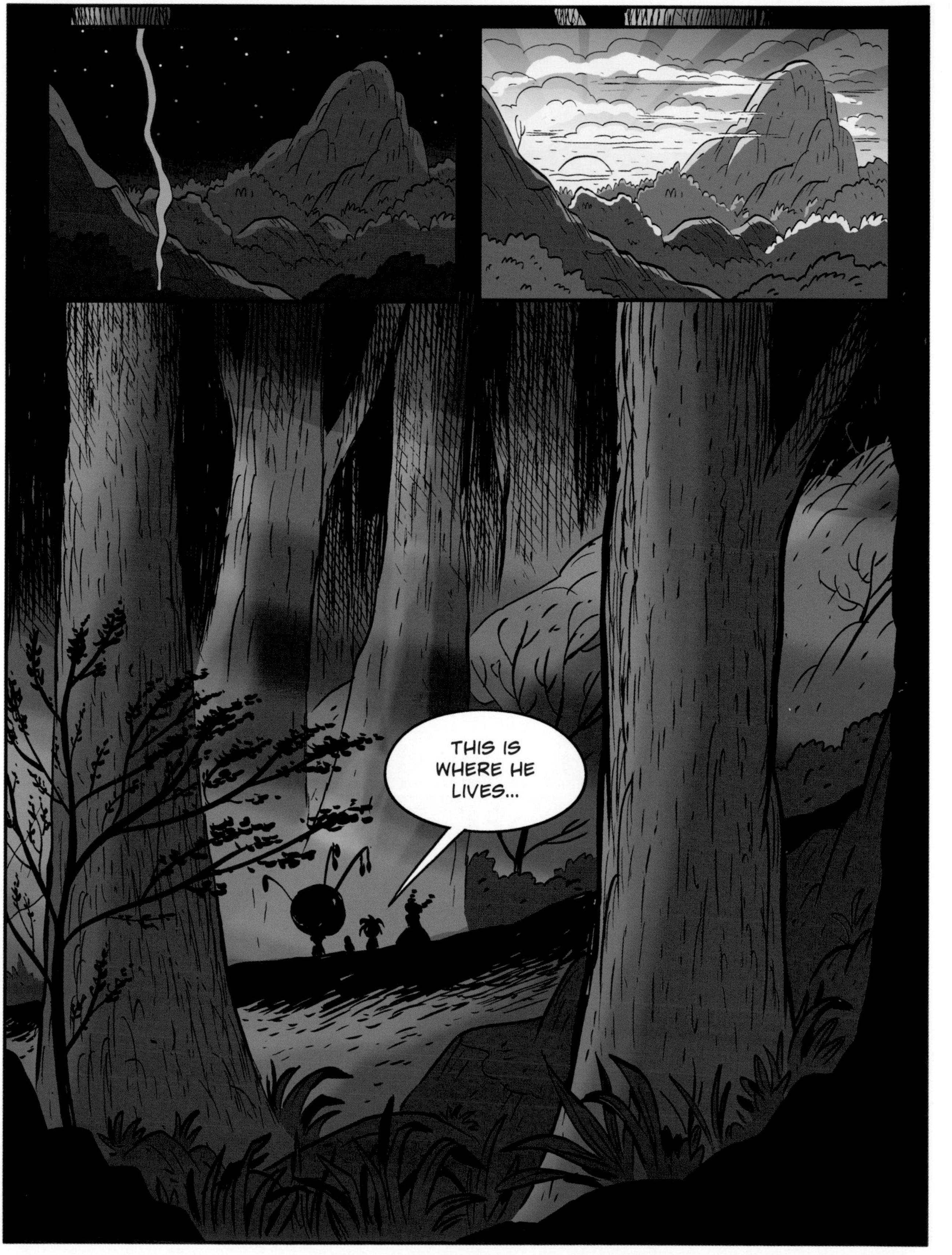
THIS IS WHERE HE LIVES...

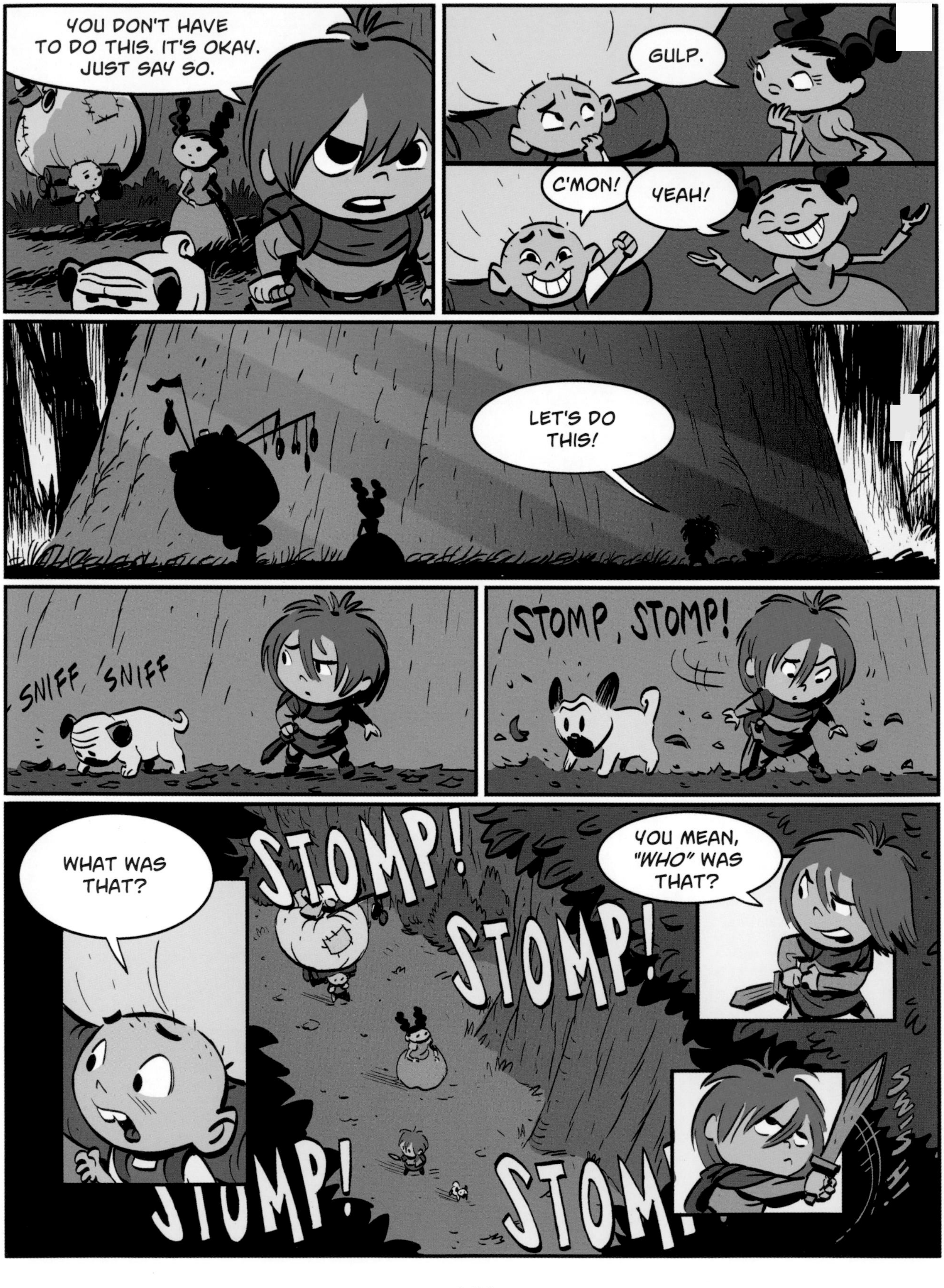
YOU DON'T HAVE TO DO THIS. IT'S OKAY. JUST SAY SO.
GULP.
C'MON!
YEAH!
LET'S DO THIS!
SNIFF, SNIFF
STOMP, STOMP!
WHAT WAS THAT?
STOMP!
STOMP!
YOU MEAN, "WHO" WAS THAT?
STOMP!
STOM!
SWISH!

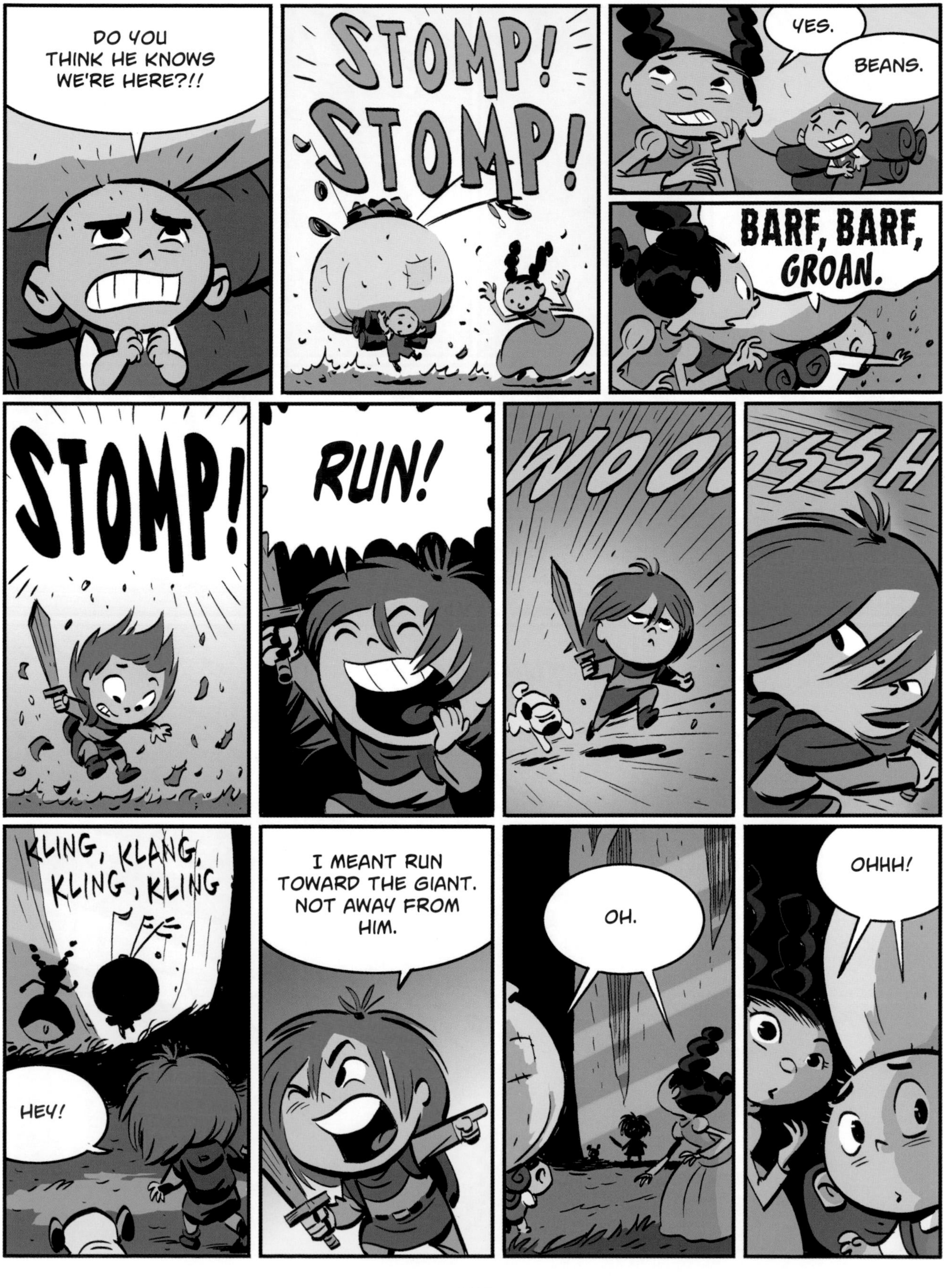
DO YOU THINK HE KNOWS WE'RE HERE?!!
STOMP! STOMP!
YES.
BEANS.
BARF, BARF, GROAN.
STOMP!
RUN!
WOOOSSH
KLING, KLANG, KLING, KLING
HEY!
I MEANT RUN TOWARD THE GIANT. NOT AWAY FROM HIM.
OH.
OHHH!

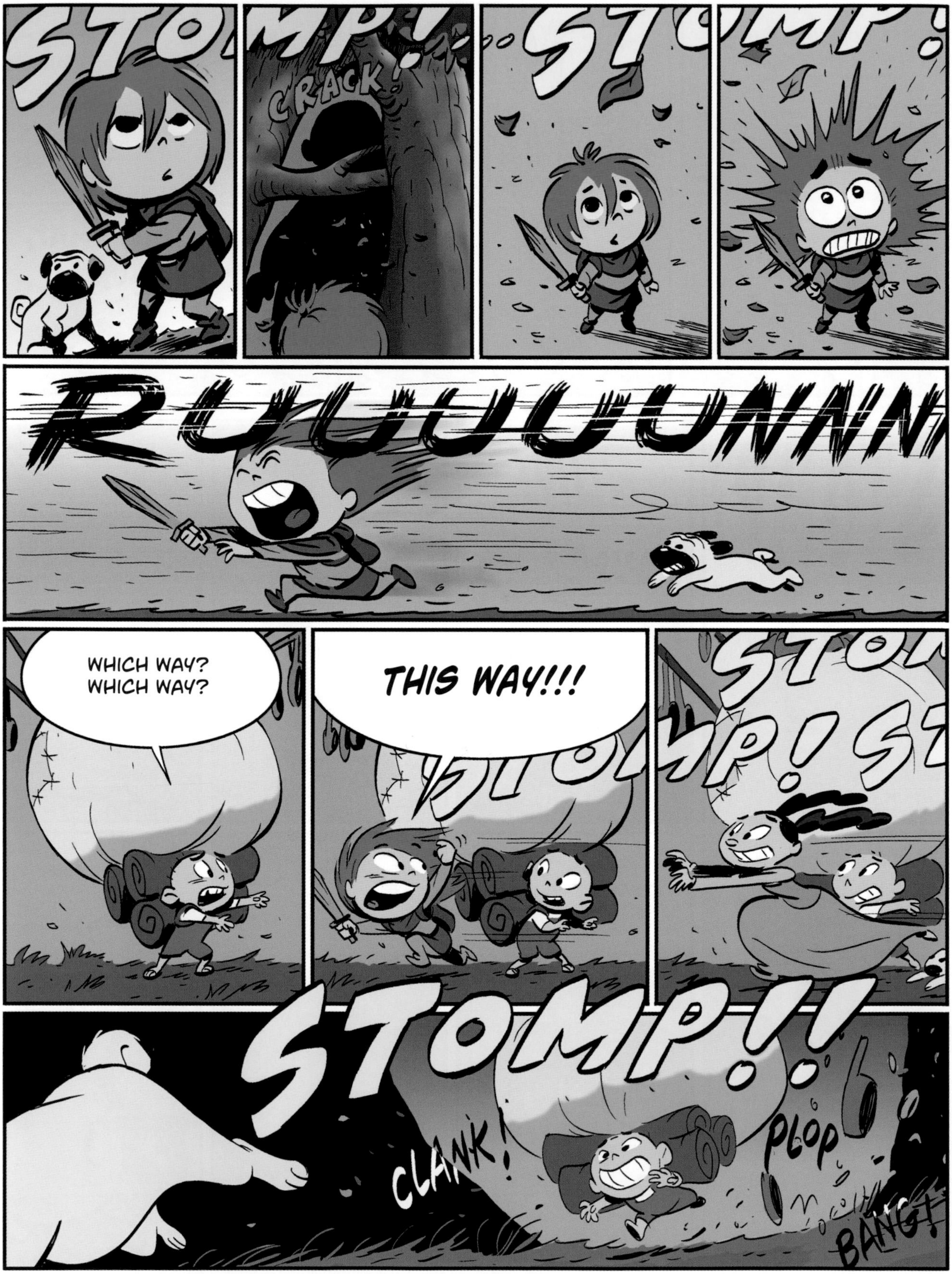
STOMP!
CRACK!
STOMP!
RUUUUUNNN
WHICH WAY? WHICH WAY?
THIS WAY!!!
STOMP! STOMP! ST
STOMP!!
CLANK!
PLOP
BANG!

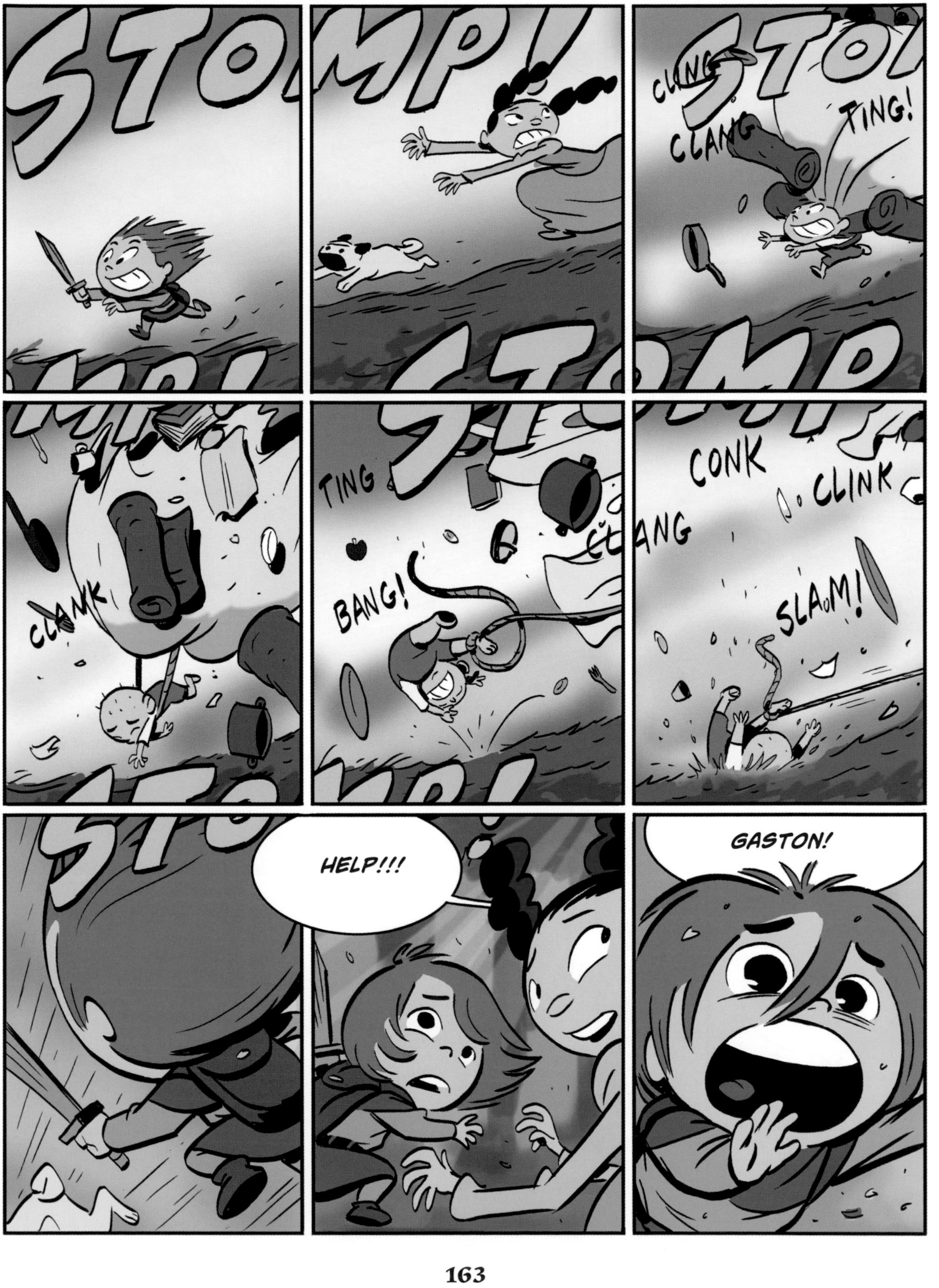
STOMP!
CLING
CLANG
TING!
STOMP!
CLANK
TING
BANG!
CLANG
CONK
CLINK
SLAM!
STOMP!
HELP!!!
GASTON!

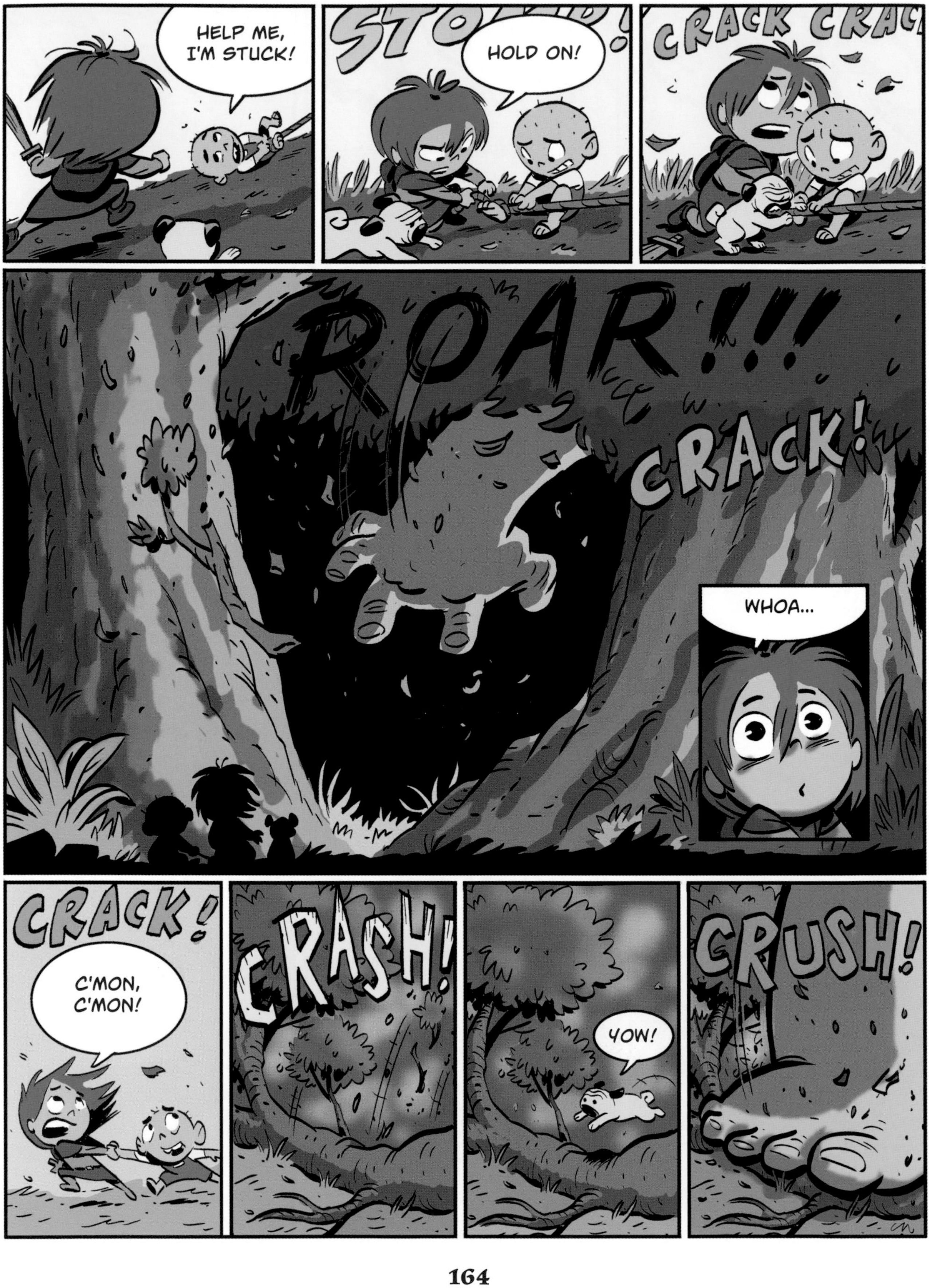
HELP ME, I'M STUCK!
HOLD ON!
CRACK CRAC
ROAR!!!
CRACK!
WHOA...
CRACK!
C'MON, C'MON!
CRASH!
YOW!
CRUSH!

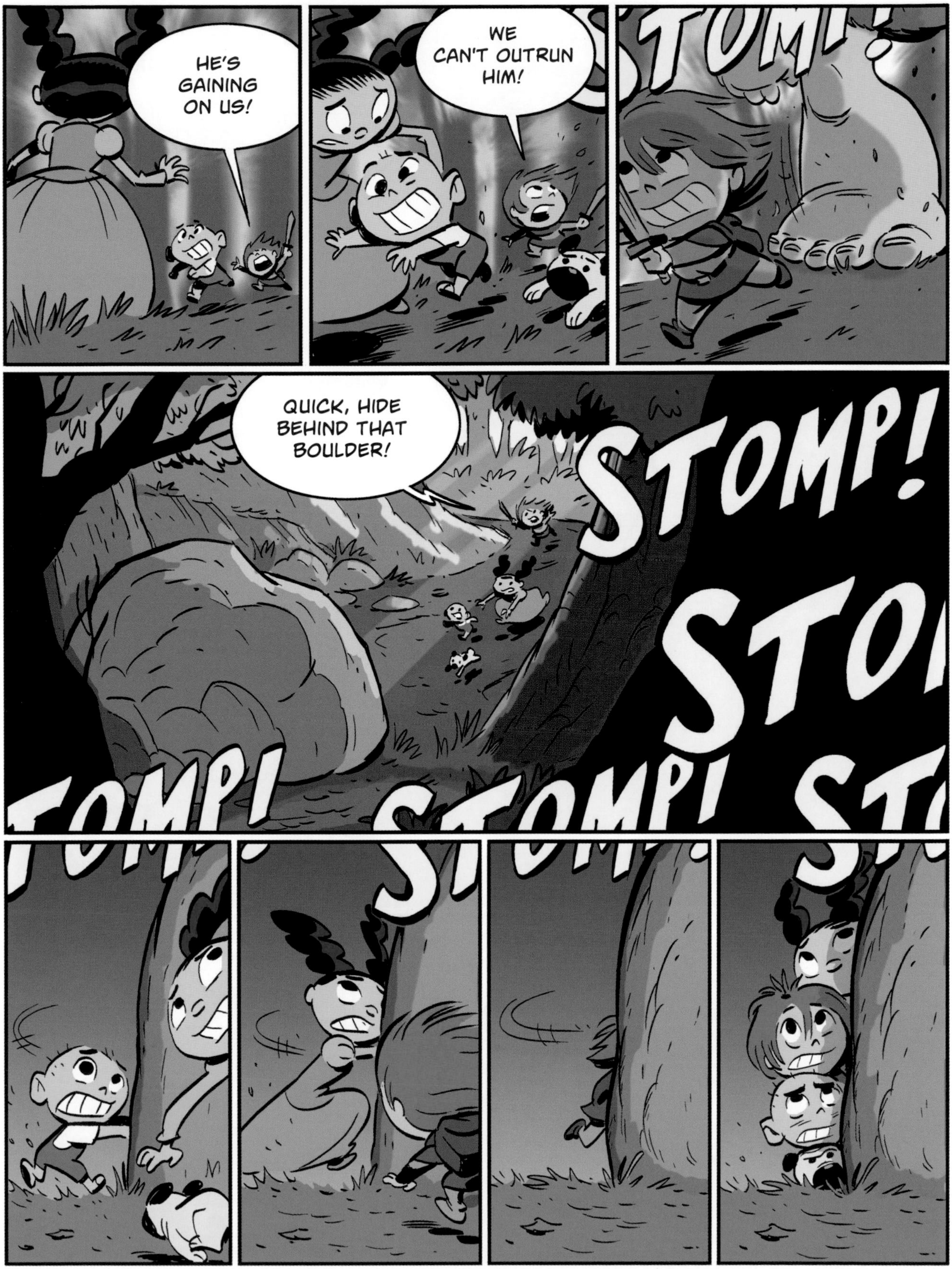
HE'S GAINING ON US!
WE CAN'T OUTRUN HIM!
STOMP!
QUICK, HIDE BEHIND THAT BOULDER!
STOMP!
STOMP!
STOMP!
STOMP!

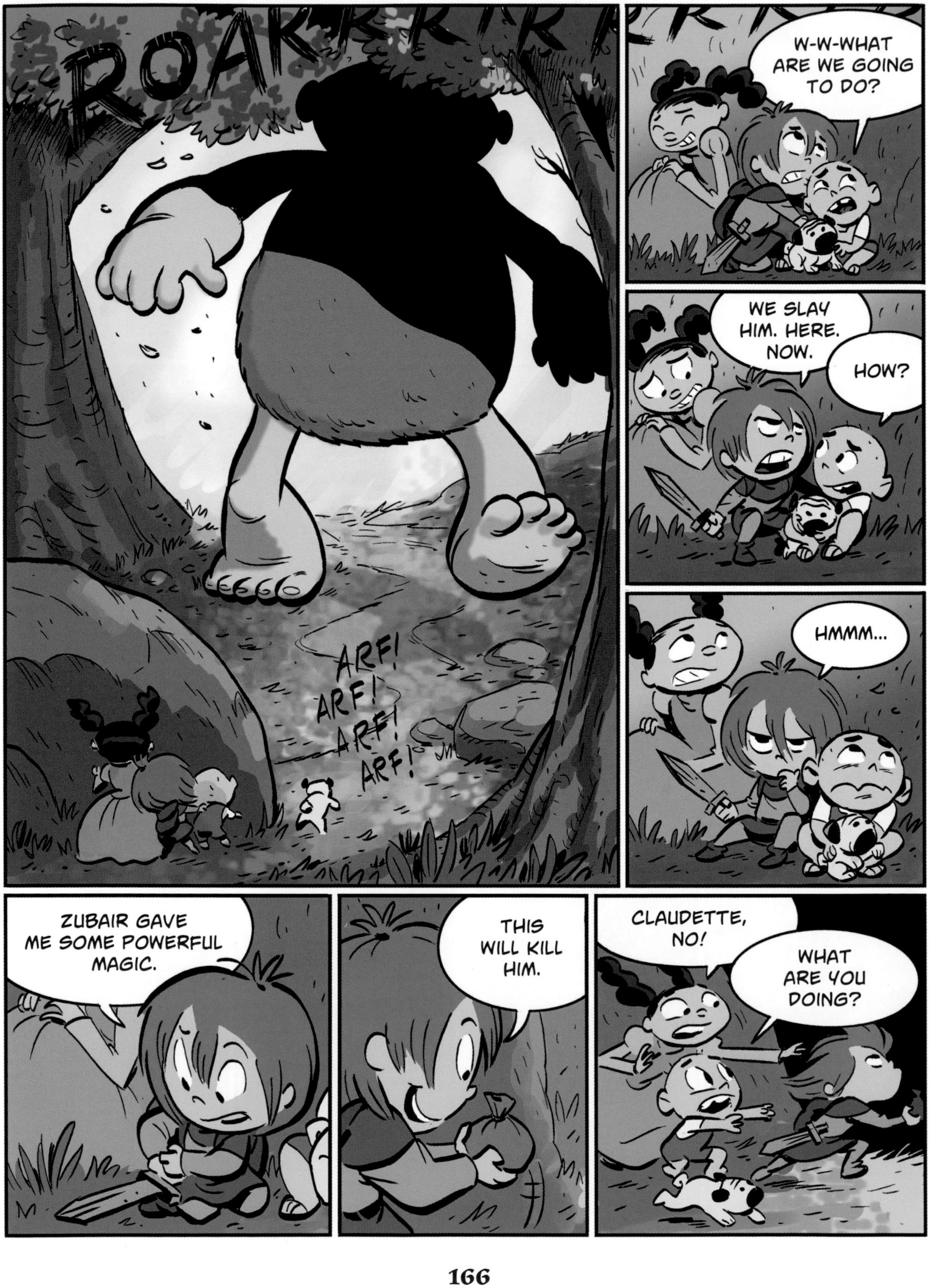
ROARRRRRRR
ARF! ARF! ARF! ARF!
W-W-WHAT ARE WE GOING TO DO?
WE SLAY HIM. HERE. NOW.
HOW?
HMMM...
ZUBAIR GAVE ME SOME POWERFUL MAGIC.
THIS WILL KILL HIM.
CLAUDETTE, NO!
WHAT ARE YOU DOING?

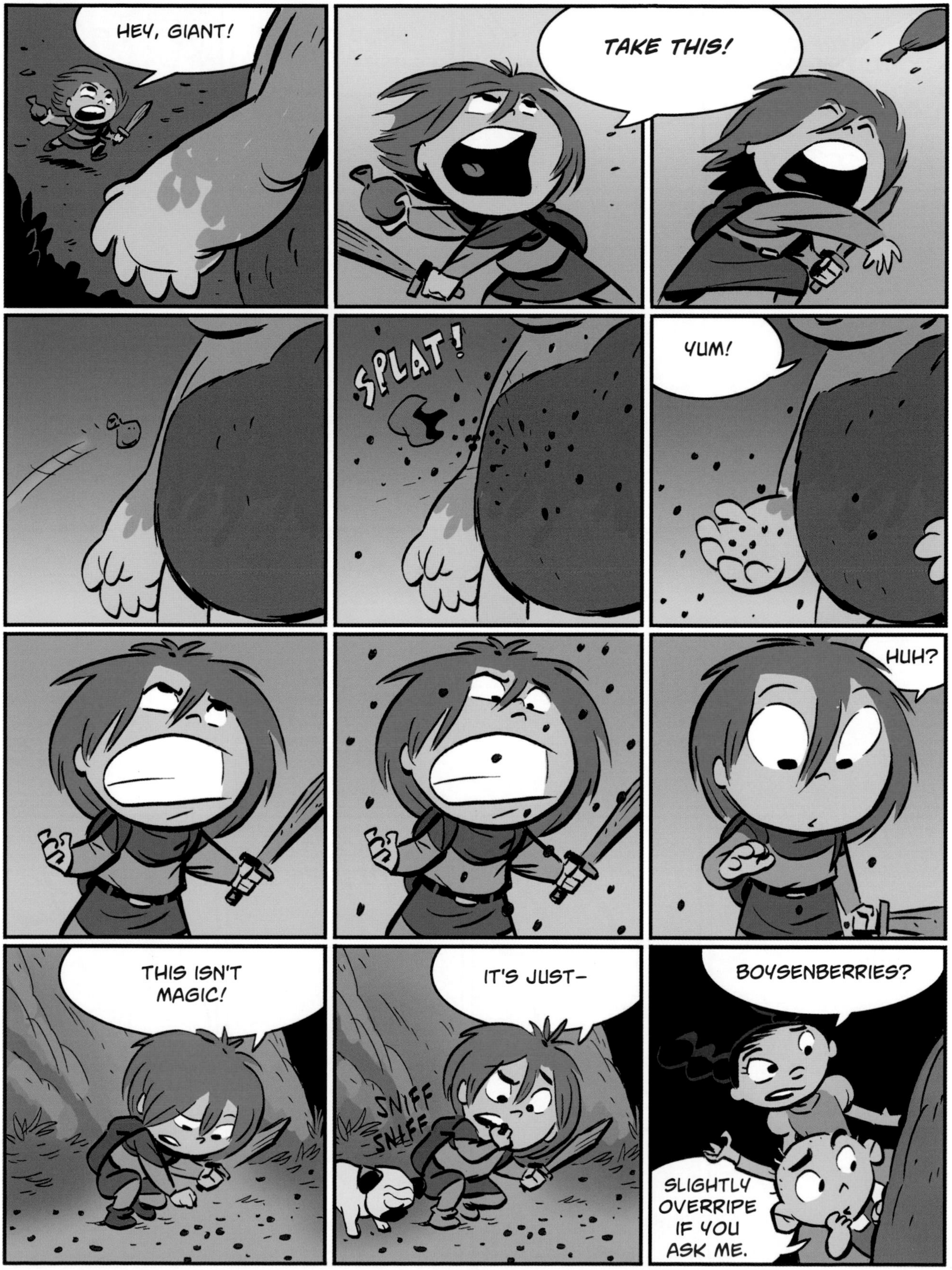
HEY, GIANT!
TAKE THIS!
SPLAT!
YUM!
HUH?
THIS ISN'T MAGIC!
IT'S JUST-
SNIFF SNIFF
BOYSENBERRIES?
SLIGHTLY OVERRIPE IF YOU ASK ME.

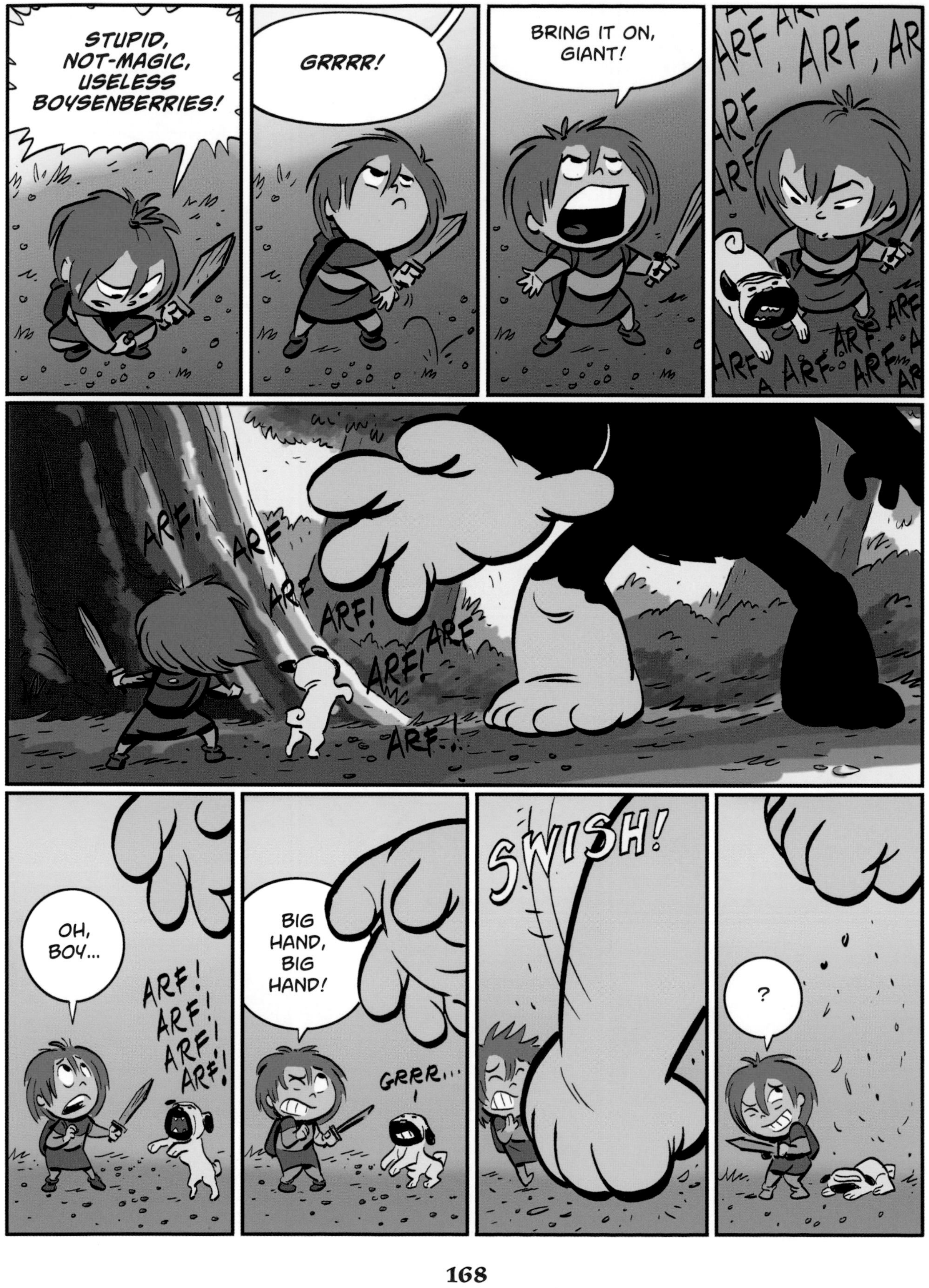
STUPID, NOT-MAGIC, USELESS BOYSENBERRIES!
GRRRR!
BRING IT ON, GIANT!
ARF, ARF, ARF
ARF! ARF ARF ARF! ARF ARF! ARF!
OH, BOY...
ARF! ARF! ARF! ARF!
BIG HAND, BIG HAND!
GRRR...
SWISH!
?

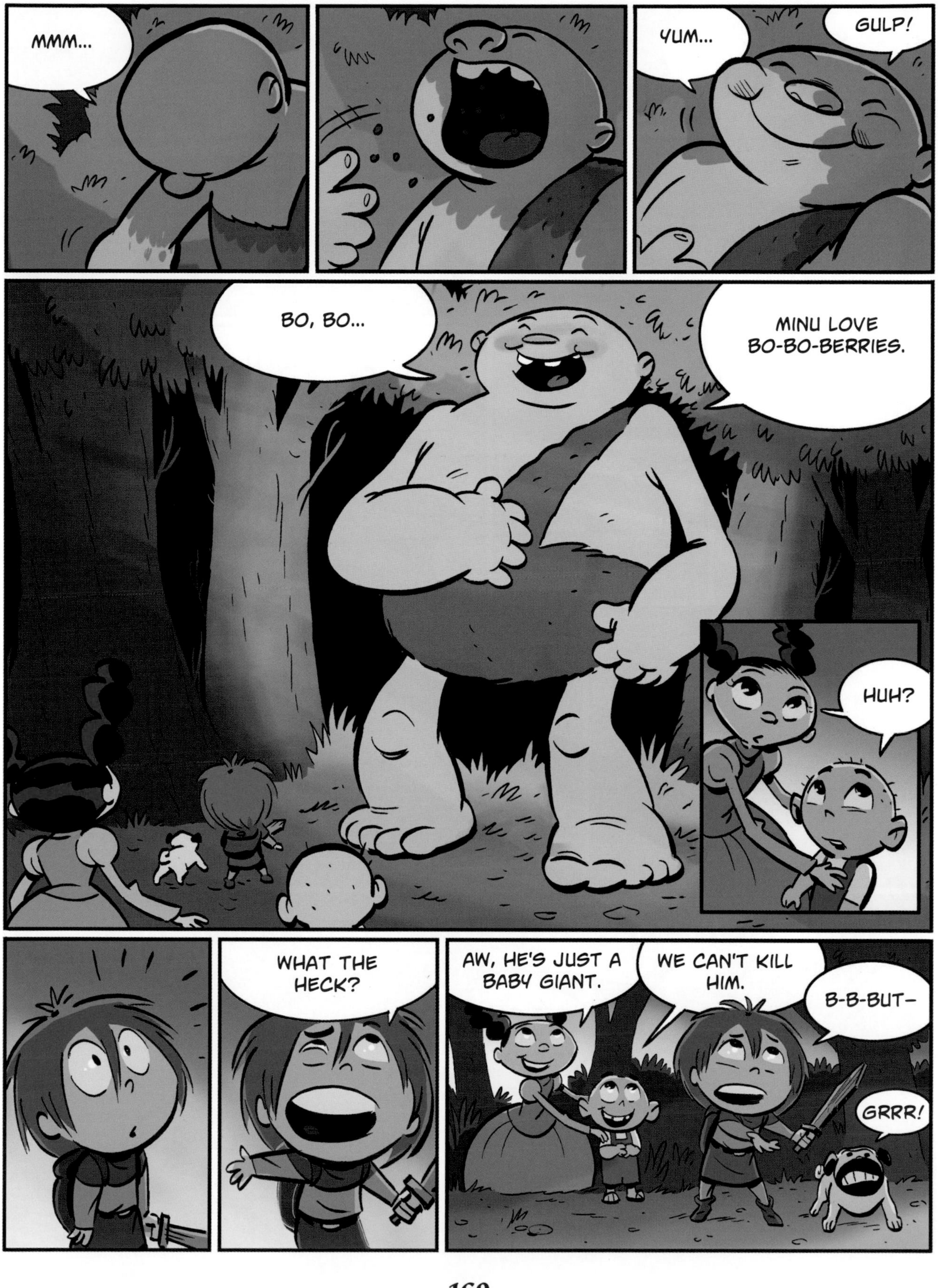
MMM...
YUM...
GULP!
BO, BO...
MINU LOVE BO-BO-BERRIES.
HUH?
WHAT THE HECK?
AW, HE'S JUST A BABY GIANT.
WE CAN'T KILL HIM.
B-B-BUT-
GRRR!

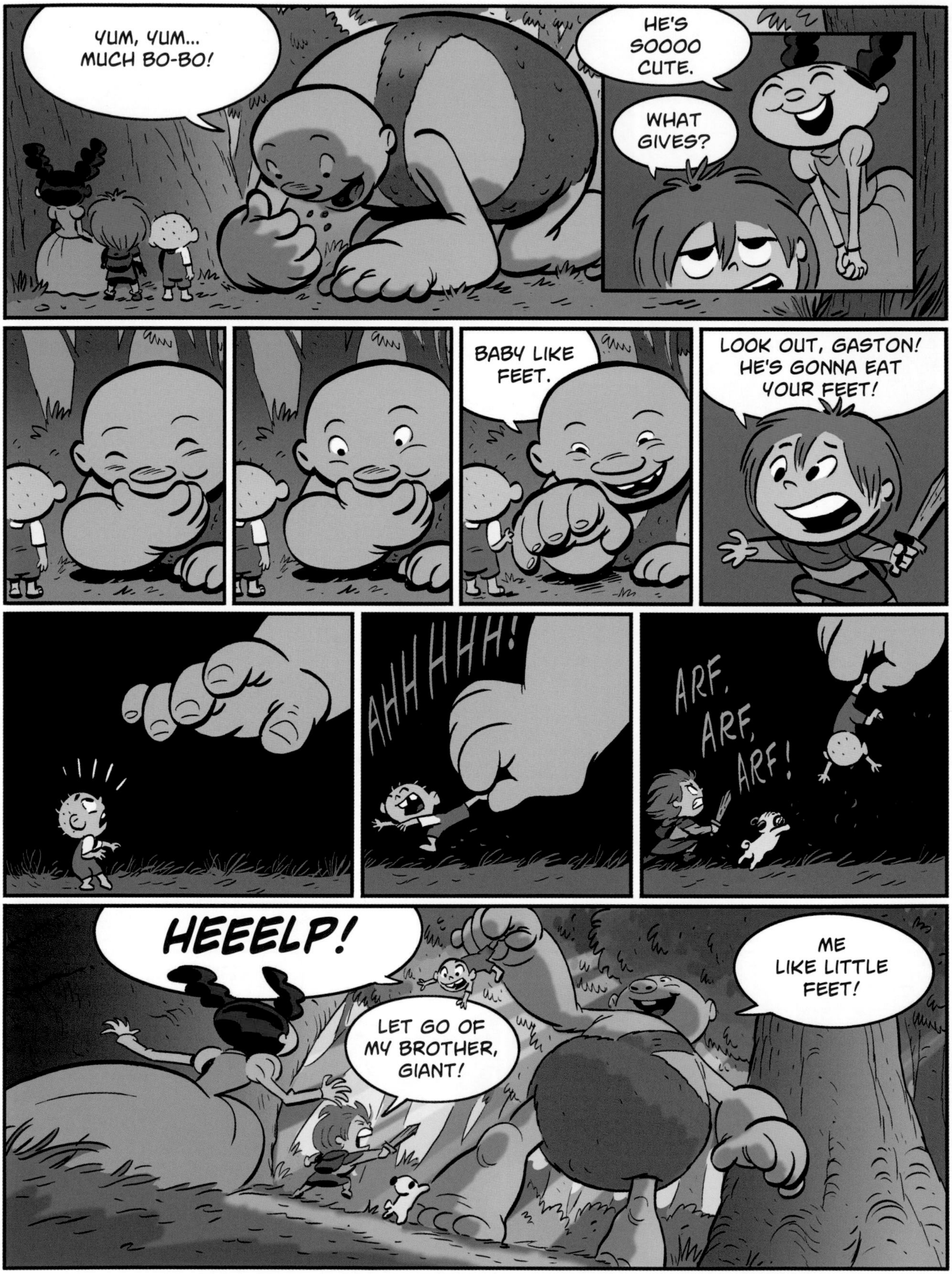
YUM, YUM... MUCH BO-BO!
HE'S SOOOO CUTE.
WHAT GIVES?
BABY LIKE FEET.
LOOK OUT, GASTON! HE'S GONNA EAT YOUR FEET!
AHHHHHH!
ARF, ARF, ARF!
HEEELP!
LET GO OF MY BROTHER, GIANT!
ME LIKE LITTLE FEET!

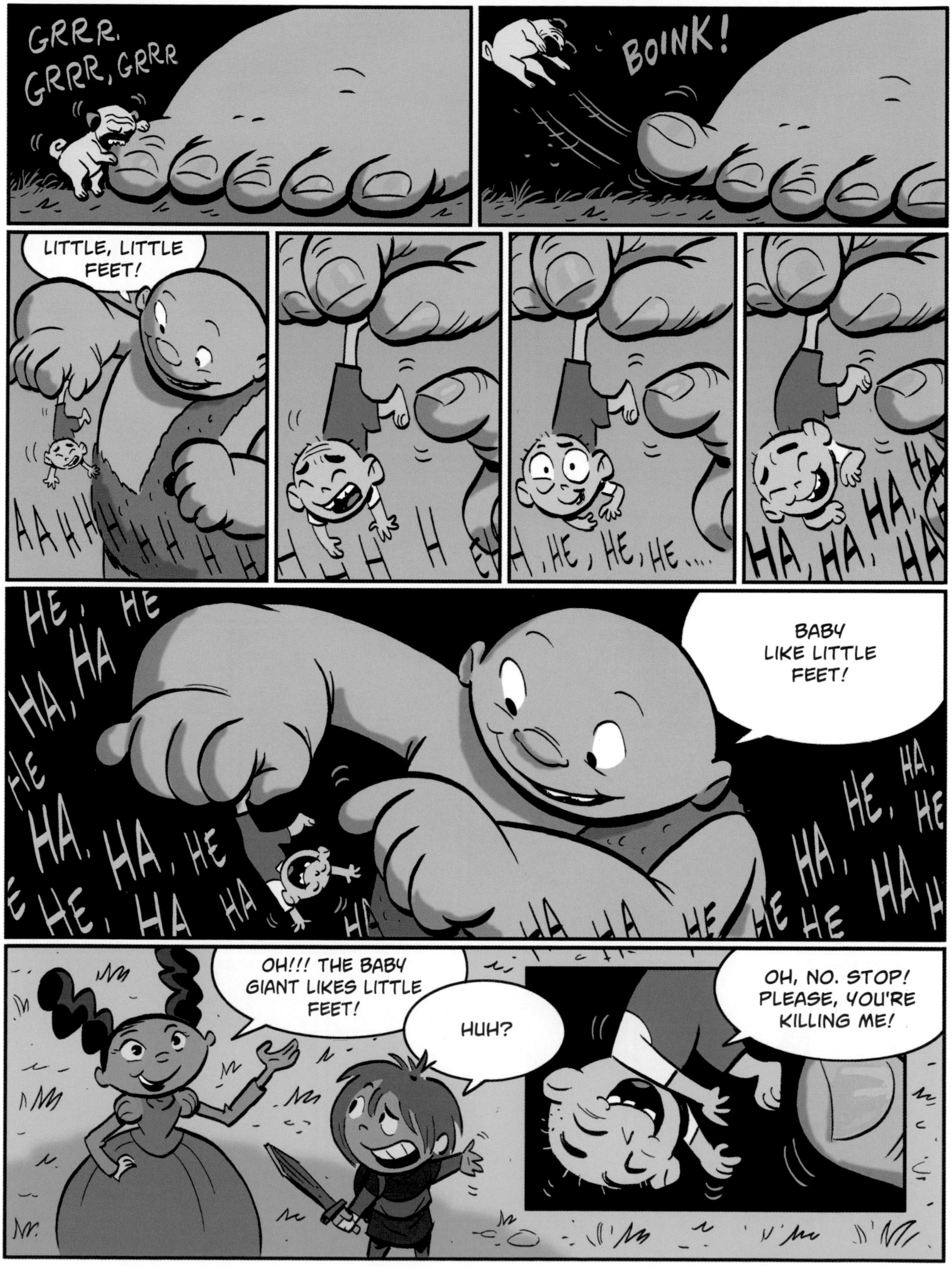
GRRR. GRRR, GRRR
BOINK!
LITTLE, LITTLE FEET!
HAHHHHHHHH
HHHHH
HE, HE, HE...
HA, HA, HA, HA
HE, HE
HA, HA
HE
HA, HA, HE
HE, HA
HA
BABY LIKE LITTLE FEET!
HA, HE
HE, HA
HA
HE
HA, HA, HE
OH!!! THE BABY GIANT LIKES LITTLE FEET!
HUH?
OH, NO. STOP! PLEASE, YOU'RE KILLING ME!

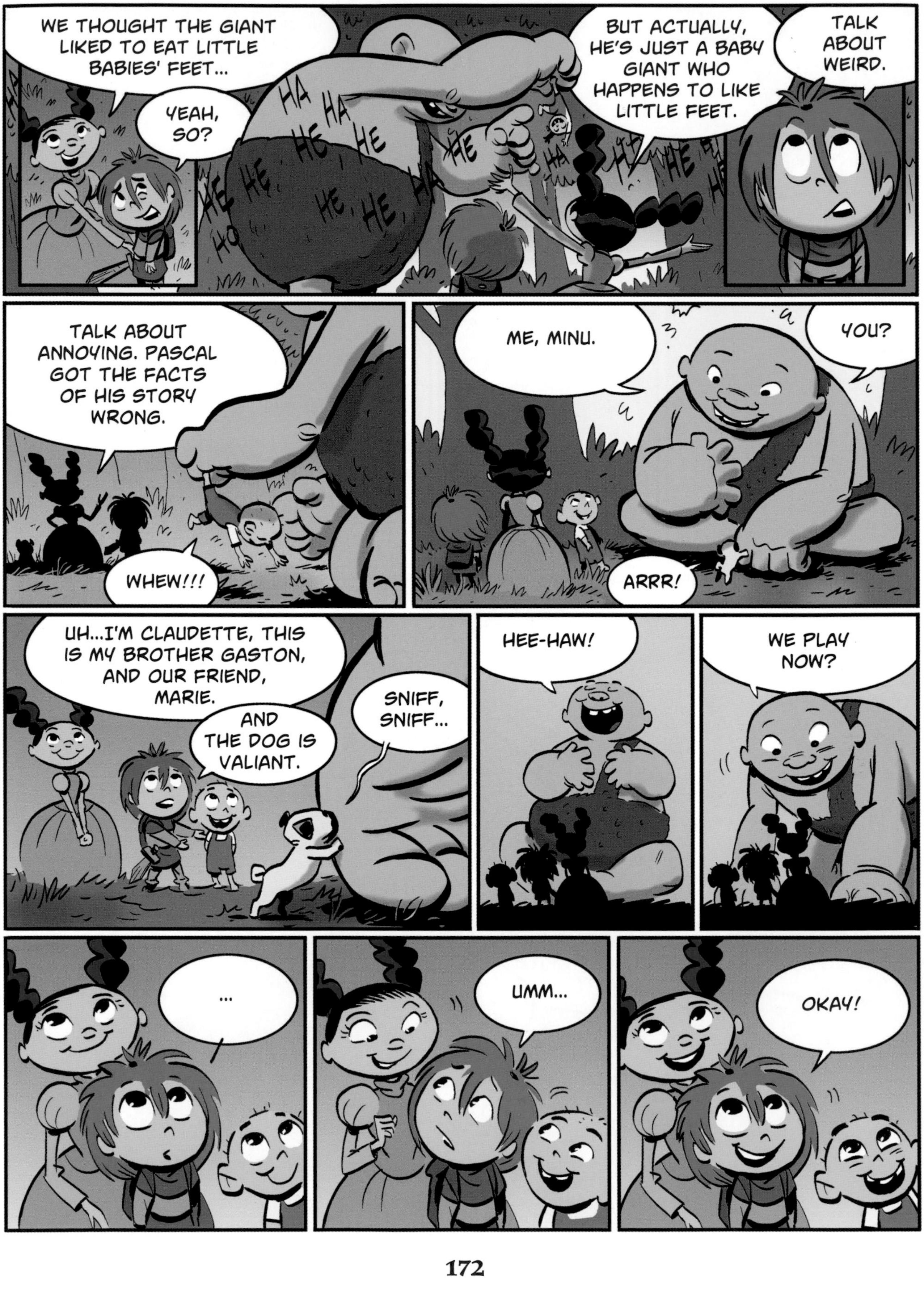
WE THOUGHT THE GIANT LIKED TO EAT LITTLE BABIES' FEET...
YEAH, SO?
HA HA HA HE HE HE HE HE HE HA HO HE HA HA HE
BUT ACTUALLY, HE'S JUST A BABY GIANT WHO HAPPENS TO LIKE LITTLE FEET.
TALK ABOUT WEIRD.
TALK ABOUT ANNOYING. PASCAL GOT THE FACTS OF HIS STORY WRONG.
WHEW!!!
ME, MINU.
YOU?
ARRR!
UH...I'M CLAUDETTE, THIS IS MY BROTHER GASTON, AND OUR FRIEND, MARIE.
AND THE DOG IS VALIANT.
SNIFF, SNIFF...
HEE-HAW!
WE PLAY NOW?
...
UMM...
OKAY!

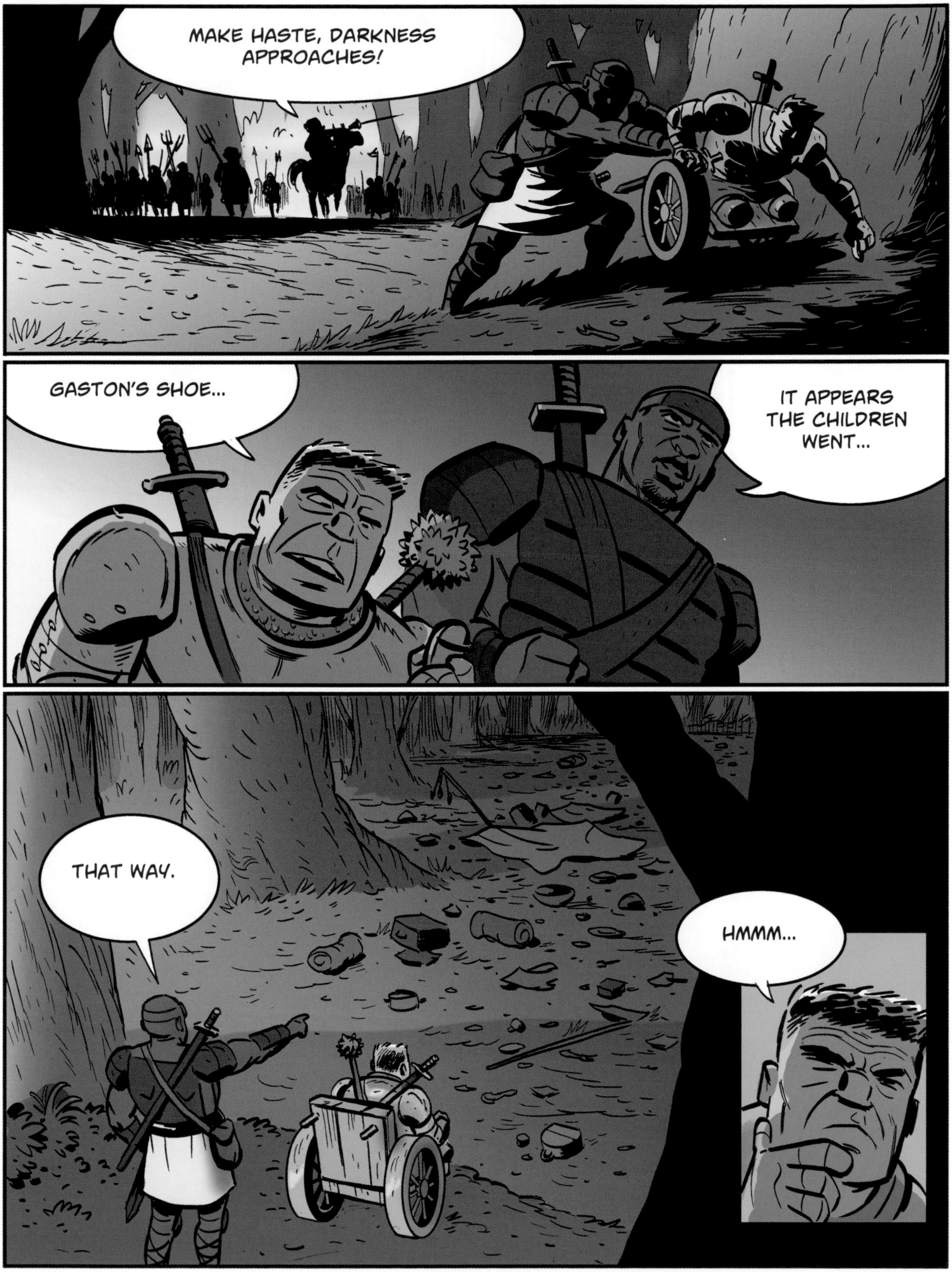
MAKE HASTE, DARKNESS APPROACHES!
GASTON'S SHOE...
IT APPEARS THE CHILDREN WENT...
THAT WAY.
HMMM...

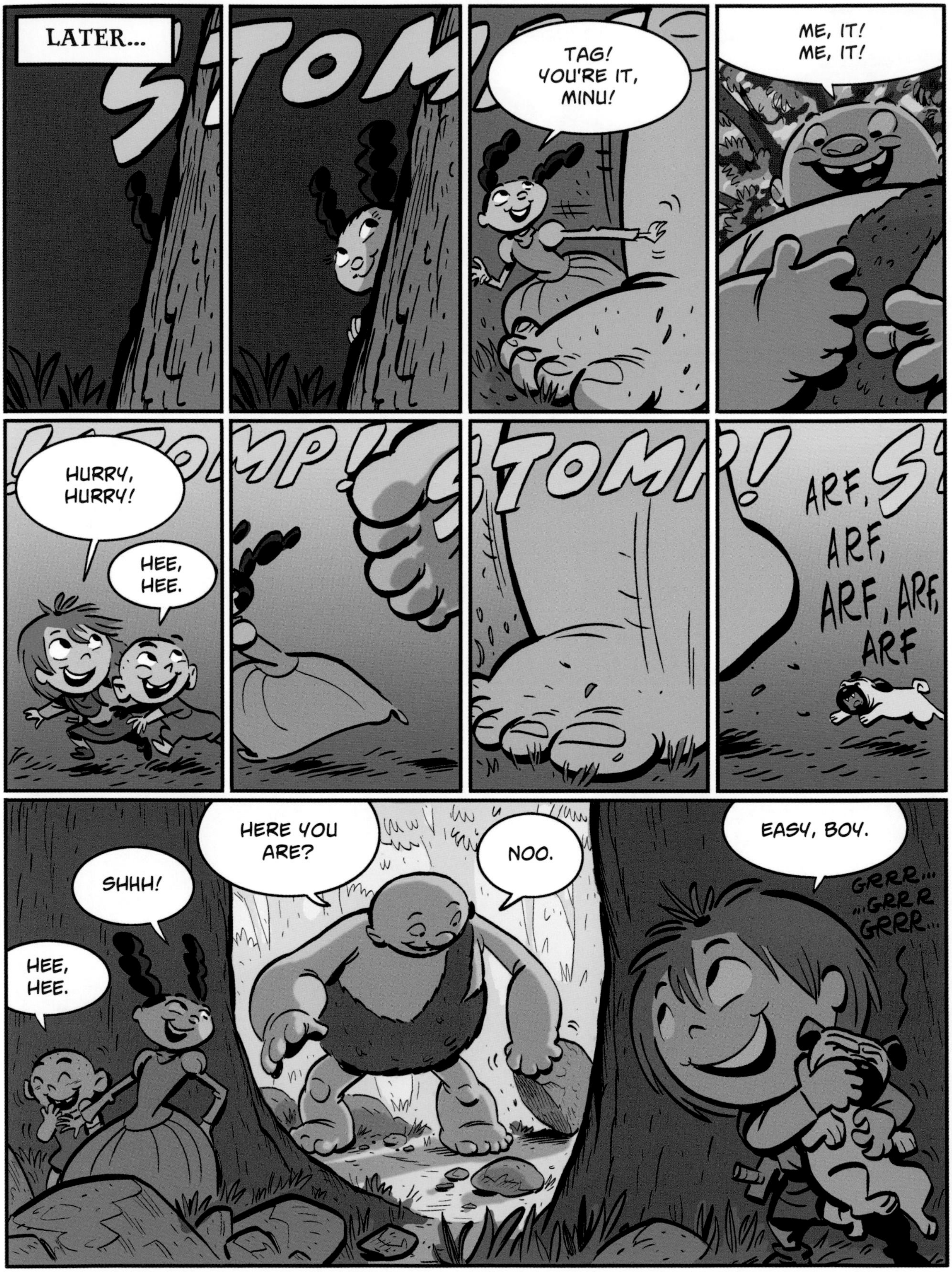
LATER...
STOMP
TAG! YOU'RE IT, MINU!
ME, IT! ME, IT!
HURRY, HURRY!
HEE, HEE.
STOMP! STOMP!
ARF, ARF, ARF, ARF, ARF
HERE YOU ARE?
SHHH!
HEE, HEE.
NOO.
EASY, BOY.
GRRR... ...GRRR GRRR...

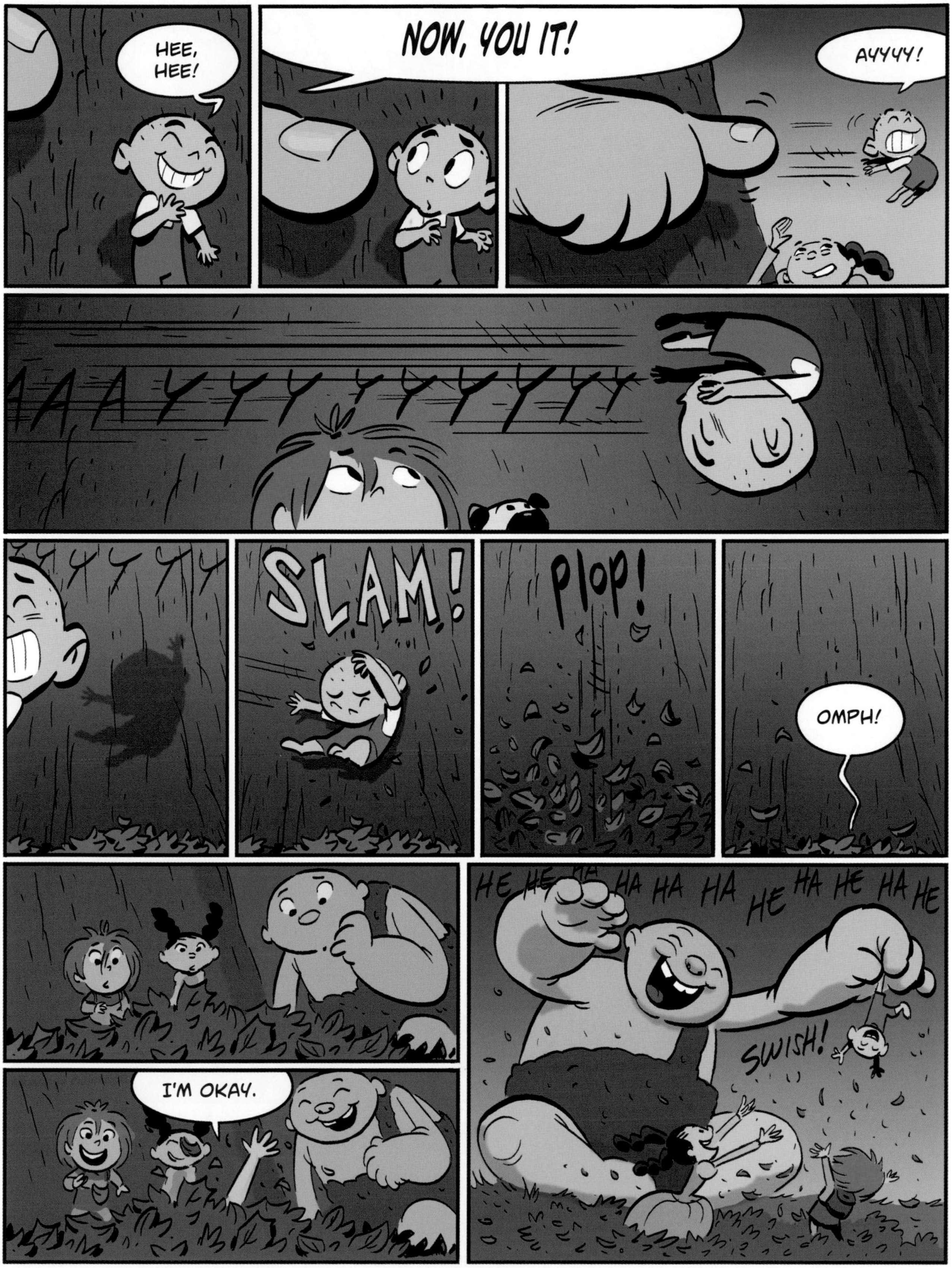
HEE, HEE!
NOW, YOU IT!
AYYYY!
AAAYYYYYYYYYY
SLAM!
PLOP!
OMPH!
I'M OKAY.
HE HE HA HA HA HA HE HA HE HA HE
SWISH!

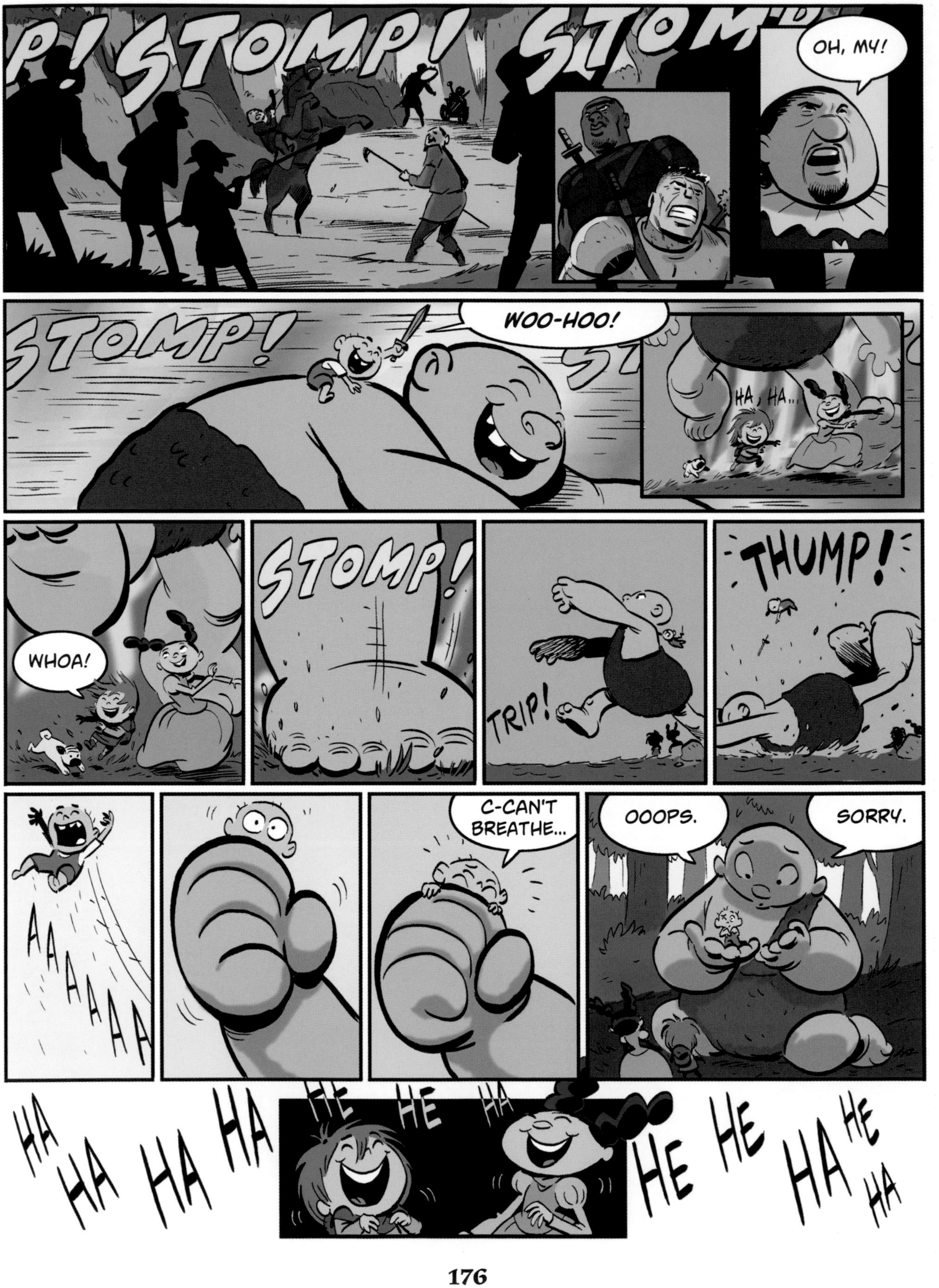
P! STOMP! STOMP
OH, MY!
STOMP!
WOO-HOO!
ST
HA, HA...
WHOA!
STOMP!
TRIP!
THUMP!
AAAAAAA
C-CAN'T BREATHE...
OOOPS.
SORRY.
HA HA HA HA
HE HE HA
HE HE HA HE HA

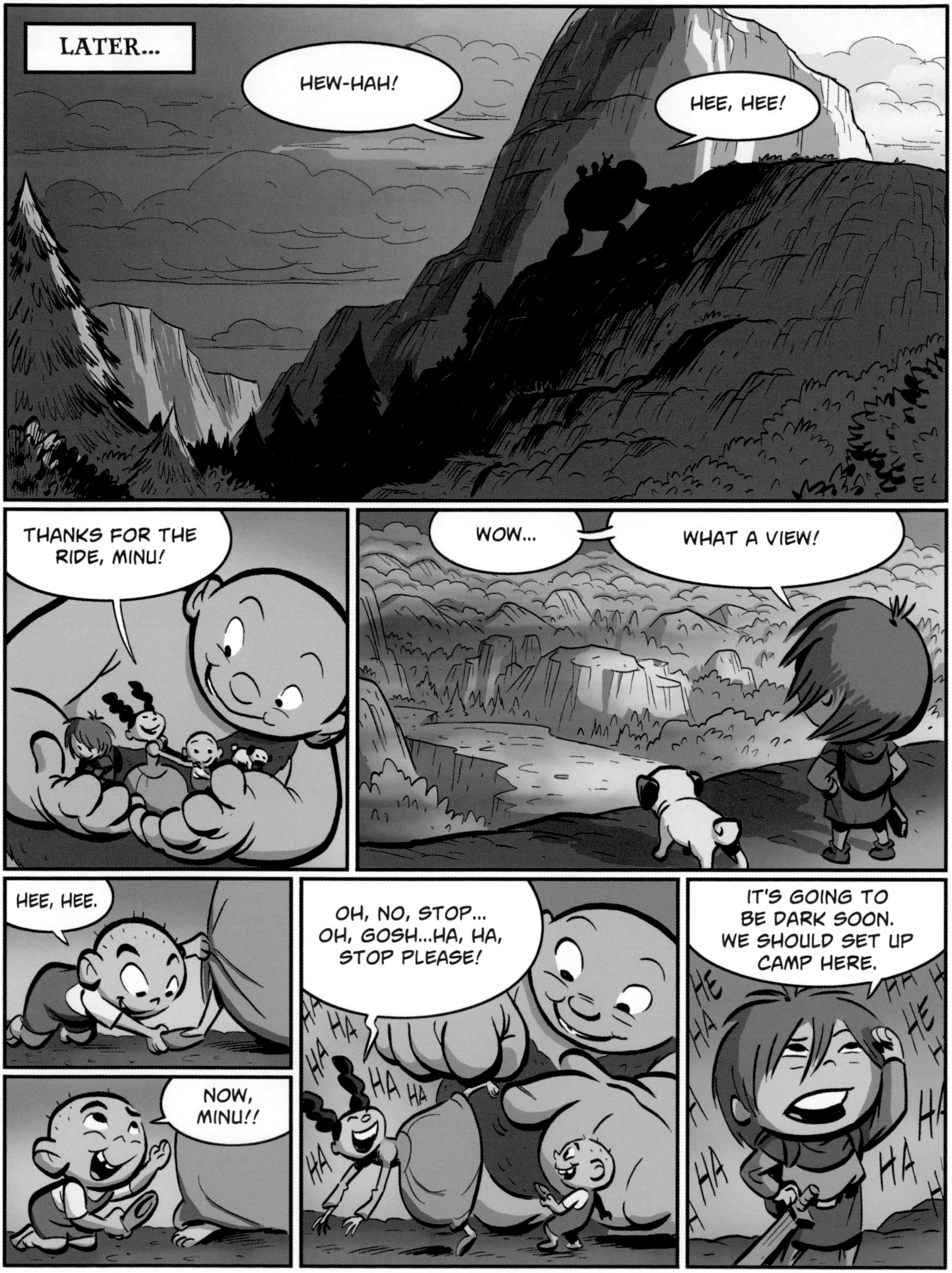
LATER...
HEW-HAH!
HEE, HEE!
THANKS FOR THE RIDE, MINU!
WOW...
WHAT A VIEW!
HEE, HEE.
NOW, MINU!!
OH, NO, STOP... OH, GOSH...HA, HA, STOP PLEASE!
HA HA HA HA
IT'S GOING TO BE DARK SOON. WE SHOULD SET UP CAMP HERE.
HE HA HA HE HA HA HA

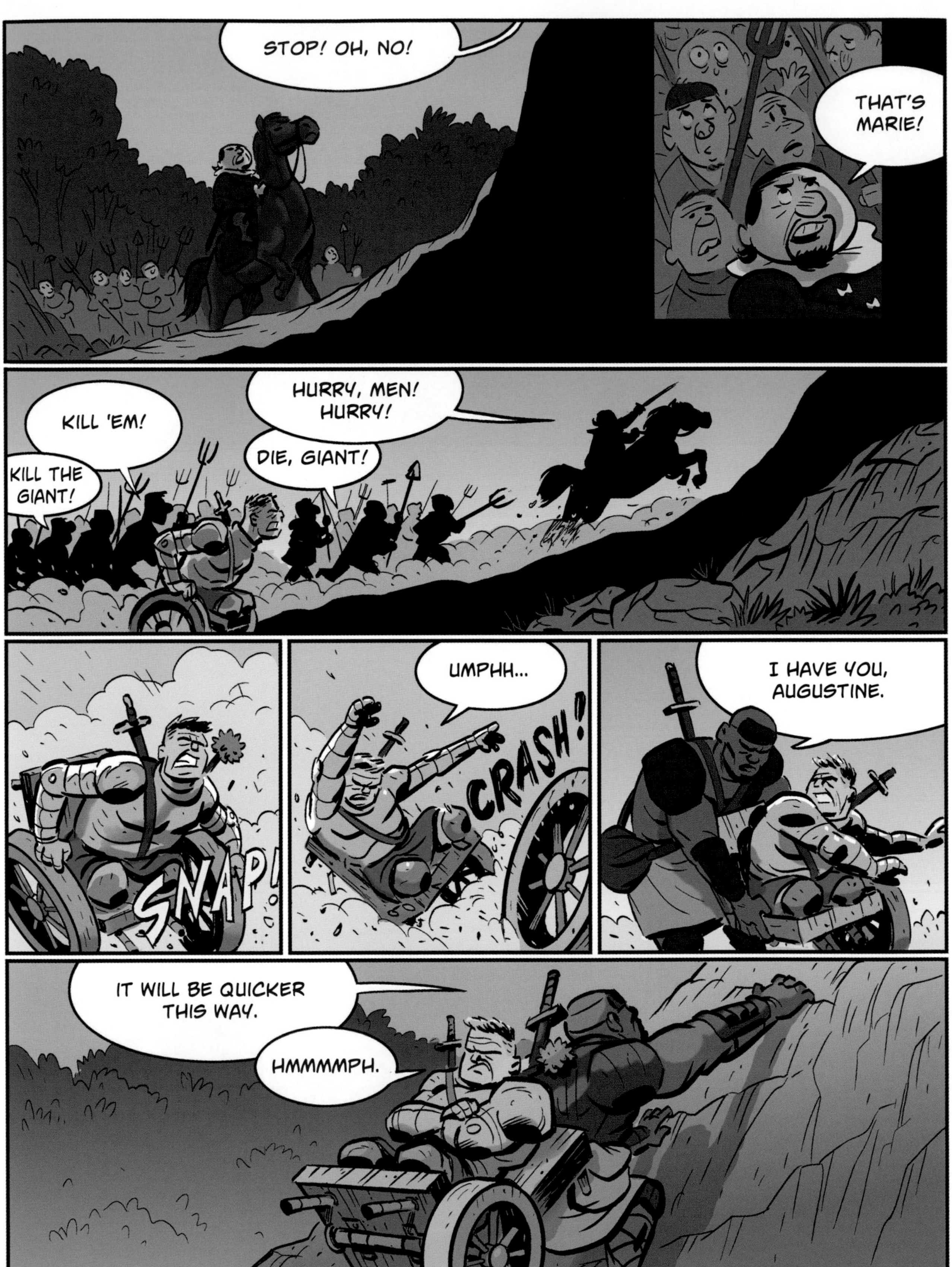
STOP! OH, NO!
THAT'S MARIE!
HURRY, MEN! HURRY!
KILL 'EM!
DIE, GIANT!
KILL THE GIANT!
SNAP!
UMPHH...
CRASH!
I HAVE YOU, AUGUSTINE.
IT WILL BE QUICKER THIS WAY.
HMMMMPH.

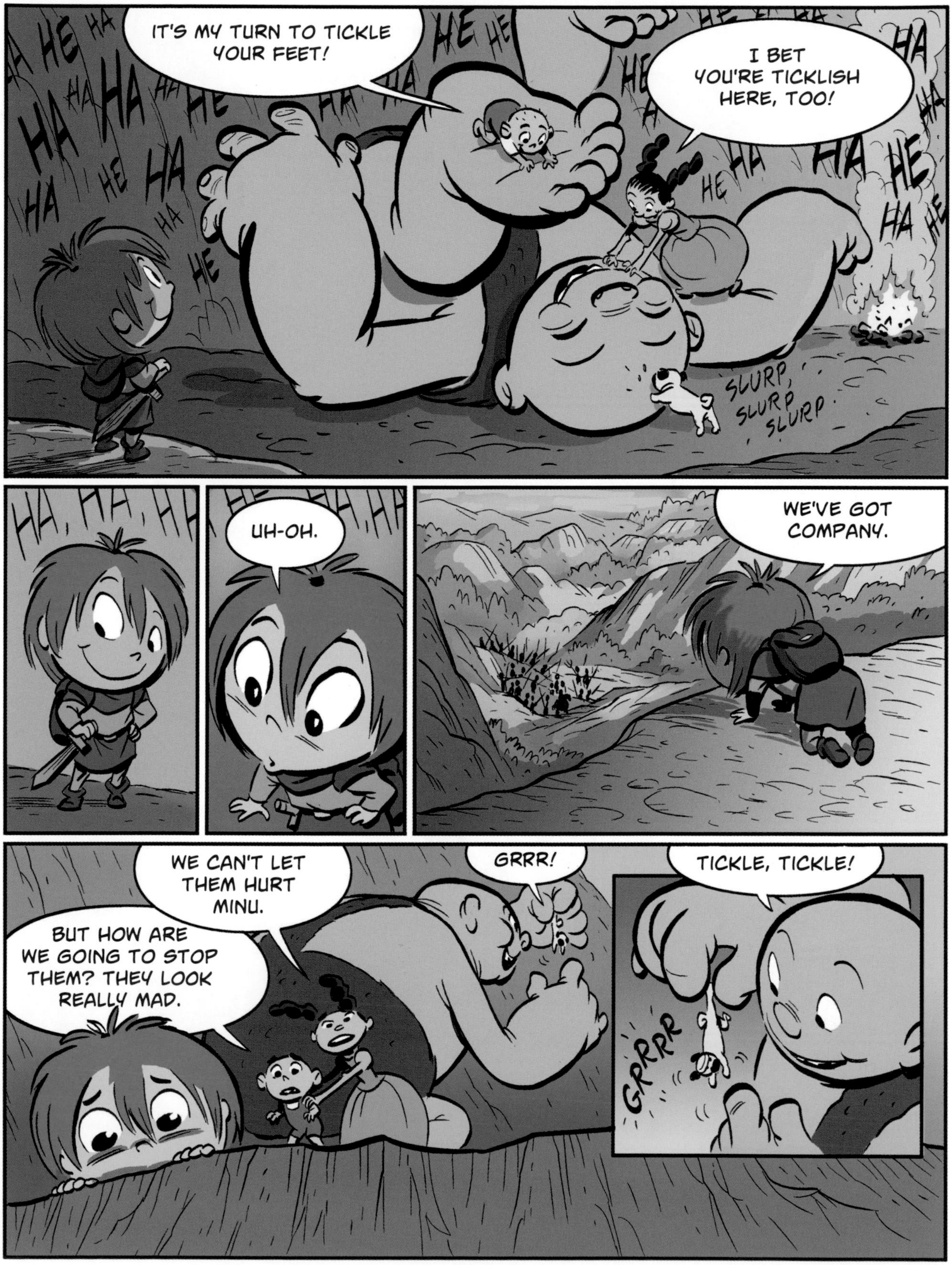

HA HE HA HA HA HE HA HE HA HA HE HA HE HE
IT'S MY TURN TO TICKLE YOUR FEET!
I BET YOU'RE TICKLISH HERE, TOO!
HA HE HA HE HA HA HE
SLURP, SLURP SLURP
HA, HA, HA
UH-OH.
WE'VE GOT COMPANY.
WE CAN'T LET THEM HURT MINU.
BUT HOW ARE WE GOING TO STOP THEM? THEY LOOK REALLY MAD.
GRRR!
TICKLE, TICKLE!
GRRRR

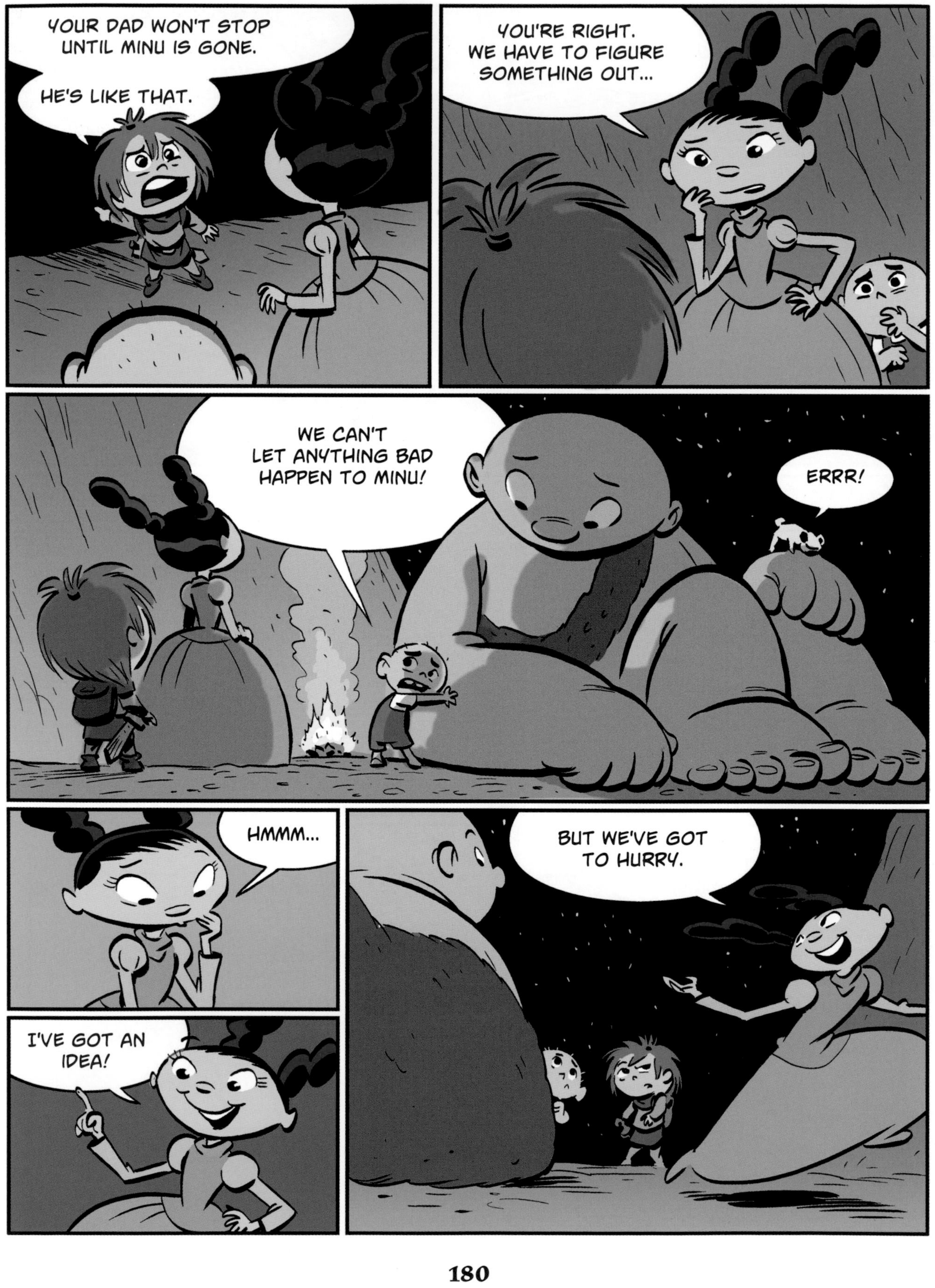
YOUR DAD WON'T STOP UNTIL MINU IS GONE.
HE'S LIKE THAT.
YOU'RE RIGHT. WE HAVE TO FIGURE SOMETHING OUT...
WE CAN'T LET ANYTHING BAD HAPPEN TO MINU!
ERRR!
HMMM...
I'VE GOT AN IDEA!
BUT WE'VE GOT TO HURRY.

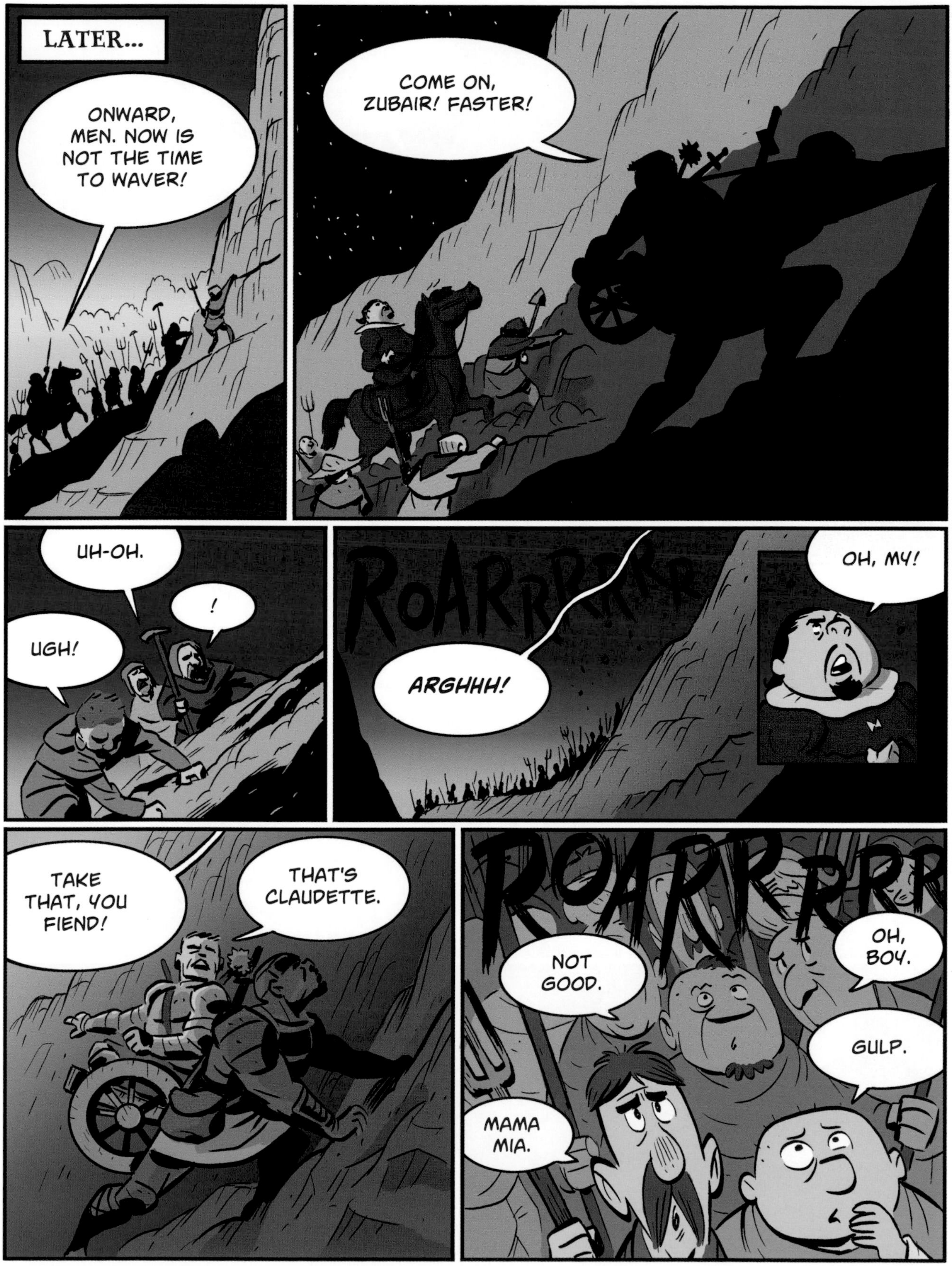

LATER...
ONWARD, MEN. NOW IS NOT THE TIME TO WAVER!
COME ON, ZUBAIR! FASTER!
UH-OH.
!
UGH!
ROARRRRRR
ARGHHH!
OH, MY!
TAKE THAT, YOU FIEND!
THAT'S CLAUDETTE.
ROARRRRRR
NOT GOOD.
OH, BOY.
GULP.
MAMA MIA.

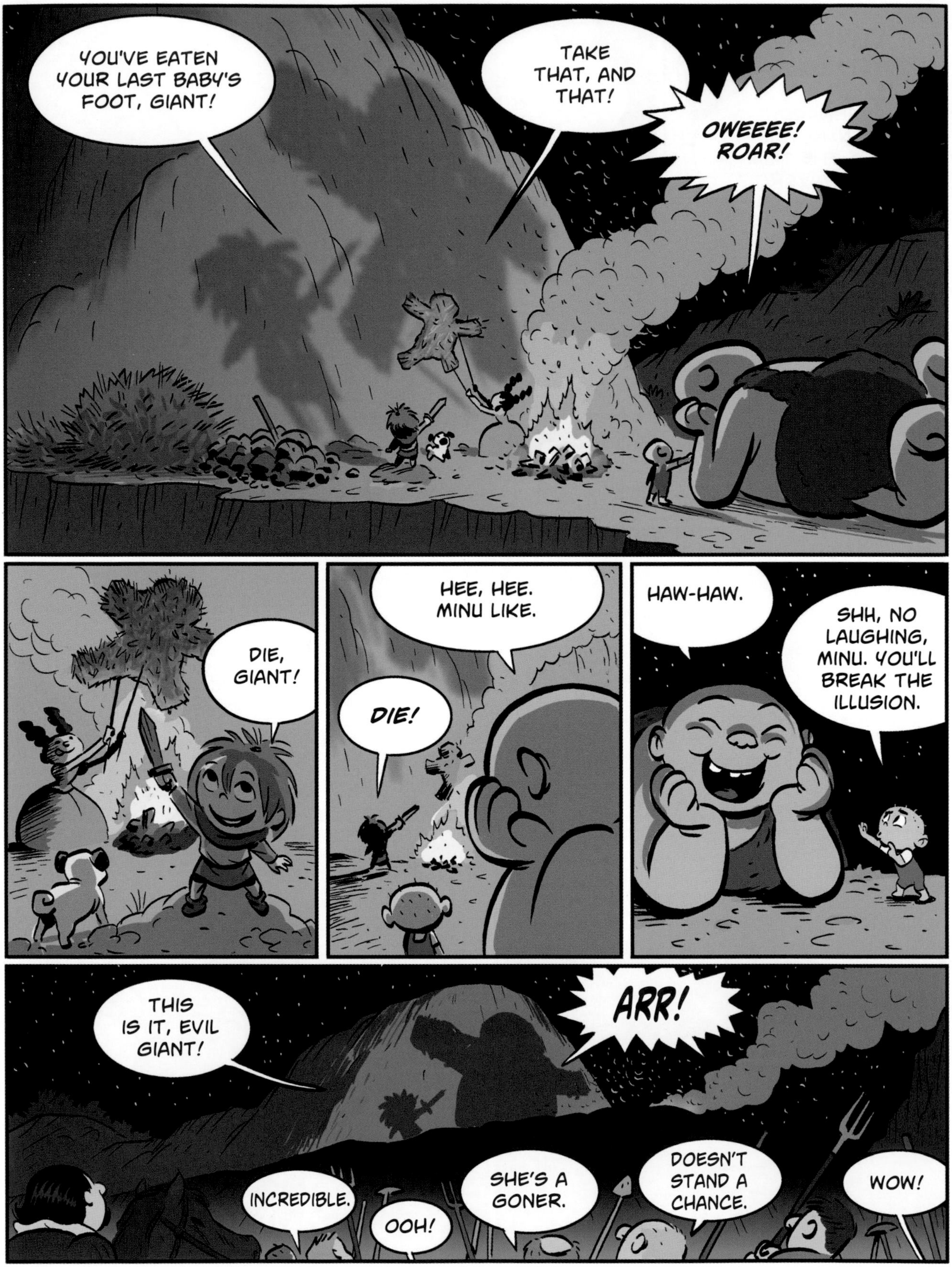
YOU'VE EATEN YOUR LAST BABY'S FOOT, GIANT!
TAKE THAT, AND THAT!
OWEEEE! ROAR!
DIE, GIANT!
HEE, HEE. MINU LIKE.
DIE!
HAW-HAW.
SHH, NO LAUGHING, MINU. YOU'LL BREAK THE ILLUSION.
THIS IS IT, EVIL GIANT!
ARR!
INCREDIBLE.
OOH!
SHE'S A GONER.
DOESN'T STAND A CHANCE.
WOW!

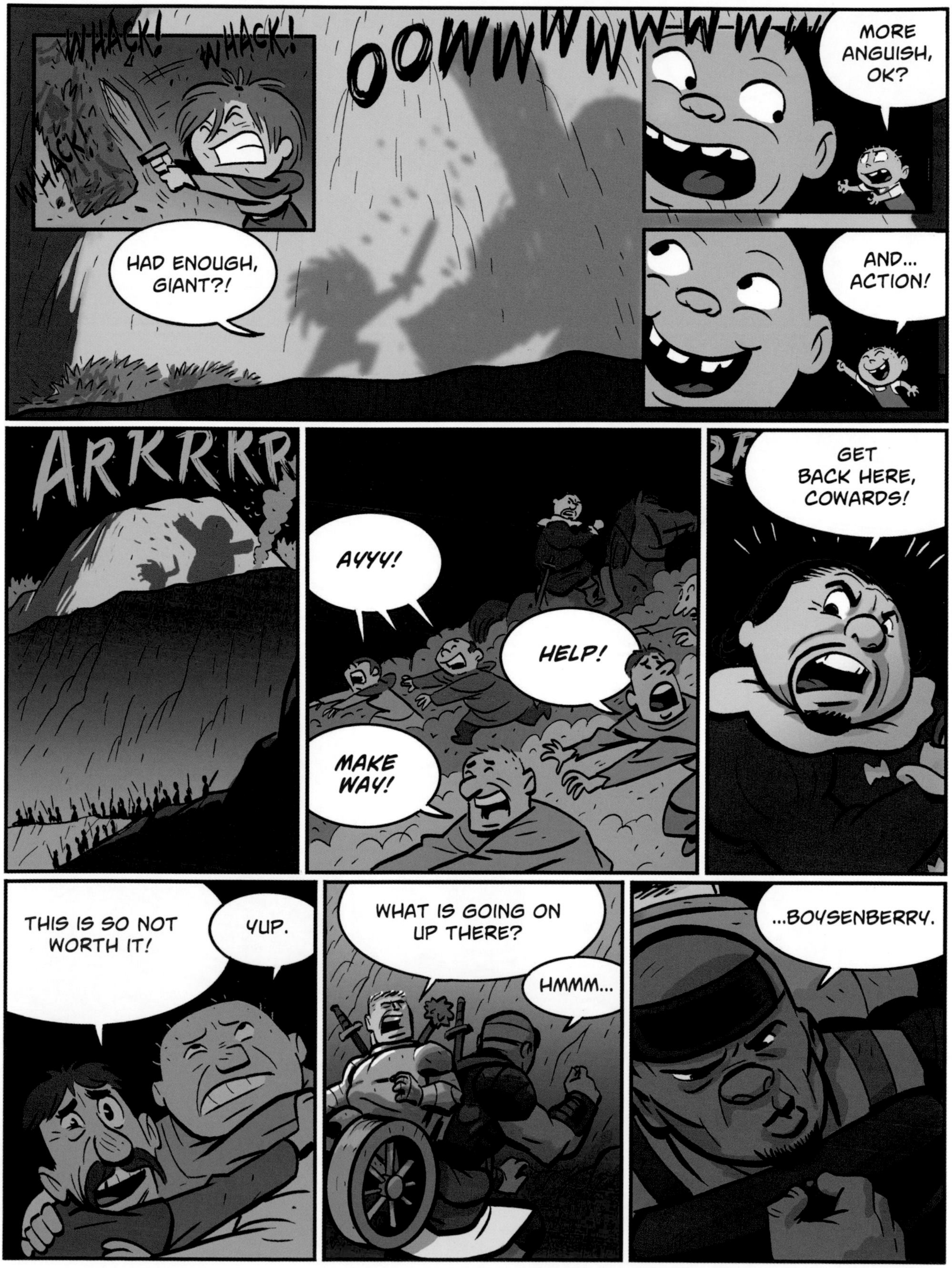
WHACK!
WHACK!
WHACK!
OOWWWWWWWWW
MORE ANGUISH, OK?
HAD ENOUGH, GIANT?!
AND... ACTION!
ARKRKR
AYYY!
HELP!
MAKE WAY!
GET BACK HERE, COWARDS!
THIS IS SO NOT WORTH IT!
YUP.
WHAT IS GOING ON UP THERE?
HMMM...
...BOYSENBERRY.

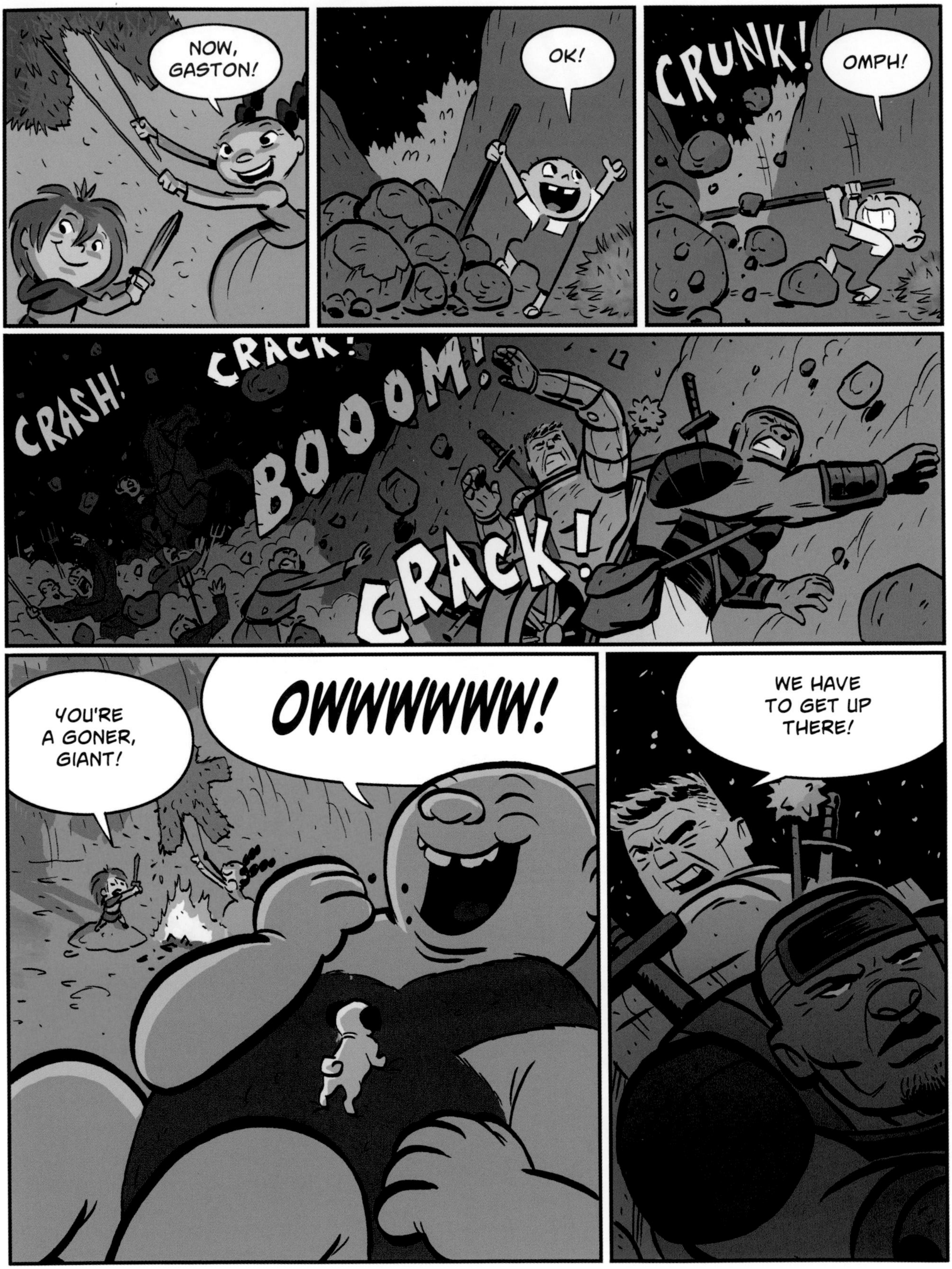
NOW, GASTON!
OK!
CRUNK!
OMPH!
CRASH!
CRACK!
BOOOM!
CRACK!
YOU'RE A GONER, GIANT!
OWWWWWW!
WE HAVE TO GET UP THERE!

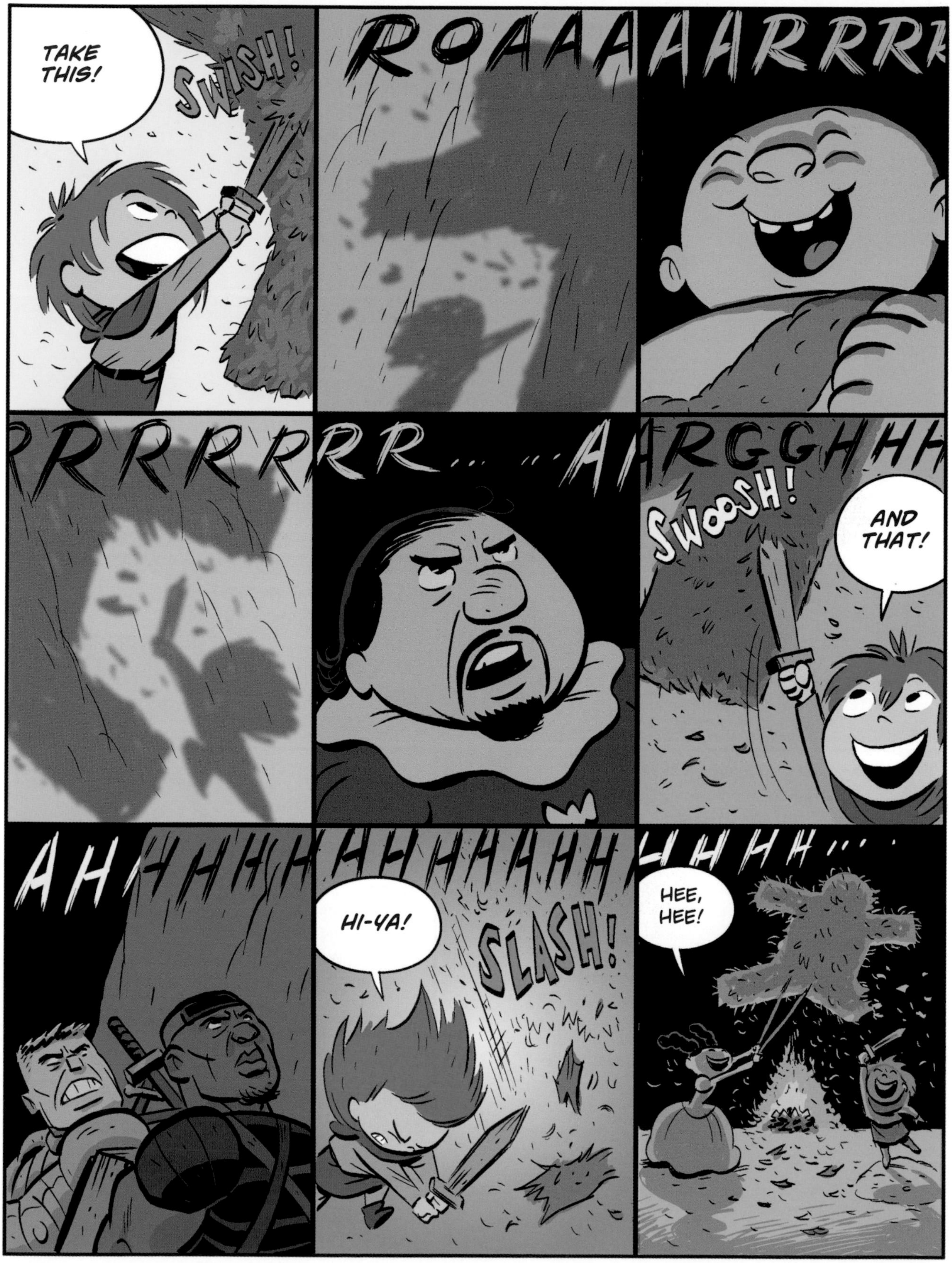
TAKE THIS!
SWISH!
ROAAAAARRRRRRRRRR... ...AAARGGHHH
SWOOSH!
AND THAT!
AHHHHHHHHHHHHHHHHH...
HI-YA!
SLASH!
HEE, HEE!

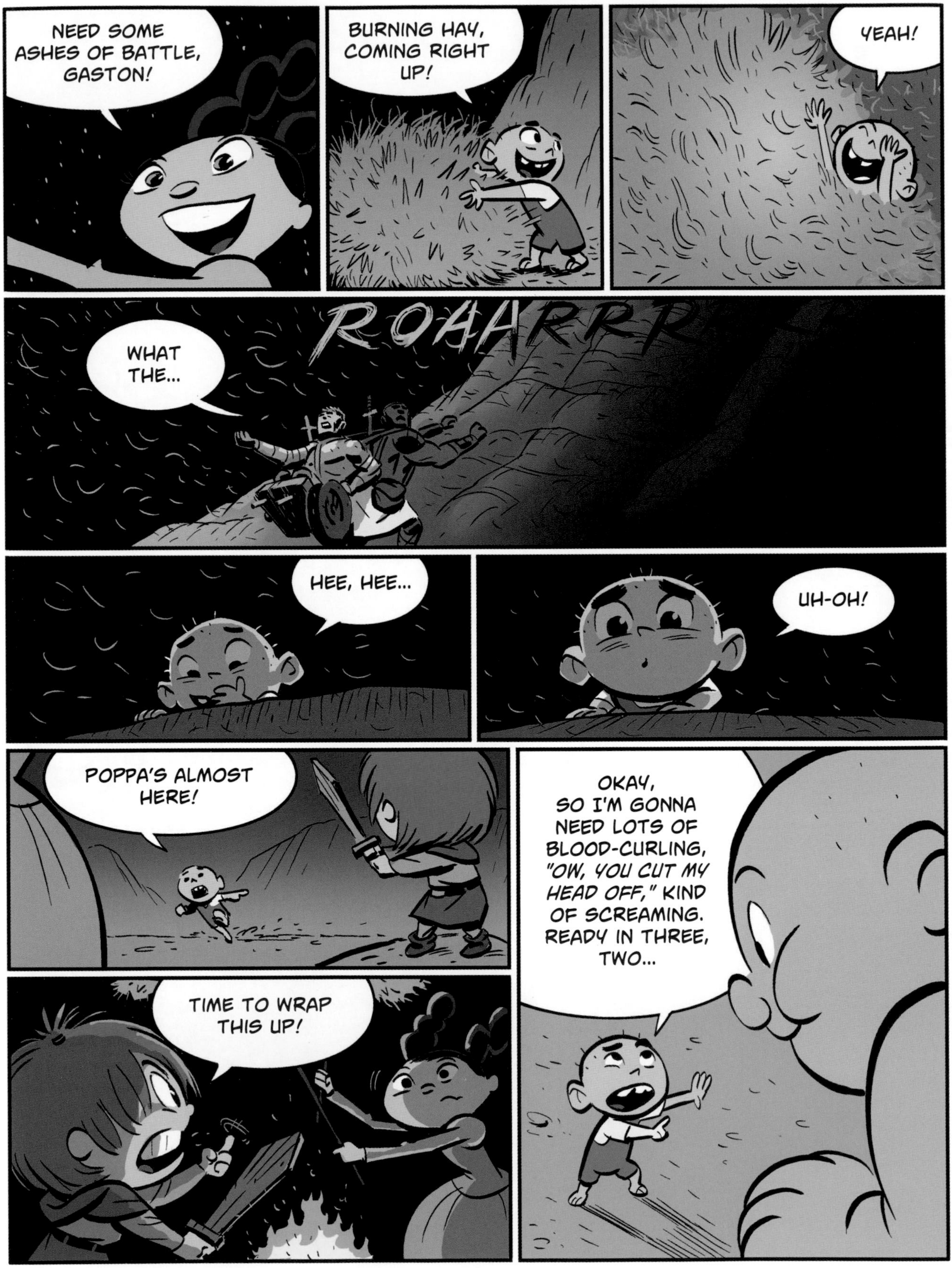
NEED SOME ASHES OF BATTLE, GASTON!
BURNING HAY, COMING RIGHT UP!
YEAH!
ROAARRR
WHAT THE...
HEE, HEE...
UH-OH!
POPPA'S ALMOST HERE!
TIME TO WRAP THIS UP!
OKAY, SO I'M GONNA NEED LOTS OF BLOOD-CURLING, "OW, YOU CUT MY HEAD OFF," KIND OF SCREAMING. READY IN THREE, TWO...

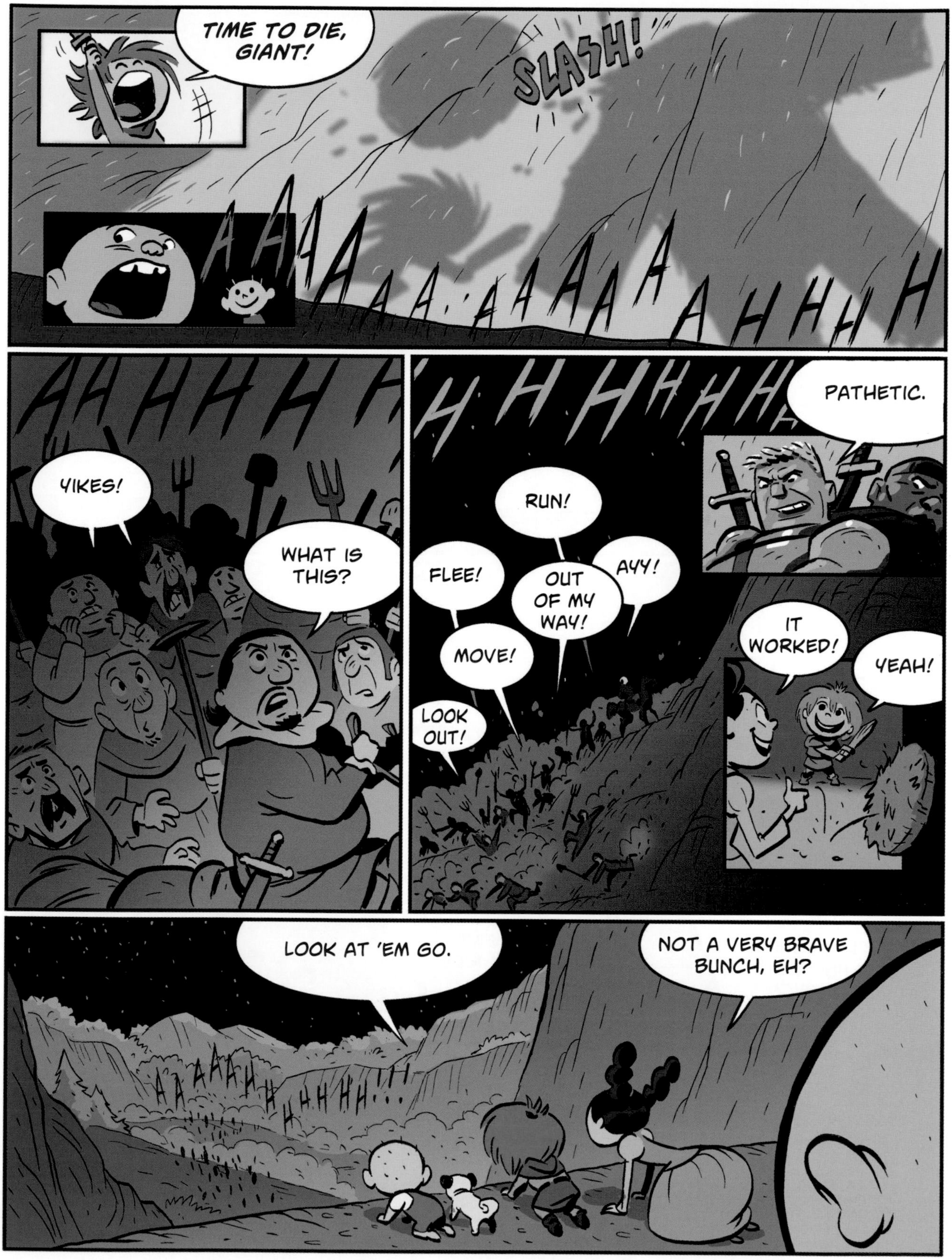
TIME TO DIE, GIANT!
SLASH!
AAAAAAAAAAAAAAHHHHH
AHHHHHH
YIKES!
WHAT IS THIS?
HHHHHHH
RUN!
FLEE!
OUT OF MY WAY!
AYY!
MOVE!
LOOK OUT!
PATHETIC.
IT WORKED!
YEAH!
LOOK AT 'EM GO.
NOT A VERY BRAVE BUNCH, EH?
AAAAHHHHHHH!!

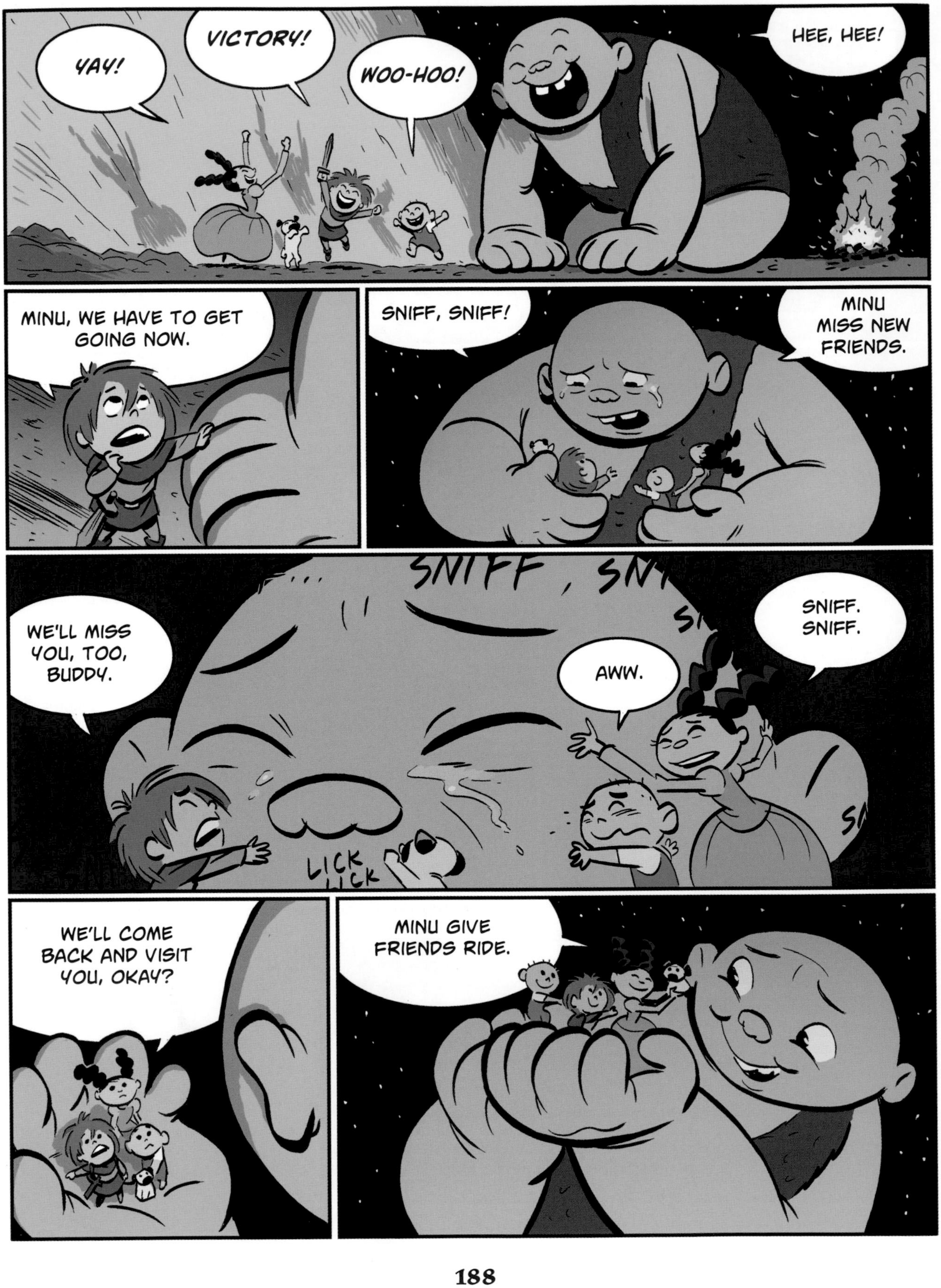
YAY!
VICTORY!
WOO-HOO!
HEE, HEE!
MINU, WE HAVE TO GET GOING NOW.
SNIFF, SNIFF!
MINU MISS NEW FRIENDS.
SNIFF
WE'LL MISS YOU, TOO, BUDDY.
SNIFF. SNIFF.
AWW.
LICK LICK
WE'LL COME BACK AND VISIT YOU, OKAY?
MINU GIVE FRIENDS RIDE.

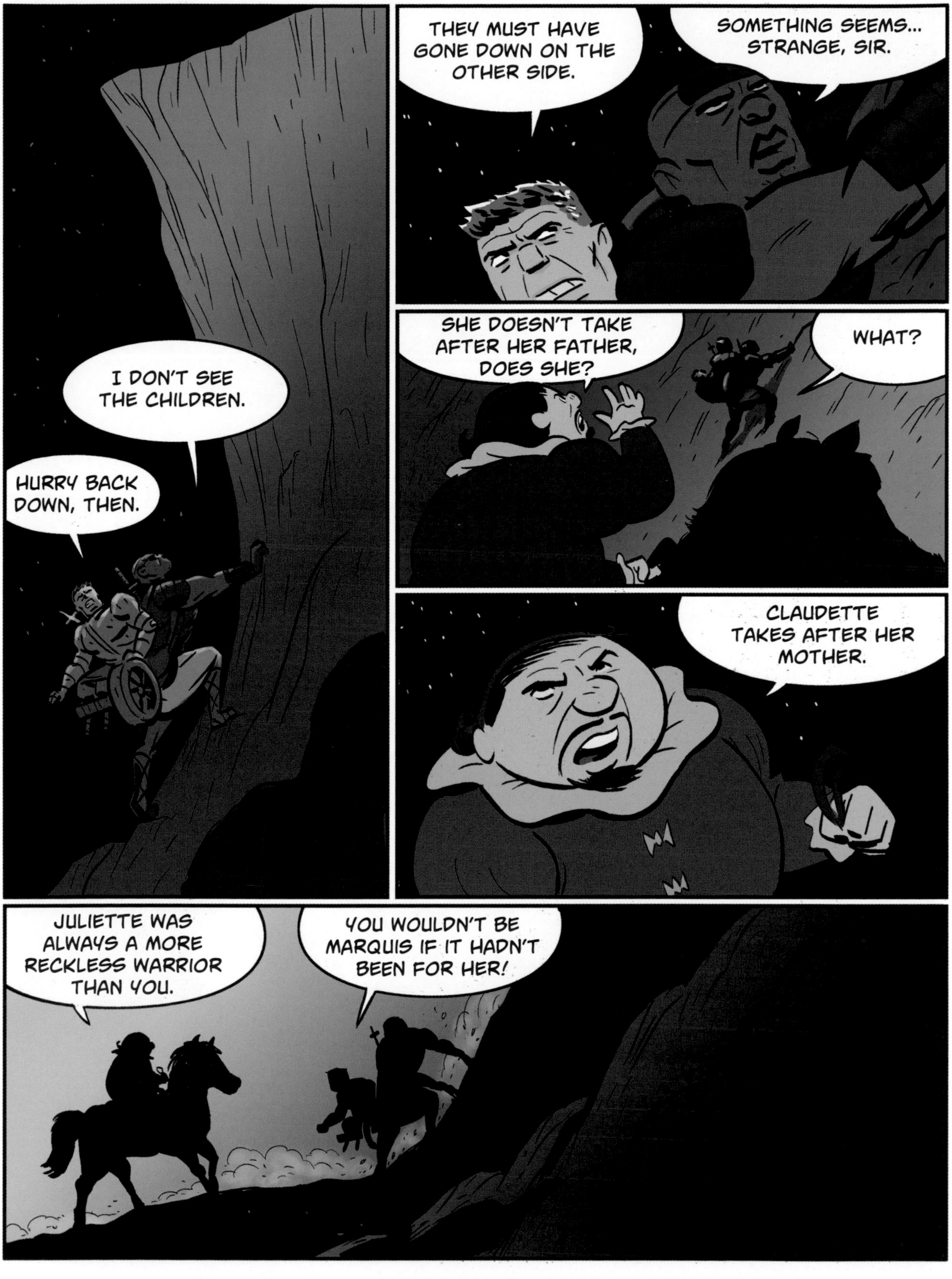
I DON'T SEE THE CHILDREN.
HURRY BACK DOWN, THEN.
THEY MUST HAVE GONE DOWN ON THE OTHER SIDE.
SOMETHING SEEMS... STRANGE, SIR.
SHE DOESN'T TAKE AFTER HER FATHER, DOES SHE?
WHAT?
CLAUDETTE TAKES AFTER HER MOTHER.
JULIETTE WAS ALWAYS A MORE RECKLESS WARRIOR THAN YOU.
YOU WOULDN'T BE MARQUIS IF IT HADN'T BEEN FOR HER!

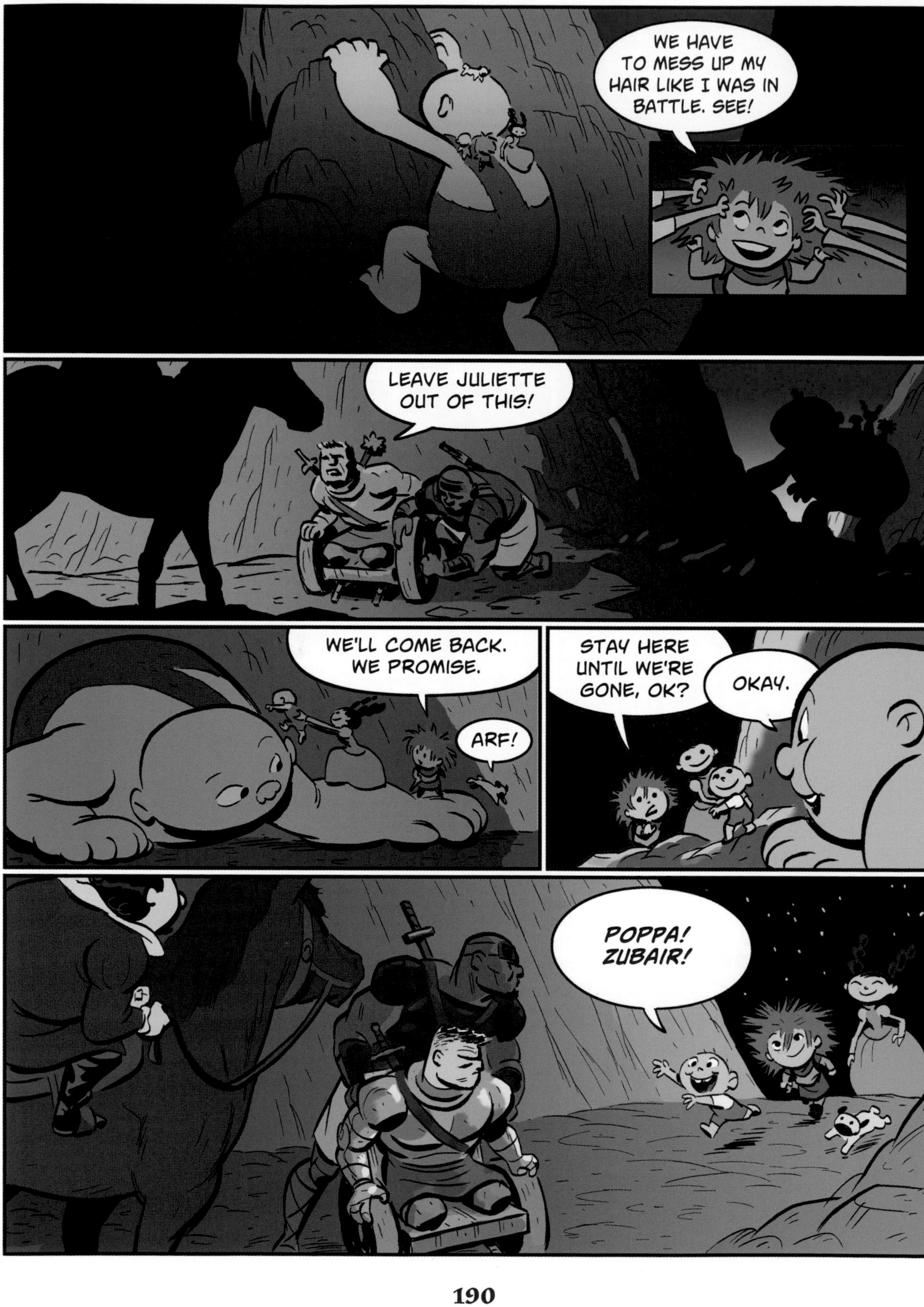
WE HAVE TO MESS UP MY HAIR LIKE I WAS IN BATTLE. SEE!
LEAVE JULIETTE OUT OF THIS!
WE'LL COME BACK. WE PROMISE.
ARF!
STAY HERE UNTIL WE'RE GONE, OK?
OKAY.
POPPA! ZUBAIR!

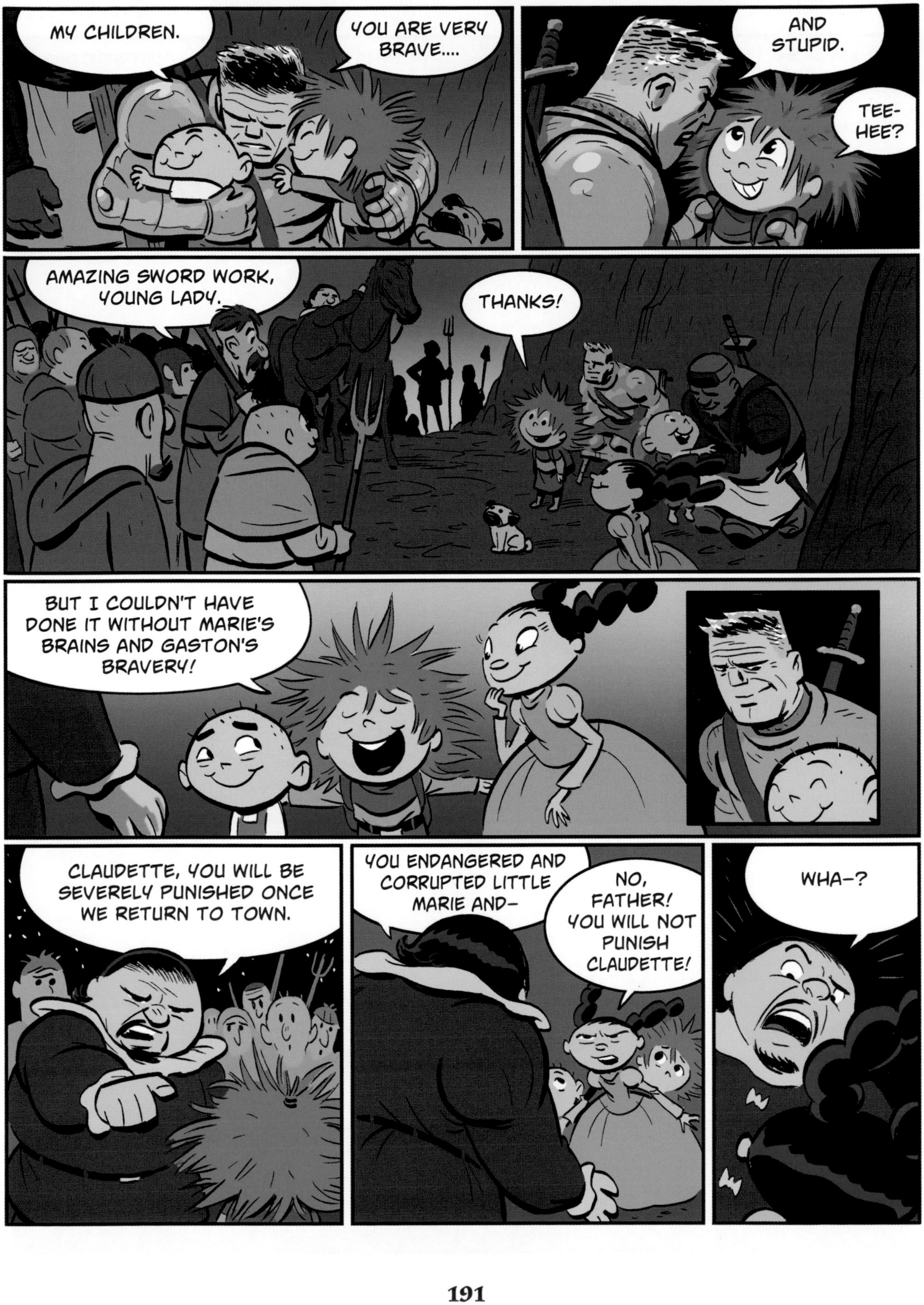
MY CHILDREN.
YOU ARE VERY BRAVE....
AND STUPID.
TEE-HEE?
AMAZING SWORD WORK, YOUNG LADY.
THANKS!
BUT I COULDN'T HAVE DONE IT WITHOUT MARIE'S BRAINS AND GASTON'S BRAVERY!
CLAUDETTE, YOU WILL BE SEVERELY PUNISHED ONCE WE RETURN TO TOWN.
YOU ENDANGERED AND CORRUPTED LITTLE MARIE AND–
NO, FATHER! YOU WILL NOT PUNISH CLAUDETTE!
WHA–?

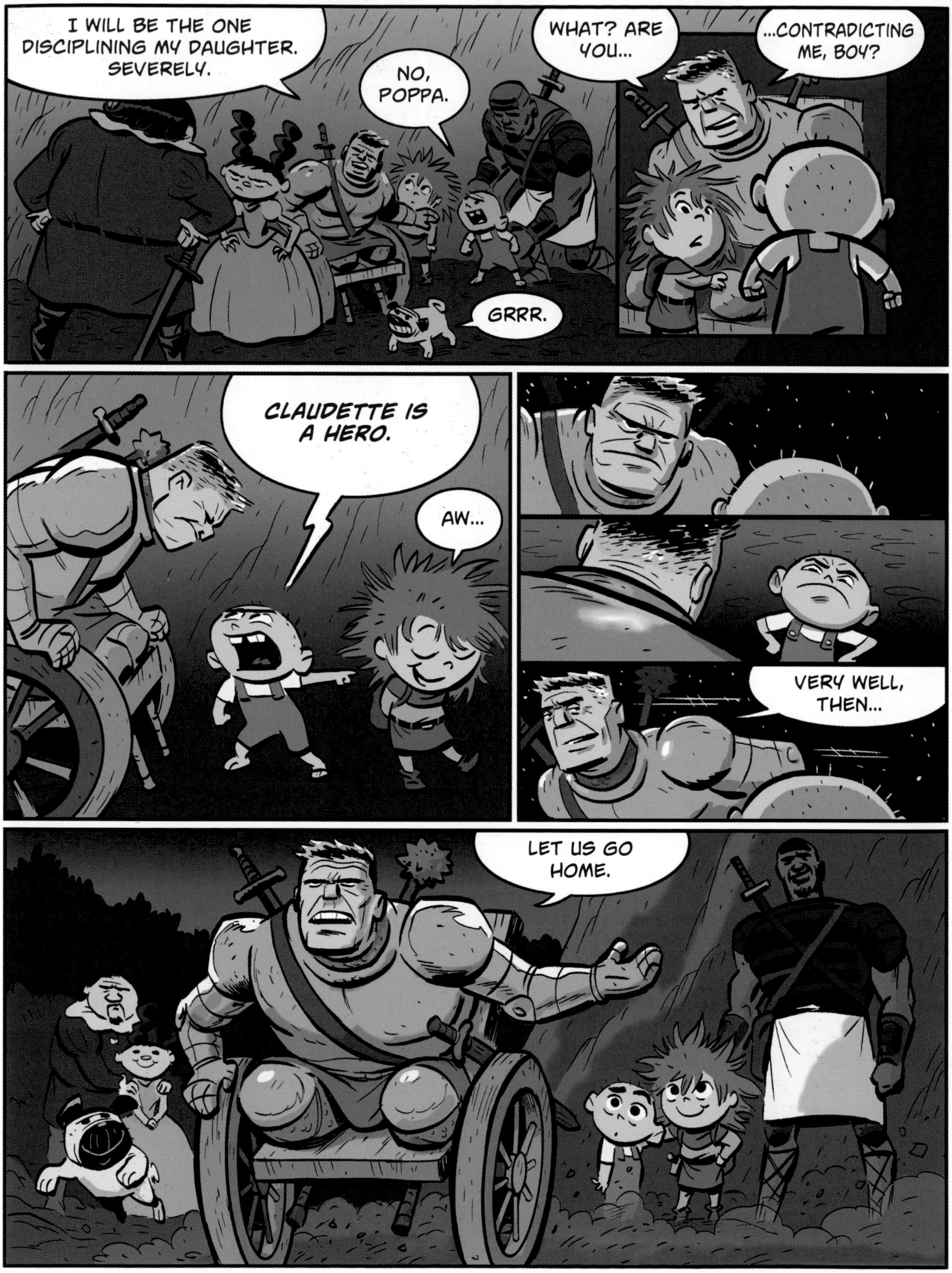
I WILL BE THE ONE DISCIPLINING MY DAUGHTER. SEVERELY.
NO, POPPA.
GRRR.
WHAT? ARE YOU...
...CONTRADICTING ME, BOY?
CLAUDETTE IS A HERO.
AW...
VERY WELL, THEN...
LET US GO HOME.

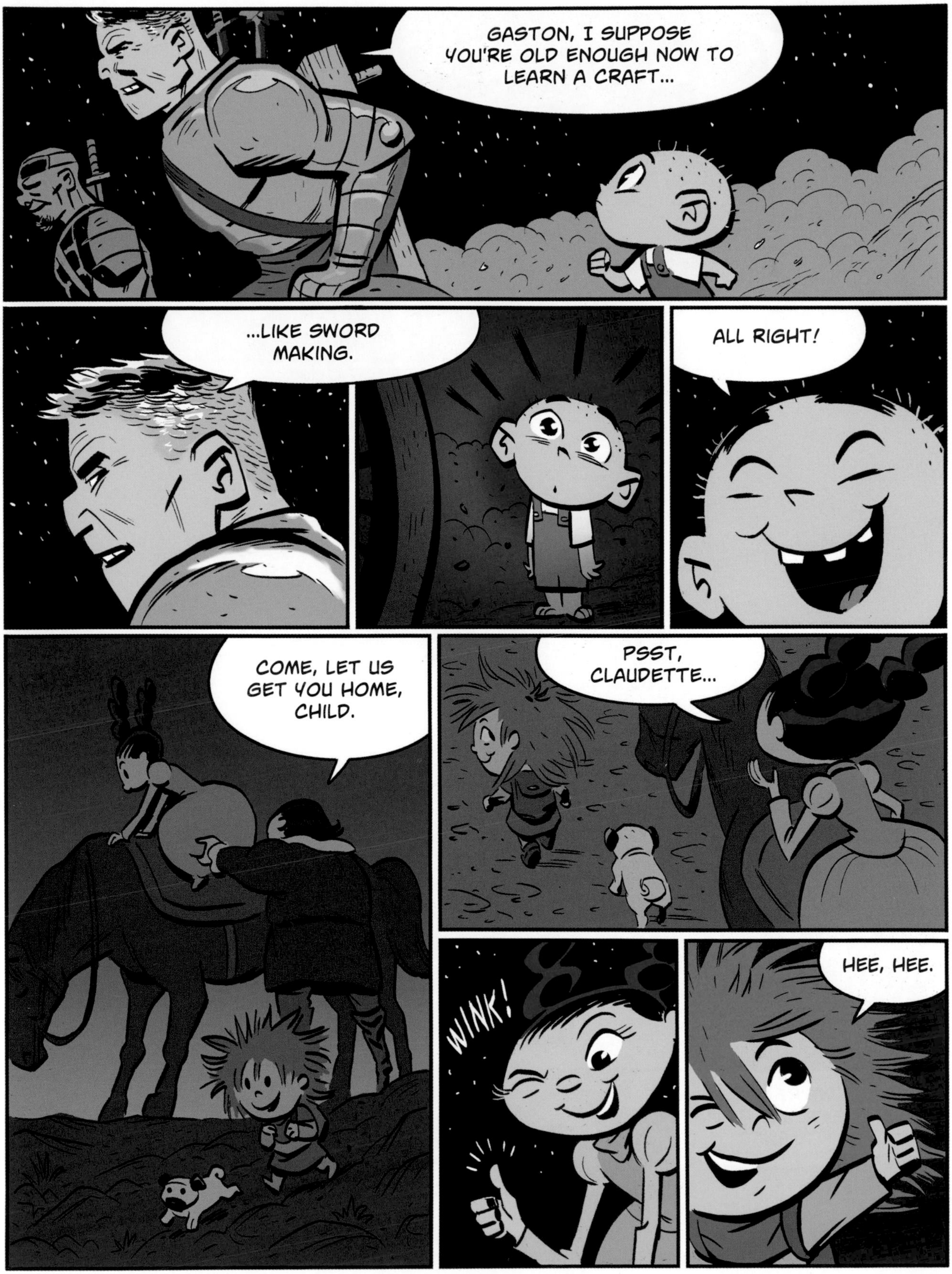
GASTON, I SUPPOSE YOU'RE OLD ENOUGH NOW TO LEARN A CRAFT...
...LIKE SWORD MAKING.
ALL RIGHT!
COME, LET US GET YOU HOME, CHILD.
PSST, CLAUDETTE...
WINK!
HEE, HEE.

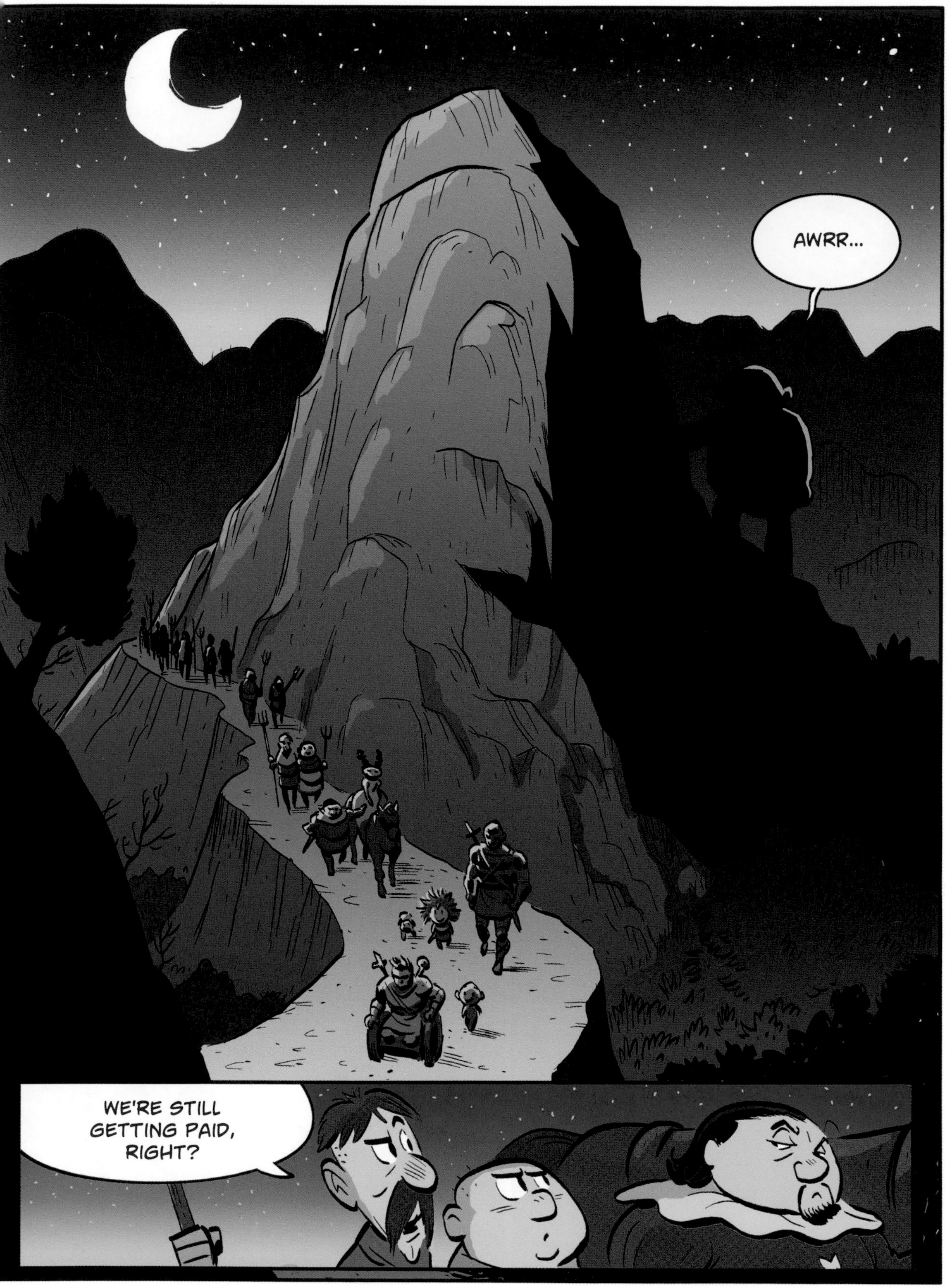
AWRR...
WE'RE STILL GETTING PAID, RIGHT?

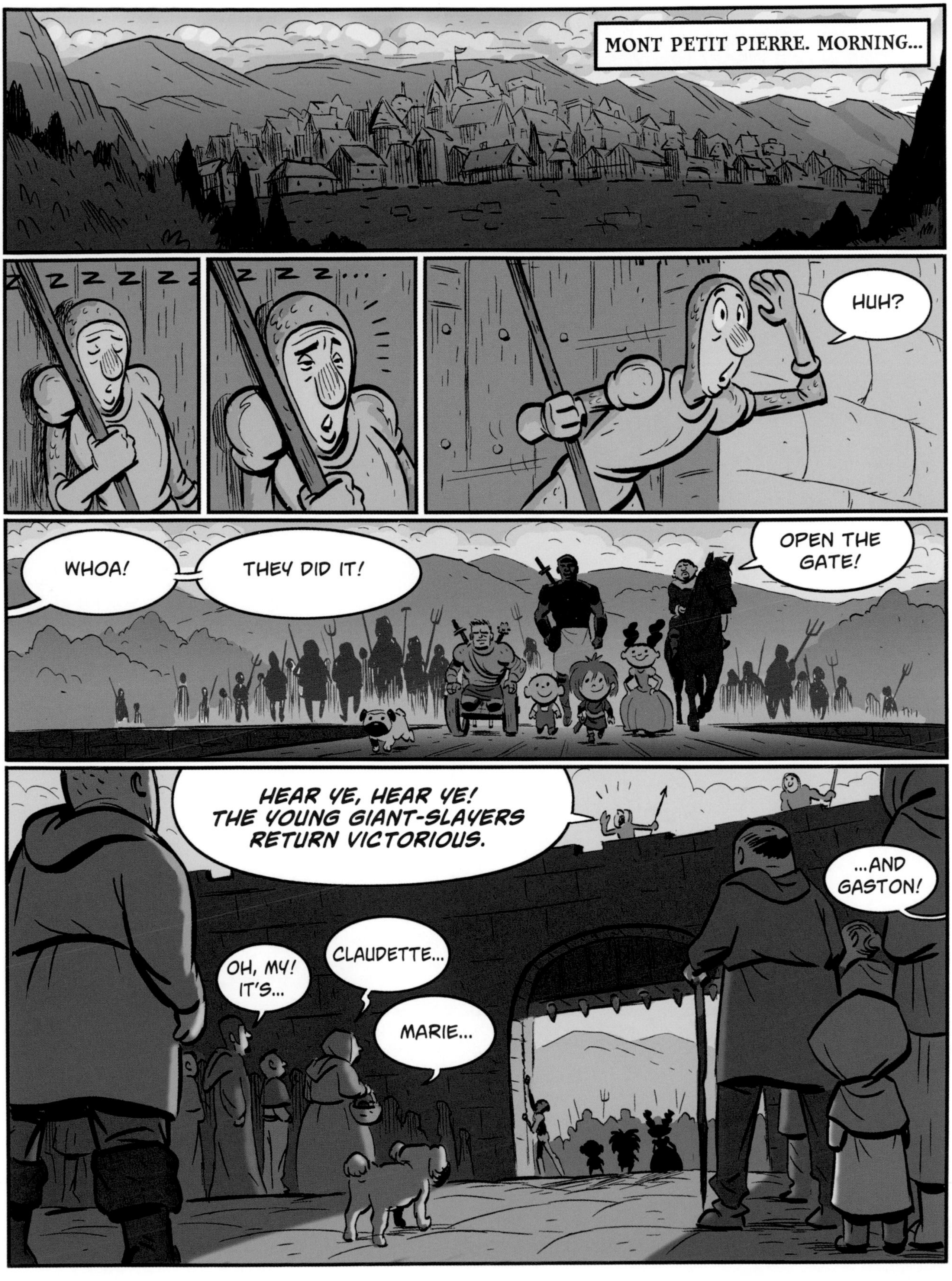
MONT PETIT PIERRE. MORNING...
Z Z Z Z Z Z
Z Z Z...
HUH?
WHOA!
THEY DID IT!
OPEN THE GATE!
HEAR YE, HEAR YE! THE YOUNG GIANT-SLAYERS RETURN VICTORIOUS.
...AND GASTON!
OH, MY! IT'S...
CLAUDETTE...
MARIE...

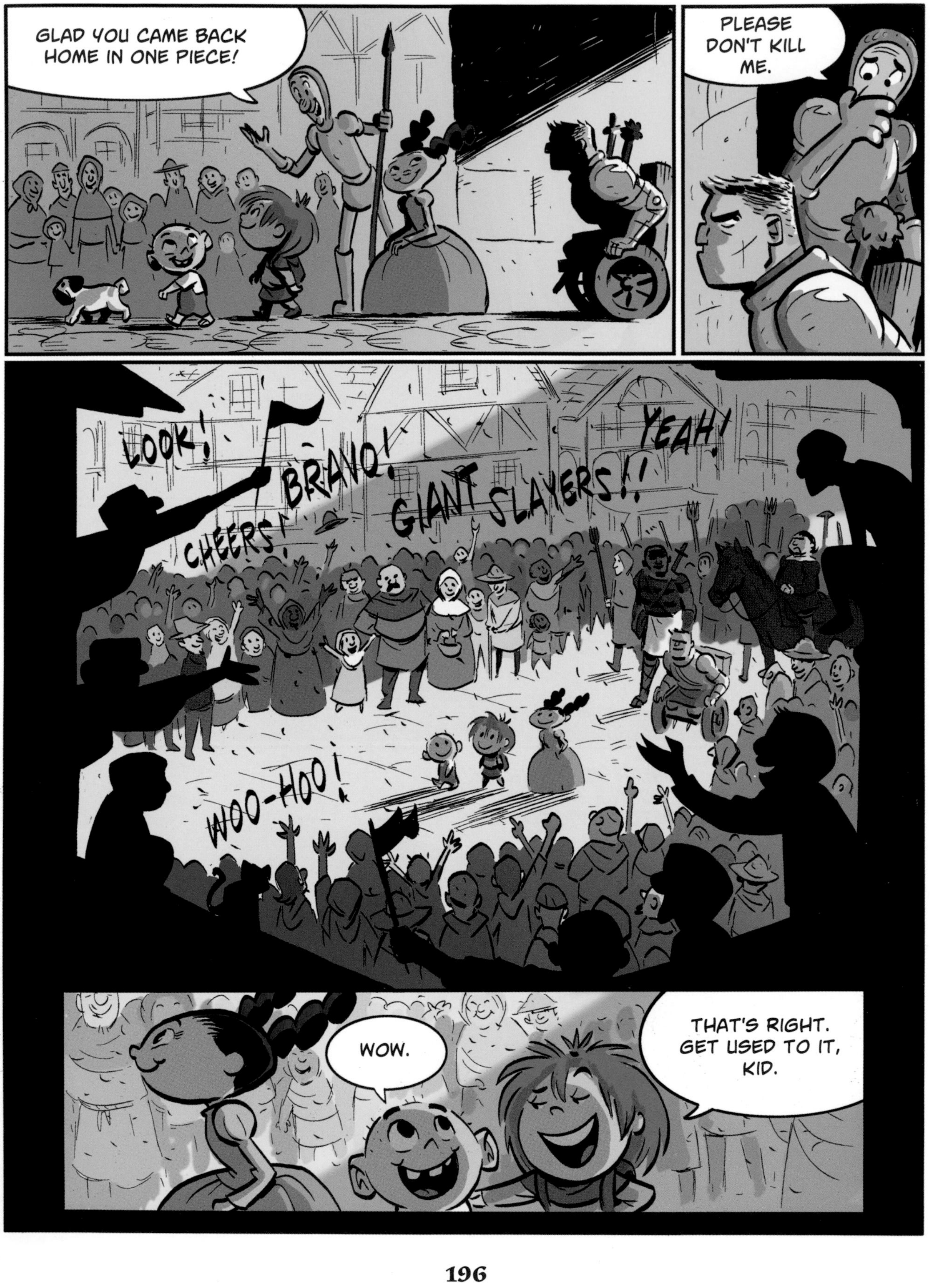
GLAD YOU CAME BACK HOME IN ONE PIECE!
PLEASE DON'T KILL ME.
LOOK!
BRAVO!
YEAH!
GIANT SLAYERS!!
CHEERS!
WOO-HOO!
WOW.
THAT'S RIGHT. GET USED TO IT, KID.

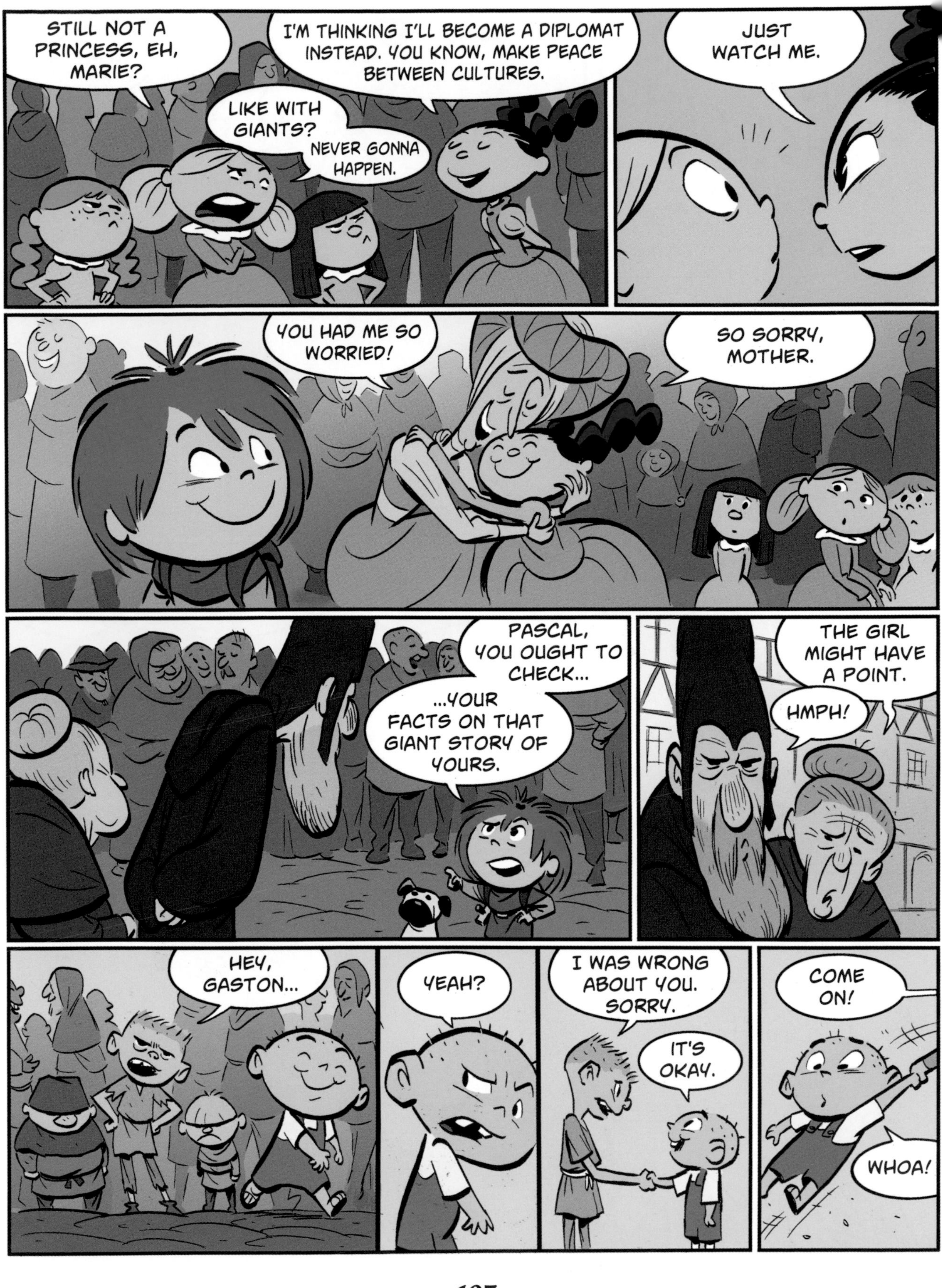
STILL NOT A PRINCESS, EH, MARIE?
I'M THINKING I'LL BECOME A DIPLOMAT INSTEAD. YOU KNOW, MAKE PEACE BETWEEN CULTURES.
LIKE WITH GIANTS?
NEVER GONNA HAPPEN.
JUST WATCH ME.
YOU HAD ME SO WORRIED!
SO SORRY, MOTHER.
PASCAL, YOU OUGHT TO CHECK...
...YOUR FACTS ON THAT GIANT STORY OF YOURS.
THE GIRL MIGHT HAVE A POINT.
HMPH!
HEY, GASTON...
YEAH?
I WAS WRONG ABOUT YOU. SORRY.
IT'S OKAY.
COME ON!
WHOA!

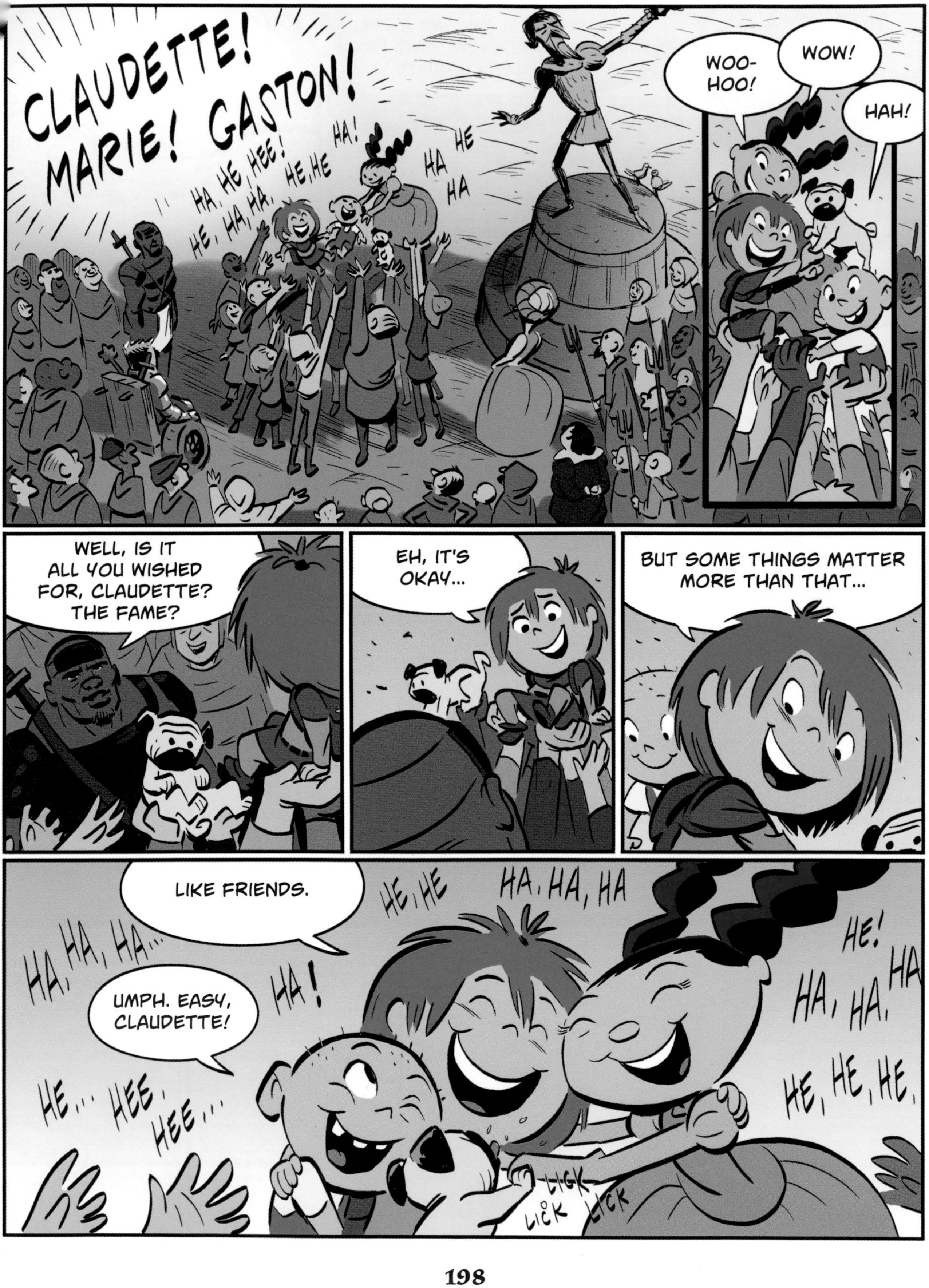
CLAUDETTE! MARIE! GASTON!
HA, HE, HEE! HE, HA, HA, HE, HE HA! HA HE HA HA
WOO-HOO!
WOW!
HAH!
WELL, IS IT ALL YOU WISHED FOR, CLAUDETTE? THE FAME?
EH, IT'S OKAY...
BUT SOME THINGS MATTER MORE THAN THAT...
LIKE FRIENDS.
HE, HE
HA, HA, HA
HA, HA, HA...
UMPH. EASY, CLAUDETTE!
HA!
HE!
HA, HA, HA
HE... HEE, HEE...
HE, HE, HE,
LICK LICK LICK

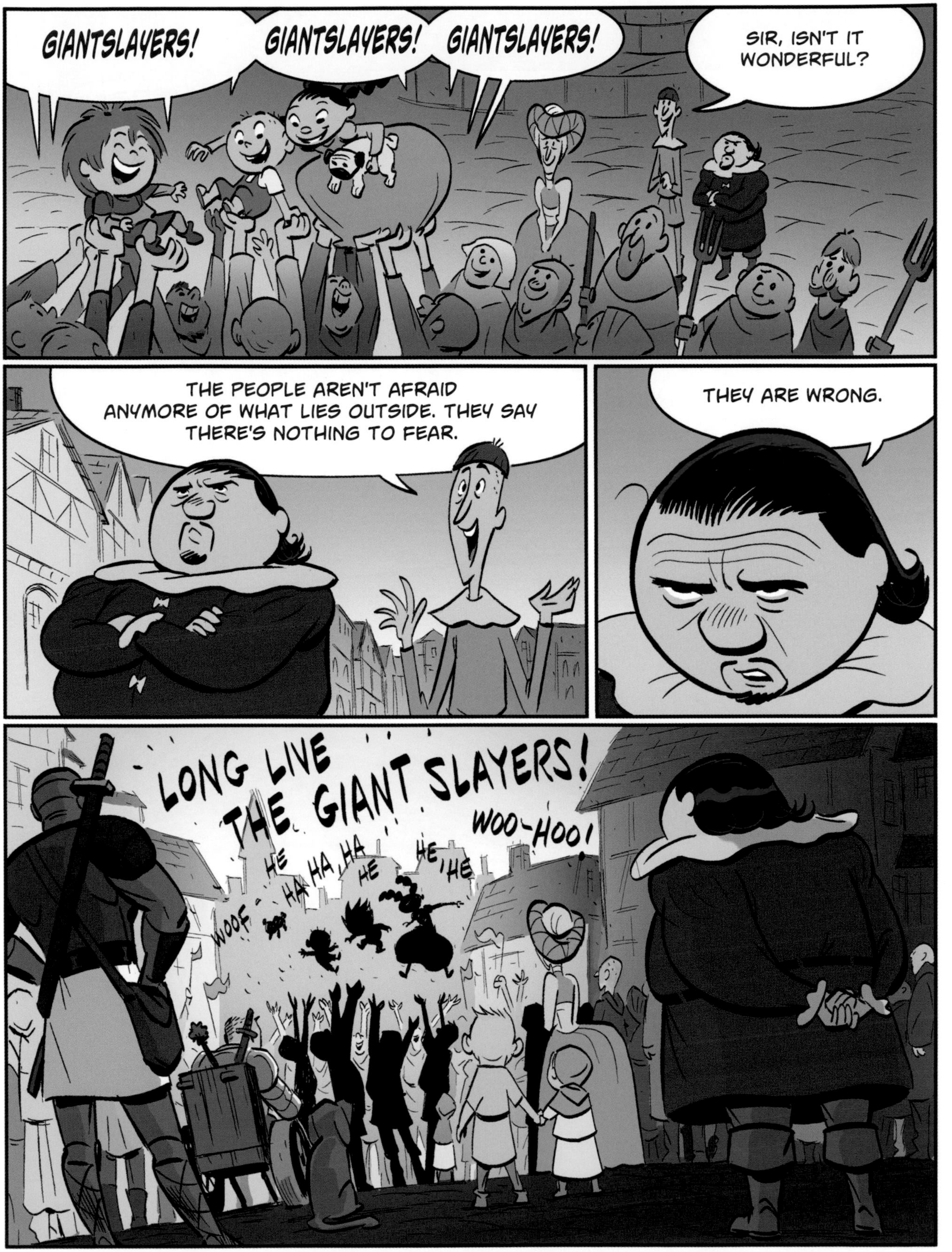
GIANTSLAYERS!
GIANTSLAYERS!
GIANTSLAYERS!
SIR, ISN'T IT WONDERFUL?
THE PEOPLE AREN'T AFRAID ANYMORE OF WHAT LIES OUTSIDE. THEY SAY THERE'S NOTHING TO FEAR.
THEY ARE WRONG.
LONG LIVE THE GIANT SLAYERS!
WOO-HOO!
HE HA HA HA HE HE HE
WOOF

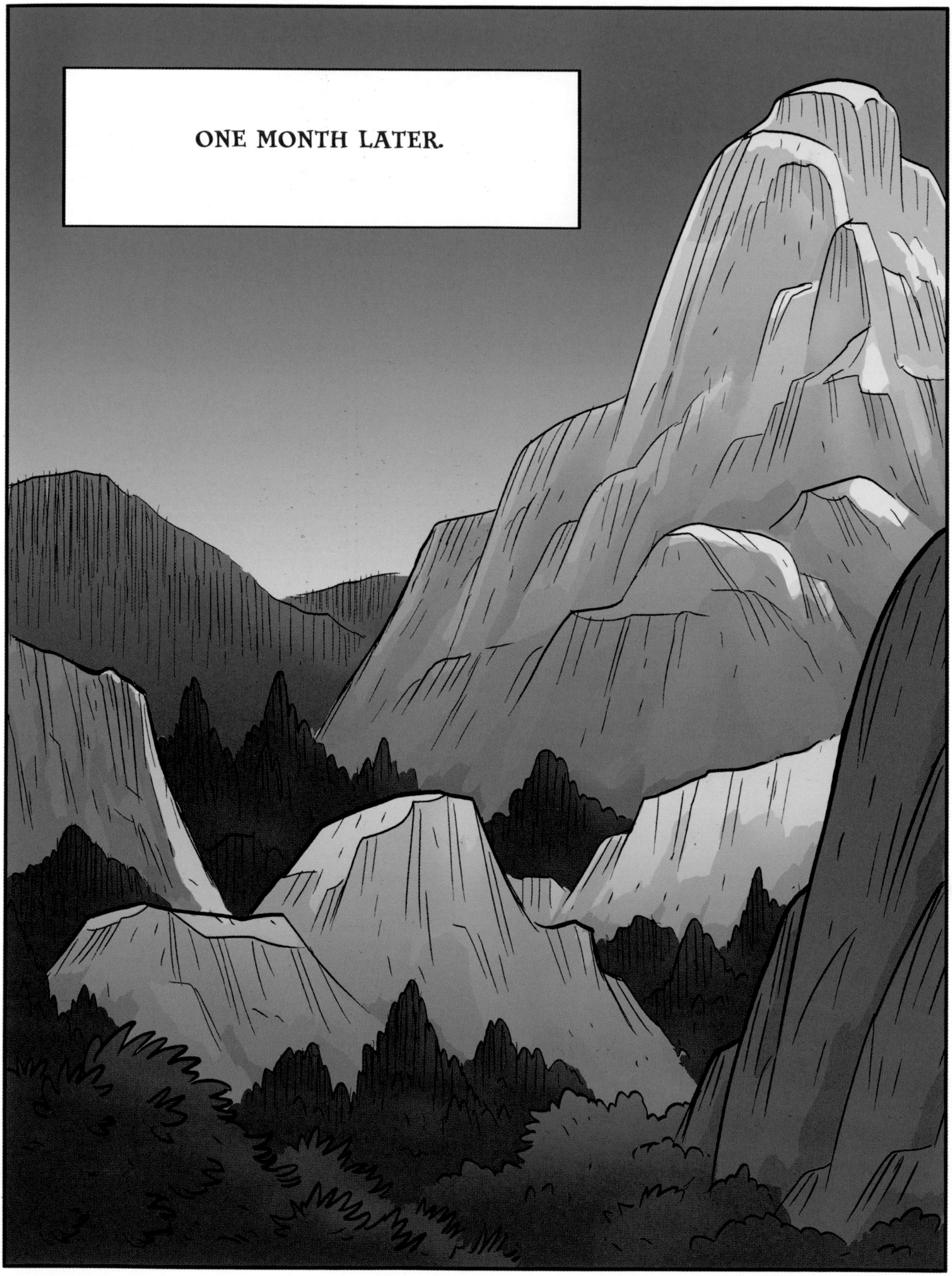
ONE MONTH LATER.

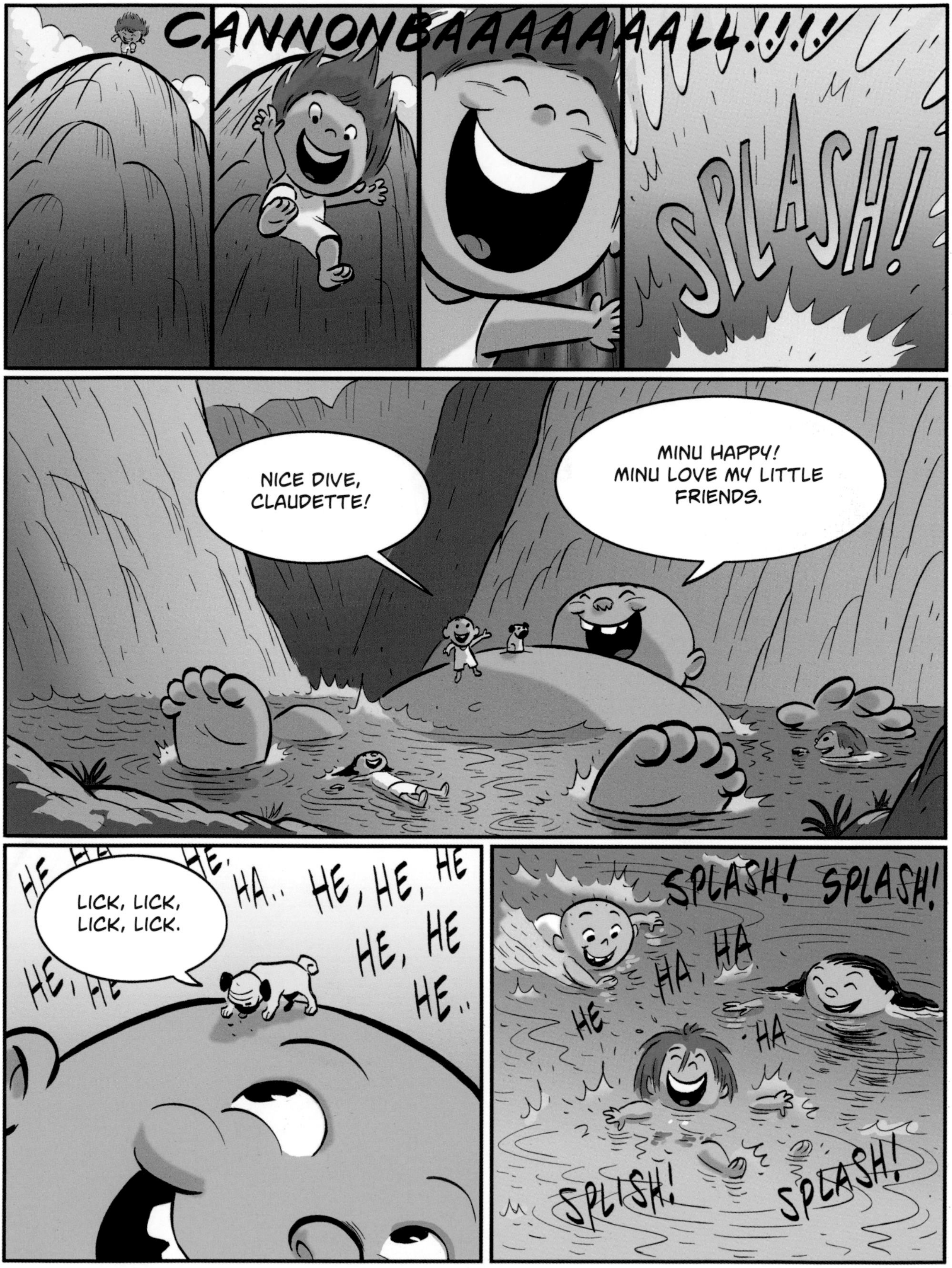
CANNONBAAAAAAAALL!!!!
SPLASH!
NICE DIVE, CLAUDETTE!
MINU HAPPY! MINU LOVE MY LITTLE FRIENDS.
HE, HE, HE, HA.. HE, HE, HE
LICK, LICK, LICK, LICK.
HE, HE HE..
HE, HE
SPLASH! SPLASH!
HA, HA
HE
HA
SPLISH! SPLASH!

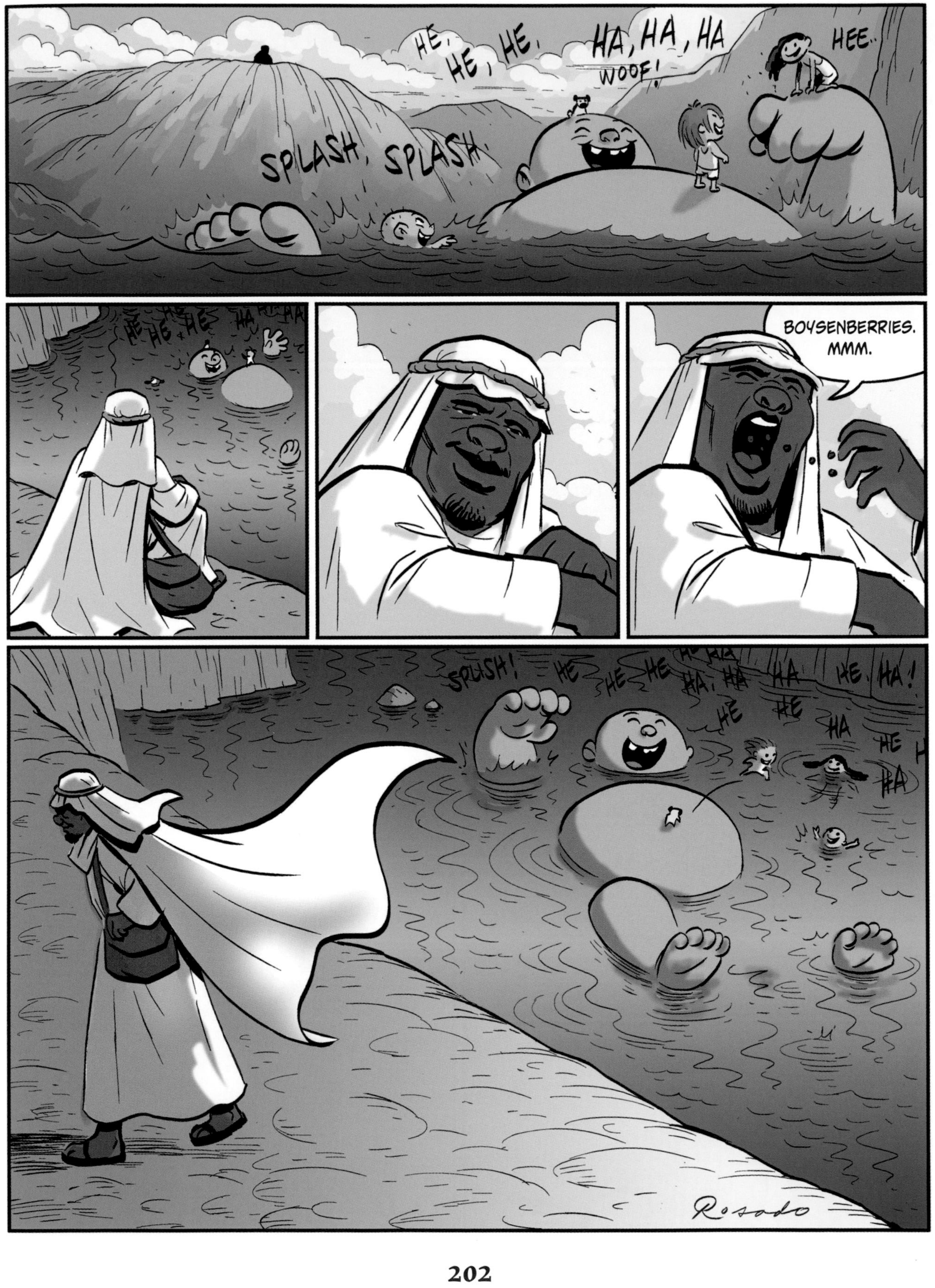
HE, HE, HE, HE,
HA, HA, HA
WOOF!
HEE..
SPLASH, SPLASH
BOYSENBERRIES. MMM.
SPLISH!
HE HE HE
HA, HA
HA
HE, HA!
HE HE
HA
HE
HA
Rosado

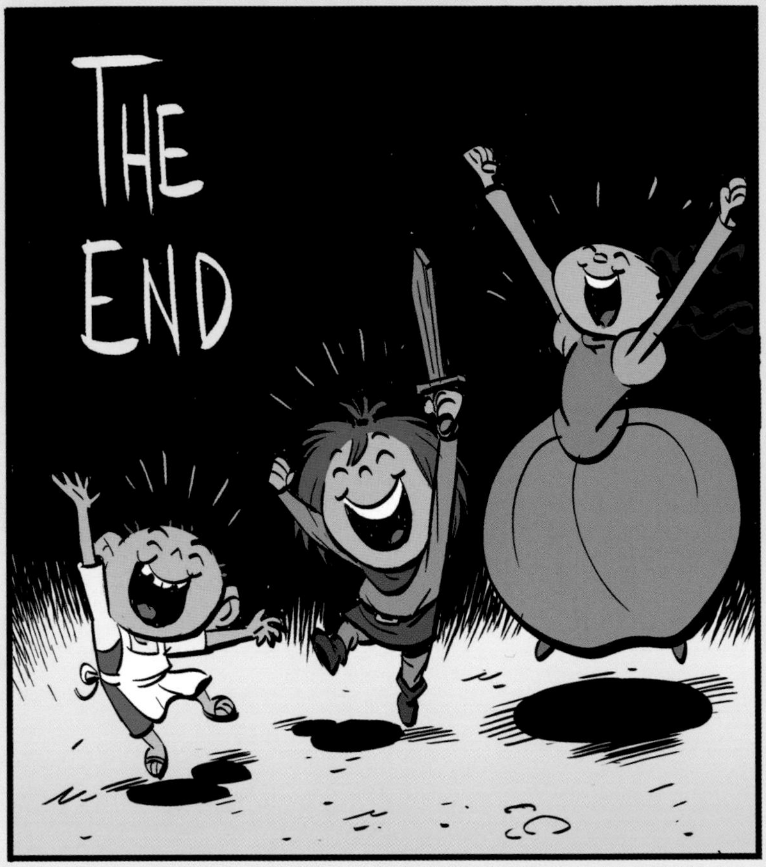
THE END

ROSADO/AGUIRRE 2010